The Legacy

Katherine Webb

An Orion paperback

First published in Great Britain in 2010
by Orion
This paperback edition published in 2010
by Orion Books Ltd,
Orion House, 5 Upper St Martin's Lane,
London WC2H 9EA

An Hachette UK company

1 3 5 7 9 10 8 6 4 2

A CIP catalogue record for this book
is available from the British Library.

ISBN 978-1-4091-1716-2

Typeset at The Spartan Press Ltd,
Lymington, Hants

Printed and bound in Great Britain by
Clays Ltd, St Ives plc

The Orion Publishing Group's policy is to use papers that
are natural, renewable and recyclable products and
made from wood grown in sustainable forests. The logging
and manufacturing processes are expected to conform to
the environmental regulations of the country of origin.

www.orionbooks.co.uk

To Mum and Dad

Prologue

1905

Gradually, Caroline returned to her senses. The numbness inside her head receded and she became aware of myriad thoughts, darting like caged birds, too fast for her to grasp. Unsteadily, she got to her feet. The child was still there, on the bed. A slick of fear washed down her spine. Part of her had been hoping that it would not be so; that somehow he would have gone, or better still never have been there at all. He had pulled himself to the far side of the bed, struggling to crawl properly on the slippery-soft counterpane. His strong fists grasped handfuls of it and he moved as if swimming very slowly across the expanse of teal-green silk. He had grown so big and strong. In another place, in another life, he would have been a warrior. His hair was midnight black. The baby peered over the bed and then turned his head to look at Caroline. He made a single sound, like *dah*; and although it was nonsense Caroline could tell it was a question. Her eyes swam with tears, and her legs threatened to fold again. He was real; he was here, in her bed chamber at Storton Manor, and he had grown strong enough to question her.

Her shame was a cloud she could not see through. It was like smoke in the air – it obscured everything, made it impossible to think. She had no idea what to do. Long minutes passed, until she thought she heard a footstep in the hallway outside the door. It sent her heart lurching, so all she knew, in the end, was that the baby couldn't stay there. Not on the bed, not in her room, not in the manor house. He just *could not*; and neither must any of the servants, or her husband, know that he ever had been. Perhaps the staff had discovered him already, had seen or heard something whilst she had been slumped, insensible, on the floor. She could only pray that it wasn't so. She had no idea how long she had waited, her mind scrambled by terror and grief. Not long enough for the child to grow bored with its explorations of the bed, so perhaps not too long after all. There was still time to act, and she had no choice.

Wiping her face, Caroline went around the bed and picked the boy up, too ashamed to look into his eyes. They were black too, she knew. As black and inscrutable as ink spots. He was so much heavier than she remembered. She lay him down and took off all his clothes, including his napkin, even though they were coarsely made, in case they could somehow lead back to her. She cast them into the grate, where they oozed smoke and stank on the embers of the morning's fire. Then she looked around, temporarily at a loss, before her eyes lit on the embroidered pillowcase at the head of the bed. It had fine, precise needlework, depicting yellow, ribbon-like flowers. The linen was smooth and thick. Caroline stripped the pillow bare and put the struggling baby into the case. She did this tenderly, her hands aware of her love for the child even if her mind could not encompass it. But she did not use it to wrap him in. Instead she turned it into a sack and carried the baby out in it like a poacher might carry rabbits. Tears wet her face, wringing themselves from the core of her. But she could not pause, she could not let herself love him again.

Outside it was raining heavily. Caroline crossed the lawn with her back aching and the skin of her scalp crawling, feeling the eyes of the house upon her. Once safely out of sight beneath the trees she gasped for breath, her knuckles white where they gripped the pillowcase shut. Inside, the child was fidgeting and mumbling, but he did not cry out. Rain ran through her hair and dripped from her chin. *But it will never wash me clean*, she told herself with quiet despair. There was a pond, she knew. A dew pond, at the far side of the grounds where the estate met the rolling downs from which sprang the stream that flowed through the village. It was deep and still and shaded; the water dark on a cloudy day like today, matt with the falling rain, ready to hide any secret cast into it. She held her breath as the thought of it rose in her mind. It turned her cold. *No, I cannot*, she pleaded, silently. *I cannot*. She had taken so much from him already.

She walked further, not in the direction of the pond but away from the house, praying for some other option to present itself. When it did, Caroline staggered with relief. There was a covered wagon, parked in a green clearing where the woods met the lane. A black and white pony was tethered next to it, its rump hunched into the weather, and thin skeins of smoke rose from a metal chimney pipe in the roof. *Tinkers*, she thought, with a flare of desperate hope in her chest. They would find him, take him, move away with him. She would never have to see him again, never be faced with him again. But he would be cared for. He would have a life.

Now the baby began to cry as rain soaked through the pillow-case and reached his skin. Hurriedly, Caroline hoisted the sack back onto her shoulder and made her way through the trees to the other side of the clearing, further away from the house so that the trail would not point in that direction. It would seem, she hoped, that somebody coming along the lane from the south had left the child. She put him amongst the knotted roots of a large beech tree, where it was fairly dry, and backed away as his cries grew louder and more insistent. *Take him and be gone*, she implored silently.

She stumbled back into the woods as quickly and quietly as she could, and the baby's cries followed her for a while before finally falling out of earshot. When they did, her steps faltered. She stood still, swaying, torn between continuing forwards and going back. *I will never hear him again*, she told herself, but there was no relief in this, in the end. It could not be any other way, but a chill spread through the heart of her, solid and sharp as ice, because there would be no getting away from what she had done, she knew then; no forgetting it. It sat inside her like a canker, and just as there was no going back, she was no longer sure that she could go on either. Her hand went to her midriff, to where she knew a child lay nestled. She let it feel the warmth of her hand, as if to prove to this child that she was still living, and feeling, and would love it. Then she made her way slowly back to the house, where she would realise, hours too late, that having carefully stripped the baby she had then left him to be found in the fine, embroidered pillowcase. She pressed her face into her bare pillow and tried to wipe the boy child from her memory.

'Tis calm indeed! so calm, that it disturbs
And vexes meditation with its strange
And extreme silentness.
Samuel Taylor Coleridge, *Frost at Midnight*

I

At least it's winter. We only ever came here in the summertime, so the place doesn't seem quite the same. It's not as dreadfully familiar, not as overpowering. Storton Manor, grim and bulky, the colour of today's low sky. A Victorian, neo-Gothic pile with stone-mullioned windows and peeling woodwork green with algae. Drifts of dead leaves against the walls and moss spreading up from behind them, reaching the ground-floor sills. Climbing out of the car, I breathe calmly. It's been a very English winter so far. Damp and muddy. The hedgerows look like smudged purple bruises in the distance. I wore bright jewel colours today, in defiance of the place, in defiance of its austerity, and the weight of it in my memory. Now I feel ridiculous, clownish.

Through the windscreen of my tatty white Golf I can see Beth's hands in her lap and the wispy ends of the long rope of her hair. Odd strands of grey snake through it now, and it seems too soon, far too soon. She was feverish keen to get here, but now she sits like a statue. Those pale, thin hands, folded limply in her lap — passive, waiting. Our hair used to be so bright when we were little. It was the white blonde of angels, of young Vikings; a purity of colour that faded with age to this uninspiring, mousy brown. I colour mine now, to cheer it up. We look less and less like sisters these days. I remember Beth and Dinny with their heads together, conspiring, whispering: his hair so dark, and hers so fair. I was cramped with jealousy at the time, and now, in my mind's eye, their heads look like yin and yang. As thick as thieves.

The windows of the house are blank, showing dark reflections of the naked trees all around. These trees seem taller now, and they lean too close to the house. They need cutting back. Am I thinking of things to do, things to improve? Am I picturing living here? The house is ours now, all twelve bedrooms; the soaring ceilings, the grand staircase, the underground rooms where the flagstones are worn smooth from the passage of servile feet. It's all ours, but only if we stay and live here. That's what Meredith always wanted. Meredith – our grandmother, with her spite and her hands in bony fists. She wanted our mother to move us all in years ago, and watch her die. Our mother refused, was duly cut off, and we continued our happy, suburban lives in Reading. If we don't move here it will be sold and the money sent to good causes. Meredith a philanthropist in death, perversely. So now the house is ours – but only for a little while, because I don't think we can bear to live here.

There's a reason why not. If I try to look right at it, it slips away like vapour. Only a name surfaces: Henry. The boy who disappeared, who just wasn't there any more. What I think now, staring up into the dizzying branches; what I think is that I *know*. I know why we can't live here, why it's even remarkable that we've come at all. *I know*. I know why Beth won't even get out of the car now. I wonder if I shall have to coax her out, the way one must coax her to eat. Not a single plant grows on the ground between here and the house – the shade is too deep. Or perhaps the ground is poisoned. It smells of earth and rot, velvety fungus. *Humus*, the word returns from science lessons years ago. A thousand tiny insect mouths biting, working, digesting the ground. There is a still moment then. Silence from the engine, silence in the trees and the house, and all the spaces in between. I scramble back into the car.

Beth is staring at her hands. I don't think she's even looked up yet, looked out at the house. Suddenly I doubt whether I've done the right thing, bringing her here. Suddenly I fear that I've left it too late, and this fear gives my insides a twist. There are sinews in her neck like lengths of string and she's folded into an angular shape in her seat, all hinges and corners. So thin these days, so fragile looking. Still my sister, but different now. There's something inside her that I can't know, can't fathom. She's done things that I can't grasp, and had thoughts I can't imagine. Her eyes, fixed on her knees, are glassy and wide. Maxwell wants her hospitalised again. He told me on the phone, two days ago, and I bit his head off for suggesting it. But I act differently around her now, however hard I try not to, and part of me hates her for it. She's my big sister. She should be stronger than me. I give her arm a little rub, smile brightly. 'Shall we go in?' I say. 'I could use a stiff drink.' My voice is loud in such close quarters. I picture Meredith's crystal decanters, lined up in the drawing room. I used to sneak in as a child, peer into the mysterious liquids, watch them catch the light, lift the stoppers for an illicit sniff. It seems somehow grotesque, to drink her whisky now she's dead. This solicitude is my way of showing Beth that I know she doesn't want to be back here. But then, with a deep breath, she gets out and strides over to the house as if driven, and I hurry after her.

Inside, the house does seem smaller, as things from childhood will, but it's still huge. The flat I share in London seemed big when I moved in because there were enough rooms not to have to peer through drying laundry to watch the TV. Now, faced with the echoing expanse of the hallway, I feel the ridiculous urge to cartwheel. We dither there, drop our bags at the foot of the stairs. This is the first time we've ever arrived here alone, without our parents, and it feels so odd that we mill like sheep. Our roles are defined by habit, by memory and custom. Here, in this house, we are children. But I must make light of it, because I can see Beth faltering, and a frantic look gathering behind her eyes.

'Stick the kettle on. I'll dig out some booze and we'll have tipsy coffee.'

'Erica, it's not even lunchtime.'

'So what? We're on holiday, aren't we?' Oh, but we're not. No we're not. I don't know what this is, but it's not a holiday. Beth shakes her head.

'I'll just have tea,' she says, drifting towards the kitchen. Her back is narrow, shoulders pointing sharply through the fabric of her shirt. I notice them with a jolt of unease – just ten days, since I saw her last, but she is visibly thinner now. I want to squeeze her, to make her be well.

The house is cold and damp, so I press buttons on an ancient panel until I hear things stirring, deep pipes complaining, water seething. There are rank ashes in the fire grates; there are still tissues and a sweetly rotting apple core in the waste-paper basket in the drawing room. Encroaching on Meredith's life like this makes me feel uneasy, slightly sick. As if I might turn and catch her reflection in the mirror – an acid grimace, hair tinted falsely gold. I pause at the window and look out onto the winter garden, a mess of leggy plants falling over, unpruned. These are the smells I remember from our summers here: coconut sun cream; oxtail soup for lunch, no matter how hot the weather; sweet, heavy clouds from the roses and lavenders around the patio; the pungent, meaty smell of Meredith's fat Labradors, panting their hot exhaustion onto my shins. So different now. That could have been centuries ago; it could have happened to someone else entirely. A few raindrops skitter onto the glass and I am a hundred years away from everything and everyone. Here, we are truly alone, Beth and I. Alone, in this house again, in our conspiracy of silence, after all this time in which nothing has been resolved, in which Beth has pulled herself apart, a piece at a time, and I have dodged and evaded it all.

First we have to sort, to make some order of all the layers of possessions, of the items that have gathered into drifts in corners. This house has so many rooms, so much furniture, so many drawers and cupboards and hiding places. I should feel sad, I suppose, to think of it sold; the line of family history down the years to Beth and me, breaking. But I don't. Perhaps because, by rights, everything should have gone to Henry. That was when it all got broken. I watch Beth for a while, as she lifts lace handkerchiefs out of a drawer and piles them on her knee. She takes them out one by one, studying the patterns, tracing the threads with her finger-tips. The pile on her knee is not as tidy as the pile in the drawer. There's no point to what she's doing. It's one of those things she does that I can't understand.

'I'm going for a walk,' I announce, rising on stiff knees, biting back irritation. Beth jumps as if she'd forgotten I was there.

'Where are you going?'

'For a walk, I just said. I need some fresh air.'

'Well, don't be long,' Beth says. She does this sometimes, as well – talks to me as if I'm a wilful child, as if I might run off. I sigh.

'No. Twenty minutes. Stretch my legs.' I think she knows where I'm going.

I follow my feet. The lawn is ragged and lumpy; a choppy sea of broken brown grasses that soak my feet. It all used to be so manicured, so beautiful. I had been thinking, without thinking, that it must have got out of hand since Meredith died. But that's ridiculous. She died a month ago, and the garden shows several seasons of neglect. We have been neglectful of her ourselves, it would seem. I have no idea how she coped before she died – *if* she coped. She was just there, in the back of my mind. Mum and Dad came to see her, every year or so. Beth and I hadn't been for an age. But our absence was understood, I think; it was never tested too hard. We were never pestered to come. Perhaps she would have liked us to, perhaps not. It was hard to tell with Meredith. She was not a sweet grandmother, she was not even maternal. Our great-grandmother, Caroline, was also here while our mother grew up. Another source of discomfort. Our mother left as soon as she could. Meredith died suddenly, of a stroke. One day ageless, an old woman for as long as I can remember; the next day no longer. I saw her last at Mum and Dad's silver wedding anniversary, not here but in an overheated hotel with plush carpets. She sat like a queen at her table and cast a cold glare around the room, eyes sharp above a puckered mouth.

Here's the dew pond. Where it always was, but it looks so different in winter colours. It sits in the corner of a large field of closely grazed turf. The field stretches away to the east, woods to the west. Those woods would shed a dappled green light onto the surface; a cool colour, cast from branches that fidgeted and sang with birds. They're naked now, studded with loud rooks clacking and clamouring at one another. It was irresistible on hot July days, this pond; but with the sky this drab it looks flat, like a shallow puddle. Clouds chase across it. I know it's not shallow. It was fenced off when we were children, but with a few strands of barbed wire that were no match for determined youngsters. It was worth the scratched calves, the caught hair. In the sunshine the water was a glassy blue. It looked deep but Dinny said it was deeper even than that. He said the water fooled the eye, and I didn't believe him until he dived one day, taking a huge lungful of air and kicking, kicking downwards. I watched his brown body ripple and truncate, watched him continue to kick even when it seemed he should have reached the chalky bottom. He surfaced with a gasp, to find me rapt, astonished.

This pond feeds the stream that runs through the village of Barrow Storton, down the side of this wide hill from the manor house. This pond is etched in my memory; it seems to dominate my childhood. I can see Beth paddling at the edge the first time I swam in it. She stalked to and fro, nervous because she was the eldest, and the banks were steep, and if I drowned it would be her fault. I dived again and again, trying to reach the bottom like Dinny had, never making it, and hearing Beth's high threats each time I popped back into the air. Like a cork, I was. Buoyant with the puppy fat on my chubby legs, my round stomach. She made me run around and around the garden before she would let me near the house, so I would be dry, so I would be warm and not white, teeth chattering, requiring explanation.

Behind me, there are distant glimpses of the house through the bare trees. That's something I've never noticed before. You can't see it through summer trees, but now it watches, it waits. It worries me to know that Beth is inside, alone, but I don't want to go back yet. I carry on walking, climbing over the gate into the field. This field, and then another, and then you are on the downs – rolling Wiltshire chalk downland, marked here and there by prehistory, marked here and there by tanks and target practice. On the horizon sits the barrow that gives the village its name, a Bronze Age burial mound for a king whose name and fame have passed out of all remembrance: a low, narrow hump, about the length of two cars, open at one end. In summer this king lies under wild barley, bright ragwort and forget-me-nots, and listens to the endless rich chortling of larks. But now it's more brittle grasses, dead thistles, an empty crisp packet.

I stop at the barrow and look down at the village, catching my breath after the climb. There's not much movement, a few ragged columns of chimney smoke, a few well-swaddled residents walking their dogs to the postbox. From this lonely hill it seems like the centre of the universe. *This populous village!* Coleridge pops into my head. I've been doing the conversation poems with my year tens. I've been trying to make them read slowly enough to feel the words, to absorb the images; but they skim on, chatter like monkeys.

The air is biting up here – it parts around me like a cold wave. My toes have gone numb because my shoes are soaked through. There are ten, twenty pairs of Wellington boots in the house, I know. Down in the basement, in neat rows with cobwebs draped around them. That one horrible time I didn't shake a boot out before putting a bare foot inside, and felt the tickle of another occupant. I am out of practice at living in the countryside; ill-equipped for changes in the terrain, for ground that hasn't been carefully prepared to best convenience me. And yet when asked I would say I grew up here. Those early summers, so long and distinct in my mind, rising like islands from a sea of school days and wet weekends too blurred and uniform to recall.

At the entrance to the barrow the wind makes a low moan. I jump two-footed down the stone steps and startle a girl inside. She straightens with a gasp and hits her head on the low ceiling, crouches again, puts both hands around her skull to cradle it.

'Shit! Sorry! I didn't mean to pounce on you like that . . . I didn't know anybody was in here.' I smile. The wan light from the doorway shines onto her, onto golden bubble curls tied back with a turquoise scarf, onto a young face and an oddly shapeless body, swathed in long chiffon skirts and crochet. She squints up at me, and I must be a silhouette to her, a black bulk against the sky outside. 'Are you OK?' She doesn't answer me. Tiny bright posies have been pushed into gaps in the wall in front of her, snipped stems neatly bound with ribbon. Is this what she was doing in here, so quietly? Praying at some half-imagined, half-borrowed shrine? She sees me looking at her offerings and she rises, scowls, pushes past me without a word. I realise that her shapelessness is in fact an abundance of shape – the heaviness of pregnancy. Very pretty, very young, belly distended. When I emerge from the tomb I look down the slope towards the village but she's not there. She is walking the other way – the direction I came from, towards the woodlands near the manor house. She strides fiercely, arms swinging.

Beth and I eat dinner in the study this first night. It might seem an odd choice of room, but it is the only one with a TV in it, and we eat pasta from trays on our knees with the evening news to keep us company, because small talk seems to have abandoned us, and big talk is just too big yet. We're not ready. I'm not sure that we ever will be, but there are things I want to ask my sister. I will wait, I will make sure I get the questions right. I hope that, if I ask the right ones, I can make her better. That the truth will set her free.

Beth chases each quill around her bowl before catching it on her fork. She raises the fork to her lips several times before putting it into her mouth. Some of these quills never make it – she knocks them back off the fork, selects an alternative. I see all this in the corner of my eye, just like I see her body starving. The TV pictures shine darkly in her eyes.

'Do you think it's a good idea? Having Eddie here for Christmas?' she asks me suddenly.

'Of course. Why wouldn't it be? We'll be staying for a while to get things sorted, so we may as well stay for Christmas. Together.' I shrug. 'There's plenty of space, after all.'

'No, I mean . . . bringing a child here. Into this . . . place.'

'Beth, it's just a house. He'll love it. He doesn't know . . . Well. He'll have a blast, I'm sure he will – there are so many nooks and crannies to explore.'

'A bit big and empty, though, isn't it? A bit lonely, perhaps? It might depress him.'

'Well, you could tell him to bring a friend. Why don't you? Call him tomorrow – not for the whole of Christmas, of course. But some of the working parents might be glad of a few extra days' grace before their little home-wreckers reappear, don't you think?'

'Hmm.' Beth rolls her eyes. 'I don't think any of the mothers at that school do anything as common as work for a living.'

'Only riff-raff like you?'

'Only riff-raff like me,' she agrees, deadpan.

'Ironic, really, since you're the real thing. Blue blood, practically.'

'Hardly. Just as you are.'

'No. I think the nobility skipped a generation in me.' I smile. Meredith told me this once, when I was ten. *Your sister has the Calcott mien, Erica. You, I fear, are all your father.* I didn't mind then and I don't mind now. I wasn't sure what *mien* meant, at the time. I thought she meant my hair, which had been chopped off short thanks to an incident with bubblegum. When she turned away I stuck out my tongue, and Mum wagged a finger at me.

Beth rejects it too. She fought with Maxwell – Eddie's father – to allow their son to attend the village primary school, which was tiny and friendly and had a nature garden in one corner of the yard: frogspawn, the dried-out remains of dragonfly nymphs; primroses in the spring, then pansies. But Maxwell won the toss when it came to secondary education. Perhaps it was for the best. Eddie boards now, all term long. Beth has weeks and weeks to build herself up, shake a sparkle into her smile.

'We'll fill up the space,' I assure her. 'We'll deck the halls. I'll dig out a radio. It won't be like . . .' but I trail off. I'm not sure what I was about to say. In the corner, the tiny TV gives an angry belch of static that makes us both jump.

Almost midnight, and Beth and I have retired to our rooms. The same rooms we always took, where we found the same bedspreads, smooth and faded. This seemed unreal to me, at first. But then, why would you change the bedspreads in rooms that are never used? I don't think Beth will be asleep yet either. The quiet in the house rings like a bell. The mattress sinks low where I sit, the springs have lost their spring. The bed has a dark oak headboard and there's a watercolour on the wall, so faded now. Boats in a harbour, though I never heard of Meredith visiting the coast. I reach behind the headboard, my fingers feeling down the vertical supports until I find it. Brittle now, gritty with dust. The piece of ribbon I tied – red plastic ribbon from a curl on a birthday present. I tied it here when I was eight so that I would know a secret, and only I would know it. I could think about it, after we'd gone back to school. Picture it, out of sight, untouched as the room was cleaned, as people came and went. Here was something that I would know about; a relic of me I could always find.

There's a tiny knock and Beth's face appears around the door.

Her hair is out of its plait, falling around her face, making her younger. She is so beautiful sometimes that it gives me a pain in my chest, makes my ribs squeeze. Weak light from the bedside lamp puts shadows in her cheekbones, under her eyes; shows up the curve of her top lip.

'Are you OK? I can't sleep,' she whispers, as if there is somebody else in the house to wake.

'I'm fine, Beth; just not sleepy.'

'Oh.' She lingers in the doorway, hesitates. 'It's so strange to be here.' This is not a question. I wait. 'I feel like . . . I feel a bit like Alice in *Through the Looking Glass*. Do you know what I mean? It's all so familiar, and yet wrong too. As if it's backwards. Why do you think she left us the house?'

'I really don't know. To get at Mum and Uncle Clifford, I imagine. That's the kind of thing Meredith would do,' I sigh. Still Beth hovers, so pretty, so girlish. Right now it's as if no time has passed, as if nothing has changed. She could be twelve again, I could be eight, and she could be leaning in to wake me, to make sure I'm not late for breakfast.

'I think she did it to punish us,' she says softly, and looks stricken.

'No, Beth. We didn't do anything wrong,' I say firmly.

'Didn't we? That summer. No. No, I suppose not.' She flicks her eyes over me now, quickly, puzzled; and I get the feeling she is trying to see something, some truth about me. 'Good night, Rick,' she whispers, using a familiar tomboy truncation of my name, and vanishes from the doorway.

I remember so many things from that summer. The last summer that everything was right, the summer of 1986. I remember Beth being distraught that Wham! were breaking up. I remember the heat bringing up water blisters across my chest that itched, and burst under my fingernails, making me feel sick. I remember the dead rabbit in the woods that I checked up on almost daily, appalled and riveted by its slow sinking, softening, the way it seemed to breathe, until I poked it with a stick to check it was dead and realised that the movement was the greedy squabble of maggots inside. I remember watching, on Meredith's tiny television, Sarah Ferguson marry Prince Andrew on the twenty-third of July – that huge dress, making me ache with envy.

I remember making up a dance routine to Diana Ross's hit 'Chain Reaction'. I remember stealing one of Meredith's boas for my costume, stumbling and stepping on it: a shower of feathers; hiding it in a distant drawer with dread in the pit of my stomach, too scared to own up. I remember reporters and policemen, facing each other either side of Storton Manor's iron gates. The policemen folded their arms, seemed bored and hot in their uniforms. The reporters milled and fiddled with their equipment, spoke into cameras, into tape recorders, waited and waited for news. I remember Beth's eyes pinning me as the policeman talked to me about Henry, asked me where we'd been playing, what we'd been doing. His breath smelt of Polo mints, sugar gone sour. I told him, I think, and I felt unwell; and Beth's eyes on me were ragged and wide.

In spite of these thoughts I sleep easily in the end, once I have got over the cold touch of the sheets, the unfamiliar darkness of the room. And there's the smell, not unpleasant but all-pervading. The way other people's houses will smell of their occupants – the combination of their washing soap, their deodorant and their hair when it needs washing; their perfume, skin; the food they cook. Regardless of the winter, this smell lingers in every room, evocative and unsettling. I wake up once; think I hear Beth moving around the house. And then I dream of the dew pond, of swimming in it and trying to dive down, of needing to fetch something from the bottom but being unable to reach. The cold shock of the water, the pressure in my lungs, the awful fear of what my fingers will find at the bottom.

Leaving

1902

I will remain steadfast, Caroline reminded herself firmly, as she watched her aunt Bathilda covertly through lowered eyelashes. The older woman cleared her plate with methodical efficiency before speaking again.

'I fear you are making a grave mistake, my dear.' But there was a glint in her aunt's eye that did not look fearful at all. More righteous, in fact, more self-satisfied, as if she, in spite of all protestations to the contrary, felt victorious. Caroline studied her own plate, where the fat had risen from the gravy and congealed into an unappetising crust.

'So you have said before, Aunt Bathilda.' She kept her voice low and respectful, but still her aunt glared at her.

'I repeat myself, child, because you do not appear to hear me,' she snapped.

Heat flared in Caroline's cheeks. She nudged her cutlery into a neater position, felt the smooth weight of the silver beneath her fingers. She shifted her spine slightly. It was laced into a strict serpentine, and it ached.

'And don't fidget,' Bathilda added.

The dining room at La Fiorentina was excessively bright, closed in behind windows that had steamed opaque with the vapours of hot food and exhalation. Yellow light glanced and spiked from glass and jewellery and polished metal. The winter had been long and hard, and now, just as spring had seemed poised to flourish with a tantalising week of bird song, crocuses and a green haze on the park trees, a long spell of cold rain had settled over New York City.

Caroline caught her reflection in several mirrors relayed around the room, her every move amplified. Unsettled by such scrutiny, she blushed more deeply. 'I do listen to you, Aunt. I have *always* listened to you.'

'You listened to me in the past because you had to, as I understand it. Now, as soon as you perceive yourself old enough, you disregard me entirely. In the most important decision you will ever make, at this most crucial juncture, you ignore me. Well, I am only glad my poor dear brother is not alive to see how I have failed his only child.' Bathilda heaved a martyr's sigh.

'You have not failed, Aunt,' Caroline murmured, reluctantly.

A waiter cleared their empty plates, brought them sweet white wine, to replace the red, and the pastry trolley. Bathilda sipped, her lips leaving a greasy smudge on the gilt rim of the glass, and then chose a cream-filled éclair, cut a large piece and widened her mouth to accommodate it. The floury flesh of her chin folded over her lace collar. Caroline watched her with distaste and felt her throat constrict.

'You have never made me feel dear to you,' Caroline murmured, so softly that the words were lost beneath the throng of voices and eating, drinking, chewing, swallowing. Smells of roast meat and curried soup clung to the air.

'Don't mumble, Caroline.' Bathilda finished the éclair and dabbed cream from the corners of her mouth. *Not long. Not much longer*, Caroline told herself. Her aunt was a fortress, she thought, angrily. Balustrades of manners and wealth around a space inside – a space most commonly filled with rich food and sherry. Certainly there was no heart there, no love, no warmth. Caroline felt a flare of defiance.

'Mr Massey is a good man, his family is respectable—' she began to say, adopting a tone of calm reason.

'The man's morals are irrelevant. Corin Massey will make you a common drudge. He will not make you happy,' Bathilda interrupted.

'How could he? He is *beneath* you. He is far beneath you, in fortune and in manners – in every station of life.'

'You've barely even met him!' Caroline cried. Bathilda shot her a censorious look.

'May I remind you that you, also, have *barely even met him*? You may be eighteen now, you may be independent from me, but have I earned no respect in raising you? In keeping you and teaching you—'

'You have kept me with the money my parents left. You have done your duty,' Caroline said, a touch bitterly.

'Don't interrupt me, Caroline. Our name is a good one and would have stood you in good stead here in New York. And yet you choose to wed a . . . *farmer*. And move away from everything and everyone you know to live in the middle of nowhere. I have indeed failed, that much is clear. I have failed to instil respect and good sense and propriety in you, in spite of all my efforts.'

'But I don't *know* anybody here, Aunt. Not really. I know only you,' Caroline said, sadly. 'And Corin is not a farmer. He's a cattle rancher, a most successful one. His business—'

'His *business*? His *business* should have stayed in the wilderness and not found its way here to prey upon impressionable young girls.'

'I have money enough.' Caroline tipped her chin defiantly. 'We will not be poor.'

'Not yet, you don't. Not for another two years. We'll see how well you like living on a farmer's income until then. And we'll see how long your wealth lasts once he has his hands upon it and finds his way to the gaming tables!'

'Don't say such things. He is a good man. And he loves me, and . . . and I love him,' Caroline declared, adamantly. He loved her. She let this thought pour through her and could not keep from smiling.

When Corin had proposed to Caroline, he had said that he'd

loved her from the first moment of their meeting, which was at a ball a month previously – the Montgomery's ball to mark the beginning of Lent. Since her debut, Caroline had envied the enjoyment that other girls seemed to derive from such functions. They danced and they laughed and they chatted with ease. Caroline, when forced to enter the room with Bathilda, found herself always at a disadvantage, always afraid to speak in case she caused her aunt to correct her, or to scold. Corin had changed all that.

Caroline chose her fawn silk gown and her mother's emeralds for the Montgomery's ball. The necklace was cool and heavy around her neck. It covered the slender expanse of her décolletage with a glow of gold and a deep glitter that sparked light in her grey eyes.

'You look like an empress, miss,' Sara said admiringly, as she brushed out Caroline's fair hair, pinned it into a high chignon on her crown and braced one foot on the stool to pull up the laces of her corset. Caroline's waist was a source of envy to her peers, and Sara always took careful pains to pull it in as far as she could. 'No man in the room will be able to resist you.'

'Do you think so?' Caroline asked, breathlessly. Sara, with her dark hair and her ready smile, was the closest thing Caroline had to a true friend. 'I fear that they will be able to resist my aunt, however,' she sighed. Bathilda had seen off more than one cautious suitor; young men she deemed unworthy.

'Your aunt has high hopes for you, miss, that's all. Of course she cares a great deal who you will marry,' Sara soothed her.

'At this rate, I will marry nobody at all, and will stay forever here listening to her disappointment in me!'

'Nonsense! The right one will come along and he will win your aunt over, if that is what he must do to have you. Just look at you, miss! You will bedazzle them, I know it,' Sara smiled. Caroline met Sara's eye in the mirror. She reached over her shoulder and grasped the girl's fingers, squeezing them for courage. 'There now. All will be well,' Sara assured her, crossing to the dresser for face powder and rouge.

Caroline, every scant inch the demure, immaculate society girl, descended the wide staircase into the incandescence of the Montgomery's ballroom. The room was alight with precious stones and laughter; ripe with the fragrance of wine and perfumed hair pomade. Gossip and smiles rippled around the room, passing like Chinese whispers; alternately friendly, amused, and vicious. Caroline saw her dress appraised, her aunt derided, her jewels admired, frank glances cast over her, and comments passed in low voices behind delicate fingers and tortoiseshell cigarette holders. She spoke little, just enough to be polite, and this at least was a trait her aunt had always approved of. She smiled and applauded with the rest when Harold Montgomery performed his party piece: the messy cascading of a champagne magnum into a pyramid of glasses. It always splashed and overflowed, wetting the stems which then stained the ladies' gloves.

The room was stuffy and hot. Caroline stood up straight, sipping sour wine that lightened her head and feeling sweat prickle beneath her arms. Fires blazed in every grate and light poured from hundreds of electric candles in the chandeliers, so bright that she could see red pigment from Bathilda's lips seeping into the creases around her mouth. But then Corin appeared in front of them and she barely heard Charlie Montgomery's introduction because she was captured by the newcomer's frank gaze and the warmth of him; and when she blushed he did too, and he fumbled his first words to her, saying, 'Hello, how are you?' as though they were two odd fellows meeting over a game of whist. He grasped her hand in its embroidered glove as if to shake it, realised his mistake and dropped it abruptly, letting it fall limply into her skirts. At this she blushed more, and dared not look at Bathilda, who was giving the young man a most severe look. 'Sorry, miss . . . I, uh . . . won't you excuse me?' he mumbled, inclining his head to them and disappearing into the crowd.

'What an *extraordinary* young man!' Bathilda exclaimed, scathingly. 'Where on *earth* did you find him, Charlie?' Charlie Montgomery's black hair was as slick as oilskin, flashing light as he turned his head.

'Oh, don't mind Corin. He's a bit out of practice at all this, that's all. He's a far off cousin of mine. His people are here in New York but he's lived out west for years now, in Oklahoma Territory. He's back in town for his father's funeral,' Charlie said.

'How extraordinary,' Bathilda said again. 'I never thought that one should have to *practise* one's manners.' At this Charlie smiled vaguely. Caroline glanced at her aunt and saw that she had no idea how disliked she was.

'What happened to his father?' she asked Charlie, surprising herself.

'He was on one of the trains that collided in the Park Avenue Tunnel last month. It was a right old mess,' Charlie said, pulling a face. 'Seventeen dead, it's now reported, and nigh on forty injured.'

'How dreadful!' Caroline breathed. Charlie nodded in agreement.

'They must run the trains with electricity. Automate the signals and remove the opportunity for sleepy-headed drivers to cause such tragedies,' he declared.

'But how could a signal work with nobody to operate it?' Caroline asked, but Bathilda heaved a gentle sigh, as if bored, so Charlie Montgomery excused himself and moved away.

Caroline searched the crowd for the stranger's bronze-coloured hair, and found herself sorry for him – for his bereavement, and for his fumbling of her hand in front of Bathilda's flat, unforgiving eye. The shocking pain of losing close family was something she could sympathise with. She sipped absently at her wine, which had gone warm in her hand and was making her throat sore. And she felt the emeralds press into her chest, felt the watery fabric of her gown on her thighs, as if her skin suddenly longed to be touched. When

Corin appeared at her side a minute later and asked her for a dance, she accepted mutely, with a startled nod, her heart too high in her throat to speak. Bathilda glared at him, but he did not even look up at her to notice, giving her cause to exclaim: 'Well, *really*!'

They danced a slow waltz, and Caroline, who had wondered why Corin had chosen a dance so slow, and so late in the evening, guessed the reason in his unsure steps, and the tentative way in which he held her. She smiled uncertainly at him, and they did not speak at first. Then he said:

'You must please excuse me, Miss Fitzpatrick. For before, and for . . . I fear I am not an accomplished dancer. It has been some time since I was lucky enough to attend such a function as this, or to dance with someone so . . . uh . . .' He hesitated, and she smiled, lowering her gaze as she had been taught. But she could not look away for long. She could feel the heat of his hand in the small of her back, as if there was nothing at all between her skin and his. She felt naked suddenly; wildly disconcerted, but thrilled as well. His face was deeply tanned, and the sun had lingered in the hair of his brows and moustache, tinting them with warm colour. His hair was combed but not brilliantined, and a stray lock now fell forward onto his brow, so that she almost reached out to brush it back. He watched her with light brown eyes, and she thought she saw a startled kind of happiness there.

As the dance ended and he took her hand to escort her from the floor, her glove snagged against the roughened skin of his palm. On impulse, she turned his hand over in her own and studied it, pushing her thumb into the callous at the root of each finger, comparing the width of it to her own. Her hand looked like a child's in his, and she drew breath and parted her lips to say this before realising how inappropriate it would be. She felt childlike indeed, and she noticed that he was breathing deeply.

'Are you quite well, Mr Massey?' she asked.

'Yes . . . I'm fine, thank you. It's a little confined in here, isn't it?'

'Come over to the window, you will find the air fresher,' she said, taking his arm to steer him through the crowd. The air was indeed close, heavy with sweat and breathing, thick with smoke and music and voices.

'Thank you,' Corin said. The long casement windows were shut against the dead cold of the February night, but that cold radiated from the glass nevertheless, providing an area of cool where the overexerted could find relief. 'I'm not used to seeing so many people under one roof all at once. It's funny, how quickly and completely a person can become unaccustomed to such things.' He hitched one shoulder in a shrug too casual for his evening coat.

'I have never left New York,' Caroline blurted out. 'That is, only for my family's summer house, on the coast . . . I mean to say . . .' but she wasn't sure what she meant to say. That he seemed foreign to her, a figure from myth almost – to have gone so far from civilisation, to have chosen life in an untamed land.

'Would you not like to travel, Miss Fitzpatrick?' he asked, and she began to understand that something had started between them. A negotiation of some kind; a sounding out.

'There you are, my dear.' Bathilda bore down on them. She could spot such a negotiation from quite a distance, it seemed. 'Do come along, I want to introduce you to Lady Clemence.' Caroline had no choice but to be led away but she glanced back over her shoulder and raised her hand in slight salute.

'Don't be ridiculous, girl!' Bathilda broke into her thoughts and returned her to the present, and the lunch table at La Fiorentina. 'You are acting like a lovesick schoolgirl! I, too, have read Mr Wister's *novel*, and it has clearly filled your head with romantic notions. I can think of no other reason why you would choose to marry a *cow-boy*. But you will learn that *The Virginian* is a work of *fiction* and bears little relation to the reality of it. Did you not also read of the dangers, and the emptiness, and the hardships of the frontier land?'

'It's not like that any more. Corin has told me all about it. He says the land is so beautiful you can see God's hand in every blade of grass . . .' At this Bathilda snorted, inelegantly. 'And Mr Wister himself acknowledges that the wild era he described is no more. Woodward is a thriving town, Corin says—'

'Woodward? Who has heard of *Woodward*? What state is it in?'

'I . . . do not know,' Caroline confessed, pressing her lips together resentfully.

'It is in no state at all, that's why you do not know. No state of the Union. It is uncharted land, full of savages and uncouth men of all kinds. Why, I heard there are no ladies to be found west of Dodge City at all – only *women* of the worst kind. No ladies! Can't you imagine how *godless* a place it must be?' Bathilda's chest swelled within the confines of her burgundy gown. A flush mottled her face all the way to her hairline, where her steel-coloured hair was gathered into a soft bouffant. She was moved, Caroline realised, incredulously. Bathilda was actually *moved*.

'Of course there are ladies! I'm sure such accounts are exaggerated,' said Caroline.

'I don't see how you can be so sure when you know nothing. How can you know anything, Caroline? You're just a child! He would tell you anything to get such a fine and wealthy wife. And you believe every word! You will leave your home and your family and all your prospects here. To live where you will have no name, no society and no comfort.'

'I will have comfort,' Caroline insisted.

A week after the ball, Corin had taken Caroline to the skating pond in Central Park, along with Charlie Montgomery and his sister Diana, who gave them a tactfully wide berth. It was late in

February and the sky was an odd yellowy-white against which the spiralling snowflakes at first looked black, then turned pale against the bare trees before they reached the ground.

'As a boy I was always half afraid to skate here. I kept waiting to fall through the ice,' Corin smiled, taking small, cautious steps more akin to walking than skating.

'You needn't have worried, Mr Massey. They drain most of the water out at the beginning of the winter, to be sure that it freezes right through,' Caroline smiled. The cold was biting. It reddened their cheeks and hung their breath in ragged white clouds around them. Caroline tucked her gloved hands into her coat pockets and skated a large, smooth circle around Corin.

'You're very good at this, Miss Fitzpatrick. Much better than I!'

'My mother used to bring me here all the time. When I was a little girl. I haven't skated in a while, though. Bathilda does not care for it.'

'Where is your mother now?' Corin asked, circling his arms clumsily to keep his balance. Snow had gathered on the brim of his hat, giving him a festive look.

'My parents died. Eight years ago,' Caroline said, skating to a halt in front of Corin, who also fell still. 'There was an explosion at a factory, as they were travelling home one evening. A wall collapsed and . . . their carriage was trapped beneath it,' she told him, quietly. Corin put his hands out as if to hold her, but then let them fall again.

'What a tragic misfortune. I'm so sorry,' he said.

'Charlie told me about your father, and I'm sorry, too,' Caroline said, wondering if he noticed the similarity, as she had, in the nightmarish, claustrophobic way in which they had both lost family. She looked down at her skates. Inside them, her toes were going numb. 'Come, Mr Massey; let's move on before we cleave to the ice!' she suggested, holding out her hand to him. He took it, smiling, then grimaced as she towed him along, wobbling like a toddler.

They drank hot chocolate in the pavilion, once the ice had become so crowded with skaters that steady progress was nigh on impossible. From their table by the window they watched young boys darting recklessly between the adults. Caroline realised that she hadn't been feeling the winter weather as she normally did. Perhaps being close to Corin was enough to warm her – it seemed to make her blood run more quickly than ever before.

'You have the most extraordinary eyes, Miss Fitzpatrick,' Corin told her, smiling bashfully. 'Why, they shine like silver dollars against the snow out there!' he exclaimed.

Caroline had no idea how to reply to him. She was not used to compliments, and so she looked down into her cup, embarrassed.

'Bathilda says that I have cold eyes. She laments that I did not inherit my father's shade of blue,' she said, stirring her chocolate slowly.

But Corin reached out a finger and lifted her chin, and she felt his touch like an electric charge. 'Your aunt is quite wrong,' he declared.

His proposal came a scant three weeks later, as the ice began to melt in the parks and the washed-out sky took on a deeper hue. He called upon her on a Tuesday afternoon, knowing he would find her alone, it being her aunt's custom to play bridge with Lady Atwell on that day. As Sara ushered him into the room, colour poured into Caroline's face and her throat went dry, and when she rose to greet him her legs were soft and uncooperative. A potent cocktail of joy and terror seemed to undo her whenever she saw him, and it grew stronger every time. Words vanished from Caroline's mind, and as Sara closed the door she smiled a tight, excited smile at her mistress.

'How kind of you to call,' Caroline managed at last, her voice trembling like her hands. 'I trust you are well?'

Instead of replying, Corin turned his hat around in his hands, began to speak but faltered, hooked a finger into his collar and tugged as if to loosen it. Caroline clasped her hands together to still them, and waited, watching him in astonishment. 'Won't . . . won't you sit down?' she offered at length. Corin glanced at her and seemed to find some resolve at last.

'No, I won't sit down,' he declared, startling Caroline with the gruffness of his tone. They faced each other for a long moment, at an impasse, then Corin crossed the room in two large strides, took Caroline's face in his hands and kissed her. The press of his mouth was so shocking that Caroline made no move to stop him, or to move away as she knew she ought. She was struck by the unexpected softness of his lips, and the heat of him. She could not breathe, and dizziness confounded her even as a peculiar warm ache began in her stomach.

'Mr . . . Mr Massey . . .' she stammered when he pulled away, still holding her face in his hands and studying her with quiet urgency.

'Caroline . . . come away with me. Marry me,' he said. Caroline could scarcely find the words to answer him.

'Do you . . . do you love me, then?' she asked at last. Her pulse jumped up in panic as she waited for his answer, for the words she so longed to hear.

'Do you not know? Can't you tell?' he asked, incredulously. 'I have loved you since the first moment I met you. The very first moment,' he murmured. Caroline shut her eyes, overwhelmed with relief. 'You're smiling,' Corin said, brushing his finger over her cheek. 'Does that mean you will marry me, or that you're laughing at me?' He smiled anxiously, and Caroline took his hand in hers, pressed it to her face.

'It means I will marry you, Mr Massey. It means that . . . I want nothing more than to marry you,' she breathed.

'I will make you so happy,' he promised, kissing her again.

Bathilda refused to announce the engagement between her niece and Corin Massey. She refused to help her assemble her trousseau, buy clothes for travelling, or pack her leather trunks for the journey. Instead, she watched her niece neatly folding away new taileds, gored skirts and embroidered shirtwaists.

'I suppose you consider yourself emancipated, to act so disastrously. Quite the Gibson Girl, I'm sure,' she remarked. Caroline made no reply, although the barb stuck because it was near to the mark. She rolled her jewellery into a blue velvet fold and tucked it into her vanity case. Later, she sought Bathilda out in their spacious house in Gramercy Park, finding her seated in a ray of spring sunshine, so startlingly bright it stripped years from the woman. Caroline asked again for her engagement to be announced. She wanted it to be done properly, officially, as it ought to be; but her request fell on deaf ears.

'It's hardly to be celebrated,' Bathilda snapped. 'I'm only glad I shan't be here to have to answer questions about it. I will be returning to London, to stay with a cousin of my dear late husband's, a lady with whom I have always shared great affection and regard. There is nothing to tie me here in New York, now.'

'You're going back to London? But . . . when?' Caroline asked, more meekly. Unhappily, she realised that in spite of the rift between them, her Aunt Bathilda represented her only family, her only home.

'Next month, when the weather is more clement.'

'I see,' Caroline breathed. She linked her hands in front of her, wound the fingers tightly together and squeezed. Bathilda looked up at her from the book she was ostensibly reading, her gaze tempered with something almost aggressive. 'Then we shall not see each other much from now on, I suppose,' Caroline murmured.

'Indeed not, my dear. But that would have been the case even if I had remained in New York. You will be far beyond the distance I could comfortably have travelled. I will give you my address in London, and of course you must write to me. And I dare say you will find company enough on the farm. There will be other farm wives in the vicinity, I am sure,' she said, smiling faintly as she returned to her book. Caroline's lace collar seemed to choke her. She felt a jolt of fear and did not know whether to run to or from Bathilda.

'You have never shown me love,' she whispered, her voice fearful and tight. 'I do not know why you should be so surprised that I run after it when it is offered to me.' And she left the room before Bathilda could scorn this sentiment.

So Caroline married with nobody to give her away and no family to represent her. She chose a gown of diaphanous white muslin, with a wide yoke of lace ruffles across the bust and crisp frills at the neck and cuffs. Her hair was piled high on her head and held with ivory combs, and pearl drop earrings were her only jewels. She wore no make-up, and her countenance, as she took a last look in the glass, was somewhat pale. Although the weather was not warm, she carried her mother's silk fan on her wrist, fingering it nervously as she travelled to a small church on the Upper East Side, close to where Corin had lived as a boy. Sara the maid sat alone on the bride's side; and as she entered the building, Caroline longed to see her parents there. Corin wore a borrowed suit and tie, his hair combed neatly back and his cheeks freshly shaven, the skin soft and slightly raw. He fidgeted with his collar as she began her approach along the aisle, but then he met her anxious gaze, and he smiled and fell still as though naught else mattered. His mother and two elder brothers were in attendance, solemn as the couple made their vows before the minister. Mrs Massey still wore her mourning dress, and although she welcomed her new daughter-in-law, her grief was too fresh for her to feel truly glad. It was another wet day, and the church was quiet and dark, smelling of damp brick dust and candle wax. Caroline did not mind. Her world had contracted to include nothing but the man in front of her, the man taking her hand, the man who looked at her so possessively and spoke with such conviction as he made his promises. With their hands joined before God, Caroline felt such an irresistible surge of elation that she could not contain it, and it spilled from her in a storm of happy tears that Corin gathered on his fingertips and kissed away. With him she would start her real life at last.

But to his new wife's dismay, Corin packed and made ready to leave New York the following day.

'We will have our wedding night in *our* home, in the house that I have built for us; not here in a place still sorrowing for my father. I came for a funeral, and I didn't bank on finding a wife,' he smiled, kissing her hands. 'I've got to sort a few things out, get the house ready for your arrival. I want it to be perfect.'

'It will be perfect, Corin,' she assured him, still unused to addressing any man by his first name alone. His kisses burned into her skin, made it hard to breathe. 'Please let me come with you now.'

'Give me a month, that's all, my sweetheart. Follow after me four weeks from today and I will have everything ready. You'll have time to say goodbye to all your friends, and I'll have time to boast to all of mine that I have married the most beautiful girl in the whole of America,' he said; and so she agreed even though his departure felt like the sky growing dark.

She called upon some of her old classmates to bid them farewell, but generally found them either occupied or not at home. Eventually, she understood herself *persona non grata*, so she spent the four weeks at home, suffering the uncomfortable silence between herself and her aunt, packing and repacking her luggage, writing letter after letter to Corin, and gazing out of the window at a view now dominated by the newly constructed Fuller Building — a wedge-shaped behemoth that towered nearly three hundred feet into the sky. Caroline had never imagined that man could build so high. She gazed at it, felt diminished by it, and the first doubts crept into her mind. With Corin gone, it almost seemed as though he had never been there at all, that she had dreamed the whole event. She turned the wedding ring on her finger and frowned, fighting to keep such thoughts at bay. But what could have been so terrible that he could not have taken her with him straight away? What had he to hide — regret for his hasty marriage to her? Sara sensed that she was troubled.

'It won't be long now, miss,' she said, as she brought her tea.

'Sara . . . will you stay a moment?'

'Of course, miss.'

'Do you think . . . do you think it will be all right? In Oklahoma Territory?' Caroline asked, quietly.

'Of course, miss! That is . . . I do not rightly know, never having gone there. But . . . Mr Massey will take good care of you, I do know that. He would not take you anywhere you would not wish to go, I am sure,' Sara assured her.

'Bathilda says I will have to work. Until I come into my money, that is . . . I will be a farmer's wife,' she said.

'That you will, miss, but hardly the common sort of one.'

'Is the work so very hard? Keeping house and all? You do it so well, Sara — is it so very hard?' she asked, trying to keep her anxiety from sounding. Sara gazed at her with an odd mingling of amusement, pity and resentment.

'It can be hard enough, miss,' she said, somewhat flatly. 'But you will be mistress of the house! You will be free to do things as you see fit, and I am sure you will have help. Oh, do not fret, miss! It may take you some while to grow accustomed to such a different kind of life to the one you have had, but you'll be happy, I am sure of it.'

'Yes. I will be, won't I?' Caroline smiled.

'Mr Massey *loves* you. And you love him – how could you not be happy?'

'I do love him,' Caroline said, taking a deep breath and holding Sara's hand tightly. 'I do love him.'

'And I'm *so* happy for you, miss,' Sara said, her voice tightening, tears springing in her eyes.

'Oh, please don't, Sara! How I wish you were coming with me!' Caroline cried.

'I wish it too, miss,' Sara said quietly, wiping her eyes with the hem of her apron.

When a letter from Corin did finally arrive, speaking words of love and encouragement, urging her to be patient for a little while longer, Caroline read and reread it twenty times a day, until she knew the words by heart and felt galvanised by them. When the four weeks were up, she kissed Bathilda's florid cheek and tried to see some mark of regret in her aunt's demeanour. But only Sara went with her to the station, sobbing inconsolably beside her young mistress as the bay horses trotted smartly along busy streets and avenues.

'I don't know how it will be without you, miss. I don't know that I'll care for London!' the girl wept; and Caroline took her hand, winding their fingers tightly together, too full of clamouring feelings to speak. Only when confronted with the locomotive, which spat steam and soot with great vigour and filled her nose with the tang of hot iron and cinders, did she finally feel that she had found some other thing in the world as glad as she was to be making the journey. She shut her eyes as the train eased forwards, and with its loud, solemn cough of steam, her old life ended and her new one began.

2

My mother's brother, my Uncle Clifford, and his wife Mary, want the old linen press from the nursery, the round Queen Anne table from the study and the collection of miniatures that live in a glass-topped display case at the foot of the stairs. I'm not sure if this is what Meredith meant when she said her children could take *a keepsake*, but I really don't care. I dare say a few more things will find their way into Clifford's lorry at the end of the week, and if Meredith would be outraged, I will not be. It's a grand house, but it's not Chatsworth. There are no museum pieces, apart from a couple of the paintings perhaps. Just a big, old house full of big, old things; valuable, perhaps, but also unloved. Our mother has asked only for any family photographs I can find. I love her for her decency, and her heart.

I hope Clifford is sending enough men. The linen press is enormous. It looms against the far wall of the nursery: acres of French mahogany with minarets and cornicing, a scaled-down temple to starch and mothballs. A set of wooden steps live behind it, and they creak and wobble beneath me. I pull stiff, solid piles of linens from the shelves and drop them to the floor. They are flat, weighty; their landings make the pictures shake. Dust flies and my nose prickles, and Beth appears in the doorway, rushing to discover what havoc I am wreaking. There is so much of it. Generations of bed sheets, worn enough to have been replaced, not worn enough to have been thrown out. It could be decades since some of these piles have been disturbed. I remember Meredith's housekeeper puffing up the stairs with laden arms; her cracked red cheeks and her broad ugly hands.

Once I've emptied the press I am not sure what to do with all the piles of linen. It could go to charity, I suppose. But I'm not up to the task of black-bagging it all, heaving it down to the car, taking it in batches into Devizes. I pile it back up against the wall, and as I do my eyes catch on one pattern, one splash of weak colour in all the white. Yellow flowers. Three pillow cases with yellow flowers, green stems, embroidered into each corner in silk thread that still catches the light. I run my thumb over the neat stitching, feel how years of use have made the fabric watery soft. There is something in the back of my mind, something I know I recognise but can't remember. Have I seen them before? The flowers are ragged looking, wild. I can't put a name to them. And there are only three. Four pillowcases with every other set but this one. I drop them back onto a pile, drop more linen on top. I find I am frowning and consciously unknit my brow.

Clifford and Mary are Henry's parents. Were Henry's parents. They were in Saint Tropez when he disappeared, which the press unfairly made a great deal out of. As if they had left him with strangers, as if they had left him home alone. Our parents did it too. We often came here for the whole of the school holidays, and for two weeks or even three, most years, Mum and Dad would go away without us. To Italy, for long walks; to the Caribbean to sail. I liked and feared having them gone. Liked it because Meredith never checked up on us much, never came outside in search of us when we'd been gone for hours. We felt liberated, we tore about like yahoos. But feared it because, inside the house, Meredith had sole charge of us. We had to be with her. Eat our dinner with her, answer her questions, think up lies. It never occurred to me that I didn't like her, or that she was unpleasant. I was too young to think that way. But when Mum got back I flew to her, gathered clammy handfuls of her skirts.

Beth kept me extra close when our parents were away. If she walked ahead, it was with one hand held slightly behind her, long fingers spread, always waiting for me to take hold of them. And if I didn't she would pause, glance over her shoulder, make sure that I was following. One year, Dinny built her a tree house in a tall beech on the far side of the wood. We'd hardly seen him for days and he'd forbidden us to spy on him. The weather had been fitful, wind dimpling the surface of the dew pond, too fresh to swim. We'd played dressing up in a spare bedroom; built castles of empty flowerpots in the orangery; made a den in the secret hollow centre of the yew topiary globe on the top lawn. Then the sun came out again and we saw Dinny wave from the corner of the garden, and Beth smiled at me, her eyes alight.

'It's ready,' he said, when we reached him.

'What is it?' I demanded. 'Go on – tell us!'

'A surprise,' was all he would say, smiling shyly at Beth. We followed him through the trees, and I was telling him about the den in the topiary when I saw it and was silenced. One of the biggest beech trees, with a silvery smooth trunk and bark that wrinkled where its branches forked, like the crook of your elbow or the back of your knee. I'd seen Dinny climb it before, with a few practised swings, to sit amidst the pale green leaves far above me. Now, high up where the tree began to spread, Dinny had built a broad platform of sturdy planks. The walls were made from old fertiliser bags, bright blue, nailed to a wooden frame and belling in and out like boat sails. The route up to this fortress was marked by knotted rope loops and chunks of scrap wood, nailed to the tree to form an intermittent ladder. In the hung silence I heard the enticing rush of the breeze, the rustling snap of the tree house walls.

'What do you think?' Dinny asked, folding his arms and squinting at us.

'It's brilliant! It's the best tree house ever!' I exclaimed, bouncing urgently from foot to foot.

'It's great – did you build it all by yourself?' Beth asked, still smiling up at the blue house. Dinny nodded.

'Come up and see — it's even better inside,' he told her, moving to the foot of the tree, reaching up for the first handhold.

'Come *on*, Beth!' I admonished her, when she hesitated.

'OK!' she laughed. 'You go first, Erica — I'll give you a boost to the first branch.'

'We should give it a name. You should name it, Dinny!' I chattered, hoisting up my skirt, tucking it into my knickers.

'What about the watch tower? Or the crow's nest?' he said. Beth and I agreed — The Crow's Nest it would be. Beth hoisted me onto the first branch, my sandals scuffing welts into the powdery green algae, but I could not reach the next handhold. My fingertips crooked over the rung Dinny had nailed into the tree, so close, but too far for me to hang on safely. Dinny joined me on the first branch, let me step on his bent knee until I could reach, but from there my leg would not stretch to the next rung.

'Come down, Erica,' Beth called at length, when I was red and cross and feeling close to tears.

'No! I want to go up!' I protested, but she shook her head.

'You're too little! Come down!' she insisted. Dinny withdrew his knee, jumped down from the tree, and I had no choice but to obey. I slithered back to the ground and stared in sullen silence at my stupid, too-short legs. I had grazed my knee, but was too disheartened to be excited about the sticky worm of blood oozing down my shin.

'Beth, then? Are you coming up?' Dinny asked, and I sank inside, to be left out, to miss out on the wonderful tree house. But Beth shook her head.

'Not if Erica can't,' she said. I glanced up at Dinny but looked away again quickly, squirming away from the disappointment in his eyes, the way his smile had vanished. He leant against the tree, folded his arms defensively. Beth hesitated for a while, as if unable to choose her next words. Then her hand reached out for me again. 'Come on, Rick. We need to go and wash your leg.'

Two days later Dinny fetched us back again, and this time the trunk of the beech tree was riddled with rungs and ropes. Beth smiled calmly at Dinny and I flew to the bottom of this ramshackle staircase, staring up at the floating house as I started to climb.

'Go carefully!' Beth gasped, sucking the fingertips of one hand as I missed my footing, wobbled. She followed me up, frowning in concentration, careful not to look down. A loose curtain of bags marked the doorway. Inside, Dinny had arranged plastic sacks stuffed with straw. There was a wooden crate table, a bunch of cow parsley in a milk bottle, a pack of cards, some comics. It was quite simply the best place I had ever been. We painted a sign, to put at the foot of the ladder. *The Crow's Nest. Trespassers will be Persecuted.* Mum laughed when she read it. We spent hours up there, adrift in whispering green clouds with patches of bright sky sparkling overhead, eating picnics, far away from Meredith and Henry. I worried that Henry would ruin it when he came to stay. I worried that he would crash through our magical place, mock it, make it seem less magnificent. But by happy, happy chance, it turned out that Henry was afraid of heights.

In my head Henry is always bigger than me, older than me. Eleven when I was seven. It seemed an enormous gap at the time. He was a *big boy*. He was loud and bossy. He said I had to do what he told me. He buttered Meredith up — she always preferred boys to girls. He went along with her on the rare occasions she came out to the woods, and more than once helped her make a nasty scheme a reality. Henry: a fleshy neck with a receding chin; dark brown hair; clear blue eyes that he would narrow, make ugly; pale skin that burnt across the nose in summer. One of those children, I see him now, who is a grown-up in miniature rather than a child, who you can look at and know, at once, what they will look like as an adult. His features were already mapped; they would grow, but not develop. He wore himself in his face, I think, charmless, obvious. But this is unfair. He never got the chance to prove me wrong, after all.

Eddie still has the face of a child, and I love it. A nondescript boy's face, sharp nose, tufty hair, kneecaps standing proud from skinny shanks in his school shorts. My nephew. He hugs Beth on the platform, a little sheepishly because some of his classmates are on the train behind him, banging on the glass, sticking up their fingers. I wait by the car for them, my hands puckered with cold, grinning as they draw near.

'Hey, Eddie Baby! Edderino! Eddius Maximus!' I call to him, putting my arms around him and squeezing, pulling his feet off the ground.

'Auntie Rick, it's just Ed now,' he protests, with a hint of exasperation.

''Course. Sorry. And you can't call me *Auntie* — you make me feel a hundred years old! Sling your bag in the back and let's get going,' I say, resisting the urge to tease him. He is eleven now. The same age Henry will always be, and old enough for teasing to matter. 'How was your train ride?'

'Pretty boring. Except Absolom locked Marcus in the loo. He screamed the place down — quite funny really,' Eddie reports. He smells of school and it starts to fill the car, sharp and vinegary. Unwashed socks, pencil shavings, mud, ink, stale sandwiches.

'Pretty funny, indeed! I had to go in and see the head a fortnight ago because he'd shut his art teacher in her classroom. They pushed a block of lockers against her door!' Beth says, voice loud and bright, startling me.

'It wasn't *my* idea, Mum!'

'You still helped,' Beth counters. 'What if there'd been a fire or something? She was in there for hours!'

'Well . . . they shouldn't have banned mobile phones then, should they?' Eddie says, smiling. I catch his eye in the rear-view mirror and wink.

'Edward Calcott Walker, I am appalled,' I say lightly. Beth

glares at me. I must remember not to conspire with Eddie against her, not even over something tiny. It can't be him and me against her, even for a second. She resents my help already.

'Is this a new car?'

'New-ish,' I tell him. 'The old Beetle finally died on me. Wait until you see the house, Ed. It's a monster.' But as we pull in and I look at him expectantly, he nods, raises his eyebrows, is not impressed. Then I think the manor might only be the size of one wing of his school – smaller than his friends' houses, perhaps.

'I'm so glad it's school holidays again, darling,' Beth says, taking Eddie's bag from him. He smiles at her sidelong, slightly abashed. He will be taller than her eventually – he reaches her shoulder already.

I tour Eddie around the grounds while Beth settles down with his report card. I take him up to the barrow, skirt the dreary woods, arrive at the dew pond. He has found a long stick somewhere and swishes it, beheading the weeds and dead nettles. It's warmer today, but damp. Flecks of drizzle in the breeze, and the empty branches knocking overhead.

'Why's it called a dew pond? Isn't it just a pond?' he asks, smacking the edge with his stick, crouching on supple, bony legs. Ripples fly out across the surface. The pockets of his jeans bulge with pilfered treasures. He's like a magpie that way, but they are things nobody would miss. Old safety pins, conkers, bits of blue and white china from the soil.

'This is where the stream starts. It was dug out a long time ago, to make this pond as a kind of reservoir. And *dew* pond because it traps the dew as well, I suppose.'

'Can you swim in it?'

'We used to – Dinny and your mum and I. Actually, I don't think your mum ever went all the way in. It was always pretty cold.'

'Jamie's parents have got this wicked lake for swimming in – it's a swimming pool, except it's not all chlorine and tiles and all that. It's got plants and everything. But it's clean.'

'Sounds great. Not at this time of year, though, eh?'

'Guess not. Who's Dinny?'

'Dinny . . . was a boy we used to play with. When we came here as kids. His family lived nearby. So . . .' I trail off. Why should talking about Dinny make me feel so conspicuous? Dinny. With his square hands so good at making things. Dark eyes smiling through his fringe, and his hair a thatch that I once stuck daisies into while he slept, my fingers trembling with suppressed mirth, with my audacity; to be so close and to touch him. 'He was a real adventurer. He built a fabulous tree house one year . . .'

'Can we see it? Is it still there?' he asks.

'We can go and look, if you like,' I offer. Eddie grins, and jogs a few paces ahead, taking aim at a sapling, tackling it with a two-handed blow.

Eddie's adult teeth haven't sorted themselves out yet. They seem to jostle for position in his mouth. There are big gaps, and a pair that cross over. They'll be clamped behind braces soon enough.

'What did I hear the other boys calling you from the train?' I call out to him.

He grimaces. 'Pot Plant,' he admits, ruefully.

'Why on *earth* . . . ?'

'Well, it's kind of embarrassing . . . do I have to say?'

'Yeah, you do. No secrets between us.' I smile. Eddie sighs.

'Miss Wilton keeps a little plant on her desk – I'm not sure what it is. Mum has them too – dark purple flowers, with furry leaves?'

'Sounds like an African violet.'

'Whatever. Well, she left us in there on detention at lunchtime, and I said I was so hungry I could eat anything, so Ben bet me a fiver I wouldn't eat her plant. So . . .'

'So you did?' I raise an eyebrow, folding my arms as we walk. Eddie shrugs, but he can't help but look a little pleased.

'Not the *whole* thing. Just the flowers.'

'*Eddie!*'

'Don't tell Mum!' he chortles, jogging on again. 'What was your nickname at school?' he calls back to me.

'I didn't really have one. Just Rick. I was always the youngest one, tagging along. Dinny called me "Pup", sometimes,' I tell him.

We are closer than many aunts and nephews, Eddie and I. I stayed with him for two months while Beth recovered, while she *got help*. It was a strained time, a time of keeping going and pretending, and being normal and not fussing. We didn't have any big conversations. We didn't bare our souls, pour out our hearts. Eddie was too young, and I am too impatient. But we shared a time of extreme awkwardness, of concentrated sadness and anger and confusion. We jarred along, the both of us feeling that way; and that's what makes us close – the knowledge of that time. His father Maxwell and I holding hushed, strangled arguments behind closed doors, not wanting Eddie to hear his father call his mother *unfit*.

All that remains of the tree house are a few ragged planks, dark and green and slimy looking; like the rotten bones of a shipwreck.

'Well, I guess it's kind of had its day,' I say, sadly.

'You could rebuild it. I'll help, if you want?' Eddie says, keen to cheer me up.

I smile. 'We could try. It's more of a summer thing though – it'd be a bit cold and mucky up there now, I should think.'

'Why did you stop coming here? To visit Great-Grandma?' An innocent question, poor Eddie, to ease the moment. What a question for him to ask.

'Oh . . . you know. We just . . . went on holiday with our parents more as we got older. I don't really remember.'

'But you always say you never forget the important things that happen when you're a kid. That's what you told me, when I won that prize for speech and drama.' I had meant it to be a positive thing when I said it. But he won the prize while I was staying with him for those two months, and what we both thought, at the same time, was that what he would always remember was coming home from school and finding Beth the way he did. I saw the thought fly across his face, shut my eyes, wished I could pull my words back out of the air.

'Well, that just goes to show that it can't have been that big a thing, doesn't it?' I say lightly. 'Come on – there's loads more to see.'

We head back towards the house, ducking into the orangery as it starts to pour with rain. From there, barely getting wet, we dodge from shed to shed, through the old stables to the coach house, which is congested with junk and spattered with bird shit. Above our heads we count the swallows' nests, clinging to the beams like fungus. Eddie finds a small axe, the blade garish with rust.

'Awesome!' he breathes, brandishing it in a swooping arc. I grab his wrist, test the comprehensive bluntness of the axe with my thumb.

'Be extremely careful with it,' I say, fixing him in the eye. 'And don't bring it into the house.'

'I won't,' he says, swooping it again, smiling at the thrum of severed air.

Outside, it grows darker and the rain falls faster. A stream of muddy water bubbles past the coach house door.

'Let's go in, shall we? Your mum'll be wondering where we've got to.'

'She should come out and see the tree house, see if she thinks we could rebuild it. Do you think she would?'

'I don't know, Ed. You know how quickly she gets cold when the weather's like this,' I say. Nothing between the core of her and the winter chill. No flesh, no muscle, no thick skin.

Beth is making mince pies again when we clatter into the kitchen. She's rolling the pastry, cutting the shapes, filling them, baking them, bagging them. She started yesterday, in preparation for Eddie's arrival, and shows no sign of stopping. The kitchen table is awash with flour and scraps, empty mincemeat jars. The smell is heavenly. Flushed, she emerges from the Rayburn with another batch, slapping the trays down onto the scarred worktop. She's filled every tin and biscuit barrel. There are several bags in the ancient freezer in the cellar. I pick two up, pass one to Eddie. The filling scalds my tongue.

'These are fabulous, Beth,' I say, by way of a greeting. She shoots me a small smile, which broadens when it moves to her son. She crosses to kiss his cheek, leaving ghostly flour fingerprints on his sleeves.

'Well done, darling. All your teachers seem very pleased with you,' she tells him. I pick up the report card from the table, blow flour from it and flick through. 'With the possible exception of Miss Wilton . . .' she qualifies. She of the African violet.

'What does she teach?' I ask him, as he squirms slightly.

'French,' Eddie mumbles, through a mouthful of pie.

'She says you aren't trying nearly hard enough, and that when you do try you prove that you should be doing much better than you currently are,' Beth goes on, holding Eddie's shoulders, not letting him escape. He shrugs ambiguously. 'And – *three* detentions this term? What's that all about?'

'French is just so *boring*!' he declares. 'And Miss Wilton is *so* strict! She's really unfair! One of those detentions I got was because Ben threw a note at me! It was hardly my fault!'

'Well, just try to pay a bit more attention, OK? French is really important – no, it is!' she insists, when Eddie rolls his eyes. 'When I'm rich and I retire to the south of France, how are you going to cope if you can't speak the language?'

'By shouting and pointing?' he ventures. Beth presses her lips together severely, but then she laughs, a rich, glowing sound I so rarely hear. She can't help it, not with Eddie. 'Can I have another mince pie?' he asks, sensing victory.

'Go on. Then go and get in the bath — you're filthy!' Eddie grabs two pies and darts out of the kitchen.

'Take your bag up with you!' Beth calls after him.

'I've run out of hands!' Eddie calls back.

'Run out of inclination, is more like it,' Beth says to me, smiling ruefully.

Later, we watch a film; Beth curled with Eddie on the sofa with a huge bowl of popcorn wedged between them. When I glance at her I see that she's hardly following the film. She turns her chin, rests it on the top of Eddie's head, shuts her eyes contentedly, and I feel some of the knots inside me loosen, slipping away into the warmth of the open fire. The weekend passes quickly this way — a trip to the cinema in Devizes, school work at the kitchen table, mince pies; Eddie out in the coach house, or marauding through the deserted stables, wielding his axe. Beth is serene, if a little distracted. She stops baking when she runs out of flour, and stands for long moments, watching Eddie through the window with a faint, faraway smile.

'I might take him to France next summer,' she says to me, not breaking off this vigil as I pass her a cup of tea.

'I think he'd love it,' I say.

'The Dordogne, perhaps. Or the Lot Valley. We could go river swimming.' I love to hear her make plans. Future plans. I love to know she is thinking that far ahead. I rest my chin on her shoulder for a moment, follow her gaze out into the garden.

'I told you he'd have fun here,' I remark. 'Christmas will be excellent.' Her hair smells faintly of mint and I pull it over her shoulder, smooth it flat against her jumper with a long sweep of my hand.

On Sunday afternoon, Maxwell arrives to collect his son. I shout for Beth as I open the door to him, and when she does not appear I give Maxwell a short tour of the ground floor and make him a coffee. Maxwell divorced Beth five years ago, when her depression seemed to be getting worse and her weight plummeted, and he said he just couldn't cope and it was no way to raise a child. So he left her and remarried pretty much straight away – a short, plump, healthy-looking woman called Diane: white teeth, cashmere, perfect nails. Uncomplicated. Beth's depression was very convenient for Maxwell, I've always thought. But he's not all bad. He met her at a good time, that's all, when she was all grace and demure beauty. She was like a swan then, like a lily. A fair-weather friend is what Maxwell turned out to be. Now his grey raincoat is dripping onto the flagstones, but the rain can't spoil the sheen of wealth on hair, shoes, skin.

'Quite an impressive place,' he says, taking a gulp of the scalding hot coffee with a loud sound I don't like.

'Yes, I suppose it is,' I agree, leaning against the Rayburn, folding my arms. I found it hard to warm to Maxwell when he was still my brother-in-law. Now, I find it near impossible.

'Needs a lot of work, of course. But huge potential,' he declares. He made his money in property, and I wonder, with a touch of spite, how the credit crunch is working out for him. Huge potential. He said that about the cottage Beth bought near Esher, after the divorce. He sees everything with a developer's eye, but Beth kept the swollen wooden doors, the fireplaces that only draw when the windows are open. She likes it half broken. 'Have you decided what you're going to do with it?'

'No, not yet. Beth and I haven't really talked about it,' I say. A flash of irritation crosses his face. He never did like diffidence getting in the way of good sense.

'Well, this legacy could make the pair of you very wealthy women—'

'We'd have to stay here, though. Live here. I'm not sure that's what either of us wants.'

'But you needn't rattle around in the whole house. Have you thought about converting it into flats? You'd need planning, of course, but that shouldn't be a problem. You could keep an apartment and the freehold for yourselves, and sell the rest off with long leaseholds. You'd make an absolute killing, and keep to the terms of the will.'

'That would cost thousands and thousands . . .' I shake my head. 'Besides, we're having a recession, remember? I thought building and developing was at a standstill?'

'We may be in recession now, but in two years' time, three? People will always need places to live, in the long term.' Maxwell tips his head, considering. 'You'd need investors. I could help you with that. I might even be interested myself . . .' I see him look around the room with renewed attention, as if drawing up plans, measuring. It gives me a spasm of distaste.

'Thanks. I'll mention it to Beth.' My tone is final. Maxwell looks at me with a stern eye but says nothing for a while.

He fixes his eyes on a painting of fruit on the opposite wall, and at length he clears his throat slightly, so I know what he will ask next.

'And how is Beth?'

'She's fine,' I shrug, deliberately vague. Again, irritation shimmers across his features, puckers his forehead into a deeper frown.

'Come on, Erica. When I saw her last week she was looking very thin again. Is she eating? Has she been acting up at all?' I try not to think about the mince pies. About the hundreds of mince pies.

'Not that I've noticed,' I lie. It's a big lie. She's getting worse again, and though I don't exactly know why, I do know when it started – when she peaked, and started to fall again: it was when Meredith died. When, by dying, she brought this place back into our lives.

'So where is she?'

'I've no idea. Probably in the bathroom,' I shrug.

'Keep an eye on her,' he mutters. 'I don't want Eddie spending

Christmas here if she's going to have one of her episodes. It's just not fair on him.'

'She's not going to have an *episode*. Not unless you try to keep Eddie away from her,' I snap.

'It's not a question of keeping Eddie away from her. It's about doing what's best for my son, and—'

'What's best for him is that he gets to spend time with his mother. And it helps her so much to have him around. She's always much better—'

'It shouldn't be up to Edward to make his mother better!'

'That's not what I meant!'

'I only agreed to Edward coming here at all because you would be here to keep an eye on things, Erica. Beth has already shown how unpredictable she can be, how unstable. Putting your head in the sand won't help, you know.'

'I think I know my sister, Maxwell, and she is *not* unstable—'

'Look, I know you only want to stick up for her, Erica, and it's admirable. But this isn't a game. Seeing her at her worst is something that might affect Edward for the rest of his life, and I am not prepared to let that happen! Not again.'

'Keep your voice down, for God's sake!'

'Look, I just want—'

'I know what you want, Maxwell, but you can't change the fact that Beth is Eddie's mother. People aren't perfect – Beth's not perfect. But she is a great mother, and she adores Eddie, and if you could just focus on that for a change, instead of watching and waiting and crying *sole custody!* every time she gets a little bit down . . .'

'*A little bit down* is something of an understatement, though, isn't it Erica?' he says, and I can only glare at him because he is right. In the pause we hear a noise from outside the room, and exchange an accusatory glance. Eddie is in the hallway, swinging his kit bag awkwardly, left to right. It twists his skinny wrist.

'Edward!' Maxwell calls, smiling broadly and crossing to engulf his son in a brief hug.

It takes me quite some time to find Beth. The house is dark today, like the world outside. A midwinter Sunday when the sun barely seemed to rise and is now fading again. I move from door to door, flinging them open, peering in, breathing the stale smell of rooms long shut. A few hours ago we all had a late breakfast, sitting at the long table in the kitchen. Beth was bright and shiny; she made hot chocolate and warmed croissants in the Rayburn for us all. Too bright and shiny, I realise now. I didn't see her slip away. I flick at light switches as I go but a lot of the bulbs have blown. I find her at last, wedged onto the window sill in one of the top floor bedrooms. From there she can see the silver car in the driveway, streaked and scattered by the rain on the dirty window.

'Maxwell's here,' I say, pointlessly. Beth ignores me. She catches her bottom lip in two fingers, pushes it against her teeth, bites it hard. 'Eddie's going, Beth. You have to come down and see him off. Come on. And Maxwell wants to speak to you.'

'I don't want to speak to him. I don't want to see him. I don't want Eddie to go.'

'I know. But it's just for a while. And you can't let Eddie go without saying goodbye.' She rolls her head to glare at me. So tired, she looks. So tired and sad. 'Please, Beth. They're waiting . . . we have to go down.' Beth draws in a breath, unfolds herself from the sill – a slow, deliberate, underwater movement.

'Found her!' My cheerful announcement is too loud. 'This place is big enough to get lost in.' Beth and Maxwell ignore me, but Eddie smiles, at a loss. I wish Beth would put on a better act sometimes. Would show that she copes. I could shake her for not showing Maxwell a better front right now. She stands before him with her arms folded, lost inside a shapeless cardigan. She didn't fight when he left. They settled amicably – that was the word both families bandied about. *Amicable*. There is nothing amicable about

Beth as she stands there now, grey-faced, raw looking. They do not touch.

'Good to see you, Beth. You look well,' Max lies.

'So do you.'

'Look, do you mind if we drop Eddie back next Saturday, rather than the Friday? Only it's Melissa's school carol concert on the Friday night and we'd all like to go together, wouldn't we, Ed?' Eddie shrugs a shoulder and nods at the same time. The poor boy could teach diplomacy. Beth's mouth pinches, her jaw knots. How she hates any mention of Max's new family, any extra second of time Eddie spends with them. But the request is reasonable, and she strives to be reasonable too.

'Of course. Of course it's no problem,' she says.

'Great,' Maxwell smiles, a quick, businesslike smile. There's a quiet pause, just the *scuff scuff scuff* of Eddie's bag, swinging to and fro. 'Have you got much planned for the week?' Maxwell asks.

'Not a lot – sorting through some of the old girl's junk, getting ready for Christmas,' I say lightly. Beth adds nothing to this summary.

'Right, well, let's get on, shall we, Ed?' Maxwell ushers his son towards the door. 'We'll see you on Saturday. Have a good week, the pair of you.'

'Wait! Eddie . . .' Beth rushes over to him and hugs him too tightly. She would go with him if she could. Keep hold of him, not let him forget her, not let him love Diane and Melissa too much. When the door is shut behind them I turn to Beth, but she won't meet my eye.

'I wish you wouldn't always be so quiet in front of Maxwell!' I burst out. 'Can't you be more . . .' I trail off, at a loss. Beth flings her arms up.

'No, I can't! I know he wants to take Eddie away from me. I can't pretend I don't know, or don't mind!' she cries.

'I know, I know,' I soothe her. She puts her hands through her messy hair. 'Eddie will be back soon,' I add. 'You know how much he loves being with you, Beth — he just adores you, and nothing Maxwell ever does will change that.' I grip her shoulders gently, try to coax a smile from her. Beth sighs, folds her arms.

'I know. I just . . . I'm going for a shower,' she says, and turns away from me.

With Eddie gone, the house is just big and empty again. By silent consensus we have stopped sorting through Meredith's things for now. The task is just too huge and seems pointless. The contents of this house have been here so long they've corroded in place. It would be an impossible task to remove it all now. They will have to use force, maybe bulldozers — I picture that, a metal-toothed bucket scraping through layers of fabric and carpet and paper and wood and dust. Hard work, like trying to scoop balls from an unripe melon. It will be a terrible act of violence. All the little traces of so many lives.

'I never thought, before, about what happens to a person's things when they die,' I say as we eat supper. The larder was full of Heinz tinned soups when we arrived but we're getting through them. I'll have to venture out into the village sometime soon.

'What do you mean?'

'Well . . . just that, I've never known anybody to die before. I've never had to deal with the aftermath, to . . .'

'Deal with the aftermath? You make it sound like a selfish thing to do, dying. Is that what you think?' Beth's voice is low and intense. Such a change in her, now that Eddie has left.

'No! Of course not. That wasn't what I was saying at all. I just meant that it's not something you think about, until it happens . . . who'll sort everything out. Where things will go. I mean, what will happen to Meredith's nighties? Her stockings? The food in the larder?' I am struggling; the conversation was meant to be flippant.

'What does it matter, Erica?' Beth snaps at me. I stop talking, break off a piece of bread, crumble it between my fingers.

'It doesn't matter,' I say. Sometimes I feel very lonely with Beth.

I never used to, not when we were younger, not before. We didn't antagonise each other much, or argue. Perhaps the age gap between us was big enough. Perhaps it was because we had a common enemy. Not even when we were shut inside for two whole days, two long sunny days, did we turn on each other. That was Henry's doing, and Meredith's. Meredith forbade us playing with Dinny from the word go; told us not to talk to any of his family, not to go near them, after we had innocently announced our new friendship to her at teatime.

We met him at the dew pond, where he was swimming. The day was warm but not hot. Early in the summer, I think it was; the landscape still fresh and green. A cool breeze blowing, so that when we first saw him, soaking wet, we shivered. His clothes were in a pile on the bank. All of his clothes. Beth took my hand, but we did not run away. Straight away, we were fascinated. Straight away, we wanted to know him – a thin, dark, naked boy with wet hair clinging to his neck, swimming and diving, all by himself. How old was I? I'm not sure. Four or five, no more than that.

'Who are you?' he asked, treading water. I shuffled closer to Beth, held her hand tighter.

'That's our grandmother's house,' Beth explained, pointing back at the manor. Dinny paddled a bit closer.

'But who are you?' he smiled, teeth and eyes gleaming.

'Beth!' I whispered urgently. 'He's got no clothes on!'

'Shh!' Beth hushed me, but it was a funny little sound, made buoyant by a giggle.

'Beth, then. And you?' Dinny looked at me. I lifted my chin a little.

'I'm Erica,' I announced, with all the composure I could muster.

Just then a brown and white Jack Russell terrier burst from the woods and bounded over to us, yapping and wagging.

'I'm Nathan Dinsdale and that's Arthur.' He nodded to the dog. After that, I would have followed him anywhere. I longed for a pet – a proper pet, not the goldfish that was all we had room for at home. I was so busy playing with the dog that I don't remember how Dinny got out of the pond without Beth seeing him naked. I suspect that he did not.

We kept seeing him, of course, in spite of Meredith's ban, and we usually managed to keep it secret by giving Henry the slip before going down to the camp where Dinny lived with his family, at the edge of the manor's grounds. Henry usually steered clear of it anyway. He didn't want to disobey Meredith, and instead absorbed her contempt for the travellers, nurtured it, let it grow into a hatred of his own. The time she shut us in our parents had gone away for the weekend. We went into the village with Dinny, to buy sweets and Coke at the shop. I turned and saw Henry. He ducked behind the phone box, but not quickly enough, and I had a prickling feeling between my shoulder blades as we walked back to the house. Dinny said goodbye and wandered off through the trees, giving the house a wide berth.

Meredith was waiting for us on the step when we got back; Henry nowhere to be seen. But I knew how she knew. She grabbed our arms, nails cutting in, bent down, put her livid face close to ours. 'If you play with dogs, you will catch fleas,' she said, the words clipped and bitten. We were towed upstairs, made to bath in water so hot our skin turned red and angry and I wailed and wailed. Beth was silent, furious.

Afterwards, as I lay in bed and snivelled, Beth coached me in a low voice. 'She wants to punish us, by keeping us indoors, so we have to show that we don't care. That we don't mind. Do you understand, Erica? Please don't cry!' she whispered, stroking my hair back with fingers that shook with rage. I nodded, I think, but I was too upset to pay attention to her. It was still broad daylight outside. I could hear Henry playing with one of the dogs on the lawn, hear Clifford's voice, blurring through the floorboards. A wide August afternoon and we had been put to bed. Confined for the whole weekend.

When our parents got back we told them everything. Dad said, 'This is too much, Laura. I mean it this time.' I felt a flare of joy, of love for him.

Mum said, 'I'll talk to her.'

At teatime, I overheard them in the kitchen. Mum and Meredith.

'He seems like a nice enough boy. Quite sensible. I really don't see the harm in it, Mother,' Mum said.

'Don't see the harm? Do you want the girls to start using that dreadful Wiltshire slang? Do you want them to learn how to steal, and to swear? Do you want them to come home lousy and degraded? If so, then indeed, there can be no harm,' Meredith replied, coldly.

'My girls would *never* steal,' Mum told her firmly. 'And I think *degraded* is overdoing it, really.'

'I don't, Laura. Perhaps you've forgotten how much trouble those people have caused us over the years?'

'How could I forget?' Mum sighed.

'Well, they are your children . . .'

'Yes, they are.'

'But if you want them to live under my roof, and in my care, then they will have to abide by *my* rules,' Meredith snapped.

Mum took a deep breath. 'If I hear that they have been locked up inside again, then they won't come here at all any more, and neither will David and I,' she said quietly, but I could hear the tension. Nearly a tremor. Meredith did not reply. I heard her footsteps coming towards me and I bolted out of sight. With the coast clear I went in to my mother, found her washing up with a quiet intensity, eyes bright. I put my arms around her legs, squeezed her tight.

Meredith was never any less averse to us playing with Dinny, but we were never shut in our room again. Mum won on that point, at least.

Monday morning is leaden and wet. The tips of my fingers and toes were chilled when I woke up, and have stayed that way; and now the end of my nose too. I can't remember when I was last this cold. In London it just doesn't happen. There's the clammy warmth of the underground, the buffeting heat of shops and cafés. A hundred and one places to hide from any dip in the outside temperature. I'm in the orangery, on the south side of the house, overlooking a small lawn ringed with gnarled fruit trees. When we were playing too loudly, when we were *trying Meredith's patience*, we would be sent here, to the small lawn, while the grown-ups sat on the west-facing terrace at a white iron table, drinking iced tea and vodka. My companions in here are the skeletal remains of some tomato plants and a toad, sitting plump by the tap that drips verdigris water onto a bright green swathe of duckweed. I had forgotten the quiet of the countryside, and it unnerves me.

It's earthy and damp in here; a fecund smell, in spite of the season. One of my earliest memories of Henry, who would have been eight or nine: on the small lawn when I was five or so; a hot August day during one of those summers that seemed to last for ever; the grass baked blonde, crisping under the onslaught; the terrace stones too hot for bare feet; the dogs too fagged to play; my nose peeling and freckles on Beth's arms. They set up one of those giant paddling pools for us on the small lawn. So big that there were steps to climb over the side and an expanse of blue plastic sheet inside, so enticing even before the water went in. I can still smell that hot plastic. It was set up, smoothed out; an illicit hosepipe threaded over to it. The water from the hose came straight from the mains and it was icy on our toasted skin. Deliciously numbing. I fidgeted about in my red swimsuit, desperate for it to fill faster.

Henry climbed in straight away, with grass on his feet that floated away. He picked up the hosepipe and waved it at us, now that the grown-ups had retreated. He sprayed us and would not let us come near. I remember being so desperate to get in, to get my feet wet. But on *my* terms. I did not want to be splashed. Feet first, then the rest, gradually. Every time I got near, he sprayed me. The water was at his anklebones, his feet white and rippling. His body was white too, soft looking, nipples pouting slightly, turned down. Then he stopped, and he swore to me – he promised. He swore an oath that I could enter safely, that he had finished spraying. I made him put the hose down before I climbed in carefully. A second of ecstatic cold on my feet then Henry grabbed me, put my head under his arm, pushed the hose right into my face. Water up my nose, in my eyes, freezing, choking; Beth shouting at him from ringside. I coughed and howled until Mum came looking.

I wish Beth would come out of the house. I read somewhere that the great outdoors is just the thing for depression. A bracing walk, a communion with nature. As if depression is like a bout of in-digestion, to be worked out of the system. I am not sure if it will work at this time of year, when the wind can blow right through your soul, but it has to be better than haunting that house. On the work bench I find a trug and some secateurs, and I head out towards the woods.

I walk in a loop via the dew pond. I do this most days. I can't seem to stay away. Standing on the steep edge of it, kicking over chalk and flints. Hints of something return to me when I stand here. Wherever I stand around Storton Manor, hints return to me – little snapshots that go with a view, or a smell, or a room. A ribbon tied behind a bed. Yellow flowers stitched on a pillowcase. Every step is an aide-memoire. Here at the pond there is something I should *remember*, something more than playing, than swimming, than the thrill of the forbidden. I shut my eyes and crouch down, hug my knees. I concentrate on the smell of the water and the ground, on the sound of the trees overhead. I can hear a dog barking, a long way off, in the village perhaps. There is definitely *something*, something I am trying to know. I put blind fingers forward until they touch the surface. The water bites, cold to the bone. I picture it thickening, ice crystals spinning hard threads through it. For one second I feel the old fear of being sucked down into it. For if water could come up from the bottom of it, from nowhere, like magic, then surely things could go the other way as well? A giant plughole. I would think this when I swam, sometimes. A delicious frisson, like swimming in the sea and suddenly thinking of sharks.

At the edge of the downs, where the trees disappear, the ground drops into a steep, round hollow. A giant scooping out of the earth, packed with hawthorn, blackthorn and elder, all bound up with old man's beard. The frost sets deeper here, lasts longer. I set my sights on a holly bush, right in the centre of it all, its bright berries like jewels in the colourless tangle, but I don't get far. I descend, slipping on the tussocky grass, and when I reach the thicket I can see no way in. The air is still, noticeably colder. My breath steams in front of my face as I make my way around, looking for a way in. No view but the slope up and away, the lip where it meets the sky. One attempt to force a way through and I retreat, badly scratched.

I head back into the woods, nothing in my trug so far but some tendrils of stripy ivy from the garden. These aren't public woods; they aren't managed, or criss-crossed with paths. The estate's pasture land is all leased or sold to local farmers these days, and I wonder if any of them ever come in here – take wood, raise pheasants, snare rabbits. I can see no sign of anything like that. The ground is choked with leaf fall and brambles, splintered logs mouldering into nothing. Unseen things move away from me with small rustling sounds and no other trace. Acorns, beech masts; around one tree a carpet of tiny yellow apples, rotting. I have to watch my feet to keep from stumbling and there are no birds singing above my head. Just a quiet breathing sound, as the wind sneaks through the naked branches.

I'm not watching where I'm going and I nearly step on a crouching person. I yelp in surprise. A young man with long dreadlocks and bright, mismatched clothes.

'Sorry! Hello,' I gasp. He stands up, far taller than me, and I see a large bracket fungus by his feet. Yellow and ugly. He was examining it, his nose virtually touching it. 'I . . . I don't think you can eat those,' I add, smiling briefly. The man faces me and says nothing. He is lean and rangy. His arms just hang by his sides as he stands there, watching me, and I feel the pull of unease towing me away from him. Some instinct, perhaps, or something missing from behind his eyes, tells me that all is not as it should be. I take a step back and turn left. He steps to his right to block me. I turn the other way and he follows. My heart beats harder. His silence is unsettling, he is somehow threatening even though he makes no move to reach out for me. He has a spicy smell about him, slightly sharp. I wonder if he's stoned. I turn left again and he smiles, a gummy smile that spreads across his face.

'Look, just get out of the bloody way, will you!' I snap, tensely. But he takes a step towards me and I try to step away but my heel catches in a web of brambles and I fall awkwardly, onto my side, feeling thorns punch into the heels of my hands and the air rush out of my lungs. Leaves fly up around me, the rotting smell of them everywhere. I turn my head and the tall man is leaning over me, blocking out the sky. I fight to free my foot from the undergrowth, but my movements are jerky and I make it worse. I think about shouting but the house is far behind me and there's no way Beth would hear me. She does not know I am out here. Nobody does. Panic makes me shake, makes the air hard to breathe. Then strong, heavy hands close tightly on my arms.

'Let go! Get off me! *Get off!*' I shout out wildly.

I hear a second voice and the hands release me, dropping me unceremoniously back into the mulch.

'Harry's no bother. You didn't mean to be a bother, did you, Harry?' the newcomer says, clapping the tall man on the shoulder. I peer up at them from the ground. Harry shakes his head and I see now that he is downcast, troubled; not fierce or lascivious in the slightest. 'He was just trying to help you up,' the other man says, with a hint of rebuke. Harry returns to his close scrutiny of the yellow fungus.

'He just . . . I was just . . . looking for greenery. For the house,' I say, still rattled. 'I thought . . . Well. Nothing really,' I finish. My heart slows slightly and I feel ridiculous. The stranger puts out a hand, pulls me to my feet. 'Thanks,' I mutter. There's an air rifle angled over his forearm, a dull gleam on the barrel. I kick the brambles back from around my feet and examine my stinging hands. Beads of blood are scattered there. I wipe them on the seat of my jeans and glance at my rescuer with a small, embarrassed smile. I find him watching me with an unsettling intensity, and then he smiles.

'Erica?'

'How did you . . . I'm sorry, do I know you?' I say.

'Don't you recognise me?' he says. I look again – a dark mess of hair, held back at the nape of his neck, a broad chest, a slight hook in the nose, straight forehead, straight brows, mouth a straight, determined line. Black eyes that shine. And then the world tips slightly, skews; features fall into place, and something stunningly familiar coalesces.

'*Dinny?* Is that you?' I gasp, my ribs squeezing in on themselves.

'Nobody's called me Dinny in a *long* time. It's Nathan, these days.' His smile is not quite sure of itself: pleased, as curious as I am to meet a figure from the past, yet guarded, held back. But his eyes never leave my face. Their gaze is like a spotlight on my every move.

'I can't believe it's really you! How . . . how are you? What the hell are you *doing* here?' I am amazed. It never occurred to me that Dinny grew up too, that he lived another life, that he would ever come back to Barrow Storton. 'You look so *different*!' My cheeks are burning, as if I have been caught out somehow. I can feel my pulse in my fingertips.

'But you look just the same, Erica. I saw a bit in the paper – about Lady Calcott dying. It made me think of . . . this place. We haven't been back here since my dad died. But suddenly I wanted to come . . .'

'Oh, no . . . I'm so sorry to hear that. About your dad.' Dinny's father, Mickey. Beth and I loved him. He had a huge grin, huge hands, always gave us a penny or a sweet – pulled it out from behind our ears. Mum met him, once or twice. Checking up, politely, since we spent so much time with them. And Dinny's mum, Maureen, always called Mo. Mickey and Mo. Our code name, to be used whenever Meredith might hear, was that we were going to visit Mickey Mouse.

'It was eight years ago. He went quickly, and he didn't see it coming. I suppose that's the best way to go,' Dinny says calmly.

'I suppose so.'

'What got Lady Calcott in the end?' I notice his tone, a slight bitterness, and that he doesn't commiserate with me on my loss.

'A stroke. She was ninety-nine – and must have been very disappointed.'

'What do you mean?'

'They were a long line of centenarians, the Calcott women. My great-grandmother lived to be a hundred and two. Meredith was always determined to outlive the queen. Good breeding stock, we are,' I say, and instantly regret it. Any mention of stock, of bloodlines, of breed.

There's a vibrant silence. I have so much to say to him I can't think where to start. He breaks off his intent gaze, looks away

~ 63 ~

through the trees towards the house, and a shadow falls over his features.

'Look, I'm sorry I swore. At . . . Harry. He startled me, that's all,' I say quietly.

'You don't need to be afraid of him, he's harmless,' Dinny assures me. We both look down at the motley figure, crouching in the leaf mould. Dinny, standing so close to me that I could touch him. Dinny, real and right here again when he was almost a myth, just minutes ago. I almost don't believe it.

'Is he . . . is there something wrong with him?' I ask.

'He's gentle and friendly and he doesn't like to talk. If that means there's something wrong with him, then yes.'

'Oh, I didn't mean anything by it. Anything bad.' My voice is too high. I take a deep breath, let it out.

'And you were looking for . . . holly?'

'Yes – or mistletoe. Or some good ivy with berries. To decorate the house.' I smile.

'Come on, Harry. Let's show Erica the big holly tree,' Dinny says. He pulls Harry up, gently propels him into a languid walk.

'Thanks,' I say again. My breathing is still too fast. Dinny turns ahead of me and I notice a brace of grey squirrels, tied by their tails with string, slung over his back. Their black eyes are half closed, drying out. Dark, matted patches in the fur on their sides.

'What are the squirrels for?' I ask.

'Dinner,' Dinny replies calmly. He looks around, sees the horror fleet across my face and smiles half a smile. 'I guess squirrel hasn't reached the menus of smart London restaurants yet?'

'Well, some of them, perhaps. Not the ones I eat in, though. How did you know I lived in London?' He turns again, glances at my smart boots, dark jeans, soft, voluminous wool coat. The sharp ends of my fringe.

'Wild guess,' he murmurs.

'Don't you like London?' I ask.

'I've only been once,' Dinny remarks, over his shoulder. 'But generally, no. I don't like cities. I like the horizon to be more than ten metres away.'

'Well, I like having things to look at,' I shrug. Dinny doesn't smile, but falls back to walk beside me, his silence almost companionable. I search for ways to fill it. He is not much taller than me, about the same height as Beth. I can see the tie in his hair, a dark red length of leather bootlace, snapped off, knotted tightly. His jeans are muddied at the hems; he wears a T-shirt and a loose cotton jumper. I see the wind circle his bare neck and I shiver, even though I am bundled beneath layers and he does not seem to notice the cold. We walk up a shallow rise, my steps by far the loudest. Their feet don't seem to find as many snags as mine.

'Over there,' Dinny says, pointing. I look ahead, see a dark holly tree, twisted and old. Harry has picked up a fallen sprig of it, is pressing the prickles into the pad of his thumb and then wincing, shaking his hand, doing it again.

I set about cutting some branches – those with the spikiest leaves, the fattest sprays of berries. One springs away from me, snagging my face. A thin scratch under my eye that stings. Dinny watches me again, his expression inscrutable.

'How's your mother? Is she here with you?' I ask. I want to hear him talk, I want to hear everything he's done since I saw him last, I want him to be real again, to still be a friend. But I remember now – his silences. They never made me uncomfortable before. A child is unperturbed by something as harmless as a silence, oddly patient in that way.

'She's well, thanks. She doesn't travel with us any more. When Dad died she gave it up – she said she was getting too old for it, but I think she'd just had enough of the road. She would never have told Dad, of course. But when he died, she quit. She's hitched to a plumber called Keith. They live in West Hatch, just over the way.'

'Oh, well. Give her my best, when you see her next.' At this he frowns slightly and I wonder if I've said the wrong thing. He has one of those faces that can be rendered so grim, so hawkish by the slightest scowl. At twelve it made him look studious, serious. I felt as silly as thistledown then and I feel it again now.

With my trug full of holly, we walk back through the woods to the clearing where they always camped before. A broad space at the western edge of the copse, surrounded by sheltering trees on three sides, with open fields to the west and a rutted green lane that takes you back to the road. The ground here is not well drained. It squelches as we get near. In summer it's such a green place; long grasses with satin stems, the ground cracked hard and safe beneath. Harry drifts along behind us, his attention flitting from one thing to another.

'And you? Are you living here now?' Dinny asks, at length.

'Oh, no. I don't know. Probably not. For the time being; for Christmas, anyway. We've inherited the house, Beth and I . . .' How pompous I sound.

'Beth's here?' Dinny interrupts, turning to face me.

'Yes, but . . . Yes, she's here.' I was going to say *but she's different, but she won't come out*. 'You should come up to the house and say hello,' I say, knowing that he won't.

There are six vehicles in the camp – more than there used to be. Two minibuses, two campervans, a big old horse lorry and a converted army ambulance, which Dinny says is his. Coils of smoke shred away from chimney pipes, and circles of cold ash scatter the ground. Harry strides ahead to sit on a stump of wood, picking something up from the ground and setting to work intently upon it. As we approach, three dogs race over to us, barking in apparent savagery. I know this drill. I stand still, let my arms hang, wait for them to reach us, to sniff me, to see me not run.

'Yours?'

'Only two of them – the black and tan belongs to my cousin Patrick. This is Blot,' Dinny scuffs the ears of a vicious-looking black mongrel, toothy and scarred, 'and this is Popeye.' A smaller, gentler dog; a rough brown coat and kind eyes. Popeye licks the fingers Dinny offers to him.

'So . . . um, are you working around here? What do you do?' I fall back on a party stalwart, and Dinny shrugs. For a second I think that perhaps he draws endless benefits, that he steals, sells drugs. But these are Meredith's thoughts, and I'm ashamed to have them.

'Nothing right now. We follow work around the country for most of the year. Farm work, bar work, festivals. This time of year is pretty dead.'

'That must be hard.'

Dinny gives me a quick glance. 'It's fine, Erica,' he tells me mildly. He doesn't ask me what I do. In the short walk to the camp I seem to have used up all the credit a childhood acquaintance afforded me.

'I like your ambulance,' I say, desperate. As I speak, the ambulance door bangs open and a girl climbs awkwardly out. She puts her hands in the small of her back, stretches with a grimace. I recognise her at once – the pregnant girl from the barrow. But she can only be fifteen, sixteen. Dinny is the same age as Beth: thirty-five. I look at the girl again and try to make her eighteen, maybe nineteen, but I can't.

The girl with the bubble-curls, a bright natural blonde that you rarely see these days. Her skin is pale and there are blue smudges under her eyes. In a tight, stripy jersey it is very clear how close to term she is. She sees me standing with Dinny and she comes across to us, scowling. I try to smile, to seem comfortable there. She looks fiercer than Blot.

'Who's this?' she demands, hands on hips. She talks to Dinny, not to me.

'Erica, this is Honey. Honey, Erica.'

'Honey? Pleased to meet you. I'm sorry for scaring you, up at the barrow the other day,' I say, in a cheery tone I secretly, horrified, think is my teaching voice.

Honey gazes at me with flat, tired eyes. 'That was you? You didn't scare me.' A noticeable Wiltshire burr to her speech.

'No, well. Not scare, but . . .' I shrug. She looks at me for a long moment. Such hard scrutiny from one so young. Palpable relief when she dismisses me, looks back at Dinny.

'The stove's not drawing right,' she says.

Dinny sighs, crouches down to put his hands through Popeye's coat. The first drops of rain land on our hands and faces.

'I'll see to it in a minute,' he tells her, soothingly. She stares at him then turns away, goes back inside without another glance. I am momentarily dumbstruck by her.

'So . . . when's the due date? Must be soon?' I ask awkwardly, hoping she won't hear me from inside.

'A little after Christmas,' Dinny says, looking away across the clearing.

'So close! You must be very excited. Has she got her overnight bag ready and everything? For the hospital?' Dinny shakes his head.

'No hospital. She wants to have it here, she says.' At this Dinny pauses, stands up and turns to me. 'I don't know if it's a good idea. Do you know anything about babies?' he sounds anxious.

'Me? No, not really. I've never . . . But the government are always on about the merits of home births these days. Every woman's right, apparently. Have you got a good midwife?'

'No midwife, no *home* birth – she wants to have it out there, in the woods.'

'In the *woods*? But . . . it's December! Is she mad?'

'I know it's December, Erica. But it's her right to choose, as you say,' he says flatly. There's a hint of exasperation there, beneath the surface. 'She's taking the idea of a natural birth about as far as she possibly can.'

'Well, you have a right to choose, too. The father has a right too. First babies can take their time, you know. Beth was in labour for thirty-six hours with Eddie . . .'

'Beth has a baby?'

'Had a baby. He's eleven now. He's coming for Christmas, so you'll probably meet him . . . Eddie. He's a fantastic kid.'

'So she's married?'

'Was married. Not married now,' I say shortly. He has questions about Beth, but none about me.

The rain is coming down harder again. I hunch, push my hands deeper into my pockets, but Dinny doesn't seem to notice it. I think about offering to talk to Honey, then I remember her hard eyes and I hope Dinny won't ask me to. A compromise, then.

'Well, if Honey wants to talk to somebody about it, maybe she could talk to Beth? Her experience could be a good cautionary tale.'

'She won't talk to anybody about it. She's . . . strong willed,' Dinny sighs.

'So I noticed,' I murmur. I can't stand another silence. I want to ask him about Christmas. About names for the baby. I want to ask about his travels, his life, our past. 'Well, I should be getting back. Getting out of this rain,' is all I can say. 'It was really good to see you again, Dinny. I'm glad you're back. And nice to meet Honey, too. I'll . . . well, we're up at the house, if you need anything . . .'

'It's good to see you too, Erica.' Dinny looks at me with his head on one side, but his eyes are troubled, not glad.

'OK. Well, bye.' I go, as casually as I can.

I don't tell Beth about Dinny when I find her, watching TV in the study. I'm not sure why not. There will be a reaction, I think, when I tell her. And I am not sure what it will be. I am agitated suddenly. I feel like we're no longer alone. I can feel Dinny's presence out there, beyond the trees. Like a niggling something in the corner of my eye. The third corner of our triangle. I switch off the TV, throw open the curtains.

'Come on. We're going out,' I tell her.

'I don't want to go out. Go where?'

'Shopping. I'm sick to death of tinned soup. Plus, it's about to be Christmas. Mum and Dad are coming for lunch, and what are you going to feed Eddie on Christmas day? Meredith's old Hovis crackers?' Beth considers this for a moment, then stands up quickly, puts her hands on her hips.

'God, you're right. You're right!'

'I know.'

'We need lots of things . . . turkey, sausages, potatoes, puddings . . .' she counts items off on her long fingers. Christmas is ten days away yet – we have plenty of time. But I don't say that. I make the most of her sudden animation, point to the door. 'And decorations!' she cries.

'Come on. You can make a list in the car.'

Devizes is prettied up for Christmas. Little fir trees lean out from the sides of shops and hotels along the High Street, strung with white lights; there's a brass band playing, and a man roasting chestnuts, plumes of acrid smoke rising from his cart. I wonder what he does for the rest of the year. Here, the darkness and the sleet draw us in, make us part of the huddled crowd. We wrap our scarves around our ears and window-shop, basking in the warm yellow light. Back in the world, the pair of us, after the solitude of the manor. It feels good, exciting, and I miss London. Inside each shop, Beth hums along to the taped carols, and as we walk I loop my arm through hers, holding her tight.

Several hours later and Beth has gone into Christmas overdrive. We have eight different cheeses, a huge ham, chipolatas, crackers – edible and the ones you pull – a turkey I struggle to carry to the car, and a cake that cost a ridiculous amount of money. We cram it all into the boot, go back for glittering baubles, strings of beads, gold paint, glass icicles, little straw angels with dresses of white muslin. There's a farm two minutes from the manor selling Christmas trees – we call in on the way back, arrange to have a tree four metres high delivered and erected on December the twenty-third.

'It can go in the hallway – they can wire it to the banister,' Beth says decisively.

Perhaps I should not let her spend when she is troubled, like now. I daren't put all the receipts together, add it all up. But Beth has money – money from Maxwell, money from her translating work. More money than I have, certainly, but it's something we never discuss. She lives small, most of the time. She squirrels it away unless Eddie needs something. All mine is absorbed by London, in getting to work, in rent, in living. Now we have enough food for ten people, when we will be five; but Beth looks happier, her face is less drawn. Retail therapy. But that's not it – she likes to be able to give. I leave her threading garlands along the mantelpiece, with a slight frown of concentration while I put the kettle on, feeling pleased and sleepy.

There's a message from my agency on my mobile phone, about some supply work at a school in Ealing, starting on January the twelfth. My thumb hovers over the redial button, but I am strangely reluctant to press it, to have real life intrude upon me. But money must be earned, I suppose; life must resume. Literature must be crammed between deaf ears. Unless it doesn't. Unless I live here, of course. No more rent. Just the upkeep, although that would probably cost more than my rent does now. Would it be worth it for five years, even ten? Trying to live here – just long enough for the legacy to stand. Then we could sell up, retire at the age of forty, once property prices are back up. But if living here makes Beth ill? And if I will always have this feeling of something stealing up behind me? I wish I could turn and look at it, I wish I could make it out. I remember everything else that happened that summer, except what happened to Henry.

We came here the two summers after that year, and our mother watched us closely. Not to protect us, not to keep us from harm; but to assess, to see how we would react. I don't know if I was different. A little quieter, perhaps. And we stayed in the garden; we didn't want to venture further any more. Mum kept us away from Meredith, who was unpredictable by then; who flew into storms of cursing and accusation. But Beth drew further and further into herself. Our mother saw and she told our father, and he frowned. And we stopped coming.

Outside, the sun sets orange and coldly pink on the horizon. I spray the holly gold, the paint burnishing the dark leaves. It looks delicious. The fumes make me dizzy, euphoric. I am hanging it from the banisters and laying it along window sills when Beth comes downstairs, arms folded, face creased with sleep. She moves from place to place where I have hung it, touching it lightly, testing the paint with her fingertips.

'Do you approve?' I ask her, smiling. I've tuned the radio to Classic FM. They're playing 'Good King Wenceslas'. Beth nods, yawns. I sing: 'Silly bugger, he fell out; on a red hot cinder!' I've no kind of singing voice.

'You're chirpy,' Beth tells me. She comes over to the window sill I am strewing with sprigs, puts my hair behind my ear for me, touches the scratch under my eye. So rare, her touches. I smile.

'Well . . .' I say. The words teeter in my mouth. I am so tempted to say them, still so unsure if they're right or wrong.

'Well, what?'

'Well, Dinny's here,' I tell her.

Loving

1902

The journey from New York to Woodward in Oklahoma Territory was a long one, covering a distance of nearly two thousand miles. State after state rolled out beneath the train, ever westwards. At first, Caroline was awed by the scene beyond the window. As they left behind the familiar towns of New York State, settlements became fewer and further between. They passed through woods so thick and dark that they seemed to belong to another age, closing the train in for mile after countless mile. They passed through fields of wheat and corn no less vast, no less astonishing; and towns that grew smaller and smaller, as if compressed by the wide expanses of land all around them. Beside the tracks in one station, rough dwellings had been built and children were playing, running alongside the train, waving, begging for pennies. With a start, Caroline saw that their feet were bare. She waved to them as the train eased away again, and turned to look back as their fragile homes shrank into miniature, and the land yawned away on either side. It was truly untamed, she thought, this land to the west. Men lived upon it, but they had not yet shaped it; not in the way they had shaped New York City. Caroline sat back in her seat and studied the distant purple hills with a pull of unease, feeling the once mighty train to be a mere speck, an insect crawling across the endless surface of the world.

By the time Caroline changed trains for the third and final time, at Dodge City in Kansas, she was heavy with fatigue and stale in her clothes. Her stomach felt hot and empty because the picnic Sara packed for her had run out a day and a half ago; Sara, who could not conceive of a journey so long that a half-dozen hard-boiled eggs, an apple and a pork pie would not be provisions enough. Caroline joined fellow passengers for lunch at El Vacquero, the Harvey Hotel beside the tracks in Dodge City. It was a brand new, brick building, and Caroline took this as proof of the new wealth and stability of what had recently been frontier land. She looked around discreetly, too curious about her surroundings to resist.

The unmade street outside thronged with people and ponies and buggies and wagons, making a muted noise quite unlike that of a New York street. Saddle horses were lined up along the hitch racks, resting their rumps on one tipped-back hoof. The reek of slurry was strong, drifting over the town from the nearby stock pens, and it mixed oddly with food smells and the hot bodies of people and animals. Confused, Caroline's stomach did not know whether to rumble or recoil. Men sauntered by with pistols strapped to their hips, their shirts untied at the throat, and Caroline stared at them in amazement, as if they had walked straight out of legend. Her heart beat hard with nervous energy and her throat was dry. For one instant, she almost missed Bathilda's indomitable presence at her side; missed having the barricade of her respectability to hide behind. Ashamed, she straightened her shoulders and reread the menu card.

The restaurant was busy with the lunch crowd, but a crisp girl in a neat uniform soon served her; bringing out consommé with vermicelli, and poached eggs, and coffee.

'Are you travelling far, miss?' a man asked her. He was sitting two seats away along the table, and he smiled and leaned towards her, so that she coloured, shocked to be spoken to so casually. The man was unshaven and his coat cuffs were shiny.

'To Woodward,' she said, unsure whether she should introduce herself before speaking, or indeed if she should speak to him at all.

'Woodward? Well, you've not too far to go now, I guess,

considering how far you've come already – New York, if I can tell by your accent?' He smiled again, wider now. Caroline nodded quickly and concentrated on her eggs. 'You got family there you visiting? In Woodward I mean?'

'My husband,' Caroline replied.

'Your husband! Now that's a crying shame. Still, lucky this place has opened up now, isn't it? The Fred Harvey place before this was in a boxcar on stilts! Did you ever see such a thing back east?' he exclaimed loudly, and Caroline tried to smile politely.

'Ah, leave the girl alone, Doon. Can't you see she wants to eat her lunch in peace?' This was another man, sitting next to the first. He had an ill-tempered look, deep creases around his eyes. He had combed his hair fiercely to one side and there it remained, held fixed by some substance or other. Caroline hardly dared look at him. Her cheeks blazed.

'Beg pardon, missus,' the first man mumbled. Caroline ate with unseemly haste and returned to the train with her hands tucked into her fox-fur muffler, in spite of the warmth of the weather.

The country after Dodge City was wide and sparsely punctuated. Mile after gently featureless mile of prairie rolled by as the train now turned southwards on the Santa Fe line. Caroline slouched in her seat and longed to loosen her stays. Too tired to keep a ladylike posture, and since she was alone in the compartment, she tipped her head against the glass and stared into the endless, eggshell sky. The horizon had never been as wide, as flat, as far away. Gradually, the mighty span of it began to give her a slippery feeling like vertigo. She had expected to see snow-capped mountains, emerald fields of farmland, and quick rivers running. But the earth looked hot and exhausted, just as she felt. She took her copy of *The Virginian* from her bag instead and fancied herself like Molly Wood, fearlessly cutting her home ties, boldly heading to a new life in an unknown land. After a while, though, she stopped feeling like Molly Wood and started to feel afraid again, so she thought of her husband, waiting for her at Woodward, and while this seemed to slow the train and prolong the interminable journey, it did at least reassure her.

The train arrived at Woodward late in the day, as the sun began to set smeared and orange against the dusty window glass. Caroline had been dozing when the conductor strode past her compartment. 'Woodward! Woodward the next stop!' His shout woke her, sent her heart skittering. She gathered her things and stood up so quickly that her head spun and she had to sit back down again, breathing deeply. *Corin*, was all she could think. To see him again, after so many days! She peered eagerly out at the station as the train squealed to a halt, desperate to catch a glimpse of him. Catching her reflection in the glass, she hastily patted her hair into shape, bit her lips to redden them and pinched some colour into her cheeks. She could not keep calm, could not keep herself from shaking.

She climbed stiffly from the train, her skirts clinging to her legs, feet swollen and hot in her boots. She looked up and down the wooden platform, her heart in her mouth, but could not see Corin among the handful of people quitting the carriages or waiting at the station. The train exhaled with a weary sound and crept towards a siding where a water tower bulked against the sky. A warm wind greeted her, singing softly in her ears, and sand on the platform ground beneath her feet. Caroline looked around again and felt suddenly empty, suddenly unbound, as if the next rush of wind might carry her off. She straightened her hat nervously, but kept her smile ready, her eyes searching. Woodward looked small and slow. The street leading into town from the rail track was wide and unmade, and the wind had carved tiny waves into the sand all along it. She could smell the tar on the station building, hot from the sun, and the pervading stink of livestock. She looked down, sketching a line in the grit with her toe.

As the locomotive moved away a new kind of quiet settled, behind the rattle of a passing buggy and the creak of the trolley as the station man pit his back against the weight of her luggage. Where was Corin? Doubts and fears bubbled up inside her — that he regretted his choice, that she was abandoned, would have to take the next train back to New York. She turned in a circle, desperate to see him. The station porter had paused with her luggage and was trying to catch her eye, to ask, no doubt, where he should take it. But if Corin was not here, Caroline had no idea. No idea where to go, where to stay, what to do. She felt the blood run out of her face and a rush of light-headedness spun her thoughts. For a terrifying moment, she thought she might faint, or burst into tears, or both. She took a deep, trembling breath and tried desperately to think what to do, what to say to the porter to conceal her confusion.

'Mrs Massey?' Caroline did not at first register this as her name, spoken with a slow drawl. She ignored the man with his hat in his hands who had come to stand to one side of her, his body curved into a relaxed slouch. He looked to be about thirty, but the weather was wearing his face as it was fading the blue from his flannel shirt. His scruffy hair was shot through with strands of red and brown. 'Mrs Massey?' he asked again, taking a step towards her.

'Oh! Yes, I am,' she exclaimed, startled.

'Pleasure to meet you, Mrs Massey. I'm Derek Hutchinson, but everybody around here calls me Hutch and I'd be happy if you would too,' he introduced himself, tucking his hat beneath his arm and holding out a hand, which Caroline shook tentatively, just with her fingertips.

'Where is Mr Massey?' she asked.

'Corin was due back in time to come and get you, ma'am, and I know he sorely wanted to, but there's been some trouble with cattle thieves and he was called upon to ride out and see to it . . . He'll be back by the time we are, I'm sure of that,' Hutch said, seeing Caroline's face fall. Tears of disappointment blurred her vision and she gripped her bottom lip in her teeth to halt them. Hutch hesitated, unnerved by her reaction.

'I see,' she gasped, swaying slightly, suddenly longing to sit down. Corin hadn't come to meet her. In sudden terror, she began to guess at reasons he might have to avoid her.

Hutch cleared his throat diffidently and shifted his feet in an awkward manner. 'I . . . uh . . . I know it truly was his wish to meet you here himself, Mrs Massey, but when there are thieves to apprehend, it's the duty of the landowners to help one another in that mission. I have come in his stead and I'm at your service.'

'It's their duty to go?' she asked, tentatively.

'Absolutely. He was duty-bound to it.'

'Are you his . . . manservant, then?' she asked.

Hutch smiled and tipped his chin. 'Well, not quite that, Mrs Massey. Not quite that. I'm foreman at the ranch.'

'Oh, I see,' Caroline said, although she did not. 'Well. Will we be there in time for dinner, do you think?' she asked, fighting to regain her composure.

'Dinner, ma'am? Tomorrow, do you mean?'

'Tomorrow?'

'It's nearing on thirty-five miles to the ranch, from Woodward here. Now, that's not far, but too far to make a start this evening, I think. There's a room waiting for you at the boarding house, and a good dinner too, for you do look in need of a square meal, if I can be as bold as to say so.' He studied her tiny form and the pallor of her skin with a measuring eye.

'Thirty-five miles? But . . . how long will it take?'

'We'll set out early tomorrow and we should get there by noon time on the second day . . . I had not reckoned on you bringing quite so many boxes and trunks with you, and that might slow the wagon down some. But the horses are fresh, and if the weather stays this fair it'll be a good, smooth ride.' Hutch smiled, and Caroline rallied herself, finding a smile for him in return in spite of the weariness that even hearing about another day and a half of travel made her feel. Hutch stepped forward, proffering his arm.

'That's more like it. Come with me now and we'll get you settled. You look fairly done in, Mrs Massey.'

The Central Hotel on Main Street was managed by a round, sour-faced woman who introduced herself as Mrs Jessop. She showed Caroline to a room that was clean if not spacious, whilst Hutch oversaw the switching of her luggage from the station trolley to the covered wagon that would take them on to the ranch. Mrs Jessop scowled when Caroline asked for a hot bath to be drawn, and Caroline hastily produced coins from her purse to sweeten the request.

'Go on, then. I'll knock on your door when it's ready,' the proprietress told her, eyeing her sternly. The latch on the bath-house door was flimsy and there was a knot in the wood through which a tiny glimpse of the hallway outside could be had. Caroline kept a careful eye on this as she bathed, terrified of seeing the shadow of a trespassing eye fall over it. The bath was shallow, but it restored her nevertheless. Blood eased into her stiff muscles and her sore back, and she rested her head at last, breathing deeply. The room smelt of damp towels and cheap soap. The last of the evening light seeped warmly around the shutters, and voices carried up to her from the street outside; voices slow and melodious with un-familiar accents. Then a man's voice sounded loudly, apparently right below the window:

'Why, you goddamned son of a *bitch*! What the *hell* are you doing here?' Caroline's pulse quickened at such obscene language and she sat up with an abrupt splash, expecting at any moment to hear more cursing, or a fight, or even gunshots ringing out. But what she heard next was a rich guffaw of laughter, and the patting of hands against shoulders. She sank back into the cooling bath-water and tried to feel calm again.

Afterwards, she dried herself with a rough towel and put on a clean white dress for dinner, forgoing any jewels because she had no wish to outshine her fellow clientèle. Without Sara's help her waist was a little less tiny, and her hair a little less neat, but she felt more like herself as she descended at the dinner hour. She looked around for Derek Hutchinson and, not finding him, enquired of Mrs Jessop.

'You'll not see him again this night, I'll bet,' the woman said with a brief, knowing smile. 'He was heading over to the Dew Drop, last I saw him.'

'Heading to where, I beg your pardon?'

'The Dew Drop Inn, over Miliken's Bridge by the depot. Whatever sustenance he's taking this evening, he'll be taking it there and not here!' At this she gave a low chuckle. 'He's been riding out a good few months. A man gets hungry.' Faced with Caroline's blank incomprehension, Mrs Jessop relented. 'Go on through and sit yourself down, Mrs Massey. I'll send Dora out with your dinner.' So Caroline did as she was bid and ate alone at the counter with no company but the inquisitive girl, Dora, who brought out a reel of questions about the east with each course of the meal. Across the room, two battered gentlemen with careworn faces discussed the price of grain at great length.

The morning dawned fair, the sky as clear as a bell, and there was a scent in the air that Caroline was unused to; an earthy smell of dampened ground and new-sprouting sage bushes on the prairie all around Woodward. So different to the brick and smoke and people smell of the city. The sun was strong as they began the final stretch of the journey. As Hutch helped her up into the wagon, Caroline noticed a gun belt now buckled around his hips, a six-shooter holstered into it. It gave her an odd tingling in her stomach. She tilted her bonnet forward to better shade her eyes against the bright light, but still could not help but squint. The sun seemed to be brighter here than it had ever been in New York, and when she commented on this, Hutch tipped his chin in agreement.

'I reckon that's so, ma'am. I've never been that far east myself, or that far north come to think of it; but I reckon any place with so much building and living and dying going on will wind up with its air all muddied up, just like its rivers.' A lively breeze picked up the sand from beneath the wagon wheels, whisking it around them, and Caroline flapped her hands to ward it off. The folds of her skirt were soon lined with the stuff. Hutch watched her, and he did not smile. 'Once we're clear of town there'll be less of that sand blowing, Mrs Massey,' he said.

It did not take long to pass through Woodward town. They drove down Main Street, which was flanked predominantly by wooden-framed buildings and just one or two of more permanent construction. There were several saloons, several banks, a post office, a large general store, an opera house. There was a fair bustle of wagons and horses, and a fair number of people going about their business, most of whom were men. Caroline looked back over her shoulder as they left town. From a distance she could see that many of the high building fronts were false, and had just a single storey crouched behind them.

'Is that the whole of Woodward?' she asked, incredulously.

'Yes, ma'am. Over two thousand souls call it home, nowadays, and growing all the while. Ever since they opened up the Cheyenne and Arapaho lands to the south, folks have been pouring in, starting to settle and farm. Some call it a pity, to see the open range fenced off and ploughed under. Me, I do call it progress, although I'm happy to say there's plenty of land left open to the cow herds yet.'

'Arapaho? What does that mean?'

'The Arapaho? They're Indian folks. From more northern parts originally, but settled here by the government, like so many others . . . Now, this land we're driving through right now belonged to the Cherokee until recently, although they themselves lived further east. They leased it out to ranchers and cattle folk for years before it was opened up to settlers in ninety-three . . .'

'But is that safe? For civilised people to live where there are

Indians?' Caroline was shocked. Hutch gave her a sidelong look, then hitched a shoulder.

'They've sold their lands and moved on east. I reckon they've as little urge to have white neighbours as some white folk have to share with Indians.'

'Thank goodness!' Caroline said. 'I could never have slept at night, knowing that such creatures were roaming around outside the window!' She laughed a little, high and nervous, and did not notice Hutch's thoughtful gaze, out over the prairie. Copying him, Caroline searched the horizon and felt her stomach flutter, to think that savages might have hunted scalps in this very place not long before. A pair of rabbits were startled from the side of the road and darted off into the brush, visible only by the black tips of their ears.

Some ten or twelve miles along the road, buildings appeared in the distance. Caroline was glad to see them. Each mile they had covered from Woodward had seemed to her another leap from safety, somehow; another mile from civilisation, even if it was also another mile closer to Corin. She shaded her eyes for a better view.

'Is that the next town?' she asked. Hutch whistled softly to the horses, two chestnut-coloured animals with hard legs and meaty behinds, and brought them to a standstill.

'No, ma'am. That's the old military fort. Fort Supply, it's called. We'll turn off the road soon, I'm afraid, so it won't be quite as smooth going.'

'Fort Supply? So there's a garrison here?'

'Not any more. It's been empty these seven or eight years.'

'But why were they here? To protect people from the Indians, I suppose?'

'Well, that was some of the reason, for sure. But more than that they was charged with keeping white folks from settling on Indian lands. So you could say, they was there to protect the Indians from the likes of you and I.'

'Oh,' Caroline said, deflating a little. She had liked the idea of soldiers guarding so close to the ranch, and had immediately pictured herself dancing a quadrille with men in neat uniforms. But as they went nearer she saw that the fort was low and rough-shod, built mostly of wood and earth rather than brick or stone. The empty black gaps of its windows seemed eerily watchful and she looked away with a shiver. 'But where does this road go to now?'

'Well, not to any place, I suppose. It runs from this here down to Fort Sill, but this end of it's mostly used by odd folk like us now, to make the run into town a bit easier on the bones,' Hutch told her. Caroline looked behind them, back along the empty road. She watched the dust resettling into their tracks. She had pictured the country virgin, untouched by any hand but God's. Here already were ghostly ruins and a road to nowhere. 'We'll be crossing the North Canadian in just a short while, Mrs Massey, but I don't want you to worry about that none. This time of year it's not going to pose us any problems at all,' Hutch said. Caroline nodded, and smiled gamely at him.

The river was wide but shallow, the water reaching only halfway up the wagon wheels, and to the horses' stomachs. Hutch let the pair take the reins from him when they reached the far side, and the animals drank deeply, kicking up sprays that spattered their dusty coats and filled Caroline's nostrils with the smell of their hot hides. She wiped at some droplets on her skirt, succeeding only in making a grubby smear. They paused for lunch on the far side, where a stand of cottonwood trees curled their roots into the sandy bank and cast a dappled shade onto the ground. Hutch spread out a thick blanket, and Caroline took his hand down from the wagon, seating herself as well as she could on the ground. Her corset would not let her be comfortable, though, and she spoke little as she ate a slice of ham that required an indelicate amount of chewing, and bread that crumbled into her lap. Grains of sand ground between her teeth as she ate. The only sound was the soft hiss and clatter of the breeze through the cottonwood leaves, which twisted and trembled, flashing muted shades of silver and green. Before they moved on again, Caroline went to some lengths to extract her scalloped silk parasol from her luggage.

The wagon made slower progress over the open prairie, bumping over knots of sagebrush, dragging sometimes in patches of shifting sand or the boggy remnants of a shallow creek. Occasionally they passed small dwellings, homesteads dug in and knocked together in haste to keep a family safe, to stake a claim, to make a new beginning. But these were far apart, and grew more infrequent the further they went. As the afternoon grew long Caroline drowsed, swaying on the seat next to Hutch. Each time her head began to droop some jolt brought her around again.

'We'll stop for the night soon, ma'am. I reckon you could use a hot cup of coffee and to bed down.'

'Oh, yes! I am rather tired. We must be very far from town, by now?'

'It seems further in this slow wagon. I have made the journey on horseback in a day before, without even trying too hard. All you need is a good, fast saddle horse, and your husband raises some of the finest such animals in all of Oklahoma Territory.'

'Where will we stop the night? Is there some other settlement nearby?'

'Oh, no, ma'am. We'll make camp tonight.'

'Camp?'

'That's right. Don't look so alarmed, Mrs Massey! I am a man of honour and discretion,' he said, smiling wryly at Caroline's expression of wide-eyed bewilderment. It was a moment before she realised he had imagined her scandalised at the thought of spending the night alone with him, just the two of them. She blushed and dropped her gaze, only to find it resting near the waistband of his trousers, where his shirt had pulled a little loose to reveal a small area of his hard, tanned stomach. Caroline swallowed and set her eyes firmly on the horizon. Her first fear had actually been of being outdoors all night, unprotected from animals, weather, and other savageries of nature.

Before sundown Hutch drew the wagon to a stop on a flat area where the ground was greener than it had been, and more lush. He helped Caroline down and she stood, aching everywhere, unsure of what to do. Hutch unhitched the wagon, took the bits from the horses' mouths and slapped their behinds. With glad expressions and swishing tails, they trotted lazily away to a near distance and began to crop huge mouthfuls of grass.

'But . . . won't the horses run away?' Caroline asked.

'Not far, I reckon. And they'll come miles for a slice of bread, anyway.' Hutch unloaded a tent from the wagon and soon had it built. He spread blankets on top of buffalo hides to make a bed, and put her vanity case inside for her. 'You'll be cosy as anything in there. As fine as any New York hotel,' he said. Caroline glanced at him, unsure if she was being mocked, then she smiled and seated herself inside the tent, wrinkling her nose at the smell of the hides. But the bed was deep and soft; and the sides of the tent belled in and out with the breeze, as if gently breathing. Caroline felt her heart slow, and a gentle calm come over her.

Hutch soon had a fire going and crouched beside it, tending to a large, flat pan that spat and smoked. He fed the flames with pieces of something dry and brown that Caroline did not recognise.

'What's that you're using as fuel?' she asked.

'Cow chips,' Hutch replied, offering no further explanation. Caroline did not dare to ask. The sky was a glory of pink and turquoise striations, marching away from the bright flare of the west to the deep velvet blue of the east. Hutch's face was aglow with firelight. 'I put that box there for you to sit on,' he said, gesturing with a fork. Caroline sat, obediently. In the darkness beyond the flames one of the horses snorted, and whinnied softly. Then a distant howl, high and ghostly, echoed across the flat plain to where they sat.

'What was that?' Caroline exclaimed, rushing to her feet once more. The blood ran out of her head and she reeled, flinging out an arm that Hutch caught, appearing at her side in an instant.

'Do sit, ma'am. Sit back down,' he insisted.

'Is it *wolves*?' she cried, unable to keep her voice from shaking.

'Nothing more than prairie wolves, is all. Why, they're no bigger than a pet dog, and no fiercer. They won't be coming anywhere near us, I promise you.'

'Are you sure?'

'Sure as I'm sitting right here, Mrs Massey,' Hutch assured her. Caroline pulled her shawl around her tightly, and huddled fearfully on the hard wooden box, her every fibre strung tight with alarm. Hutch seemed to sense her disquiet and began to talk. 'Coyotes, they also get called sometimes. They run around in packs and squabble over leftover bones here and there. That's all they're singing about – who's found the best old cow bones to chew. The most mischief they get up to is stealing chickens from home-steaders, but they only do that when they have to. I reckon they've learnt not to go too close to folk, unless they want to take a bullet in the tail that is . . .' And so he talked on, his voice low, and soothing somehow, and Caroline was reassured by it. Now and again the coyote song drifted over the camp, long and mournful.

'They sound so lonely,' she murmured.

Hutch glanced at her, his eyes lost in shadow. He carefully passed her a tin cup.

'Take some coffee, ma'am,' he said.

The sunrise woke her, light glowing irresistibly inside the tent. Caroline had been dreaming of Bathilda, watching over her shoulder as Caroline ran scales up and down the piano, exclaiming *Wrists! Wrists!* as she had been wont to do. For a moment, Caroline could not remember where she was. She poked her head cautiously out of the tent and was relieved to see no sign of Hutch. The eastern sky was dazzling. Caroline had never in her life been up so early. She stood up and stretched, hands in the small of her back. Her hair was in disarray and her mouth was sour with last night's coffee. She rubbed her eyes and found her brows full of sand. Her whole face, in fact, and her clothes. There was a line of dirt inside her cuffs, and she could feel it inside her collar too, rubbing at the skin. Rumpled blankets beside the cooling embers of the fire spoke of where the foreman had spent the night.

'Good morning, Mrs Massey,' Hutch called, giving her a start. He was approaching from the green expanse beyond the parked wagon, a chestnut horse held by a halter rope in each of his hands. 'How did you find your first night as a cow-puncher?' he smiled. Caroline smiled back, not really understanding him.

'Good morning, Mr Hutchinson. I slept well, thank you.'

'I'm taking these two to water at the creek over this way, then I'll get some breakfast cooking,' he said. Caroline nodded, and glanced around. 'I put a can of water there, in case you wanted to freshen up any,' he added, smiling again as he made his way past the camp.

Caroline's real want, however, was for plumbing. She dithered for a while and then realised, to her dawning horror, that she would have to relieve herself amidst the bushes, and that Hutch's ostentatious departure in the other direction was probably meant to reassure her that he would be nowhere around to witness this indignity. He had placed a wad of torn up news sheets and a thin cotton towel next to the solicitous can of water. With a horrified grimace, Caroline made as best use of these meagre facilities as she could. Upon his return, Hutch, with great delicacy, neither looked for nor asked after any of the items he had set out for her.

By midday the sun was scorching, but Caroline's arm, clutching her dusty parasol, was heavy with fatigue. She gave up and folded it into her lap. Looking up into the vast, fathomless sky, she saw two distant dark spots, circling high above.

'Are those eagles?' she asked, pointing skywards, and noticing as she did how brown with dirt her lace glove was. Hutch followed her gaze, squinting.

'Just buzzards, I'm afraid. Not really many eagles down here on the prairie. If you go up into the Rockies you'll see some beautiful birds. Those are some sharp eyes you've got there, Mrs Massey,' he told her. He looked back out over the horses' ears and sang quietly to himself: *Daisy, Daisy, give me your answer do . . .'* Caroline let her eyes drift to the horizon, then she straightened in her seat and pointed again.

'Somebody's coming!' she exclaimed, excitedly.

'Well, we're not at all far from the ranch now, ma'am. It could be one of our own riders,' Hutch nodded, with a subtle smile.

'Is it Corin?' Caroline asked, her hands flying to her dishevelled hair. She began to tuck wayward strands of it beneath her bonnet. 'Do you think it's Mr Massey?'

'Well,' Hutch smiled again, as her frantic grooming continued, 'I know of no other man who rides a mare as black as that in this vicinity, so I think it just might be your husband after all, ma'am.'

Caroline was still brushing her skirts and pinching her cheeks, not caring if Hutch witnessed these efforts, when the rider drew near, and she at last saw Corin for the first time since she'd wed him over a month before. She let her hands fall neatly into her lap, and sat up straight even though she was bubbling with nerves inside. The black horse covered the ground in an easy lope, kicking up sprays of sand, and when at last he reached them Corin pulled the kerchief down from his face to reveal a wide grin. He was as golden and lovely as she remembered him.

'Caroline!' he cried. 'It's so good to see you!' He swung down from his horse and came to stand by her foot. There she remained, seated high on the wagon, transfixed with fear and anticipation.

'Are you well? How was the journey?' When she didn't reply Corin's face fell a little and a puzzled look came into his eyes. This was her undoing. Still lost for words, and more relieved to see him than she would ever have admitted, Caroline surrendered all propriety and toppled herself from the bench into his waiting arms. Only the sparseness of her prevented the couple ending up in the prairie sand. Behind them, reins held casually in one hand, Hutch watched with a laconic smile, and gave his boss a genial nod.

There was a scattering of people around the ranch house when the wagon bringing Corin Massey's new wife finally pulled up outside. They were young men mostly, with worn, dusty clothes, who seemed, nevertheless, to have made some attempts to comb their hair and tuck in their shirts. Corin smiled at the trepidation on Caroline's face as she gave her own filthy attire another despairing glance. The men nodded, tipped their hats and murmured greetings as she climbed down from the wagon, and she smiled and acknowledged them politely.

'I so want to take you on a tour of the ranch, Caroline. I'm so excited to show you everything! Unless you're too tired after your journey?' said Corin, swinging down from his horse.

'Oh, I am so tired, Corin! Of course you must show me everything, but first I need to lie down, and then take a bath,' she said. Corin nodded readily, although he looked a little disappointed. The tall, white house Caroline had envisaged was instead a low, wood-frame building; and although the front had indeed been painted white, prairie sand had blown up against it and given the bottom half a grubby look. Corin followed her gaze.

'A spring wind blew up before the paint had a chance to dry,' he told her, sheepishly. 'We'll paint over it, don't worry. Luckily we only had time to do the front, so not too much work was undone!' Caroline peered around the corner of the house, and sure enough the sides remained bare wood.

'I'll see to Strumpet. You take Mrs Massey on into the house,' Hutch said, taking the reins from Corin.

'Strumpet?' Caroline asked, bewildered.

'My mare,' Corin grinned, giving the horse's forehead a rub. Caroline knew little enough about horses, but the animal appeared to scowl. 'The most contrary, bad-tempered soul you'll find on these lands, and that's a known fact.'

'Why do you keep her, if she is so unpleasant?'

'Well,' Corin shrugged, as if this had never occurred to him, 'she's my horse.'

Inside, the walls were bare and no curtains hung at the windows. There was furniture enough but it was placed higgledy-piggledy, at odds with the angles of the room. An easy chair drawn up to the burner, with piles of livestock journals and seed catalogues beside it, was the only thing that looked to be in its right place. Many boxes and cartons stood around the floor. Caroline turned a slow circle, gazing at all this, and sand rasped beneath her boot heels. When she next looked at her husband she could not hide her dismay. Corin's smile faded from his face.

'Now, I deliberately didn't have it all fixed up because there was no point, I thought, until you'd arrived and told me *how* it should be fixed. We'll get it set up quickly enough, now that you're here,' he explained, hurriedly. Caroline smiled, drawing in a shaky breath rich with the scent of newly hewn oak. 'It just . . . it took me longer than I had planned to get the place built . . . I'm sorry, Caroline.'

'Oh, no! Don't be!' she exclaimed, anguished to see him crestfallen. 'I'm sure it will be wonderful – I know just how we should finish it. You've done *so* well.' She turned and leant her head against his chest, and revelled in the smell of him. Corin pushed strands of hair back from her forehead and held her tightly. His touch made her warm inside, and gave her a tight feeling, like hunger.

'Come with me,' he murmured, and led her through a door in the far corner of the main room, to a smaller room where a large iron bedstead dominated. It was draped with a fine, multicoloured quilt, and Caroline ran her fingers lightly over it. The fabrics were satins and silks, cool and watery to the touch. 'I had the bed freighted all the way from New York,' Corin told her. 'It arrived right before you did; and the quilt was my mother's. Why don't you try it?'

'Oh, no! I'd dirty it. It's so lovely, Corin,' Caroline enthused.

'Well, I'm dirty too; and I say we try it out.' Corin took her hands and then her waist, and then linked his arms around her.

'Wait! No!' Caroline laughed, as he pulled them both down to land, bouncing, on the mattress.

'We never did get our wedding night,' he said softly. The sun streaming in from the window lit his hair with a soft coronet and threw his brown eyes into shadow. Caroline was very aware of the stale smell of her own unwashed body, and the dryness of her mouth.

'No. But it's not bedtime yet. And I need to bathe . . . and someone might see in.'

'We're not in New York any more, love. You don't have to do as your aunt tells you, and we don't have to do what society tells us . . .' Corin placed his hand flat on her midriff and Caroline caught her breath, fast and shallow in her chest. He worked each button of her blouse free and smoothed it gently aside.

'But, I—'

'But *nothing*,' Corin murmured. 'Turn over.' Caroline obeyed, and Corin fumbled slightly as he undid the laces of her corset. Released, the sudden rush of air into Caroline's lungs made her head spin, and she closed her eyes. Corin turned her to face him and traced the lines of her body with the roughened palms she had noticed the first time they met. He kissed her eyelids softly. 'You're so beautiful,' he said quietly, and his voice was deep and blurred.

'Eyes like silver dollars.' Alarmed by the force of the passion she felt, Caroline kissed him as hard as she could. She had little enough idea what to expect, knowing only that Corin now had rights to her body that nobody had had before. Bathilda had hinted darkly at pain that was to be borne, and duties that were to be performed, but the press of Corin's skin against her own was a feeling more wonderful than any she had yet experienced; and the gentle insistence of his touch, the shift of his weight between her thighs, filled her with a sensation that was hot and cold and almost painful and so far beyond anything she had felt before that she cried out in astonished joy, no longer aware that there was any impropriety, or anybody else in the world to hear her.

Corin toured his new wife around the ranch in a buggy, since it was too far to walk and she had never ridden horseback before. He had seemed stunned by this fact, but then he'd shrugged and said, 'Don't worry; you'll learn soon enough.'

But Caroline did not trust the animals, with their ugly teeth and brute strength, and the thought of sitting atop of one did not appeal to her in the slightest. When Corin proudly introduced her to his brood mares, and to the stallion Apache, Caroline nodded and smiled and struggled to tell them apart. The creatures all looked the same to her. He drove her around the various corrals, stock pens and cattle chutes, and the low, roughly built bunkhouses where the line-riders slept. Caroline noticed how comfortable her husband seemed, without a trace of the uncertainty or diffidence he had shown in New York society. They passed a pitiful-looking hovel, half dug into the ground and then roofed with planks and sod.

'That would have been our home, if you'd come to me much sooner!' Corin told her with a smile.

'That?' Caroline echoed, appalled. Corin nodded.

'That dugout's the very first dwelling I put here when I staked my claim in ninety-three. And I wintered in it twice before I got a proper house set up – I found one out on the prairie and dragged it here – if you can believe that!'

'You stole a *house*?'

'Not stole! No, not that. I suppose it had been put up by some boomer, trying to settle the land before it was legal. Well, whoever built it had moved on, or been moved on. It was just sitting there, sheltering nothing but rattlesnakes; so I shook them out, loaded it on a flatbed wagon and dragged it back here. It was a good little house, but certainly not roomy enough for a family.' As he said this he took her hand and squeezed it; and Caroline looked away bashfully.

'A *large* family?' she queried, tentatively.

'I reckon four or five kids ought to do it,' Corin grinned. 'How about you?'

'Four or five ought to do it,' she agreed, smiling widely.

'Here, now; this is the shelter we bring the mares into when they're due to foal.'

'What's that?' Caroline asked, pointing to a conical tent beyond the mare's corral.

'That's where Joe's family lives. See the dugout beside? Joe and his wife sleep there, but his folks wanted a teepee like they'd always had, and so that's what they live in still. They're a traditional sort of people.'

'Why would . . . Joe's family live in a teepee?' Caroline asked, perplexed. Corin looked at her, as puzzled as she.

'Well, they're Indians, sweetheart. And they like to live as they ever have, although Joe himself is more forward-thinking. He's worked the trails for me since the very beginning, when I could only pay him in clothes and five-cent tins of Richmond tobacco. One of my best riders—'

'Indians? There are *Indians* here?' Caroline's heart quickened and her stomach twisted. She would not have been more shocked if he'd told her he let wolves roam amidst his cattle. 'Hutch told me they were all gone!' she whispered.

'Well, most of them have. The rest of Joe's people are on the reservation, east of here, on land that reaches the banks of the River Arkansas. Those that remained here in Oklahoma Territory, that is – Chief White Eagle leads them. But some went north again a few years back. Chief Standing Bear led them back to their Nebraska lands. I guess they were more homesick than the others . . .' he explained, but Caroline scarcely heard this brief history of the tribe. She could not believe her ears, or her eyes, that here camped on her doorstep were the savages of whose atrocities lurid stories had circulated in the east for decades. Fear froze her to the core. Wildly, she grabbed the reins from Corin and dragged the horse's head around, back towards the house.

'Hey – wait, what are you doing!' Corin exclaimed, trying to wrestle the reins from her as the horse tossed its head in protest, the bit clanking against its teeth.

'I want to go! I want to get *away* from them!' Caroline cried, shaking all over. She put her hands over her face, desperate to hide. Corin steadied the horse and then peeled her hands into his.

'Now, look!' he said seriously, eyes pinioning hers. 'Listen to me, Caroline. They are good people. *People*, just like you and me. They just want to live and work and raise their families; and no matter what you've heard back east where they like to paint Indians as the worst kind of villains, I am telling you that they don't want to trouble you or anybody else. There's been strife in the past, strife that often enough we white men brought with us, but now all any of us wants to do is get on as best we can. Joe has brought his family here to live and work alongside us, and that's taken a kind of courage you and I can't understand, I do believe. Are you listening to me, Caroline?' She nodded, although she could hardly credit what he was saying. Tears rolled down her cheeks. 'Don't cry, my darling. Nothing you've been told about Indians applies to Joe. I can guarantee you that. Come along now and I'll introduce you.'

'No!' she gasped.

'Yes. They're your neighbours now, and Joe is a firm friend of mine.'

'I can't! Please!' Caroline sobbed. Corin took out his hand-kerchief and wiped her face for her. He tipped her chin up and smiled affectionately.

'You poor thing. Please, don't be afraid. Come on, now. The second you meet them you'll see you've got nothing to be frightened of.'

Clicking his tongue at the beleaguered buggy horse, Corin turned it again and drove them towards the teepee and dugout. Surrounding the two dwellings was an array of washing lines and drying racks, ropes, tools and harnesses. A fire was burning outside the tent, and as they approached a small, iron-haired woman emerged with a blackened pot to place over the embers. Her back was bowed, but her eyes sparkled from deep within the creases webbing her face. She said nothing, but straightened up and nodded, eyeing Caroline with quiet interest as Corin jumped down from the buggy.

'Good morning, White Cloud, I've come to introduce my wife to you,' Corin said, tipping the wide brim of his hat respectfully at the old woman. Caroline's legs, as he helped her down, felt unsteady beneath her. She swallowed, but there remained a lump in her throat that made it hard to breathe. Her thoughts swirled inside her head like a blizzard. A man came out of the dugout, followed by a young girl, and another woman came from the teepee, middle-aged and severe looking. She said something incomprehensible to Corin, and Corin, to Caroline's utter amazement, replied.

'You speak their tongue?' she blurted out, and then recoiled when all eyes turned to her. Corin smiled, somewhat diffidently.

'Indeed, I do. Now, Caroline, this is Joe, and this is his wife Magpie, most commonly known as Maggie.' Caroline tried to smile, but she found that she could not hold the gaze of either one of them for more than a few seconds. When she did she saw a stern, dark man, not tall but broad across the chest; and a plump girl, her long hair prettily braided with coloured strings woven through it. Joe's hair was also long, and they both had high, feline cheekbones and a serious line to their brows. Magpie smiled and ducked her head, trying to catch Caroline's eye.

'I'm very pleased to meet you, Mrs Massey,' she said, and her English was perfect even if her accent was strong. Caroline gaped at her.

'You speak English?' she whispered, incredulously. Magpie gave a cheerful chuckle.

'Yes, Mrs Massey. Better than my husband, although I have been learning for less time!' she boasted. 'I'm so glad you are here. There are far too many men at this ranch.'

Caroline took a longer look at the girl, who was wearing a simple skirt and blouse, with a brightly woven blanket wrapped around her shoulders. Her feet were shod with soft slippers of a kind Caroline had never seen before. Her husband, who wore a heavy, beaded vest beneath his shirt, muttered something sharp in their own tongue, and Magpie scowled, answering him with something short and indignant. Joe did not smile as readily as his wife, and his expression seemed, to Caroline, most hostile. The blackness of his eyes alarmed her, and his mouth was a straight, implacable line.

'I have never met any Cherokee . . . people before,' Caroline said, somewhat emboldened by Magpie's cheerful demeanour.

'Still you have not.' Joe spoke for the first time, wryly. His accent was so guttural that it took a little while for her to understand him. Caroline glanced at Corin.

'Joe and his family are of the Ponca tribe,' he explained.

'But . . . Hutch told me these lands were Cherokee before . . .'

'They were. It's . . . well, put simply, there are many tribes in this country. It was Indian Territory before it was Oklahoma Territory, after all. Joe and his family are a little out of the ordinary, in that they have chosen to adopt some of the white man's ways of living. Most of his people choose to stay with their own, on reservation lands. Joe here got a taste for cattle driving and has never looked back — isn't that right, Joe?'

'Got a taste for beating you at cards, mostly,' the Ponca man said, twisting his mouth to one side sardonically.

As they moved away from the teepee, Caroline frowned.

'Joe seems an odd name for an . . . for a Ponco . . .'

'Ponca. Well, his real name, in his own tongue, is just about unpronounceable. It means Dust Storm, or something of that kind. Joe's just a lot easier for folk to say,' Corin explained.

'He does not seem to show you much respect, considering you are his employer.'

At this Corin glanced at Caroline, and a frown shaded his eyes for a moment. 'He has plenty of respect for me, I assure you; and it's respect I've had to earn. People like Joe don't give out respect because you're white, or because you've got land, or you pay their wages. They give it when you can show you have integrity and a willingness to learn, and can show respect to them where it's due. Things are a little different out here than in New York, Caroline. People have to help themselves and help each other when a flood or a freeze or a tornado might wipe out everything you have in an instant . . .' He trailed into silence. A warm wind blew off the prairie, singing through the spokes of the buggy wheels. Stinging with his rebuke, Caroline sat in unhappy silence. 'You'll soon settle in, don't you worry,' Corin said, in a lighter tone.

A few days later, they took their honeymoon picnic; setting out in the buggy while the sun was skirting the eastern horizon, and heading due west of the ranch for three hours or so, to a place where the land rolled into voluptuous curves around a shallow pool, fed by a slow-running creek. Silver willows leaned their branches down, shading the water's edge and touching it in places, pulling wrinkles in the wide reflected sky.

'It's so pretty here,' Caroline said, smiling as Corin lifted her down from the bench.

'I'm glad you like it,' Corin said, planting a kiss on her forehead. 'It's one of my favourite places. I come here sometimes, when I need to think about things, or when I'm feeling low . . .'

'Why didn't you live here, then? Why did you fix the ranch over to the east?'

'Well, I wanted to fix it here but Geoffrey Buchanan beat me to it. His farmhouse is another two miles that way, but this land is in his claim.'

'Won't he mind us coming here?'

'I doubt it. He's a pretty relaxed kind of fellow but, more importantly, he won't know we're here,' Corin grinned, and Caroline laughed, crossing to the edge of the pool and dipping her fingers into the water.

'Do you come here often then? Do you get low, out here?'

'I did sometimes, when I was first here. Wondered whether I'd staked the right claim, wondered if it was too far from my family, if the land was right for the cattle. But I've not been back here for many months,' he shrugged. 'It soon became clear to me that I never did a better thing than staking the claim I did, and making those choices. Everything happens for a reason, is what I believe, and now I know that's right.'

'How do you know?' she asked, turning to him, drying her fingers on her skirt.

'Because I have you. When my father died, I thought . . . I thought for a time that I should move back to New York and look after my mother. But the second I got back there I knew I couldn't stay. And then I found you, and you were willing to come away with me . . . and if any good thing could come from losing my father, then you are that good thing, Caroline. You're what was missing from my life.' He spoke with such clarity, such resolve, that Caroline was overwhelmed.

'Do you really think that?' she whispered, standing close to him, feeling the sun's heat flush her skin. It shone brightly in his eyes, turned them the colour of caramel.

'I really think that,' he said quietly; and she stood up on her toes to kiss him.

In the shade of the willow trees they spread out their rugs, unpacked the hamper and unhitched the buggy horse, which Corin tethered to a tree. Caroline sat with her legs tucked carefully beneath her, and poured Corin a glass of lemonade. He lay down easily beside her, propped on one elbow, and undid the buttons of his shirt to let the cool air in. Caroline watched him almost shyly, still not used to the idea that he belonged to her, still not used to his relaxed manner. She had not known until her arrival at the ranch that men grew hair on their chests, and she examined it now, curling against his skin and damp with the heat of his body.

'Corin?' she asked him suddenly.

'Yes, love?'

'How old are you?'

'What? You know that!'

'But I don't! I just realised . . . I don't know how old you are. You seem so much older than me — not in appearance, I mean! Well, partly in appearance, but also in . . . in other ways,' she floundered. Corin smiled.

'I'll be twenty-seven next birthday,' he said. 'There now — are you appalled that you've married such an old-timer?'

'Twenty-seven is not so very old! I shall be nineteen in just a couple of months. But . . . you seem to have lived here for a lifetime already. You're as settled here as if you'd been here fifty years!'

'Well, I first came out here with my father, on a business trip — prospecting for new beef suppliers. My father traded in meat, did I tell you that? He sold to all the best restaurants in New York, and for a time I was destined to go into the business with him. But I knew as soon as I got out here that we were at the wrong end of that chain of supply, and I never left. I was just sixteen when I decided to stay on out here and learn about raising the beeves instead of just buying their dead flesh.'

'Sixteen!' Caroline echoed. 'Weren't you scared, to leave your family like that?' she asked. Corin thought for a moment, then shook his head.

'I've never been much afraid of anything. Until I asked you to dance,' he said. Caroline blushed happily, straightening her skirts.

'It really is hot, isn't it? Even here in the shade,' she commented.

'You want to know the best way to cool down?'

'What is it?'

'Swimming!' Corin declared, springing to his feet and pulling his shirt up over his head.

'*Swimming!* What do you mean?' Caroline laughed.

'I'll show you!' he said, sliding off his boots, kicking his pants to one side and charging into the pool, as naked as Adam, with a wild whooping and splashing. Caroline stood up and watched in utter amazement. 'Come in, sweetheart! It's the best feeling!' he called.

'Are you *crazy*?' she cried. 'I can *not* swim here!'

'Why ever not?' he asked, swimming the length of the small pool with broad strokes of his arms.

'Well . . . well, it's . . .' she waved an incredulous arm. 'It's muddy! And it's out in the open — anybody could see! And I don't have a bathing suit.'

'Sure you do! It's right there under your dress,' Corin grinned.

'And who's to see? There's nobody around for miles – it's just you and me. Come on! You'll love it!'

Caroline walked uncertainly to the edge of the bank, unlaced her boots and hesitated. Sunlight danced prettily on the water's surface and tiny fish were lazing in the warm shallows. The sun beat down on her, scorching the top of her head and making her clothes feel tight and stifling. She bent down, pulled off her boots and stockings and put them carefully on the bank, then, gathering her skirt to her knees, she stepped in until the water lapped her ankles. The relief of cold water on her clammy skin was her undoing.

'Oh, my goodness,' she breathed.

'Now, how much better does that feel?' Corin called to her, coming over to where she stood. The white of his buttocks gleamed, distorted, beneath the surface, and Caroline laughed.

'You look just like a frog in a bucket!' she told him.

'Oh, really?' he asked, flicking a spray of water up at her. With a squeal she retreated. 'Come on, come in and swim! I dare you!'

Caroline looked over her shoulder, as if an audience might have appeared, ready to gasp in dismay at her wantonness, then she undid her dress and stays and draped them over a willow branch. She kept her chemise on, the bare skin of her shoulders crawling, feeling utterly conspicuous, then went back to the edge of the pool with her arms wrapped protectively around her. There she paused, mesmerised by the feel of the mud as it squeezed up between her toes. She had never felt anything like it, and hitched up her petticoat to look down, flexing her feet and smiling. When she looked up to remark upon it, she found Corin watching her with a rapt expression.

'What is it?' she asked, alarmed.

'You. Just look at you . . . You're so brave. And so beautiful. I've never seen anything like it,' he said simply. Water had splayed his hair across his forehead, making him younger, boyish.

Caroline had only intended to paddle, but the touch of the water and the thrill of Corin's words made her bold, and she waded in up to her waist, the water swirling the translucent folds of her chemise around her legs. With a nervous laugh she lay back and let the water buoy her up. It felt chilly as it fingered through her hair.

'Come here and kiss me,' Corin demanded.

'With regret, sir, I am far too busy swimming,' Caroline replied grandly, paddling away with an ungainly stroke. With a start, she realised she hadn't swum since childhood, at her family's summer house.

'I shall have a kiss, even if I must chase you down for it,' Corin told her. Laughing and kicking her legs Caroline tried to escape; but she did not try very hard.

The sun was setting as they came over the last rise and saw the lights of the ranch house glimmering below them. Caroline's skin felt hot and raw where the sun had singed it, and her dress felt odd without the chemise underneath, which was laid out drying on the back of the buggy. She licked her lips, tasted the mineral tang of the creek water. They both carried the smell of it on their skin, in their hair. They had made love on the riverbank, and the languor of it lingered in her muscles, leaving her heavy and warm. Suddenly, she did not want to arrive back at the house. She wanted the day to last for ever; she and Corin in a shady place on a hot day, making love over and over again, without another thought or care in the world. As if reading her mind, Corin reined the horse to a halt, surveying his home for a moment before turning to her.

'Are you ready to go back?' he asked.

'No!' Caroline said fiercely. 'I . . . I wish every day could be like today. It was so perfect.'

'It truly was, sweetheart,' Corin agreed, taking her hand and raising it to his lips.

'Promise me we'll go back there. I won't go one *inch* closer to the house until you promise me.'

'We have to go back to the house! Night's coming . . . but I do promise you we'll go there again. We can go back whenever we want to – we *will* go back, and we'll have many more days like today. I swear it,' he said.

Caroline looked at the outline of him in the indigo twilight, caught the gleam of his eye, the faint shape of a smile. She put her hand out and touched his face. 'I love you,' she told him simply.

With a shake of the reins the horse began a lazy descent towards the wooden house below, and with each step it took, Caroline felt a sense of vague foreboding growing inside her. She turned her eyes to the dark ground ahead and was suddenly afraid, in spite of Corin's pledge, that no day to come would be as sweet as that which had just passed.

mine eye
Fixed with mock study on my swimming book:
Save if the door half opened, and I snatched
A hasty glance, and still my heart leaped up,
For still I hoped to see the stranger's *face,*
Samuel Taylor Coleridge, *Frost at Midnight*

3

I have been trying to remember good things about Henry. Perhaps we owe him that, because we got to grow up, live lives, fall in love, fall out again. He liked to tell stupid jokes, and I loved to hear them. Beth was always kind, and took me with her, and helped me, but she was rather serious, even as a child. Once I laughed so hard at Henry's jokes that I nearly wet myself – the fear of it abruptly stopped the giggles, sent me scrambling for the toilet with one fist corked between my legs. *What do you call a dinosaur with only one eye? Do-you-think-he-saw-us. What do you call a deer with no eyes? No idea. Why do elephants paint the soles of their feet yellow? So they can hide upside down in custard. What's orange and sounds like a parrot? A carrot. What's small, brown and wrinkly and travels at two hundred miles an hour? An electric currant.* He could keep it up for hours, and I pushed my fingers into my cheeks where they ached.

He was telling me stupid jokes one day when I was about seven. It was a Saturday, because the remains of a cooked breakfast were still scattered on the dining room table; sunny outside but still cool. The French doors onto the terrace were open, letting a breath of air sneak in, just cold enough to tickle my ankles. I wasn't really watching what Henry was doing as he reeled out his jokes. I wasn't paying attention. I just followed him, stood close enough behind him to trip him, prompted him whenever there was a pause: *Say another one! How do you know when there's an elephant in your bed? You can see the 'E' on his pyjamas. What's brown and sticky? A stick.* He had the biscuit barrel and he was cementing two plain short-breads together with a thick daub of English mustard. The extra strong stuff, ugly coloured, that Clifford liked on sausages. I was trying to remember a good thing about him, and now this.

I didn't think to ask why. I didn't ask where we were going. He wrapped the biscuits in a napkin, pocketed them. I followed him across the lawn like a tame monkey, demanding more jokes, more jokes. We went west, not south into the trees but to the lane instead; skirted along it, behind the hedge, until we got to Dinny's camp. Henry hunkered down in the ditch, pulled me in with him. A foaming, pungent wall of cow parsley to sink behind. At this point only did I think to whisper, 'Henry, what are you doing? Why are we hiding?' He told me to shut up so I did. A spying game, I thought; tried not to rustle loudly, checked beneath myself for nettles, ants' nests, bumble bees. Dinny's grandpa was sitting on a folding chair outside his battered white motor home, waxed hat pulled low over his eyes, arms folded, hands tucked into armpits. Asleep, I think. Deep, dark creases running from the sides of his nose to the corners of his mouth. His dogs lay either side of him, chins on paws. Two black and white collies called Dixie and Fiver, who you weren't allowed to touch until Grandpa Flag had said it was OK. *They'll 'ave those fingers, you give 'em cause*.

Henry threw the sandwiched biscuits over the hedge. The dogs were on their feet in an instant, but they smelt the biscuits and they didn't bark. They crunched them down, mustard and all. I held my breath. I said *Henry!* in my head. Dixie made a hacking noise, sneezed, put her muzzle down on one paw and rubbed at it with the other. Her eyes squinted up; she sneezed again and shook her head, whimpered. Henry had his knuckles in his teeth, his eyes bright, intent. Lit up inside, he was. Grandpa Flag was murmuring to the dogs now, awake. He had his hands in Dixie's ruff, was peering at her as she retched and snuffled. Fiver walked a small, slow circle to one side, heaved, threw up a disgusting yellow mess. A sob of laughter escaped around Henry's fist. I was strangled with pity for the dogs, boiling with guilt. I wanted to stand up and shout, *It wasn't me*. I wanted to disappear, run back to the house. I stayed, rocked on my crouched legs, hid my face in my knees.

But the worst of it was that when I was finally allowed to leave, a pinch on the arm to rouse me, we'd gone a scant twenty paces before Dinny and Beth appeared. The hems of their jeans soaked with dew, a small green leaf in Beth's hair.

'What have you two been doing?' Beth asked. Henry scowled at her.

'*Nothing,*' he said. Able to inject a world of scorn into a single word.

'Erica?' She looked at me sternly, incredulous that I should be with Henry, that I should look guilty. That I should betray them that way. But where had *they* been, without me? I wanted to shout. *They* had left *me*. Henry glowered at me, gave me a shove.

'Nothing,' I lied. I was quiet and sullen for the rest of the day. And when I saw Dinny the day after, knowing that he had been home, I couldn't look at him. I knew he knew. Because of Henry's jokes.

'Rick? Can we go now?' Eddie's head appears at the door to my room, where I, for once, have been skulking. Staring through the foggy glass at the white world beyond. Tiny crystals in the corners of the pane, feathery and perfect.

'*The frost performs its secret ministry, Unhelped by any wind,*' I quote at him.

'What's that?'

'Coleridge. Sure, Eddie, we can go. Give me five seconds.'

'One-two-three-four-five?'

'Ha, ha. Push off. I'll be down in a moment – I can hardly go out in my dressing gown.' I was defiantly still in it when I opened the door to Maxwell earlier.

'Not today,' Eddie agrees, retreating. 'It's cold enough to freeze the arse off a penguin out there.'

'Charming, dear,' I call. The frost has cast the trees in white. It's like another world out there – a brittle, albino world where white and opalescent blues have replaced dead grey and flat brown. It's dazzling bright. Every tiny twig, every fallen leaf, every blade of grass. The house is made new; no longer the ghost, or the corpse, of a place I remember. I am soaring with optimism today. It would be hard not to be. After so many overcast days, the sky seems to go up for ever. It's giddy, all that space up there. And Beth has said she'll come with us – that's how vibrant the day is.

When I told her Dinny was here she froze. I was scared for a minute. She didn't seem to breathe. The blood could have halted in her veins, her ticking heart gone silent, such was the stillness in her. A long, hung moment in which I waited, and watched, and tried to guess what was next. Then she looked away from me and licked her lower lip with the tip of her tongue.

'We'd be strangers, now,' she said, and walked slowly into the kitchen. She didn't ask me how I knew, what he looked like now, what he was doing here. And I found I didn't mind not telling her. I didn't mind keeping it to myself. Keeping the words he had spoken in my head alone. Owning them. She was relaxed again when I went to find her, as we made mugs of tea and I dunked Hobnobs in mine. But she didn't eat that night. Not a Hobnob, not the plate of risotto I put in front of her, not the ice cream afterwards.

It's the twentieth of December today. The car steams up as I drive east through the village and then turn north onto the A361.

'One more day, guys, and then it's all downhill until spring!' I announce, flexing fingers stiff with chill inside my gloves.

'You can't wish the winter away until Christmas has been,' Eddie tells me firmly.

'Really? Not even when my hands have frozen to the wheel? Look, I'm trying to let go and I can't! Frozen on – look!' Eddie laughs at me.

'Keeping hold of the steering wheel while you drive could be considered a good thing,' Beth observes wryly from the passenger seat.

'Well then, it's a good job I'm frozen on, I guess.' I smile. I take the turning to Avebury. Eddie's been doing prehistory this term. Wiltshire's riddled with it. We park, decline to join the National Trust, join instead the steady trickle of people going along the path towards the stones. The ground twinkles, the sun is overwhelming.

A fine Saturday and there are lots of other people at Avebury, all bundled up like we are, shapeless and dark, moving in and out of the ancient sarsen stones. Two concentric rings, not as high as Stonehenge, not as grand or orderly, but the circles far, far bigger. A road runs right through them; half the village is scattered amidst them, although the little church sits chastely without. I like this set-up. All those lives, all those years, piled up in one place. We walk all the way around the ring. Beth reads from the guidebook but I am not sure Eddie is listening. He has a stick again. He is sword-fighting somebody in his head and I wish I could see whom. Barbarians, perhaps? Or somebody from school.

'The Avebury Stone Circles are the largest in Britain, located in the third largest henge. In all, the surrounding bank and ditch and the area enclosed cover eleven point five hectares . . .'

'Beth!' I cry. She is wandering close to the edge of the bank. The grass is slick with frost-melt.

'Oops.' She corrects her course, gives a little laugh.

'Eddie, I'm going to test you on this later!' I shout. My voice blares in the still air. An elderly couple turn to look. I just want him to listen to Beth.

'The quarrying methods used include antler picks and rakes, ox-shoulder blades and probably wooden shovels and baskets . . .'

'Cool,' Eddie says, dutifully. We pass a tree grown into the rampart, its roots cascading above ground like a knotty waterfall. Eddie scrambles down it, commando-style; crouches down, clings to it, peers up from three metres below us.

'Are you an elf?' Beth asks.

'No, I'm a woodsman, waiting to rob you,' he replies.

'Bet you can't get me before I pass this tree to safety,' Beth challenges him.

'I've lost the element of surprise,' Eddie complains.

'I'm getting away!' Beth goads, sauntering onwards. With a rebel yell Eddie scales the roots, slipping and sliding, bashing his knees. He grabs Beth with two hands, makes her squeal. 'I submit, I submit!' she laughs.

We walk out, away from the village along the wide avenue of stones that leads away to the south. The sun shines on Beth's face — a long time since I saw it lit this way. She looks pale, older, but there are blooms in her cheeks. She looks serene too. Eddie leads us, sword aloft, and we walk until our toes get too cold.

On the way back I pull up at the Spar in Barrow Storton for some ginger beer for Eddie. Beth waits in the car, quieter again now. Eddie and I are pretending not to notice. There's a horrible feeling of her teetering, being on the edge of something. Eddie and I hesitate, wanting to pull her one way, scared of accidentally nudging her, tipping her the wrong way.

'Can't I have Coke instead?'

'Yes, if you'd rather.'

'I'm really not that bothered about alcohol, to be honest. I had some vodka last term, in dorm.'

'You've been drinking *vodka*?'

'Hardly drink*ing*. Drank, once. And I felt sick, and Boff and Danny *were* sick, and it stank the place out. Gross. I don't know why grown-ups bother,' he says, airily. His cheeks have a glorious pink flare from the bite outside. Eyes bright as water.

'Well, you might change your mind later on. But for Christ's sake don't tell your mother! She'll have a fit.'

'I'm not *stupid*, you know.' Eddie rolls his eyes at me.

'No. I know.' I smile, wincing at the weight as two huge bottles of Coke go into the basket. As we approach the till, Dinny comes in. The bell rings above his head, a jaunty little fanfare. At once I don't know where to look, how to stand. He has walked right past Beth, in the car. I wonder if she saw him, if she knew him.

'Hullo, Dinny,' I greet him. I smile. Casual neighbours, nothing more, but my heart is high in my chest. He looks up at me, startled.

'Erica!'

'This is Eddie – I mean Ed – who I was telling you about. My nephew – Beth's boy.' I pull Eddie to my side, he grins affably, says *hi*. Dinny studies him closely, then smiles.

'Beth's son? It's nice to meet you, Ed,' he says. They shake hands, and for some reason I am moved, I am choked. A simple gesture. My two worlds coming together with the press of their skins.

'Are you the Dinny my mum used to play with when she was little?'

'Yes. I am.'

'Erica was telling me about you. She said you were best friends.' Dinny looks at me sharply, and I feel guilty, even though what I said was true.

'Well, we were, I suppose.' His voice calm and low, always measured.

'Stocking up for Christmas?' I butt in, inanely. The Spar is hardly bursting with seasonal fare; threadbare tinsel taped to the edges of the shelves. Dinny shakes his head, rolls his eyes slightly.

'Honey wants salt and vinegar crisps,' he says, then looks away sheepishly.

'Did you see Mum, outside? She's out there in the car – did you say hello?' Eddie asks. A flutter in the pit of my stomach.

'No. I didn't. I'll . . . I will now,' Dinny says, turning to the door, looking out at my grubby white car. His eyes are intent; he moves straight, shoulders tense, as if compelled to go to her.

I can see him, through the glass in the door. Between the

spray-on drifts of fake snow in its corners. He bends down at the window, his breath clouding the air. Beth rolls the window down. I can't see her face with Dinny in the way. I see her hands go up towards her mouth and then flutter away again, drifting as if weightless. I duck; I crane my neck to see. I strain my ears, but all I can hear is Slade on the radio behind the counter. Dinny leans his bare arm on the roof of the car and I feel the ache of that cold metal on my own skin.

'Rick – it's our go,' Eddie says, nudging me with his elbow. I heave the basket onto the counter, am forced to break off my surveillance and smile at the gloomy-looking man at the till. I pay for the Coke, a Twix and some ham for lunch, and rush to get back out to the car.

'So what do you do now? You always wanted to be a concert flautist, if I remember rightly?' Dinny is saying. He straightens up from leaning on the car, folds his arms. He looks defensive suddenly, and I notice that Beth has not got out of the car to talk to him. She barely looks at him, keeps rearranging the ends of her scarf in her lap.

'Oh, that didn't quite pan out,' she says with a thin little laugh. 'I got to grade seven and then . . .' She pauses, looks away again. She got to grade seven the spring before Henry disappeared. 'I stopped practising as much,' she finishes, flatly. 'I do some translating now. French and Italian, mostly.'

'Oh,' Dinny says. He studies her, and the moment hangs, so I blunder in.

'I struggle enough with English – trying to teach it to teenagers is like trying to push water uphill with a fork. But Beth always did have a gift for languages.'

'You have to listen, that's all, Rick,' Beth says to me, and it is a reproof of some kind.

'Never was my strongest suit,' I agree with a smile. 'We've just been to Avebury. Ed was keen to see it because they've been doing it at school. Mind you, once we got there you were more interested in having a hot fudge sundae in the pub, weren't you, Ed?'

'It was *amazing*,' Eddie assures us. Dinny gives me a quizzical smile, but when Beth asks him nothing more, his face falls slightly and he steps back from the car.

'So, how long are you staying?' he asks, and he addresses this to me, since Beth is staring straight ahead.

'For Christmas, definitely. After that, we're not really sure. There's a lot of sorting out to be done,' I say. Which is honest and ambiguous enough. 'How about you?'

'For the time being,' Dinny shrugs; even more ambiguous.

'Ah.' I smile.

'Well, I'd better be getting on. Good to see you again, Beth. Nice to meet you, Ed,' he says, nodding to us and walking away.

'He didn't get the crisps,' Eddie observes.

'No. He must have forgotten,' I agree, breathless. 'I'll get some and take them over later.'

'Cool.' Eddie nods. He pulls open the back door with one hand, the other hand fighting its way into the Twix. So flippant. No idea how huge the thing that just happened is, here at the car window. I go back into the shop, buy salt and vinegar crisps, and when I get back into the car I start the engine and take us home, and I don't look at Beth because I feel too awkward, and the things I would ask I won't ask in front of her son.

Eddie is lying on his bed, in pyjamas, tethered to his iPod. On his front with his heels swinging over his back. He's reading a book called *Sasquatch!* and with his music on he can't hear the owls outside, calling to each other between trees. I leave him. Downstairs, Beth is making mint tea, her fingers pinching the corner of the teabag and dipping it, over and over, into the water.

'I hope Dinny didn't startle you, appearing at the car window like that?' I say. Lightly as I can. Beth glances at me, presses her lips together.

'I saw him go into the shop,' she says, still dipping.

'Really? And you recognised him? I don't think I would have — not just from glimpsing him go by.'

'Don't be ridiculous — he looks exactly the same,' she says. I feel inadequate — that she saw something I didn't.

'Well,' I say. 'Pretty amazing to see him again after all this time, isn't it?'

'Yes, I suppose so,' she murmurs.

Now I can't think what to ask. She should not be this careless about it. It should matter more. I search her face and frame for signs. 'Perhaps we should ask them up to the house. For a drink or something?'

'They?'

'Dinny and Honey. She's his . . . well, I'm not sure if they're married. She's about to have his baby. You could talk her out of having it in the woods. I think he'd be grateful for that.'

'Having it in the woods? How extraordinary,' Beth says. 'What a pretty name though — Honey.' There is more to it than this. There has to be.

'Look, are you sure you're OK?'

'Why wouldn't I be?' she says, that same bemused tone that I don't believe. She looks at me again, and I see that her fingers are in the hot water, mid-dip. Steaming hot water, and she does not flinch.

'But you hardly spoke to him. You two used to be so close . . . didn't you want to talk to him? Catch up?'

'Twenty-three years is a long time, Erica. We're totally different people now.'

'Not *totally* different — you're still you. He's still him. We're still the same people who played together as kids . . .'

'People change. They move on,' she insists.

'Beth,' I say, eventually, 'what happened? To Henry, I mean?'

'What do you mean?'

'Well, I mean, what happened to him?'

'He disappeared,' she says flatly, but her voice is like thin ice.

'No, but, do you remember, that day at the pond? The day he vanished? Do you remember what happened?' I press. I don't think I should. I partly want to know, I partly want to move her. And I know I shouldn't. Beth's hand slips down to the worktop. It knocks her cup roughly aside, slops tea. She takes a deep breath.

'How can you ask me that?' she demands, constricted.

'How can I? Why shouldn't I?' I ask, but when I look up I see she is shaking, eyes alight with anger. She doesn't answer for a while.

'Just because Dinny's around . . . just because he's here it doesn't mean you need to go raking up the past!' she says.

'What's it got to do with Dinny? I just asked a simple question!'

'Well, don't! Don't keep asking bloody questions, Erica!' Beth snaps, walking away. I sit quietly for a long time, and I picture that day.

We got up early because it had been such a hot night. A night when the sheets seemed to wrap themselves around my legs, and I woke up again and again with my hair stuck in clammy rat-tails to my forehead and neck. We helped ourselves to breakfast and then listened to the radio in the conservatory, which faced north and was cool in the morning. Terracotta tiled floor, ranks of orchids and ferns on the window sill. We wallowed in Caroline's swing chair, which had blue canvas cushions that smelt faintly sharp, almost feline. Caroline was dead by then. Dead when I was five or six years old. I ran past that swing chair once, a very little girl, and did not see her in it until her stick shot out and caught me. *Laura!* she snapped, calling me my mother's name, *Go and find Corin. Tell him I need to see him. I must see him!* I had no idea who Corin was. I was terrified of the limp bundle of fabric in the swing chair, the incongruous strength behind that stick. I ducked beneath it, and ran.

We got dressed at the last possible minute, went reluctantly to church with Meredith and our parents, ate lunch in the shade of the oak tree on the lawn. A special little table laid there just for the three of us. Beth, Henry and me. Peanut butter and cucumber sandwiches, which Mum had made for us because she knew we were too hot and fractious to eat the soup. The itchy press of the wicker chair into the backs of my legs. Some small bird in the tree crapped on the table. Henry scraped it up with his knife, flicked it at me. I ducked so violently that I fell off my chair, kicked the table leg, spilt my lemonade and Beth's. Henry laughed so hard a lump of bread went up his nose, and he choked until his eyes streamed. Beth and I watched, satisfied; we did not thump him on the back. He was vile for the rest of the day. We tried everything to lose him. The heat made him groggy and violent, like a sun-struck bull. Eventually he was called inside to lie down because he was caught tying a Labrador's legs together with string while it panted, long-suffering and bewildered. Meredith would not stand for the torment of her Labradors.

But he came out again later, as the afternoon broadened. He found us at the dew pond. The three of us by then, of course. I had been swimming, pretending to be an otter, a mermaid, a dolphin. Henry laughed at my wet saggy knickers, at the bulge of water in the gusset. *Have you pissed your pants, Erica?* Then something, *something*. Running. Thoughts of the plughole at the bottom of the pond, of Henry being sucked down through it. That must have been why I said to them, again and again: *Look in the pond. I think he's in the pond. We were all at the pond*. Even though they had looked, they told me. Mum told me, the policeman told me. They had looked and he wasn't there. No need for divers – the water was clear enough to see. Meredith took me by the shoulders, shook me, shouted, *Where is he, Erica?* A tiny bubble of spit from her mouth landed warm and wet on my cheek. *Mother, stop it! Don't!* Beth and I were given dinner in the kitchen, our mother spooning beans onto our toast, her face pale and preoccupied. As dusk bloomed the evening smelled of hot grass getting damp, and air so good you could eat it. But Beth did not eat. That was the first time, that evening. The first time I saw her mouth close so resolutely. Nothing in, and nothing out.

'What's with all the crisps?' Beth asks, poking the multipack of salt and vinegar amongst the breakfast detritus on the table.

'Oh . . . they were supposed to be for Honey. I forgot to take them down to her yesterday,' I say. Eddie is sitting on the bench with his back to the kitchen table, throwing a tennis ball against the wall and catching it. The ball's flat, threadbare; it probably belonged to a Labrador once. He throws it with a maddening lack of rhythm. 'Eddie, can you give it a rest?' I ask. He sighs, aims, throws the ball into the bin in one smooth arc.

'Great shot, darling,' Beth smiles. Eddie rolls his eyes. 'Are you bored?' she asks him.

'A bit. No, not really,' Eddie flounders. The equal pull of honesty and tact.

'Why don't you deliver those crisps to Honey?' I suggest, swigging the remains of my tea.

'I've never even *met* Honey. And I only met that bloke once, yesterday. I can hardly go marching into their front yard waving crisps, can I?'

'I'll go with you,' I say, swinging my legs around and getting up. 'Do you want to come, Beth? The camp's just where it always was,' I can't resist adding. I don't know how she can not want to go back, to see.

'No. No thanks. I'm going to . . . I'm going to walk into the village. Get the Sunday paper.'

'Can I have a Twix?'

'Eddie, you're going to turn into a Twix.'

'Please?'

'Come on, Eddie. We're going. Boots on, it's pretty muddy on the way,' I say.

I take us to the camp the long way, via the dew pond. It's becoming a daily pilgrimage. It's just a cold brown day today, none of the ice and sparkle of yesterday. I pause to walk to the edge, look into the depths of it. It's unchanged. It gives me no answers. I wonder if I just wasn't paying attention, when whatever it was happened? My mind wanders sometimes – gets snagged on a background thought, gets coaxed away. When other teachers talk to me, sometimes it happens. I don't like to think about repressed memories, about trauma, amnesia. Mental illness.

'I think you're a bit obsessed with this pond, Rick,' Eddie tells me gravely. I smile.

'I'm not. What makes you say that, anyway?'

'Every time we come near it you go all Luna Lovegood. Staring into space like that.'

'Well, *excuse* me, I'm sure!'

'I'm only *joking*,' he exclaims, pushing me awkwardly with his shoulder. 'But it does kind of look the same every time. Doesn't it?' He turns away a few paces, crouches to pick up a stone, hurls it into the water. The surface shatters. I watch him and suddenly my knees ache, sickeningly, as if I've missed my step on a ladder.

'Come on, then,' I say, turning away quickly.

'Did something happen here?' Eddie asks in a rush. He sounds tense, worried.

'What makes you ask, Eddie?'

'It's just . . . you keep coming back out here. You get that look in your eye, like Mum gets when she's sad,' Eddie mumbles. I curse myself silently. 'And Mum seems . . . she doesn't seem to like it here.' It's easy to forget how clearly a child can see things.

'Well, something did happen here, Eddie. When we were small

our cousin Henry disappeared. He was eleven, the same age as you are now. Nobody ever found out what happened to him, so we've kind of never forgotten about it.'

'Oh.' He kicks up sprays of dead leaves. 'That's really sad,' he says, eventually.

'Yes. It was,' I reply.

'Maybe he just ran away and . . . I don't know, joined a band or something?'

'Maybe he did, Eddie,' I say, hopelessly. Eddie nods, apparently satisfied with this explanation.

Dinny is standing with a man I don't recognise as the dogs come charging over to us, circling proprietorially. I smile and wave as if I pop in every day, and Dinny waves back, more hesitantly. His companion smiles at me. He's a thin man, wiry, not tall. He has fair hair, cropped very close, the tattoo of a tiny blue flower on his neck. Eddie walks closer to my side, bumping me. We move nervously into the circle of vehicles.

'Hi, sorry to interrupt,' I say. I try for bright, but to my own ears I sound brassy.

'Hello there, I'm Patrick. You must be our neighbours up at the big house?' the wiry man greets me. His smile is warm and real, his handshake rattles my shoulder. At such a welcome I feel a knot in my stomach begin to loosen.

'Yes, that's right. I'm Erica and this is my nephew, Eddie.'

'Ed!' Eddie hisses at me sideways, through unruly teeth.

'Ed, good to meet you.' Patrick rattles Eddie's shoulder too. I notice Harry sitting on the step of a van behind the two of them. I think about calling out a greeting, but change my mind. Something in his hands again, something the focus of immense concentration. Most of his face is hidden behind hanging hair and thick whiskers.

'Well, uh, this might sound a little odd but we noticed you'd forgotten to get Honey's crisps yesterday. In the shop. So, we brought some over for her. That's if she's not craving pickles this morning instead?' I wave the big sack of crisps. Patrick gives Dinny a look – not unkind, slightly puzzled.

'I know how fed up *I* get when Mum forgets my food when she goes shopping,' Eddie rescues me. At the sound of his voice, Harry looks up. Dinny shrugs one shoulder. He turns.

'Honey!' he yells at the ambulance.

'Oh! There's no need to disturb her . . .' I feel colour in my cheeks. Honey appears at one of the small windows. It frames her face. Pretty, petulant.

'What?' she shouts back, far louder than she needs to.

'Erica has something for you.' I squirm. Eddie edges closer to Harry, trying to see what he's working on. Honey appears, picking her way carefully down the steps. All in black today, hair arrestingly pale against it. She stands at a distance from me and watches me suspiciously.

'Well. Silly really. We got you these. Dinny said you fancied some, so . . .' I trail off, I dandle the bag. Slowly, Honey steps forward and takes them from me.

'How much do I owe you?' she asks, scowling.

'Oh, no, don't worry. I don't remember. Forget it.' I wave my hand. She shoots Dinny a flat look and he puts his hand in his pocket.

'Two quid cover it?' he asks me.

'There's really no need.'

'Take it. Please.' So I take it.

'Thanks,' Honey mutters, and goes back inside.

'Don't mind Honey,' Patrick grins. 'She was born in a bad mood, and then it got worse in puberty, and now that she's expecting . . . well, forget it!'

'Fuck you, Pat!' Honey shouts, out of sight. He grins even wider.

Eddie has got closer and closer to Harry. He is peering at the man's hands, and probably blocking his light.

'Don't get in the way, will you, Ed?' I say, smiling cautiously.

'What is it?' Eddie asks Harry, who doesn't reply, but looks at him and smiles.

'That's Harry,' Dinny tells Ed. 'He doesn't really like to talk.'

'Oh. Well, it looks like a torch. Is it broken? Can I see?' Eddie presses. Harry opens his hands wide, displays the tiny mechanical parts.

'So, will you be down for our little solstice party this evening, Erica?' Patrick asks.

'Oh, well, I don't know,' I say. I look at Dinny and he looks back, steadily, as if working out a problem.

'Of course you are! The more the merrier, right, Nathan? We're lighting a bonfire, having a bit of a barbecue. Bring some booze and you're most welcome, neighbour,' Patrick says.

'Well, maybe then.' I smile.

'Your dreadlocks are wicked,' Eddie tells Harry. 'You look a bit like *Predator*. Have you seen that film?' He has his fingers in the mess of torch parts, picking bits out, putting them in order. Harry looks faintly astonished.

'I've got to run. I'll catch you later.' Patrick nods at Dinny and me. He leaves the camp with a springing step, hands thrust into the pockets of a battered wax coat.

I look at the muddy toes of my boots, then at Eddie, who is piecing the torch back together before Harry's incredulous eyes.

'Ed seems a good lad,' Dinny says then, and I nod.

'He's the best. He's a great help.' There's a long silence.

'When I spoke to Beth . . . she seemed, I don't know,' Dinny says, hesitant.

'She seemed what?'

'Not like she used to be. Almost like there was nobody home?'

'She suffers from depression,' I say, hurriedly. 'She's still the same Beth. Only she's . . . she got more fragile.' I have to explain, even though I feel treacherous. He nods, frowns. 'I think it started here. I think it started when Henry disappeared,' I blurt out. This is not what Beth has told me, but I do think it's true. She told me it started one stormy day, driving home at dusk. The clouds were heavy, but on the western horizon as she drove towards it, they broke into slivers, and stripes of bright pale sky showed behind them. One of those wet mackerel skies. She said she suddenly couldn't tell what was the horizon and what was the sky. Hills or clouds. Earth or air. It was so bewildering that she almost drifted into the oncoming traffic, and she felt seasick all evening, as if the ground were moving beneath her feet. After that, she told me, she wasn't sure what was real any more, what was safe. That's when she thinks it started. But I remember her the evening Henry vanished. Her silence, and the uneaten beans on her plate.

'I would hate to think that what happened then has made her ill all this time,' Dinny says quietly. He knows what happened. He *knows*.

'Oh?' I say. If only he would go on, say more. *Tell me*. But he doesn't.

'It wasn't . . . well. I'm sorry to hear that she's not happy.'

'I thought coming back here would help, but . . . I'm worried it might be making her worse. You know, bringing it all back. It could go either way, I think. But it's good that Eddie's here. He takes her mind off things. Without him I think she'd even forget it was Christmas.'

'Do you think Beth will come to the party tonight?'

'Truthfully, no. I'll ask her, if you like?' I say.

Dinny nods, his face falling. 'Ask her. Bring Eddie too. He and Harry seem to be getting on well. He's great with kids — they're less complicated for him.'

'If you asked her, I'm sure she'd come. If you came up to the house, that is,' I venture. Dinny shoots me a brief, wry smile.

'Me and that house don't really get along. You ask her, and

perhaps I'll see you both later.' I nod, bury my hands in the back pockets of my jeans.

'Are you coming, Ed? I'm going back to the house.' Eddie and Harry look up from their work. Two sets of clear blue eyes.

'Can't I stay and finish this, Rick?' I glance at Dinny. He shrugs again, nods.

'I'll keep an eye out,' he says.

We smuggled Dinny into the house once, when Meredith had gone into Devizes for a dental appointment. Henry was at the house of a boy in the village with whom he had taken up. A boy whose house had a *proper* swimming pool.

'Come *on*!' I hissed at Dinny. 'Don't be such a baby!' I was desperate to show him the big rooms, the huge stairs, the enormous cellars. Not to impress him, not to show off. Just to see his eyes widen. To be able to show *him* something for a change, to be the one in charge. Beth hunkered down at the back of the three of us, smiling tensely. There was nobody about except the housekeeper – who never paid us much attention – but still we crouched to scuttle in. Behind the last sheltering bush, I was close enough to feel Dinny's knee pressing into my hip; smell the dry, woody smell of his skin.

Dinny was reluctant. He had been told enough times, heard enough stories from his grandpa, Flag, and his parents; had even had fleeting encounters with Meredith. He knew he wasn't welcome there, and that he shouldn't want to look. But he was curious, I could tell. As a child will be when a place is forbidden. I had never seen him that unsure; I'd never seen him hesitate, and then choose to carry on. We went from room to room, and I gave a running commentary: 'This is the drawing room, only nobody ever does any drawing in it, not that I've seen. This is the way to the cellar. Come and see! It's the size of another whole house! This is Beth's room. She gets the bigger room because she's older but from my room you can see right into the trees and I saw an owl, once.' On and on I went. The Labradors followed us, grinning and wagging excitedly.

But the more I went on, and the more we showed him, the more rooms we dragged him into, the quieter and quieter Dinny got. His words dried up, eyes that were wide fell flat again. Eventually even I noticed.

'Don't you like it?'

A shrug, a tip of the eyebrows. And then the sound of the car on the driveway. Freezing, panicking, hearts lurching. Trying to hear: were they coming in the front, or the back? A calculated risk and I chose wrong. We ran out onto the terrace as they appeared at the side of the house. Meredith, my father, and worst of all Henry, back from his visit. He grinned. After a hung moment I grabbed Dinny's arm, yanked it, and we tore across the lawn. The greatest act of insurrection I think I ever performed and it was to save Dinny. To save him from hearing what Meredith would say to him. She was shocked into silence, just for a second. Standing tall and thin in a crisp linen suit, duck-egg blue; hair set, immaculate. Her mouth was a hard red line of pigment, and then we were away and it cracked open.

'Erica Calcott, you come back here this *instant*! How dare you bring that *filth* into my house? How *dare* you! I *insist* that you come back here immediately! And you, you thieving gypsy! You'll scuttle off like vermin, will you? Like the vermin that you are!' I like to think my father said something. I like to hope Dinny didn't hear, but of course deep down I know that he did. Running away like a thief. Like a trespasser. I thought I was being brave, I thought I was being a hero for him. But he was angry with me for days. For making him go into the house, and then for making him run away.

I'm up in Meredith's room. This is the biggest bedroom, of course, with an ugly four-poster bed, heavy with carvings. The base is high and the mattress deep. How will the next owners move this bed? It's huge. Only by taking an axe to it, I think. To be replaced with something contemporary and probably beige. I fling myself across it, over the stiff brocaded bedspread, and count how long it takes me to stop bouncing. Who made this bed? The housekeeper, I suppose. The morning that Meredith collapsed on her way into the village. Gradually I become still and realise that I am bouncing on my dead grandmother's bed. The very sheets she slept in the night before she died.

In here more than anywhere the ghostly remains of her seem to linger. As is only natural, I suppose. Part of me wishes that I'd come to see her as an adult. That I'd pinned her down, made her tell me where all that bad feeling came from. Far too late now. Her dressing table is a huge thing – deep, wide; several drawers in columns on either side, a wide drawer in the middle that opens into my lap; a triptych mirror set on a box of yet more drawers. The top is satin smooth, a patina wrought by centuries of soft female fingers. I think Mum should have jewellery as well as photos. Meredith made no bones about telling us she'd sold off her best pieces, like the best of the estate's land, to pay for repairs to the roof. She told my parents this accusingly, as if they ought to have put their hands in their pockets, looked under the sofa cushions and produced thirty thousand pounds. But there has to be something left for my thieving hands to find.

Lipsticks and eyeshadows and blushers in the top right-hand drawer. Small dunes of loose make-up powder, shimmering underneath all the metal tubes and plastic compacts. Belts in the next, coiled like snakes. Handkerchiefs, hair clips, chiffon scarves. This drawer smells powerfully of Meredith, of her perfume, and the slightly doggy notes of the Labradors. In the bottom right drawer are boxes. I take them out, put them up where I can see them. Most are full of jewellery – dress pieces by the looks of it. One box, the biggest, shiny and dark, is full of papers and photographs.

With a prickle of excitement, I sift through the contents. Letters from Clifford and Mary; holiday postcards from my mum and dad;

odd bank statements, secreted away into this secretive box for who knows what reason. I read odd snatches of each, feeling the illicit thrill of prying. Some photographs too, which I put to one side; and then I find the newspaper clippings. About Henry, of course. Local papers started the coverage. *Lady Calcott's Grandson Missing. Search for Local Boy Intensifies. Clothes found in Westridge woods did not belong to missing boy*. Then the nationals joined in. Abduction fears, speculation, a mysterious hobo spotted walking the A361 with a bundle that could have been a child. Boy matching the description seen lying in a car in Devizes. *Police very concerned*. I can't take my eyes from it. As if a hobo could have carried Henry any distance at all. Big-boned, solid Henry. We never saw any of this, Beth and I. Of course we didn't. Nobody reads the paper when they're eight years old, and we weren't allowed to watch the news at the best of times.

It looks like she bought several papers, different ones every day. Did she cut these out at the time, or later, years afterwards, as a way to keep hope alive, to keep *him* alive? I had no idea it was such a big story. I hadn't connected, until right now, the reporters milling at the gates with any kind of national infamy. Of course, I realise now why they were there, the reporters; why the story ran and ran, getting fewer and fewer column inches as the months went on, until it disappeared altogether. Children shouldn't just vanish without trace. That's the worst fear, worse even than finding the body, perhaps. Having no answers, having no idea. Poor Meredith. She was his grandmother, after all. She was meant to be looking after him.

I am staring, staring hard at a grainy, enlarged photo of Henry. A school photo, neat and tidy in a blazer and stripy house tie. Hair combed; toothy, decorous smile. That photo on posters in the shop window, on telegraph poles, on newspaper pages, in doctors' waiting rooms and supermarkets and garages and pubs. No websites back then, but I remember seeing this photo all over the village. The one in the shop window was in colour. It quickly faded in the sunshine, but it was bright when I first saw it. *Can I go to the shop? No! You're to stay indoors!* I couldn't understand why. Mum went with me in the end, and held my hand, and politely asked the reporters to let us through, to not follow us. A couple of them did anyway, took some pointless shots of us emerging from the shop with orange ice lollies. One tiny cutting from late August, 1987. A full year later. The regretful last line: *Despite an extensive police investigation, no trace of the missing boy has yet been found.*

There's an ache in my ribs and I realise I've been holding my breath. As if in anticipation; as if the story could have had any other ending. I notice the rain falling faster, louder. Eddie is out in the woods. He'll be soaked. It seems so unreal, reading about Henry in the press, reading about that summer. Unreal, and at the same time all the more real. All the more terrible. It did happen, and I was there. I put the clippings back in the box, careful not to crease them. I will keep these, I think; in the very same box, so coffin-like, that Meredith put them in twenty-three years ago.

I pick up the pile of photographs and flick through them, shaking off the shadow of the newspaper clippings. Random family portraits and holiday shots for the most part – the sort of thing Mum was after. A small black and white photo of Meredith and Charles on their wedding day – my grandfather Charles, that is, who was killed in World War II. Charles wasn't in the armed forces, but he went up to London on business one week and a stray V2 found its way to the club where he was having lunch. The best shots of their wedding day are on the piano in the drawing room, in heavy silver frames, but in this little shot Meredith is bent at an odd angle, twisting to look back over her shoulder, away from Charles, as if the hem of her dress has caught on something. They are emerging from the church, coming out of the dark into the light. In profile Meredith's face is young, painfully anxious. Her hair is very fair, eyes huge in her face. How did such a lovely girl, such a nervous young bride, ever become Meredith? The Meredith I remember, cold and hard as the marble shelves in the pantry.

Only one other photo arrests me. It's very old, battered around the edges; the image surfaces from a sea of fox marks and fade. A young woman, perhaps in her early twenties, in a high-necked dress, hair pinned severely back; and on her lap a child in a lace dress, not more than six months old. A dark-haired baby, its face slightly smeared, ghostly, as if it wriggled just as the exposure was taken. The woman is Caroline. I recognise her from other pictures around the house, although in none of them does she look as young as this. I turn it over, read the faint stamp on the back: *Gilbert Beaufort & Son, New York City*; and hand written, in ink that has almost vanished, *1904*.

But Caroline did not marry Henry Calcott, my great-grandfather, until 1905. Mary was seized by a genealogy fad a few years back – traced the Calcott family lineage that she was so proud to have married into and sent us all a copy in our Christmas card that year. They married in 1905, and they lost a daughter before Meredith was born in 1911. I frown, turn the picture to the light and try to find any more clues within it. Caroline stares calmly back at me, her hand curled protectively around her baby. Where did this child go? How did it fall from our family tree? I slip the photo into my back pocket, begin to pick through the jewellery, hardly seeing it. A brooch pin catches my fingertip, and I sit there a while, tasting my blood.

After dinner Eddie escapes from the table to watch TV. Beth and I sit among the dirty plates and bowls. She has eaten a little. Not enough, but a little. When she senses Eddie watching her, she tries harder. I steal one last potato from the bowl and lean back, feel something stiff in my back pocket.

'What's that?' Beth asks, as I pull out the photo of our great-grandmother. She hasn't spoken to me much since I asked her about Henry, and now her voice is slightly stiff. But I know an olive branch when I see one.

'I found it up in Meredith's room — it's Caroline,' I tell her, passing it over.

Beth studies the young face, the pale eyes. 'Gosh, yes, so it is. I remember those eyes — even when she was ancient, they stayed that bright silver colour. Do you remember?'

'No, not really.'

'Well, you were pretty small.'

'I used to be so scared of her! She hardly seemed human to me.'

'Were you really? But she never bothered us. Never paid us much attention.'

'I know. She was just so . . . *old*!' I say, and Beth chuckles.

'That she was. From another era, well and truly.'

'What else do you remember about her?' I ask. Beth leans back from the table, pushes her plate away from her. Half of her slice of quiche is still on her plate, untouched.

'I remember that look Meredith used to get on her face whenever she had to feed her, or dress her. That look of such careful neutrality. I always remember thinking she must have been having terrible thoughts, such terrible thoughts to have been so careful not to let them show on her face.'

'But what about Caroline? Do you remember anything she said, anything she did?'

'Well, let me think. I remember the time she went mad at the summer party — when was it? I can't remember. Not long before she died. Do you remember it? With the fireworks and all the lanterns strung along the driveway to light the way up to the house?'

'God! I'd totally forgotten about that . . . I remember the fireworks, of course, and the food. But now you remind me I do remember Meredith wheeling Caroline inside, because she'd been shouting something about crows . . . what was it about? Can you remember?' I ask. Beth shakes her head.

'It wasn't crows,' she says. And as she tells me, the scene slides into focus in my mind, as if it had always been there, waiting for Beth to point it out to me.

The Storton Manor summer party was an annual affair, usually held on the first Saturday in July. Sometimes we were there in time for it, sometimes not, depending on the school calendar. We always hoped to be – it was the one occasion when we wanted to take part in something of Meredith's, because the lights and the people and the music and the dresses turned the manor into another place, another world. That year, Beth spent hours doing my hair for me. I'd been crying because my party dress had got too small for me, something we hadn't discovered until I put it on earlier in the evening. It was too tight under the arms and the smocking pinched my skin. But there was no alternative so I had to wear it, and to cheer me up Beth braided turquoise ribbons into my hair, fifteen or twenty in total, which came together in a plume of curled ends at the back of my head.

'Last one – sit still! There. You look like a bird of paradise, Erica!' she smiled, as she knotted the last one. I tipped my head this way and that, liked the brush of the ribbons against the back of my neck.

Flaming torches marched up the driveway, reeking of paraffin and guttering in the night air. They made a sound like flags flying. There was a string quartet on the sun terrace near where long tables had been set up, draped with white cloths and loaded with ranks of shining glassware. Silver ice buckets on long legs held chilled bottles of champagne, and the waiters raised their eyebrows at me when I dipped my fingers in, filching ice cubes to suck. The food was probably wonderful, but I remember snatching a caviare bliny, cramming it into my mouth and then spitting it into the nearest flowerbed. Adult conversation that we didn't understand volleyed over our heads; gossip and hearsay bandied back and forth, oblivious of we little spies, infiltrating the crowd.

Most of our extended family, people I never see any more, attended, as well as everyone who was anyone in county society. A photographer from *Wiltshire Life* circulated, snapping the more attractive women, the more titled men. Horsey women with flat hair and big teeth, who wore garishly expensive evening gowns in shades of pink, peacock and emerald. They dug out their diamonds for the occasion – rocks glittering against freckled English skins. The whole garden was flooded with the smell of their perfumes, and later, when the dancing started, that of fresh sweat. The men wore black tie. My dad fidgeted with his collar, his cummerbund, not used to the stiff edges, the layers of fabric. Insects swirled around the lanterns like sparks from a fire. The lawns rang with voices and laughter, a steady roar that grew with the number of empty bottles. Only the fireworks silenced it, and we children stared, rapt, as the purple night sky exploded into light.

A whole crew of staff was brought in to cater the party. Wine waiters; cooks who took over the kitchen; waitresses to ferry the trays of hot canapés they produced; calm, implacable butlers who lingered indoors, politely directing people to the downstairs bathrooms and discouraging the curious from peering into the family rooms. It was one of these anonymous workers that Caroline attacked, inexplicably. She had been positioned in her chair on the veranda, near enough to the terrace to hear the music, but still within the shelter of the house. People drifted over to pay their respects, bending forward awkwardly so as not to tower over her, but they drifted away again as soon as it was polite to do so. Some of them Caroline acknowledged with a faraway nod of her head. Some she just ignored. And then a waitress went over with a smile, offered her something from a tray.

She was dark, I remember that. Very young, maybe only in her teens. Beth and I had noticed her earlier in the evening because we envied her hair. Her skin was a deep olive and she had the most luxurious black hair, hanging in a thick plait over her shoulder. It was as deep and glossy as ink. She had a neat rounded body, and a neat rounded face with dark brown eyes and apples high in her cheeks. She might have been Spanish, or Greek perhaps. Beth and I were nearby because we'd been following her. We thought her incredibly lovely. But when Caroline looked up and focused on the girl her eyes grew huge and her mouth dropped open – a damp, lipless hole in her face. I was close enough to see that she was shaking, and to see a frown of alarm pass over the waitress's face.

'Magpie?' Caroline whispered, a ragged breath forming the word so loosely I thought I'd heard it wrong. But she said it again, more firmly. 'Magpie, is that you?' The waitress shook her head and smiled, but Caroline threw up her hands with a hoarse cry. Meredith looked over at her mother, drawing down her brows.

'Are you all right, Mother?' she asked, but Caroline ignored her, continuing to stare at the dark-haired waitress with a look of pure terror on her face.

'It can't be you! You're dead! I know you are . . . I *saw* it . . .' she wailed.

'It's OK,' the girl said, backing away from the old woman. Beth and I watched, fascinated, as tears began to slide down Caroline's cheeks.

'Don't hurt me . . . please don't,' she croaked.

'What's going on here?' Meredith demanded, appearing next to her mother, glaring at the hapless waitress, who could only shake her head, at a loss. 'Mother, be quiet. What's the matter with you?'

'No! Magpie . . . how can it be? I was sure I didn't . . . I didn't mean for it . . .' she begged, putting trembling fingers over her mouth. Her face was aghast, haunted. The waitress moved away, apologising, smiling an uncomfortable smile. 'Magpie . . . wait, Magpie!'

'That's quite enough! There's nobody here called Magpie! For goodness' sake, Mother, pull yourself together,' Meredith admonished her, sharply. 'We have guests,' she said pointedly, leaning forwards to speak right into Caroline's ear. But Caroline just kept staring after the black-haired girl, frantically searching the crowd for her.

'Magpie! Magpie!' she shouted, still weeping. She grasped Meredith's hand, fixed her daughter with wide, desperate eyes. 'She's come back! Don't let her hurt me!'

'Right. That's enough. Clifford — come and help me.' Meredith beckoned sharply to her son and between them they turned Caroline's chair and manoeuvred her in through the tall glass doors. Caroline tried to fight them, kept craning her head to look for the girl, kept saying the name, over and over again. *Magpie, Magpie.* It was the first and only time I remember feeling sorry for her, because she sounded so frightened, and so very, very sad.

'Magpie, that was it. Funny name,' I say, as Beth stops speaking, undoes her own long plait and runs her fingers through her hair. 'I wonder who she thought that girl was?'

'Who knows? She was obviously pretty confused by then. She was over a hundred, remember.'

'Do you think Meredith knew? She was so brusque with her about it!'

'No. I don't know,' Beth shrugs. 'Meredith was always brusque.'

'She was horrible that night.' I get up, clatter the kettle onto the hotplate for coffee.

'You should go and have a root around in the attic if it's old pictures and papers you're after,' Beth says, suddenly keen.

'Oh?'

'That old trunk up there — when we came here for Caroline's funeral I remember Meredith putting everything she could find of hers up in that old red leather trunk. It was almost as if she wanted everything of Caroline's out of her sight.'

'I don't remember that. Where was I?'

'You stayed in Reading with Nick and Sue next door. Dad said you were too young to go to a funeral.'

'I'll go and have a look up there later, then,' I say. 'You should come up, too.'

'No, no, I've never been that bothered about family history. You might find something interesting, though,' she smiles. I notice how keen she is for me to investigate this distant past rather than our more recent one. How keen she is to distract me.

Longing

As spring became summer, Caroline grew more used to the presence
of Joe and Magpie and the other Ponca women, who were Joe's
mother White Cloud and widowed sister, Annie. She did not call
upon them again, but Corin warned her that it was traditional for
Indian womenfolk to drop in on one another, and to exchange gifts,
and she received several such visits before the Ponca seemed to lose
interest. Caroline dreaded seeing the trio approach the house, and
she sat awkwardly through their visits, crippled by nerves, unsure of
how to speak to them, or what to give in return for their gifts of
honey, mittens and an elegantly carved wooden ladle. In the end
she usually gave them money, which White Cloud accepted with a
closed expression on her face. Caroline made them tea and longed
for them to leave, but when their visits ceased she could not help but
feel that she had failed in some way. And she watched Joe from the
window as he went about the ranch, her eyes ever curious for the
alien oddity of his features, his black mane of hair. He wore a long
knife in a tooled leather sheath on his hip, and each time she saw it a
cold shiver scurried down her spine.

She did not get used to the heat, which increased with each
passing day. By noon the sun was a flat, white disc that seemed to
press like a giant hand on her head whenever she stepped outside,
pushing her down, making her heavy and half-blind. When the
wind blew it seemed as hot as the blast from an oven. Accustomed
all her life to rising at ten in the morning, Caroline now took to
getting up with Corin, at first light, in order to have some time to
exist, some time to live before the heat became unbearable. At that

hour the sky in the east was violet and azure, pricked by faint, glimmering stars that winked out of existence as the day broadened. Corin drove her back to Woodward to order fabric for curtains, and rugs, and a large mirror to hang above the mantel, and he paid for all of these things with a slightly bemused expression. Caroline chafed with impatience in the intervening weeks it took for the goods to come by train from Kansas City, and she clapped her hands with excitement when they arrived. Gradually, she dragged the furniture in the house into a better arrangement, and she swept and swept to keep the sand out on windy days, until her hands blistered and she gave up in frustration, stopping up whatever gaps she could find around the windows and doors with rags.

It was even harder for her to get used to the work required, on a daily basis, just to keep the household up and running. She knew that as Corin's wife she should make his coffee and breakfast in the morning before he set out onto the ranch, but by the time she had put up her hair and washed her face and laced herself into her corsets, he had provided for himself and gone out to work.

'Why do you take such time with your hair, love? There's nobody here that's going to think badly of you if you just pin it back in a simple fashion,' Corin pointed out gently, scooping her hair from her damp neck and running his thumb across the fine strands.

'*I* would think badly of it,' Caroline replied. 'A lady can't go around with her hair unbound. It's just not decent.' But she took what she thought to be his meaning and began to rise even earlier in order to make herself presentable and still have time to cook breakfast.

When the cistern was dry, water had to be drawn from the well at the top of a rise to the north of the house; a well Corin was quick to point out was nothing short of a miracle, since most of the county's groundwater was tainted with gypsum that rotted the guts and tasted foul.

'Not even the finest house in Woodward has a supply of water this close and this sweet. They're still hauling it in from the south by wagon!' he told her proudly.

It took a long time to boil water on the stove and, since timber was so scarce, more often than not the cow chips Caroline had encountered in Hutch's camp fire were the only fuel. Upon finding out what these were – chunks of dried-out cattle manure – Caroline promptly refused to collect them, and could only be induced to use them by poking them into the stove with iron tongs. Not far away from the ranch was a shallow stream that the ranchers referred to as Toad Creek, along the banks of which grew a thin line of straggly cottonwoods, sand plums and walnut trees, giving the ranch a welcome dash of foliage.

'Why can't we just cut timber from the creek?' Caroline asked, wrinkling her nose as Hutch, a little disgruntled at the task, delivered a basket of cow chips to the door.

'Well, ma'am, we could. But only for a couple of months and then we'd be back to the chips and without any trees to pretty up the view,' Hutch told her, drily.

And each morning there was the water to bring in, the stove to sweep out and re-lay, breakfast to make and then pots to clean, laundry to wash – Caroline was used to dirty clothes being taken away and then returned to her two days later, clean, pressed and neatly folded; she was astonished to discover how much work went into those intervening two days – and then the endless battle with the sand in the house and on the porch. She had also to tend to her wilting, stunted vegetable garden. Corin had presented her with the seeds proudly, having traded them with a neighbour. Watermelons and marrows, peas and beans. He also bought her two tiny cherry trees, which she watered with great care and attention, fretting when the wind buffeted them. They struggled in the red soil, and did not flourish no matter how she cosseted them. Then there was lunch to prepare, clothes to be mended and then dinner. Caroline was not a good cook. She scorched the eggs and forgot to salt the beef. Vegetables went soft, meat went tough and stringy. Her beans had hard, gritty centres. Her coffee was weak, and her bread refused to rise, emerging from the oven solid and chewy. Each time she apologised, Corin reassured her.

'You've not been brought up to do it, that's all. You'll get the hang of it,' he smiled, manfully swallowing down whatever she put in front of him. Every time her hands got grimy she washed them at once, hating the feel of dirt on her skin, the dark crescent of earth and smuts beneath each nail. She scrubbed her hands so many times in a day that the skin grew red and angry and began to crack, and she sat mourning their lost softness, cradling them in her lap at the end of the day.

Hot baths could only be had by laboriously filling a large copper drum and lighting the fire beneath it, and then filling the tin tub by the bucketful, behind a wooden screen that Caroline had ordered for the express purpose of private bathing. Corin chafed at such wanton use of precious water, but at the end of her day's labour, with her movements hampered by her corsets, Caroline's body ached from fingertips to toes. She could feel each knobbly protrusion of her spine as it uncurled against the back of the tub, feel a tender crease between every single rib. Her hands, as she wrung out her washing cloth, trembled with fatigue. In the yellow glow of the kerosene lamps, she examined her broken nails and the tan colour of her arms where she had taken to pushing up her sleeves in the heat. She rubbed her thumb over her calluses now, massaging rose-scented vanishing cream into them to soften them, as lonely coyote song filled the darkness outside.

She did not complain of the work, not even to herself. Whenever she caught herself flagging, she pictured Bathilda, smiling in mocking triumph; or she thought of Corin, so full of admiration, calling her brave and beautiful, and how she would hate to prove him wrong. But on the occasions that her spirits did begin to sink, Corin seemed to sense it. He brushed the sand from her hair at the end of the day, singing softly as he pulled the bristles through in long, smooth strokes; or telling her tall stories to make her laugh: about the super-smart cow that drank beer and had learnt to count, or the impatient settler who'd painted himself all over with the wet red mud of Woodward County to pass himself off as Indian and settle on their lands. Or, as she lay in the tub and rubbed her calluses, he would appear around the bath screen and work his fingers into the tight muscles of her neck and shoulders until she was all but drowsing in his hands; then he would gather her up and carry her, dripping wet, to the bed. In the consuming, blinding joy of his lovemaking, she forgot all other aches.

One night they lay side by side on the bed, catching their breath after their exertions. Propping himself up on his elbow, Corin wiped the commingled sweat from Caroline's chest and slid his hand down to her stomach. She smiled and shifted under the heavy weight of it, the hot press of his skin.

'Boy or girl to start with?' he asked.

'Which would you rather?' she replied.

'I asked first!' he smiled.

Caroline sighed happily. 'I truly don't mind. Maybe a girl . . . a little girl with your brown eyes and hair the colour of honey.'

'And then a boy?' Corin suggested.

'Of course! You'd rather a boy first?'

'Not necessarily . . . although it would be good to get him up and running, get me some more help around the ranch . . .' he mused.

'Poor baby! Not even born yet and you've got him out riding the fences!' Caroline cried.

Grinning, Corin put his lips to her belly and kissed her damp skin. '*Psst!* Hey, you in there – come out a boy and I'll buy you a pony!' he whispered.

Caroline laughed, putting her hands around Corin's head to cradle it, no longer noticing their roughness.

It was two months before a neighbour dropped by to visit. Caroline heard a shout at the front of the house, as she was glumly examining a sunken honey cake that she'd just taken from the oven. 'Hullo, Masseys!' the shout came again and, startled, Caroline realised it was a woman's voice. She smoothed back her hair, brushed flour from her apron, and opened the front door, stepping onto the porch with regal grace. Then she gaped. The woman, if such she was, was not only dressed as a man – in slacks, leather chaps and a flannel shirt tucked into a wide leather belt – but she was sitting *astride* a rangy bay horse, slouching as comfortably in the saddle as if she had been born there. 'You're home! I was beginning to think I was hollering at an empty house,' the woman declared, swinging her leg over the horse's back and dropping abruptly to the ground. 'I'm Evangeline Fosset. Pleased to meet you, and do call me Angie since everybody else does,' she continued, approaching with a smile. A long ponytail of orange hair swung behind her, and although her face was as tanned as Corin's it was also strong and handsome. Her blue eyes shone.

'I'm Caroline. Caroline Massey.'

'Figured you were.' The keen blue eyes swept over her. 'Well, Hutch told me you were a beauty, and Lord knows that man never lies,' she said. Caroline smiled, uncertainly, and said nothing. 'I'm your neighbour, by the way. My husband Jacob and I have a farm about seven miles that way.' Angie pointed to the south-east.

'Oh! Well . . . um . . . won't you come inside?' Caroline faltered.

She cut little squares from the outside edge of her honey cake, where it was indeed more or less like a cake, and served them on a large plate, with tea and water. Angie took a long draught.

'Oh! How I envy you that sweet well of yours! To have water not tasting of gyp or the cistern is something wonderful, I can tell you,' she exclaimed, draining the glass. 'Did Corin tell you how they found it? The well, that is?'

'No, he hasn't . . .'

'Well, they'd tried digging about a hundred different holes and found nothing but gyp, gyp, and some more stinking gypsum water. They were relying on the creek but that dries up half of the year, as you'll soon see. And they were being so darn careful with the supply that not one of the men on this ranch had washed himself for more than a month. I tell you, no word of a lie: I could smell them from my front step! Well, one day a funny old man came riding by on a beaten-up mule and said did Corin want him to find sweet water on his land? Ever one to give a person a chance, although he didn't see how the old fellow was going to achieve what he hadn't managed in months, Corin tells him by all means.' Angie paused for breath and popped a square of cake into her mouth. Caroline watched her, mesmerised. 'This old fellow takes out a narrow, forked branch of wood that's all worn smooth with years of touching, and off he goes, wandering here, there and everywhere, holding this twig in his fingertips. The midday sun starts pounding down and still he goes hither and thither, back and forth, until he gets to the top of the rise and bam! That twig of his twists in his grip and points straight down at the turf like an arrow. 'Here's your sweet water, sir,' the old fellow announces. And digging down, sure enough, there was the well. Can you believe that, now?' Angie finished her tale with a nod and a smile, and watched Caroline, expectantly.

'Well, I . . .' Caroline began, her voice sounding frail after Angie's bold narrative. 'If you say so, of course,' she finished, smiling slightly. Angie's face fell a little, but then she smiled again.

'So, how are you settling in? You getting used to ranch life?'

'Yes, I think so. It's rather different . . . to New York.'

'I'll bet it is! I'll bet!' Angie chuckled; a low, throaty sound.

'I've never seen a woman ride astride before,' Caroline added, feeling rude to mention it, but too astonished not to.

'Oh, it's the only way to travel around here, believe me! Once you've tried it, you'll never go back to fiddling around sideways. When I heard Corin was bringing a gal back from the city, I thought, that poor thing! She can't know what she's getting into! Not that I don't love this place. It's my home, although Lord knows Mother Nature can be a bitch around here at times, pardon my language – but really, she can.' Again, Angie looked at Caroline, and Caroline smiled nervously, at a loss. She poured her guest some more tea. The china cup, with its pattern of pink roses and blue ribbons that had seemed so charming in the catalogue, looked as fragile and childish as a toy in Angie's strong hand. 'The loneliness gets to some women. Not seeing anyone – well, any other women – for weeks at a time. Months, sometimes. It can get to a person, being in the house by yourself all day.'

'I've been . . . keeping very busy,' Caroline said hesitantly, startled by the woman's forwardness.

'As we all do, for sure,' Angie shrugged. 'Kids'll help, when they start coming. Nothing like a houseful of little ones to keep you distracted, I can tell you!' Caroline smiled, and blushed a little. She could hardly wait to have her first baby. She longed for a tiny child to cradle, for the softness of its skin, the wholeness of a new family. The permanence of roots put down.

'Corin wants to have five,' she said, smiling shyly.

'Five! My good Lord, you've got your work cut out for you, girl!' Angie exclaimed with a wide grin. 'But – you're young yet. Spread them out, that's my advice. That way the older ones'll be able to help you with the tiddlers. Well, when you fall, be sure to let me know. You'll want more help then, and advice from an old hand. Just remember where I am, and send word if you need anything.'

'That's really very kind of you,' Caroline said, secretly sure she would need no such help. She knew, in her heart, that while her cooking refused to improve and her body would not harden to the housework, it was in motherhood that her calling lay.

When Angie left, an hour or so later, she did not set off in the direction of her home, but towards the corrals where some of the men were at work. Caroline tended not to venture there herself, feeling too shy of the men and too unsure of the nature of their work, despite Corin's urgings that she learn the running of the ranch. What she had seen she had found brutal. Animals brought roughly to the ground, their horns sawn off, their heads pushed beneath stinking, stinging dip to kill parasites, the Massey Ranch emblem, *MR*, burned into their skins. She hated the way they rolled their eyes in terror, so white and vulnerable looking. But seeing Angie lead her horse calmly over to Hutch, who was overseeing the branding of new calves in the nearest corral, Caroline suddenly felt left out and left behind. She hurriedly removed her apron, grabbed her bonnet and walked quickly in the same direction.

Hutch had come over to the fence and was leaning upon it, continuing to watch the branding even as he talked to Angie. Wondering how to announce her presence, feeling high strung with nerves, Caroline heard her name spoken and stopped instead, stepping sideways so that the shadow of the bunkhouse engulfed her. The stink of burning hair and skin made her gag, and she put her hand over her mouth to stifle the sound.

'She's none too friendly, is she?' Angie said, folding her arms. Hutch shrugged one shoulder.

'She's trying her best, I reckon. Can't be easy, with her brought up so soft. I don't think she ever walked more than a quarter mile at a time before, and I hear from Corin that she surely never cooked before.'

'Shame he didn't set up nearer town – she could have taught class or something. Made better use of those fine manners than she will out here,' Angie said, shaking her head as if in disapproval. 'What do the boys make of her?'

'Hard to say, really. She doesn't come out of the house much; she doesn't ride out, sure as heck doesn't bring us lemonade on a hot day,' Hutch grinned. 'Feels the heat a bit strongly, I think.'

'What was Corin thinking, marrying such a green tenderfoot and leaving her out here by herself?'

'Well, I reckon he was thinking she was a fine-looking girl with a good head on her shoulders.'

'Hutchinson, one of these days I'll hear you speak a hard word about someone or something and I will fall clean off my horse. Good head on her shoulders in the city maybe, but out here? Why, she's even setting about the chores with corsets on so tight she can hardly breathe! Does that sound like good sense to you?' Angie exclaimed. Hutch said something that Caroline could not hear above the calves' frightened bellows, and then he turned towards Angie. Fearing she would be seen, Caroline skirted the side of the bunkhouse and walked swiftly back to the house, angry tears smarting her eyes.

Later, at dinner, Caroline watched her husband as he ate the bland food she had given him without complaint. He had come in late from rounding up two stray beeves, arriving at the table ravenous and having performed no toilette but to splash his hands and face with water from the trough. In the lamplight he looked rough, older than he was. His hair stuck out at wild angles and there was prairie sand along his hairline. After a day outside he seemed to soak up the sun and then glow all night long, she thought. The sun loved him. It did not love her. It scorched her pale skin, burnt freckles into her cheeks and made her nose peel most unattractively. She watched him and felt a surge of love that was at once wonderful and somehow desperate. He was her husband, and yet she felt as though she might lose him. She had not known that she was failing until she met Angie Fosset and heard her verdict on Corin's soft new wife. She swallowed her tears because she knew she would not be able to explain them to him.

'Evangeline Fosset came by here today,' she said, her voice a little constricted.

'Oh? That's wonderful! She's such a good neighbour, and always so friendly. Didn't you find her so?' he asked. Caroline sipped from her water glass to forestall her reply. 'If ever there was an example of how the West gives women freedoms that they've never had, and of how best a woman might make good on those freedoms, Angie is that example,' Corin went on.

'She didn't leave a calling card before visiting. I wasn't prepared for a guest,' Caroline said, hating the cold tone in her voice, but also hating to hear her husband praise another woman.

'No, well . . . when you've got to ride seven miles to say you're going to call on a person, seems like sense to just go ahead and call on them once you get there, I suppose.'

'I heard her talking about me to Hutch. She called me tenderfoot. What does it mean?'

'Tenderfoot?' Corin smiled briefly, but stopped when he saw his wife's tight expression, the glimmer in her eyes. 'Oh, now, sweetheart – I'm sure she didn't mean anything bad by it. Tenderfoot just means you're not used to the West, that's all. To the outdoor kind of life.'

'Well, how can I be used to it? Is it my fault, where I was born? Is that any reason to talk about a person, and use names? I'm *trying* to get along with life out here!'

'I know you are! I know.' Corin took Caroline's hands and squeezed them. 'Don't fret about it. You're doing great—'

'No, I'm not! I can't cook! I can't keep up with all the work! The plants aren't growing . . . the house is full of sand!' she cried.

'You're exaggerating—'

'Hutch knows I can't cook, so you must have told him! I *heard* him say it!'

At this Corin paused, and a little colour came into his cheeks. 'I'm sorry, sweetheart. I shouldn't have said it and I'm sorry that I did. But, my love, if you need some help just tell me, and we'll find you some help!' he assured her, stroking her face where tears were wetting the skin.

'I need help,' she said, miserably; and as she admitted it she felt the weight of it lighten on her shoulders. Corin smiled.

'Then you shall have it,' he told her gently, and he murmured soft words to her until she smiled back at him and stopped her crying.

So Magpie was recruited to come into the house and share the housework, and although Caroline was not sure that she wanted the Ponca girl beside her all day long, Magpie came with a ready smile and an ease of doing things that came from being born to it. Happily, Caroline relinquished the cooking to her and watched as old bones and dried beans became thick, tasty soup; and bread dough rose willingly between damp cloths when left in the sun on the window sill; and handfuls of mysterious herbs picked from the prairie made sauces savoury and delicious. The washing took less than half the time it had previously taken, and came up cleaner; and Magpie did the heavier jobs, like fetching water and carrying the wet linens out to the line so that Caroline, for the first time since her arrival, found time in the day to sit and read, or to start some sewing. She never thought she would feel anything other than glad to have another person take on these tasks, but at the same time she envied the ease with which Magpie performed them. Magpie worked with good cheer, and she taught Caroline tactfully, never implying that she ought to know such things, and never making Caroline feel inadequate, so it was impossible to resent the girl.

But she did find it hard to concentrate with Magpie in the house. The girl drew the eye and she sang softly to herself as she worked — odd melodies like none Caroline had ever heard, as alien and eerie as the voices of the prairie wolves. And she moved softly, so softly that Caroline hardly heard her. She was sitting at her sewing one morning, stitching a tiny flower garland into the corner of a table runner, when she sensed a presence behind her and turned to find Magpie right by her shoulder, appraising the work.

'Very good, Mrs Massey,' she smiled, nodding approvingly. 'You stitch very well.'

'Oh . . . thank you, Magpie,' Caroline said breathlessly, startled by the girl's sudden appearance. The sun, catching the long braid of the Ponca girl's hair, showed no sign of red, or of brown. It was as black as a crow's wing. Caroline noticed the thickness of it, and its inky sheen, and thought it coarse. With her round face and wide cheekbones, Magpie almost resembled the Celestial women Caroline had occasionally seen in New York, although Magpie's skin was darker and redder. Caroline could not help shuddering slightly when their arms accidentally brushed. But she was fascinated by the girl, and caught herself watching her in whatever task she was performing. In the heat of the day, while sweat blistered Caroline's brow and itched beneath her clothes, Magpie seemed unaffected. The sun had no power to discomfort her, and Caroline envied her this, too.

One suffocatingly hot day, when Caroline thought she would run mad if she had no relief from it, she went into the bedroom, shut the door, stripped off her blouse and corset and threw them to the floor. She sat still and felt the relative cool of the air in the room touch her sticky, stifling skin and, slowly, the light-headedness that had dogged her all that morning began to diminish. It was so humid, the air so thick, the sky so blindingly, glaringly bright that Caroline seemed to feel her blood thickening, simmering in her veins. When she dressed again, she left the corset off. Nobody seemed to notice, and indeed there was little *to* notice. The heat and her own cooking had reduced her appetite and the work had taken its toll. Beneath the rigours of her underclothes, Caroline had grown very thin.

Later that week it rained. It rained as though the sky were blackly furious with the ground and aimed to injure it. It rained in torrents, not in drops but in solid rods of water that lanced down from the glowering clouds and stirred the topsoil into a soup that ran away towards Toad Creek. That modest creek became an angry cascade. The horses stood stoically, nose to tail, with water streaming from their manes. Out on the pasture, the cows lay down and narrowed their eyes. Corin was in Woodward with Hutch, having driven seven hundred head of cattle to the stock pens, and Caroline lay on the bed in the early evening and prayed as hard as she could that the North Canadian would not flood, would not stay long in spate, would not prevent Corin's return. She left the shutters open, listening to the rain hammer the roof above her, waiting, arms outflung, for the air creeping in through the window to feel cooler – for the water to wash the heat away.

There was a tentative knock at the door, and Magpie appeared.

'What's wrong?' Caroline asked abruptly, sitting up with a start.

'Nothing wrong, Mrs Massey. I have brought you something. Something to make you relieved,' the girl said. Caroline sighed, smoothing back her sweaty hair.

'Nothing can make me relieved,' she murmured.

'Come and try,' Magpie pressed. 'It's not good to lie down too much. You don't grow used to things that way,' she insisted, and Caroline dragged herself to her feet, following the Ponca girl to the kitchen. 'Watermelon. The first one of the summer! Try some.' Magpie passed Caroline a wide slice of the fruit: a bloody-coloured crescent moon that stickied her fingers.

'Thank you, Magpie, but I'm really not very hungry . . .'

'Try some,' Magpie repeated, more firmly. Caroline glanced at her, met her bright black eyes and saw only goodwill there. She took the fruit and nibbled at it. 'It's good, yes?'

'Yes,' Caroline admitted, taking bigger bites. The melon was neither sweet nor sharp. It tasted mild and earthy, softly easing the parched, torn feeling at the back of her throat.

'And drink this.' Magpie passed her a cup of water. 'Rainwater. Straight from the sky.'

'Well, there's no shortage of that today!' Caroline joked.

'This is water from the land, this is water from the sky,' Magpie explained, pointing to the fruit and the cup. 'To eat and drink these things, it makes you . . . it makes you balance with the land and the sky. Do you see? That way, you don't feel so much like you are punished. You will feel like you are a part of this land and sky.'

'That would be good. Not to feel punished,' Caroline smiled slightly.

'Eat more, drink more!' Magpie encouraged her, smiling too. They sat together at the kitchen table, with the rain hissing down outside and their chins slick with melon juice; and soon Caroline felt a blessed cool begin to spread outwards from inside her, sluicing the fevered burn from her skin.

There was a dun-coloured mare called Clara, who had short, slender legs, a compact body, ribs like a barrel, neck a little scrawny. She was in her twilight years and had foaled a half-dozen times for Corin; foals that had grown into fine saddle horses, with just one exception — a colt who was never right between the ears, and could not be broken, and who snapped the bones of several fine bronco busters before his heart finally gave out with the strain of his own fury.

'Clara hung her head all sorrowful the day it happened, even though that colt was over the other side of Woodward by then,' Hutch told Caroline, as she stroked the mare's bony face tentatively. The pungent reek of horse and the leather of the tack was strong in the morning sunshine. Caroline squinted up at the foreman from the shade of her bonnet. Hutch's eyes were bright slivers between the furrows of his brows and the crow's feet scoring his temples. These marks on his face were deep, though he was only a little older than Corin.

'You think she knew her baby had died? How sad!' Caroline said.

'I reckon she knew. Inferno, we called that colt. He was the colour of fire, and when you walked up to him he fixed you a look in the eye that made grown men tremble.'

'How horrible! How could an animal as gentle as Clara have such an evil offspring?'

'Many a murderer was born to a decent, God-fearing woman, and I guess the same applies for horses as for humans,' Hutch shrugged. 'Now, Clara here wouldn't hurt a fly. You could get up on her back, yell at the top of your voice and give her a mighty wallop with a stick and she wouldn't even hold that against you.'

'Well! I don't think I'm going to do any of those things!' Caroline laughed.

'Well, sure you are – the getting up on her back part, that is,' Hutch smiled.

'Oh, no! I thought I was just learning how to put the saddle on today?' Caroline said, a note of alarm in her voice.

'That's right, and that's taken all of five minutes. And what's the point of a horse with a saddle on it if nobody gets up and sits in it?'

'Hutch, I . . . I don't know that I can . . .' she faltered.

'Only one way to find out,' he said, but gently, and he took her elbow to draw her closer to the horse's side. 'Come on now, Mrs Massey. There's no way the wife of a rancher can go around not knowing how to ride. And it's nothing to be scared of. It's as easy as sitting in a chair.'

'Chairs don't run around! Or kick!' Caroline argued.

'No, but they don't get you from point A to point B in half the time a wagon does, neither,' Hutch chuckled. His smile was crooked and warm, and when he held out his hand to her she found it impossible not to take it.

'I'm really not sure about this,' she said, nerves making her voice small.

'In about ten minutes' time, you're going to be wondering what all the fuss was about,' Hutch assured her.

Hutch cupped his hand around her shin and boosted her into the side saddle, where she perched, her face pale, expecting at any moment to be cast back into the sand. He showed her how to hook her right leg around the pommel to keep herself secure, and to take her weight in the left stirrup for balance.

'All right now. Comfy?' he asked.

'Not really,' she said, but she found the beginnings of a smile for him.

'Now, give her a little nudge with that heel, loose those reins and say, "Get up, Clara!"'

'Get up, Clara! Please,' Caroline said, with as much conviction as she could manage, and then gave a little shriek as the mare moved obediently forwards.

'OK, now you're riding!' Hutch exclaimed. 'Just relax, she's not going anywhere. Relax, Mrs Massey!' he called, walking beside her with one hand loosely on the rein. 'You're doing a great job,' he told her.

For half an hour or so Hutch escorted her around the empty corral. Clara walked steadily, stopping and starting and turning left and right without the least hint of bad attitude or boredom. Caroline listened to what she was told, and tried to remember it all, tried to feel the movement of the horse and make it her own, as Hutch instructed, but she could not shake the feeling that the animal had no choice but to resent her being there, and would at any given moment revert to the wild and throw her as far as she possibly could. Her back and legs were soon aching, and when she commented on this to Hutch, he gave the side saddle a disparaging look.

'Well, that's bound to happen when you do something for the

first time. But, to be honest, Mrs Massey, you'd be a heck of a lot more comfortable riding astride than you are sat sideways like that . . .'

'Men ride astride. Ladies take the side saddle,' Caroline said firmly.

'You're the boss,' Hutch shrugged.

At that moment, Corin came cantering in off the pasture with two of the line-riders. Sunlight rippled from Strumpet's black coat, and sweat was running down the mare's forelegs. Caroline sat up straighter, rigid with embarrassment. The line-riders, whose names she still could not remember, tipped their hats to her, and slowed their horses, and she thought for a hideous moment that they were going to stop and watch the rest of her riding lesson. She gave them a small wave, and her cheeks flared scarlet. They rode as naturally as Magpie cooked and worked, slouching in the saddle as though their bodies had been designed for that very purpose. To her immense relief, they carried on towards the water troughs and only Corin pulled up at the corral fence.

'Well, now! Look at you! You look fantastic up there, sweetheart!' he beamed, pulling off his hat and rubbing his hot scalp.

'You want to go on over?' Hutch asked, and Caroline nodded. 'Well, go on then. You know how,' he urged her. Cautiously, Caroline turned the mare's head and persuaded her to walk over to the fence.

'That's fantastic, Caroline! I'm so happy to see you up on a horse at last!' Corin told her.

'I'll never be able to saddle her alone — it's so heavy!' Caroline smiled, anxiously.

'Well, that's as may be. But you can just ask any one of the boys and they'll help you with it. There's always somebody around, and they'd jump through hoops if a pretty girl like you asked them to!' Corin grinned.

'Can I get down now, Hutch?' she asked.

'I think we've done enough for one day,' Hutch nodded, hitching up his jeans at the waist. 'Couple more goes like today and we'll change your name to Annie Oakley!' he smiled.

Feeling altogether less of a tenderfoot, Caroline listened as Hutch described the best way to dismount, but somehow her foot got snarled up in the stirrup, and her skirts tangled her knees, so she sprawled forwards on the descent, landing on her front in the corral sand with the air whooshing out of her lungs. Behind her, Clara gave a small snort of surprise.

'Damn! Are you all right, Caroline?' Corin swore, scrambling out of his own saddle.

'Well, that wasn't exactly how it was supposed to go,' Hutch remarked calmly, taking her arm and helping her to sit up. 'Hang on there, catch your breath,' he instructed, but Caroline had no intention of staying in the dirt, or so close to Clara's hooves, for any longer than she had to. She climbed shakily to her feet, coughing, her eyes streaming where grit had got into them. Her neck was jarred and one wrist badly over-bent where it had taken the weight of her fall. She was covered in dust from hair to hemline. She glared at Corin, furious with herself and crippled with embarrassment.

'Why, you look every bit as fierce as Inferno, when you fire up like that!' Hutch said, admiringly.

'And every bit as red, too,' Corin grinned.

'Don't . . . *laugh* at me!' Caroline bit the words off, frustration and anger burning her up inside. She turned on her heel and stalked away towards the house, shaking with the shock of the fall, her legs jellied by the riding. She was more disappointed than she could bear – to have failed again, to have made herself a laughing stock.

'Ah, hell, Caroline! Come back! I wasn't laughing at you!' She heard Corin call out behind her, but she squared her shoulders the best she could and kept walking.

*

Autumn arrived on the prairie with a string of vicious thunder-storms and pounding hailstones rent from blackened skies. Hutch came in from the range one evening and warmed himself by the stove as he reported the loss of three head of cattle, felled that day by a bolt of lightning that had struck the ground amidst the herd and thrown them into the air like confetti. Caroline paled at the tale, and Corin gave his foreman a censorious look that the poor man, his teeth chattering and his hands curled into scalded red claws, failed to notice. This glowering season was short, and soon the true winter began. Corin came in for dinner with his move-ments stiff and clumsy, and granules of sleet clinging to his eyebrows; but he always found a smile for his wife, declaring:

'There's one *hell* of a blue norther blowing out there!'

Caroline, who would once have been shocked by such language, no longer was. Still, she frowned slightly, out of habit, and pulled her shawl tightly around her against the wave of cold air that entered with her husband. She, who never thought she would miss the summer's heat, found herself longing for the sun.

They saw out the end of 1902 and welcomed in 1903 with a party at the Fosset's farm, to which all of the nearby ranchers, their families and riders had been invited. The night was still and dry, the air hanging like a chill blanket, and on the buggy ride over, Caroline's fingers, toes, her nose and the tips of her ears grew quite dead with cold. There was no moon, and the lantern on the buggy lit the prairie a scant few yards ahead. The dark all around was like a living thing, like solid flesh that watched. Caroline shivered, and huddled closer to Corin. Behind them, she could hear the hooves of the Massey riders following, keeping close as if they too felt pursued. When the Fosset place hove into view ahead, lights blazing out into the night, Caroline uttered a short, silent prayer of relief, and breathed a little easier.

There were fires burning about the yard, and meat smoking and spitting on the griddle, and a mass of people and horses all gathered into this oasis of light and life on the dead, dark plains. Corin's arm was shaken, his shoulder clapped, and they were soon engulfed by the friendly crowd of their neighbours. An accordion, a fiddle and a drum struck up in the barn, and the heat given off by dancing bodies warmed it, filled it with the animal smell of breath and sweat. Angie's children had made a painted banner out of a ragged old sheet, and it hung above the gate, reading *happy new yere!* and easing to and fro in the slow shifting air. Angie had two girls, aged twelve and eight, and a little boy aged four, who had his mother's red hair and the bluest eyes anyone had ever seen. Even as she danced and laughed and talked, Angie kept one eye on this perfect, happy little lad, and when she saw Caroline admiring him, she called him over.

'Kyle, this here is our good neighbour Caroline Massey. Now, what do you say to her?' she whispered to the boy, swinging him up onto her hip.

'Please' t' meetya, Missus Massey,' Kyle mumbled shyly, around the fingers he was chewing.

'Oh, well I'm pleased to meet you too, Kyle Fosset,' Caroline smiled, taking the hand that wasn't in his mouth and shaking it gently. Angie set him down and he darted away, ungainly on his short chubby legs. 'Oh, Angie! He's just the most *beautiful* child!' she exclaimed, and Angie beamed.

'Yeah, he's my little angel all right, and don't he just know it!'

'And the girls too . . . you must be so proud of . . .' Caroline said, but she could not keep her voice steady and had to stop.

'Hey there, now – stop that! This here is a celebration of the new year, and all the wonderful new things it's going to bring. You hear me?' Angie said, significantly. 'It's going to happen for you. You just have to be patient. You hear?' Caroline nodded, and wished she could feel as sure as Angie sounded.

'Mrs Massey? Will you dance with a rough rider like myself?' Hutch asked, appearing beside them.

'Of course!' Caroline smiled, hastily blotting her eyes with her fingertips. The band played one tune into the next without pause, and Hutch led her in a swaying dance that was almost a waltz, but not quite so. The room was a blur of smiling faces, some of them none too clean, and Caroline remembered the Montgomery's ball, still not yet a year gone but seeming to belong to another lifetime altogether. She had come such a long way, she told herself. It was no wonder that she did not yet find herself feeling at home.

'Is everything all right, Mrs Massey?' Hutch asked, seriously.

'Yes, of course! Why wouldn't it be?' she said, too brightly, her voice thin.

'No reason,' Hutch shrugged. He was wearing his best shirt, and she noticed that the top button was hanging by a thread. She made a mental note to add it to the pile of mending back at the ranch. 'Are you ready for another riding lesson, yet? You did great, that first time we tried it, but I never saw you go back for another try.'

'No, well . . . I'm not sure I'm the world's most naturally gifted horsewoman. And besides, now the weather's turned so cold I would surely freeze if I tried it!' she said.

'There are some people that take naturally to it, that's for sure, and others that don't. But I've seen those that once struggled get to grips with it in the end, with practice. But you have to be willing to get back on the horse, Mrs Massey. You do have to get back on the horse,' Hutch said, intensely, and she was no longer sure that he was talking about riding.

'I . . .' she started, but could not think what to say. She looked down at her feet and saw how dusty her shoes were, and found her eyes swimming with tears.

'You're going to be just fine,' Hutch said, his voice so low that she hardly heard him.

'Hutchinson, I'm cutting in! That's my wife you're cradling and she's by far the handsomest girl in the room,' Corin announced, taking Caroline's hands and spinning her into his embrace. His eyes were alight with happiness, cheeks flushed from sipping whisky and dancing, and he looked glorious, so glorious that Caroline laughed and threw her arms around his neck.

'Happy new year, my darling,' she whispered into his ear, letting her lips brush lightly against his neck, so that he held her tighter still.

In February snow fell deeply, lying in thick drifts and making the world too bright to look upon. Caroline stared at the featureless scene beyond the window in wonder, and stayed close to the stove as much as she could, her hands curled inside the fingerless mittens the Ponca had given her, which kept as much of her skin covered as possible whilst still allowing her to do the mending. Her chilled fingers fumbled the needle and dropped it often.

'Now you are glad to have them,' Magpie said, nodding at the thick mittens. 'When White Cloud gave them to you, I saw in your face you thought you would never need them!' she smiled.

'I should have paid her double,' Caroline agreed, at which Magpie frowned slightly.

'Will you tell a story, while I do this work?' Magpie requested. She was kneeling at the wash tub, rubbing the stains out of Corin's work wear on a ridged wooden washboard.

'What kind of story?'

'It doesn't matter. A story of your people,' Magpie shrugged. So Caroline, unsure who her people were, told her the story of Adam and Eve in the Garden of Eden, and of the treacherous serpent, the delicious apple, and the subsequent fall from grace. She put down her sewing as she reached the finale, describing their sudden shame at their nakedness, and the scramble to find something with which to cover themselves. Magpie chuckled, which made her cheeks even rounder and her eyes sparkle.

'This is a good story, Mrs Massey – a missionary man told this same story to my father once, and do you know what my father said?'

'What did he say?'

'He said this is typical of a white woman! An Indian woman would have picked up a stick and killed the snake and all would have been well in the garden!' she laughed. Caroline, stung for a moment by the implied criticism, soon found herself smiling, and then catching the girl's infectious laughter.

'That's probably about right,' she conceded, and they were still laughing when Corin came in, brushing the snow from his shoulders. He looked at Caroline, sitting by the stove with her sewing to one side, and at Magpie on her knees by the tub, and he frowned. 'Corin? What's wrong?' Caroline asked; but he shook his head and came over to the stove to warm himself.

Later, as they were eating supper, Corin spoke his mind.

'When I came home today, I . . . I didn't like what I saw, Caroline,' he said.

'What do you mean?' she asked, her heart high in her throat.

'You just sitting there, keeping warm, when Maggie was working so hard—'

'It wasn't like that! I was working at the mending! Ask Magpie . . . I just stopped to tell her the story of Adam and Eve . . .' Caroline trailed off, unhappily.

'I know you're used to having servants, Caroline, but Maggie is no servant. I meant for her to help you in the house, of course, but she does not have time to do *everything* here. She has her own home to tend to, and soon she won't be able to do as much. You need to help her more, love,' he finished gently. He broke a piece of bread from the loaf and crumbled it distractedly between his fingers.

'She does help me! I mean, I help her too – we share the work! What do you mean, soon she won't be able to do as much? Why won't she?'

'Sweetheart,' Corin looked up at her through his rough golden brows. 'Maggie's pregnant, Caroline. She and Joe are going to have a baby. Their first.' He looked away again, his face sombre, and in that expression Caroline read an accusation. Tears sprang to her eyes and she was choked with an emotion a little like ire, a little like grief, a little like guilt. An insufferable mixture of the three that burned in her gut and made a roaring noise in her ears. She clattered up from the table, ran to the bedroom and closed the door behind her.

In a light buggy, harnessed to a bay horse with a high, proud head carriage, the journey to Woodward could be made in a day, with a dawn start and a break to rest and water the horse at noon time. Most of the ranch hands and riders accompanied them on horseback, including Joe and Magpie. Caroline watched the Indian girl, who rode a wiry grey pony, and wondered how she could have failed to spot the telltale swell at her middle, the slight deference in her movements.

'Is it wise for Magpie to ride in her condition?' Caroline whispered to Corin, although there was little chance of being heard above the thudding of hooves, the wind and the creak and whirr of the buggy wheels.

'I said the very same thing to Joe,' Corin smiled. 'He just laughed at me.' He shrugged. 'I guess Ponca women are a bit tougher than white women.' A few tiny flecks of rain blew out of the sky. Caroline made no reply to Corin's remark, but she felt the sting of it. The implication she heard, whether he had intended it or not, was that she was weak and that she was failing here in the West, as a woman and as a wife.

They arrived in Woodward as dark was falling and took a room at the Central Hotel. Joe, Magpie and the ranch boys melted into the town: to the Equity, Midway, Shamrock and Cabinet saloons, to the brothel run by Dollie Kezer at the Dew Drop Inn, and to the houses of friends. Caroline's back ached from the long drive and she was tired, but she nevertheless urged Corin to lie with her, and she shut her eyes as she felt him spend himself within her, praying that whatever magic it was that made a child coalesce into being, it would happen this time – *this time*.

Caroline's spirits had soared with the prospect of coming into town for the spring gala day, and for dancing. Visits away from the ranch were precious scarce and they had not ventured forth for four long months since the Fosset's shindig on new year's eve. Woodward, which had seemed upon her arrival from New York to be a one-horse town indeed, now seemed a vibrant hub of life and activity. But there was something about this very fact, even, that saddened Caroline. The following day dawned fair and the streets thronged with people, cowboys and settlers alike. They formed two thick cords that ran for several blocks along the length of Main Street, undulating where a raised sidewalk ran in front of a shop. The air thronged with the smells and sounds of thousands of bodies and excited voices, the stink of horses and manure, and the parched wood and paint fragrance of the buildings. Store fronts were strung with colourful bunting and had their doors flung wide open to welcome the unprecedented opportunity for new custom that day.

The crowd was entertained with a roping and riding contest, a mock buffalo hunt, and shooting competitions. There were fancy lariat tricks and a display of bull-dogging that looked unduly violent to Caroline, who turned her face away as the steer's head was pulled around, its lip clamped as they both crashed to the ground. Joe far outperformed all other competitors in a knife-throwing competition, sending his blade again and again into the centre of a paper target pinned to hay bales to win a box of fine cigars and a brand new Bowie knife. The applause for his victory was muted compared to that lavished upon the white victors of other events, but Joe smiled his wry half-smile nonetheless and admired the new blade. They ate barbecue, fresh peaches, ice cream and honey cakes, and the ladies drank iced tea while the men took beer. Caroline, who had been without ice or refrigeration since leaving New York, found the chilled drink in her mouth to be not far short of heavenly. They caught up with neighbours, and Corin swapped the current prices of wheat and beeves with fellow ranchers; and they ran into Angie and Jacob Fosset, Angie clad in a lurid lilac gown with too much colour on her face. When Corin complimented her, she laughed and exclaimed:

'Oh, I look like a show girl, I know I do; but we gals don't get to dress up often enough! And I need a little help to look festive, Lord knows – we can't all be pretty as paint like your wife here, Corin Massey!'

'Well,' Corin told her, with a generous tip of his hat, 'you look just fine to me, Angie Fosset.' While the men talked, Angie took Caroline to one side.

'Any news, honey?' she asked in a low tone, in answer to which Caroline could only grip her lower lip in her teeth and shake her head. 'Well, I've thought of some things you could try . . .' Angie told her.

In the evening the band played waltzes and polkas, as well as some square dances – large sheets of canvas were laid over the sand of Main Street to facilitate the dancing, since no hall in town could accommodate such a large number of pairs. Caroline danced with the grace of her upbringing, even though Corin's steps were marred by beer and there were wrinkles in the canvas to snag unwary feet. With buildings all around her, and people, Caroline felt better than she had in months as they marked a Mexican waltz amongst the jostling shoulders of Woodward's citizens. For a while, the smile she wore was not a brave one, or a dissembling one, but a genuine one.

But later, as she stood talking to a circle of Woodward wives, Caroline saw Corin across the street, bending down in front of Magpie and putting his hands on her midriff. He seemed to cradle the bulge in her abdomen gently, almost reverently, and whilst Magpie looked embarrassed she also looked pleased. Caroline caught her breath and blood flooded her cheeks. Corin was in his cups, she knew, but this behaviour was too much. Soon, though, it was not for this reason that her cheeks burned. Corin's face was turned away, his gaze was unfocused. Waiting, she realised; waiting for the child to move inside the Ponca girl. And as she witnessed this act of intimacy, she suddenly thought she saw something possessive in her husband's touch – something altogether too interested.

4

It's cold as we walk down towards the woods on the longest night of the year. All three of us. Eddie pestered Beth into coming, and in the end she seemed almost curious. There's a brisk, bitter breeze that finds its way inside our coats, so we walk quickly, on stiff limbs. In the clear dark our torch beams stagger haphazardly. The moon is bright and the flowing clouds make it seem to sail across the sky. A vixen shrieks as we get near the trees.

'What was that?' Eddie gasps.

'Werewolf,' I say, matter-of-fact.

'Ha, ha. Anyway, it's not a full moon.'

'All right, then, it was a fox. You're no fun any more, Edderino.' I am in high spirits. I feel unfettered, like my strings have been cut and I can float free. Bright, restless nights do this to me. There is something about a wind blowing in the dark. The way it brushes by, its nonchalance. It seems to say: *I could pick you up; I could carry you away, if I wanted to.* There is a promise to this evening.

We can hear music now, and raised voices, laughter; and now the glow of the bonfire shines at us between the trees. Beth hangs back. She folds her arms tightly across her chest. The firelight follows every anxious line of her face. If Eddie wasn't with us I think she would stay here, in the sheltering woods, darting from shadow to shade and watching. I pull a flat bottle of whisky from my coat pocket, fight to open it with gloved hands. The three of us, in a circle, our breath pouring up into the sky.

'Swig. Go on. It'll warm you up,' I tell her, and for once she doesn't argue. She takes a long pull.

'Can I have some?' asks Eddie.

'Not on your life,' Beth replies, as she wipes her chin and

coughs. She sounds so real, so there, so like Beth that I grin and take her hands.

'Come on. I'll introduce you to Patrick. He's super nice.' I take a drink myself, feel the fire in my throat, and then we move.

There's a moment of nerves as we step into the firelight. The same as before, of being unsure of our welcome. But then Patrick finds us and introduces us to a myriad people, and I struggle to keep their names in my head. Sarah and Kip – long hair shining in the firelight, stripy knitted hats; Denise – a tiny woman with a deeply lined face and ink-black hair; Smurf – a huge man, hands like shovels, a gentle smile; Penny and Louise – Penny the more butch of the pair, her head shaved, her eyes fierce. Their clothes and hair are bright. They look like butterflies against the winter ground. There's a sound system in the back of a pick-up and vehicles parked all the way up the lane. Children too, dodging in and out of the crowd. Eddie vanishes and I see him a little while later with Harry, threading thick wads of dead leaves onto long twigs and thrusting them into the fire.

'Who's that with Eddie?' Beth asks, a note of alarm in her voice.

'That's Harry. I've met him, don't worry. He's a little bit on the slow side, you could say. Dinny says he's always got on well with children. He seems totally harmless to me,' I tell her, speaking loudly, right into her ear. The fire has put a dew of sweat along our lips and brows.

'Oh,' Beth says, not quite convinced. I see Honey, moving across the clearing, preceded by her enormous bump. Her face is alive this evening, she's smiling, and she is lovely. I feel a small prickle of despair.

'That's Honey, there. The blonde,' I say to Beth, in defiance of myself. Watching expressions veer wildly across Honey's face, I am sure of it – I have taught girls older than her: she is too young to be having that baby. I feel something close to anger, but I can't tell who or what it's aimed at.

Then Dinny appears beside Beth, smiling his guarded smile. His hair is unbound and it hangs around his jaw, messy and black. He stands half turned towards the fire, half away, so the light cuts him in two, throws his face into sharp relief. It stops a breath in my chest, holds it until it burns.

'Glad you came down to join in, Beth, Erica,' he says, and as he smiles again I see the faint blurring of alcohol about him – a true warmth, for the first time since I saw him again.

'Yes, well, thank you very much for having us,' Beth replies, looking around at the party and nodding as if we are at some society do.

'You've got lucky with the weather tonight, anyway. It's been foul,' I say. Dinny gives me an amused look.

'I don't believe in foul weather – it's all just weather,' he says.

'No bad weather, only the wrong clothes?' I ask.

'Exactly! Have you tried my punch? It has a certain . . . punch. Don't take any naked flames near it, whatever you do,' he smiles.

'I tend to avoid punch,' I say. 'There was an incident with punch, I'm told. Although, they might be lying because I sure as hell don't remember anything about it.'

'Beth, then? Can I tempt you?' Beth nods, lets herself be led away. She still looks slightly dazed, almost bewildered to be here. Dinny's hand is on her elbow, guiding her. For a moment I am left alone as he pulls her away, and some emotion scuttles through me. A familiar old emotion, to be left behind by Beth and Dinny. I give myself a shake, find faces that I know and foist myself upon them.

I can feel the whisky heat in my blood and I know I should be careful. Eddie tears past me, grabs my sleeve and pulls me round.

'You haven't seen me! Don't tell them you've seen me!' he gasps, breathless, grinning.

'Tell who?' I ask, but he's gone, and seconds later a small tangle of children, and Harry, scurry by in his wake. I take another long pull of whisky then pass the bottle to a pixie-faced girl with rings in her nose, who laughs and thanks me as she passes. The stars wheel over my head and the ground seems to vibrate. I can't remember when I was last drunk. Months and months ago. I had forgotten how good it can feel. And I see Beth standing next to Dinny, in a knot of people, and even though she is not speaking, she looks almost relaxed. She is part of them, not locked up inside herself, and I am happy to see it. I dance with Smurf, who spins me until I feel a little sick.

'Don't fall in love with her, Smurf. These Calcott girls don't stick around,' Dinny shouts to him as we pass by. I am too slow to ask him what he means. I get as close to the fire as I dare, use a poker to rake a jacket potato from the ashes at the edge, then burn my tongue on it. It has the tang of the earth. I greet Honey, and even though her reply is stilted I don't care. And I watch Dinny. It's not even conscious after a while. Wherever I am I seem to know where he is. As if the fire lights him a little brighter than it does everybody else. The night spins out around the camp, dark and alive; then I see flashing blue lights, coming along the lane towards us.

The police have to park and walk down to the camp. Two cars, disgorging four officers. Marching in with an air of diligence, they start checking for drugs, asking people to turn out their pockets. The music goes quiet, voices fall away. A hung moment in which the fire snaps and roars.

'Is there a Dinsdale here?' a young officer asks. A pugnacious gleam in his eye. He is short, square, very tidy.

'Several!' Patrick calls back at him.

'Can I see some identification to that effect please, sir?' the policeman asks stiffly. Dinny waves Patrick back, dips quickly into his van and presents the officer with his driving licence. 'Well, even so I'm required to ask you all to disperse, as this is an illegal gathering in a public place. I have reason to believe that things may escalate, constituting an illegal rave. There have been several complaints—'

'This isn't an illegal gathering in a public place. We have the right to camp here, as you well know. And we have the same right as the rest of the population to have a few friends around for a party,' Dinny says coldly.

'There have been complaints about the noise, Mr Dinsdale—'

'Complaints from who? It's only ten o'clock!'

'From people in the village, and at the manor house . . .'

'From the manor house? Really now?' Dinny asks, glancing over his shoulder at me. I go over, stand next to him. 'Have you been complaining, Erica?'

'Not me. And I'm pretty sure Beth and Eddie haven't either.'

'And who might you be, madam?' the officer asks me, somewhat dubiously.

'Erica Calcott, the owner of Storton Manor. And that's my sister Beth, and since we're the only people *living* at Storton Manor, I think we can safely say all residents there give this party their full endorsement. And who might *you* be?' The whisky makes me bold, but I am angry too.

'Sergeant Hoxteth, Ms . . . Lady . . . Calcott, and I . . .' I have flustered him. At the edge of my sight, I see Dinny's eyes light up.

'It's *Miss* Calcott. Are you any relation of Peter Hoxteth, the old bobby?' I interrupt.

'He's my uncle, not that I think that has any relevance to—'

'Yes, well. I remember your uncle. He had better manners.'

'There have been complaints, nevertheless, and I am authorised to break up this gathering. I don't wish for there to be any unpleasantness about it, however—'

'The Hartfords over at Ridge Farm have their summer ball every year, with twice this number of people and a live band with a massive amp. If I ring up and complain about *that*, will you go trooping in and break it up? Start searching for drugs?'

'I hardly think—'

'And anyway, this isn't a public place. This is my land. Which, I suppose, makes this *my* party. My *private* party. To which you boys are not, I fear, invited.'

'Miss Calcott, surely you can understand—'

'We'll turn the music down now, and off at midnight, which we were planning to do anyway. The kids need to get to bed,' Dinny interjects. 'But if you want to send us all packing without making some arrests, you'd better come up with a better reason than made-up complaints from the manor house. *Officer*.'

Hoxteth bridles, his shoulders are high and tense. 'It is our *duty* as police officers to investigate complaints—'

'Well, you've investigated. So piss off!' Honey chips in, waving her belly aggressively at the man. Dinny puts a restraining hand on her arm. Hoxteth's eyes flicker over Honey's youth, her beauty, the swell of her midriff. He flushes, knots forming at the corners of his jaw. He nods at his officers and they begin to file away.

'Music off. And everybody gone by midnight. We'll be back to check,' he says, raising a warning finger. Honey raises a finger of her own, but Hoxteth has turned away.

'Tosser,' Patrick mutters. 'Full of youthful zeal, that one,' he adds. Once the cars have pulled away, Dinny turns to me with a smile, an arched eyebrow.

'*Your* party, is it?' he asks, amused.

'Oh, come *on*. It did the trick,' I reply.

'That it did. I never had you down as the anti-establishment type,' he says wryly.

'Shows what you know. I even got arrested once – do I get some kudos for that?'

'Depends what you got arrested for.'

'I . . . I threw an egg at our MP,' I admit, reluctantly. 'Not very anarchic.'

'Not very,' he says, flashing me a grin. 'But it's a start.'

'That was wicked,' Eddie tells me, appearing at my side, breathless. I put my arm around his shoulders and squeeze him before he can escape.

Beth is cooking something for lunch that's filling the ground floor with garlic-scented steam. The windows cloud with it and rain cloaks the outside world so that the house feels like an island. Eddie's gone off into the woods with Harry, and strains of Sibelius's fifth come creeping up the stairs with the steam. Beth's favourite. I take it as a good sign that she has looked it out in Meredith's music collection, and is preparing food that she might even eat. I wonder what Dinny and Honey are doing. In such rain, on such a depressing day. No rooms to wander through, no rows and rows of books or music, no television. Their lifestyle is a matter of pure speculation for me. If it were me, I suppose I'd be in the village pub. For a second I consider seeking them out there, but my stomach gives a lurch of protest and I remember the hangover I'm nursing. Instead I head for the attic stairs.

I do remember Sergeant Hoxteth's uncle. We would see him in the village sometimes, when we went for sweets or ice cream from the shop. He had a ready smile. And he came to the house, on more than one occasion. Either because Meredith had called him, or because the Dinsdales had. They have the right to camp there, just as Dinny said. There's a legal deed or warrant or whatever, from the time of my great-grandfather, before he married Caroline. He and Private Dinsdale were in the army together, in Africa I think. The full story has been lost down the years, but when they came back Dinsdale wanted a place to park up, and Sir Henry Calcott gave it to him. And to all members of his family, in perpetuity. They have a copy of it, and our family lawyer holds a copy. It really got Meredith's goat.

We'd see Sergeant Hoxteth standing in the hallway, waiting uncomfortably for Meredith to appear with her Gorgon glare. The time she made one of the farmers park a massive baler across the top of the track to keep the travellers out. The time she learnt that not all those at the camp were Dinsdales and wanted the *hangers-on* evicted. The time she saw someone drawing water from one of the estate troughs and wanted to press charges. The time food kept vanishing from the larder, and small articles from around the house, and Meredith insisted that it was the Dinsdales until it turned out that the housekeeper had an elderly mother to support. The time one of the travellers' dogs got into the garden and she *put the wind up it* with a twelve-bore shotgun. People in the village thought that they were under attack. *They will spread diseases to my animals*, was Meredith's clipped explanation.

We used to come up here to the attic sometimes, to root around in the junk. It always looked like there should be something exciting to discover, but it didn't take long for us to tire of the packing crates, broken lamps, offcuts of carpet. The hot-water tank, gurgling and hissing like a sleeping dragon. On such a wet day it is dark up here, the far reaches of the space hung in shadow. The tiny dormer windows are few and far between and they are crusted up with water marks and algae. It is so quiet I can hear the soft breathing sounds of the house, the rain making a musical chuckle as it filters through the choked guttering. Unconsciously, I tiptoe.

The leather of the old red trunk is so dry and brittle that it feels sandy when I touch it, comes away as grit between my fingers. I strain my eyes to see inside, dragging it around to face the nearest window. It leaves the ghost of itself in the dust on the floor and I wonder when it was last moved. Inside are wads of papers; boxes; a small, dilapidated valise of some kind; a few mystery objects wrapped in yellowed newspaper pages; a leather writing case. It doesn't look much, if this is all of Caroline's personal things. Not much for a hundred years of life. But then, old houses like this come ready-made, I suppose. The lives within come and go, but most of the contents stay the same.

I search avidly through the papers. Invitations to various functions; a government leaflet about what to do in an air raid; Caroline's telegram from the queen on the occasion of her one hundredth birthday; some prescriptions written out in a doctor's hand so typically wild that I can't make out the words. I unwrap a few of the paper parcels. There's a gold face-powder compact and matching lipstick; an exquisite tortoiseshell fan, so fragile I hardly dare touch it; a silver dressing table set, inlaid with mother of pearl, the brushes silky soft, the mirror cracked across its face; a curious bone ring, satin smooth, with a silver bell hanging from it that tinkles, startling me in the stillness. I wonder what sets these objects apart, what made them wholly Caroline's, what stopped Meredith selling them off like she did with so many of the other precious things. After a while, I notice it. They are all engraved, marked as hers. *CC*, drawn with a flourish into the metal. I turn the bone ring over in my fingers, looking for the same mark. The script, when I find it on the rim of the tarnished silver bell, is small and almost worn away, and it makes me pause. *For A Fine Son*, it reads.

I re-wrap these treasures and put them back in the trunk. I am not sure what will become of them. Technically, they belong to Beth and me now, but they don't really, of course. Any more than they belonged to Meredith, which was why she stowed them away up here. The valise, which has a wide, hinged-opening top, is empty. It once had a pink silk lining, now just in tatters. I take out the writing case instead, which is so full that the laces struggle to tie around the bulge of it. Inside are her letters, many of them still in their envelopes. Compact, white envelopes, much smaller than are commonly used these days. I flick through, realise that most of them have been addressed in the same hand – a small, slanting script in black ink. Just slightly too cramped to be called elegant. I open one carefully and skip straight to the end. Most of these letters are from Meredith and have a Surrey postmark.

My heart gives a strange little twist. I turn back to the first page of the one I am holding, and read.

April 28th 1931.

Dear Mother,

I hope this letter finds you well, and less troubled by your rheumatism than of late? You will be pleased to hear that I am settling in well here, and am gradually becoming accustomed to running my own household — even though I do of course miss you, and Storton. Charles is rather relaxed about the arrangements — his only stipulation is that breakfast be served at eight and dinner at nine! An easy man to please, and I have had the freedom to find my own way of doing things. The house is so much smaller than Storton, you would doubtless be amused by how many and varied the instructions have been that I've needed to give the staff in order to bring things along! I fear they have grown rather too used to having a gentleman alone in the house, and one unlikely to pay much mind to the rotation of linen, the freshening of flowers or the airing of guest bedrooms.

It does seem rather unusual to be alone in the house all day whilst Charles is at his offices. There is a singular quiet in the afternoons here — I often look to my left to remark upon something to you, only to find the room empty! I suppose I ought to make the most of the peace and quiet before it is carried away by the patter of little feet . . . I find myself entirely pulled between two emotions: the thrill of anticipating the birth of your first grandchild, and utter dread of the same event! I remind myself daily that women have been giving birth successfully for a great many years, and that I am certain there can be nothing another woman might do that I might not. Were you afraid, when you were first expecting? I do hope you will come and visit, Mother — I should dearly love to have your advice. The house is smaller than you are used to, as I have said, but it is nevertheless quite comfortable. I have fitted out the largest guest bedroom with new drapes and bed linen — the existing ones were quite worn out — so it is every bit ready for your arrival. The garden is a riot of daffodils, which I know you like, and the countryside hereabouts is really very charming for a gentle walk. Write and let me know if you will come, and when you might like to. In anticipation of our happy event, Charles has sworn me off driving the motorcar, but I can arrange for our man Hepworth to collect you from the station at any time — it is a short drive, not at all arduous. Do come.

With much affection,
Meredith.

In 1931 Meredith would have been just twenty years old. Twenty years old, married and expecting a baby that she must have lost, because my mother was not born for some time after that. I read the letter again, try to re-imagine Caroline as a mother somebody loved, as somebody Meredith clearly missed. The letter makes me sad, and I have to read it again to work out why. It is such a *lonely* letter. From far below, I hear Beth calling me for lunch. I slip the letter back into the case and tuck it beneath my arm before going down to her.

The rain doesn't stop until Tuesday afternoon, and I am itching to get outside. I envy Eddie, who comes back as it gets dark, hair in damp curls and mud up to the knees of his jeans. At what age do you start to notice the cold and the wet and the mud? About the same time you stop moving everywhere at a run, I suppose. In the nursery the gap where the linen press stood yawns at me from the wall. An imprint of dust and cobwebs and unfaded paint. I cross to the piles of cloth I evicted from it, start to go through them, putting cot sheets, lacy sleep-sacks, tiny pillow cases and an exuberant christening gown to one side. A pile of muslin squares that I find tucked away, and a small feather eiderdown as well. I have no idea if any of it will be any use to Honey and her baby, when it comes. Will she even have a cot? But it is good, heavy linen, smooth to the touch. Luxurious. She might like that idea, perhaps: swathing the child in expensive bedding, even if the ambulance will be a more basic nursery. I catch sight of those pillowcases again, with the yellow stitched flowers. I make a mental note to look the flowers up, identify them, in case that will tell me why they tug at my subconscious so.

'Where are you going with that lot?' Beth asks, as I lug it down the stairs.

'I'm taking it over to Honey. It's all baby stuff – I thought she could use it.' Beth frowns. 'What's wrong?' I ask.

'Erica, why are you trying to . . .'

'What?'

'You know. I don't think you should be trying so hard to be friends with them again, that's all.'

'Why not? Anyway, I'm not trying that hard. They are our neighbours though. You seemed happy enough to chat to Dinny at the party the other night.'

'Well, you made me go, you and Eddie. It would have been rude not to talk to him. But I . . . I don't think we have much in common any more. In fact I'm not sure we ever knew him as well as we thought we did. And I don't see what purpose it serves, trying to pretend everything is how it was before.'

'Of course we knew him! What's that supposed to mean? And why shouldn't things be how they were before, Beth?' I ask. She seals her lips, looks away from me. 'If something happened between the two of you that I don't know about . . .'

'Nothing happened that you don't know about!'

'Well, I'm not so sure,' I say. 'Besides, just because you don't want to be friends with him any more, doesn't mean I shouldn't be,' I mutter, dragging the bag to the door and pulling on my coat.

'Erica, wait!' Beth comes across the hall to me. I turn, search her face for clues. Troubled blue eyes, closely guarded. 'We *can't* go back to the way things were. Too much has happened. Too much time has passed! It's far better to just . . . move on. Leave the past alone,' she says, her eyes sliding away from mine. I think of Dinny's hand, its gentle, proprietorial grip on her elbow.

'It sounds to me,' I say, steadily, 'that you don't want him any more, but you don't want me to have him either.'

'*Have* him? What is that supposed to mean?' she says sharply. I feel colour flare in my cheeks and I say nothing. Beth draws in a deep, uneven breath. 'It's hard enough being back here as it is, Erica, without you acting like an eight-year-old again. Can't you just stay away, for once? We're supposed to be spending time here *together*. Now Eddie is off with that Harry all day long, and you'd rather chase after Dinny than . . . I don't have to stay, you know. I could take Eddie and go back to Esher for Christmas . . .'

'Well, that's a great idea, Beth. Just the kind of unpredictable behaviour that Maxwell is always looking out for!' I regret this as soon as I say it. Beth recoils from me. 'I'm sorry,' I say quickly.

'How can you say things like that to me?' she asks softly, her eyes growing bright, blurred. She turns and walks away.

Outside, I take a deep breath, listen to the muted calls of the rooks, the gentle dripping and unfurling of soaked foliage. A living sound, a living smell in the middle of winter. I've never really noticed it before. I drop the bag of linens, suddenly unsure of myself, and sit down on a rusting metal bench at the edge of the lawn; feel the dead cold of it bite through my jeans. Perhaps I will take it down later. I can hear voices coming from the stream beyond the eastern edge of the garden. I make my way over, through the little gate at the side of the lawn and down across the scrubby slope. After the rain the ground is heavy with water. It squeezes up around my feet as I walk.

Eddie and Harry are in the stream, the water swirling perilously close to the tops of their wellies. All the rain of late has made the water fast, and even faster in the centre, channelled deep because

Eddie and Harry have built a dam of flints and sticks reaching out from each bank. Harry's trousers are wet all the way up to his hips, and I know how cold the water must be.

'Rick! Check it out! We almost got it right the way across a moment ago, but then part of it collapsed,' Eddie calls, excited, as I reach them. 'But before it did the water got really high! That's when we got soaked, actually . . .'

'I can see that. Boys, you must be freezing!' I smile at Harry, who smiles back and points at a rock by my feet. I bend down and pass it to him gingerly, slipping on the muddy bank, and he adds it to the dam.

'Thanks,' Eddie says absently, unconsciously speaking for his friend. 'It's not that cold once you get used to it,' he shrugs.

'Really?'

'No, not really — my feet are bloody freezing!' he grins.

'Language,' I say, automatically and without conviction. 'It's a good dam, I have to admit,' I continue, standing in the mud with hands on hips. 'What are you going to do if you manage to finish it? It'll make a huge lake.'

'That's the idea!'

'I see. God, Eddie, you are *covered* in mud!' It's all up the sleeves of his jumper, where he has pushed them up with muddy hands; all up the legs of his cords where he's wiped his hands. There's a smear across his forehead, sticking his hair into clumps. 'How have you managed to get so filthy? Look — Harry's managed to stay clean!'

'He's further from the ground than I am!' Eddie protests.

'True enough,' I concede.

Grabbing a fistful of Harry's coat to steady himself, Eddie makes his way towards me, feet rocking over the stony stream bed.

'Is it lunch time yet? I'm starving,' he declares, losing his balance and bending forwards to steady himself, hands in the freezing mud.

'Yes, almost. Come back and get cleaned up — you can always finish this later. Here.' I hold out my hand and Eddie grabs it, taking a huge stride out of the stream, heaving on my arm. 'No — don't pull, Eddie, I'll slip!' I cry, but too late. My legs scoot from under me and I sit down abruptly, with an audible splash.

'Sorry!' Eddie gasps. Behind him Harry grins, makes an odd huffing noise, and I realise he is laughing.

'Oh, you think that's funny, do you?' I ask, slithering back to my feet, wet mud seeping into my knickers. I pull my trousers up, leaving vast muddy smears across them in doing so. Eddie wobbles again, takes a sloshing step forwards that kicks a wave of water over the tops of my boots. *'Eddie!'*

'Sorry!' he says again, but this time he can't keep from smiling, and Harry laughs harder.

'You little buggers! It's freezing! Here,' I find my muddiest finger, wipe it on Eddie's nose. 'Have some more!'

'Wow, thanks Rick! And here . . . here's some for you! Happy Christmas!' Eddie scoops some mud into his hand, chucks it at me. It lands messily on the front of my sweater, which is pale grey. I gasp, peer down at it. Eddie freezes, as if suddenly afraid he's gone too far. I scrape the worst of it off, weigh it in my palm.

'You. Are. *Dead!*' I say, lunging at him. With a yelp of laughter, Eddie darts past me, up the bank and into the scrub.

It takes me some distance to catch up with him and I have to discard the mud and swear a truce before he'll let me near him. I put my arm around him , more to warm my own throbbing fingers than anything else. Behind us, Harry had been following but he stops, stares up into a hawthorn tree where two robins are cursing one another.

'Is he coming?' I ask. Eddie shrugs.

'He's always stopping to watch birds and stuff like that. I'll see you later, Harry!' he shouts, giving him a wave. We ought to go in through the scullery, but it's locked and we have no choice but to use the front door. We discard our boots outside — a hollow gesture, since our socks are every bit as wet and muddy. Beth puts her head around the kitchen doorway.

'What on *earth* have you been doing?' she gasps. 'Your clothes!' Eddie looks a little contrite, glances at me for support.

'Um, being eight years old again?' I venture, painting my face with innocence. Beth gives me a hard look, but she cannot hold it. The ghost of a smile twitches her mouth.

'Perhaps you might like to get changed, the pair of you, before we have lunch?' she says.

I phone my mum in the afternoon, to check that all is well, and ask what time they plan to arrive.

'How is it going there? How's Beth?' Mum asks, in a casual tone that I recognise. The casual tone she uses to ask important things. I pause, listen for sounds of my sister close by.

'She's OK, I think. A little bit up and down, I suppose.'

'Has she said anything? Anything about the house?'

'No – what kind of thing?'

'Oh, nothing in particular. I'm looking forward to seeing you both – and Eddie of course. Is he having fun there?'

'Are you kidding? He loves it! We hardly see him – he's out playing in the woods all day. Mum – could you do me a favour?'

'Yes, of course, what is it?'

'Could you possibly dig out your copy of that family tree Mary drew up? And bring it along?'

'Yes, I think so. If I can find it. What do you want it for?'

'I just want to check something. Did you ever hear of Caroline having a baby before she was married to Lord Calcott?'

'No, I never did. I would doubt it very much – she was very young when she married him. What on earth makes you ask that?'

'It's just this photo I found – I'll show you when you get here.'

'Well, all right then. But you know any questions about family history really ought to be directed at Mary. She did all that research the other year, after all . . .'

'Yes, I suppose so. Well, I'd better crack on here – I'll see you very soon.'

I can't call my Aunt Mary – Henry's mother. I can't speak to her on the phone. I get a feeling that I can hardly bear, as if the air in my lungs is hardening. At Meredith's funeral, I hid. To my shame. I actually hid from her behind a vast spray of lilies.

For bedtime reading, I prop Caroline's writing case on my knees and read a few more of Meredith's letters. Some of the earlier ones date from her time away at college and speak of a fierce deportment tutor, dormitory politics, shopping trips into town. Then the lonely letters from Surrey begin. I flick through a few more of them and then, tucked into one of the pockets of the case, I find an envelope addressed in quite a different hand. The paper inside is like dried leaves, and I touch it lightly, unfold it with consummate care. Just one page, with one paragraph of script. Far larger lettering than Meredith's, written with emphatic pen pressure, as if in some urgency. The date given is the fifteenth of March, 1905.

Caroline

I received your letter this morning and with no slight concern. Your recent marriage and delicate condition are matters to be much celebrated, and no one could be more satisfied than I to see you settled and joined to a man such as Lord Calcott, who is well positioned to give you everything you require for a happy life. To put your current position in unnecessary jeopardy would be foolhardy in the extreme. Whatever it is that you feel you must confess, may I strongly urge you that all matters arising from your previous existence in America should by every means possible remain in America. No purpose can be served by revisiting such matters now. Be grateful for the new start you have been given, for the happy circumstance of your fortuitous marriage, and let that be the last word upon it between us. Should you bring embarrassment or infamy of any kind upon yourself or our family, I should have no other choice but to sever all ties with you, however it would grieve me.

Your Aunt,
B.

The scoring beneath the phrase *remain in America* has all but torn the paper. A heavy, violent strike. In the quiet after I read these ringing words, I see all the secrets within this house lying in drifts as deep as the dust and shadows in the corners of the room.

On Christmas Eve our parents arrive, and their familiar car pulling into the driveway seems a small miracle of some kind. Proof of an outside world, proof that this house, Beth and I, are part of it. I meant to keep Eddie in this morning – I suggested to Beth that we should – but he is up before us and gone. An empty bowl in the kitchen sink, cornflakes drying hard, and half a glass of Ribena on the table.

'We've lost your grandson, I fear,' I say, as I kiss Dad and take bags from the back of the car. Perhaps not the cleverest thing I could say. Mum hesitates.

'What's happened to Eddie?' she asks.

'He's got a friend – Harry. He camps here, just like . . . Well. They're always off in the woods. We hardly see him these days,' Beth says, and we can hear that it bothers her. Just a little.

'Camping? You don't mean . . . ?'

'Dinny's here. And his cousin, Patrick, and some others,' I say casually. But I can't help smiling.

'Dinny? You're *kidding*?' Mum says.

'Well, well!' Dad adds.

'Hmm, well, now you know how we used to feel, I suppose,' Mum says to Beth, kissing her on the cheek as she goes indoors. Beth and I share a look. This hadn't ever occurred to us.

Beth looks like our mother. She always has, but it's getting more pronounced the older she gets. They both have Meredith's willowy figure, the delicate bones of her face, long artistic hands. Meredith cut her hair short and set it, but Mum has always left hers natural, and Beth's is long, unchecked. And they have an air about them, which I lack. Grace, I suppose it is. I take more after our father. Shorter, broader, clumsier too. Dad and I stub our toes. We catch our sleeves on door handles, knock our wine glasses over, bruise ourselves on coffee table edges, chair legs, worktops. I have a huge affection for this trait, since it comes from him.

We drink coffee and admire the Christmas tree that came yesterday and now towers up into the stairwell. All the decorations we bought weren't quite enough. They look a little lost on such vast branches. But the lights twinkle and the resinous smell of it reaches every corner of the house, a constant reminder of the season.

'Bit extravagant, isn't it, love?' Dad asks Beth, who tips her eyebrows, dismissively.

'The house needed cheering up. For Eddie,' she says.

'Ah well, yes, fair enough,' Dad concedes. He's wearing a red jumper; grey hair standing up in tufts just like Eddie's does, and the hot coffee flushing his cheeks pink. He looks jovial, kind – just as he is.

There's a thump on the door, which I open to find Eddie and Harry on the step, out of breath, as ever, and damp.

'Hi, Rick! I came to say hello to Grandma and Grandpa. And I told Harry he could come and see the tree. That's OK, isn't it?'

'Of course it's OK, but kick those boots off before you take another step!'

Eddie is hugged, kissed, questioned. Dad proffers a hand to Harry for him to shake, but Harry just looks at it, bemused. He drifts over to the tree instead, crouches down to gaze up into it, as if trying to see it at its biggest, its most imposing. Dad shoots me a quizzical look and I mouth, *I'll tell you later*. We decide to keep

Eddie, since lunch is not far off, and send Harry home with a box of Beth's mince pies, which he dips into even as he shambles off across the lawn.

'He seems a funny old thing,' Mum says mildly.

'He's wicked. He knows all the best places to go in the woods — where to find mushrooms and badgers' nests,' Eddie defends his friend.

'Badgers have setts, not nests, Eddie; and I hope you haven't been playing with fungi — that's really very dangerous!' Mum says. I see Eddie bridle.

'Harry knows which ones you can eat,' he mutters, defensively.

'I'm sure he does. It's fine, Mum,' I say, to quieten her. 'Old people don't know that wicked means good,' I whisper to Eddie. He rolls his eyes, escapes up the stairs to get changed.

'It's good for him, to have such an outdoor friend. He spends so much time cooped up at school,' Beth says firmly.

Mum raises a hand. 'I meant no criticism! Lord knows you two spent enough time out in the woods with Dinny when you came to stay here.'

'You didn't mind, though, did you?' Beth asks anxiously. She is all the more sensitive now to the slights of children against their parents. Mum and Dad exchange a glance, and Dad gives Mum a fond smile.

'No, not really, I suppose,' Mum says. 'It might have been nice if you'd wanted to spend a bit more time with us . . .' In the shocked pause after she says this, Beth and I exchange a guilty look and Mum laughs. 'It's fine, girls! It was the beginnings of my empty nest syndrome, that's all.'

'I don't know what I'll do when Eddie goes off to university. It's bad enough now that he boards all week,' Beth murmurs, folding her arms.

'You'll miss him like mad, you'll spoil him rotten when he comes down, and you'll find a new hobby — just like all mothers do, darling,' Mum tells her, putting an arm around her bony shoulders.

'It's a long way off yet, anyway,' I remind her. 'He's only eleven, after all.'

'Yes, but five seconds ago he was a tiny baby!' Beth says.

'They grow up fast,' Dad nods. 'And be happy about it, Beth! After six years of having a teenage boy around the house, I expect you'll be thrilled to have him go off to study!'

'And just think of all the fun stages you've got before then — the arguments about curfews, and driving lessons, and first girlfriends staying over. Finding porno mags under his bed . . . peering into his dazed eyes in the morning and wondering what drugs he took the night before . . .'

'Erica! Really!' Mum admonishes me, as Beth's eyes grow wide with horror.

'Sorry.' I smile.

'Rick, I think you've been teaching too long,' Dad chuckles. Beth raises her eyebrows at me.

'Smug aunt syndrome — that's your problem. You get to watch me go through all of this and laugh into your sleeve as I get it all wrong and tear out my hair,' she says accusingly.

'Come on, Beth. I'm joking. You've never put a foot wrong as a mother,' I tell her, rushing on before a pause can form, before we all remember the huge wrong stride she took, not too long ago. 'Come and have some mince pies — Beth's outdone herself with them.'

Later on, I show Mum the photographs I've found for her. She identifies the people I didn't recognise — more distant relatives, people now dead, faded away, leaving only their faces on paper and traces of their blood in our veins. I show her the one of Caroline, taken in New York with the baby cradled in her left arm. Mum frowns as she scrutinises it.

'Well, that's definitely Caroline – such pale eyes! She was striking, wasn't she?'

'But what was she doing in New York? And whose baby is it, if she only married Lord Calcott in 1904? Do you think they had one before they got married?'

'What do you mean, what was she doing in New York? She was *from* New York!'

'Caroline? She was American? How can nobody have told me that before?'

'Well, how can you not have realised? With that accent of hers . . .'

'Mum, I was five years old. How would I have noticed her accent? And she was ancient by then. She hardly spoke at all.'

'True, I suppose,' Mum nods.

'Well, that explains why she was in New York in 1904. So, who's the baby?' I press. Mum takes a deep breath, inflates her cheeks.

'No idea,' she says. 'There's no way she could have had a child with Henry before they wed, even if that wouldn't have caused a huge scandal. She only met him late in 1904, when she came over to London. They married in 1905, soon after they met.'

'Well, was she married before? Did she bring the baby over with her?'

'No, I don't think so. You really would be better off asking Mary. As far as I know, Caroline came over from New York, a rich heiress at the age of around twenty-one or twenty-two, married a titled man at quite some speed, and that was that.'

I nod, oddly disappointed.

'Perhaps it was a friend's baby. Perhaps she was its godmother. Who knows?' Mum says.

'Could have been,' I agree. I take the picture back, study it closely. My eyes seek out Caroline's left hand, her ring finger, but it's hidden in the folds of the ghostly child's dress. 'Do you mind if I keep this one? Just for a while?' I ask.

'Of course not, love.'

'I've . . . been reading some of her letters. Caroline's letters,' I am strangely reluctant to confess this. Like reading somebody's diary, even after they're dead. 'Have you got that family tree? There was a letter from an Aunt B.'

'Here you are. Caroline's side of things is a bit sketchy, I'm afraid. I think Mary was more interested in the Calcott line – and all of Caroline's family records would have been in America, of course.' There is nothing, in fact, on Caroline's side, except the names of her parents. No aunts or uncles, a very small twig to one side before Caroline joined the main tree in 1905. Caroline Fitzpatrick, as she was then.

I study her name for some time, waiting, although I'm not sure what for.

'In this letter, her aunt – Aunt B – says that whatever happened in America should stay in America, and she shouldn't do anything to mess up her marriage to Lord Calcott. Do you know anything about that?' I ask. Mum shakes her head.

'No. Nothing at all, I fear.'

'What if she did have a baby before she came over here and got married?'

'Well, for one thing she wouldn't have managed to get married if she had! Well brought up girls did not just have babies out of wedlock back then. It would have been unthinkable.'

'But what if she did get married to someone else before Lord Calcott? I found something up in the loft – in the trunk where Meredith put all of Caroline's stuff – and it says *To a Fine Son* on it,' I say.

Mum raises her eyebrows a little, considers. 'It was probably Clifford's. What kind of something?'

'I don't know – it's some kind of bell. I'll fetch it down later and show you.'

We have drifted into the drawing room. Mum picks up each

photo from the piano and studies it at length, her face hung between expressions. She runs her thumb over the glass of Charles and Meredith's wedding portrait. A futile little caress.

'Do you miss her?' I ask. Normally a stupid question when somebody's mother dies. But Meredith was different.

'Of course. Yes, I do. It would be hard not to miss somebody who knew how to fill a room quite the way my mother did.' Mum smiles, puts the photo down, wipes her fingermarks away with the soft cuff of her cardigan.

'Why was she like that? I mean, why was she so . . . *angry*?'

'Caroline was cruel to her,' Mum shrugs. 'Not physically, or even verbally . . . perhaps not even deliberately; but who can say what damage is done when a child grows up unloved?'

'I can't imagine. I can't imagine how a mother could fail to love her child. But, *how* was she cruel to her?'

'Just in a thousand and one little ways,' Mum sighs, thinks for a moment. 'For example, Caroline never brought her a present. Not once. Not on birthdays or at Christmas, even when Meredith was small. Not on her wedding day, not when I was born. Nothing at all. Can you imagine how something like that might . . . chip away at you?'

'But if she'd never had a present, perhaps she didn't know to expect one?'

'Every child knows about birthday presents, Erica – you've only to read a storybook to learn about them. And the staff used to get her little things when she was small – Mother told me how much they meant to her. A rabbit – I remember her mentioning that. One year, the housekeeper gave her a pet rabbit.'

'That's . . . really sad,' I say. 'Didn't Caroline believe in presents?'

'I just don't think she was aware of the date, most of the time. I honestly don't think she knew when Meredith's birthday was. It was as though she hadn't given birth to her at all.'

'But if Caroline was so awful, why was Meredith so devoted to her? Why did she move back here with you and Clifford when your father died?'

'Well, difficult or not, Caroline was her mother. Meredith loved her, and she was always trying to . . . prove herself to her.' Mum shrugs sadly, opens the piano lid and presses the top note. It floats out, fills the room, in perfect tune. 'We were never allowed to play this piano. Not until we'd reached a certain standard. We had that battered old upright in the nursery to practise on instead. Clifford never did get good enough, but I did. Just before I went away to university.'

'There are lots of letters from Meredith in Caroline's things. They all sound rather sad, as if she was always more or less by herself – even when she was married.'

'Well,' Mum sighs. 'I don't remember my father, so I don't know how things were before he died. She loved him, very much I think. Perhaps too much. Caroline once said to me that losing love like that left a hole you could never fill. I remember it clearly because she so rarely spoke to me. Or to Clifford – she hardly seemed to notice us children at all. I'd been watching Mum out in the garden, and I jumped when she spoke because I hadn't heard her sneak up behind me.'

'She could still walk, then?'

'Of course she could! She wasn't always ancient.'

'But why didn't Caroline love Meredith? I don't understand.'

'Neither do I, dear. Your great-grandmother was a very strange woman. Very distant. Sometimes I would go and sit next to her and try to talk to her, but I soon realised she wasn't listening to a word I said. She would just stare right through you, with those grey eyes of hers. No wonder Meredith married so soon – she must have been thrilled to find somebody who would listen to her!'

'It's amazing how normal you are. What a great mother you are.'

'Thank you, Erica. Your father helped, of course. My knight in shining armour! If I'd moved back here after my degree, if I'd stayed here long enough to resent them both . . . who knows?'

'Perhaps not everyone is cut out for parenthood. I can't imagine Meredith was the cuddliest . . .'

'No, but she was a good mother, for the most part. Strict, of course. But she wasn't as . . . sharp when we were small, as she was after we'd been living back here for a few years. As Caroline grew frail, she needed a lot of looking after. I think Mother resented that. She did her best for us, but I don't think she got over losing my father, or the disappointment of having life begin and end here — she and Caroline, cooped up in this old house. But we turned out OK, didn't we? Clifford and I?' she asks me, her face shaped with sudden sadness. I cross the room, hug her.

'More than OK.'

'I've come to collect some kisses!' Dad announces, finding us, brandishing mistletoe and a grin.

After dinner we put all our presents under the tree. Eddie looks like a miniature gent in his navy blue monogrammed dressing gown, stripy pyjamas and red felt slippers. He checks the gift tags and positions each parcel carefully, according to some private scheme. We drink brandy, listen to carols. Outside the rain is lashing at the house in waves. It sounds like handfuls of gravel, thrown against the windowpanes. It makes me shiver.

Sometime around midnight the rain stops, the clouds roll away, and a bright moon bedazzles the night sky. It lights the green paper vines climbing the walls in my room, the single wardrobe, the arched window looking east over the driveway. There's a rookery in the naked chestnut tree outside, the nests like clots in the twiggy branches. I can't get to sleep. My brain scrambles to life each time I start to drift, sending up a starburst of faces and names and memories to confound me. Brandy does this to me sometimes. I have to unpick each thought from the knotted mess, work it loose from my mind and let it float away. I keep the memories of Dinny, though; I don't let them go. New ones I've made, to add to the well-worn, sunshine ones. Now I know how he looks in winter light, in rain. I know how he looks in firelight. I know how alcohol takes him; I know how he makes a living, how he lives. I know how that wide, lazy childhood smile has grown up, changed, become a quick flash of teeth in the darkness of his face. I know he resents us, Beth and me. And soon, perhaps, I might begin to understand why.

Christmas morning passes in a rushed, comforting haze of food preparation, champagne and piles of torn shiny paper. Dad helps Eddie unpack his new games console, and they experiment with it on the inadequate television in the study while we women occupy the kitchen. The turkey barely fits into the Rayburn. We have to poke its legs in, and the tips of them blacken where they touch the sides.

'Never mind. Everyone prefers breast, anyway,' Mum says to Beth, who waves a nervous hand through the tendrils of smoke rising from the oven. It will take hours to roast and, pleading a slight headache, Beth retires to lie down. She shoots us a mute, angry glance as she goes. She knows we will talk about her now. I don't know if she sleeps at such times or if she just lies there, reading wisdom in the cracks in the ceiling, watching spiders enmesh the light shade. I hope she sleeps.

Mum and I slide ourselves onto the kitchen benches, link hands across the table, our conversation hanging awkwardly around the urge to talk about Beth. I break the silence.

'I found a load of newspaper clippings in with the photos in one of Meredith's drawers. About Henry,' I add, unnecessarily. Mum sighs, withdraws her hands from mine.

'Poor Henry,' she says, and strokes her fingers over her forehead, brushing back an imaginary hair.

'I know. I've been thinking about him a lot. About what happened—'

'What do you mean, about what happened?' Mum asks sharply. I look up from the thumbnail I was picking.

'Just, that he vanished. His disappearance,' I say.

'Oh.'

'Why? What do you think happened to him?'

'I don't know! Of course I don't know. I thought, for a while that . . . that perhaps you girls knew more than you were saying . . .'

'You think we had something to do with it?'

'No, of course not! I thought that, maybe, you were protecting somebody.'

'You mean Dinny.' Something flares inside me.

'Yes, all right then, Dinny. He had a temper, your young hero. But, Erica, Henry vanished! He was taken, I'm sure of it. Somebody took him, carried him off and that was the end of it. If anything had happened to him here on the estate, anything at all, then the police would have found some evidence of it. He was taken away, and that's all there is to it,' she finishes, calm again. 'It was a terrible, terrible thing, but nobody is to blame except the person who took him. There are just a few very dangerous people out there, and Henry was unlucky enough to meet one of them.'

'I suppose he was,' I say. None of this rings true to me. None of it convinces me. Eddie by the pond, throwing a stone; and that watery ache in my knees.

'Let's not talk about it today, shall we?'

'OK, then.'

'How has Beth been?'

'Not great. A bit better now. We went to a party at the camp the other night, and she chatted to Dinny a bit; and she seemed to pick up a little. And now that you and Dad are here too . . .'

'You went to a *party* with *Dinny*?' Mum sounds incredulous.

'Yes. So what?'

'Well,' she shrugs, 'it just seems so odd, after all these years. Taking up with him again . . .'

'We're not *taking up with him*. But we are neighbours now. For the time being, anyway. He's . . . well. He's not really much different, and neither am I, so . . .' For a terrifying moment, I think I will blush.

'He was so in love with Beth, you know. Back when they were twelve,' Mum says, staring into the past and smiling. 'They say you never forget your first love.'

I down the last of my champagne, get up to fetch the bottle. The heat of my blush remains, moves up to my nose, threatens to become tears. 'Come on. These spuds won't peel themselves!' I smile, proffering a paring knife at her.

'How long will Beth rest for?'

'A hour, perhaps. Long enough to dodge the potato peeling, that's for certain.'

My eyes strain against the gathering dark. It's not yet five o'clock but my feet are indistinct. They snag on tufts and twigs and roots that I can't see. I've come to fetch Eddie. I make a pass of the camp but all is quiet. I am still not sure who each vehicle belongs to, and they look so tight, so closed up against the world that I am too afraid to go knocking on doors, asking for Harry. I cut into the woods but the darkness is even deeper here. I should have brought a torch. Night is coming fast; the light feels exhausted.

'Eddie!' I call, but it's a pathetic sound. I can see the strict formations of the search teams, going through these woods twenty-three years ago. Five days after he vanished, but still they kept trying. Their faces grim; the dogs pulling at their leads. The crackle and click of CB radios. *Henry!* Their shouts were loud and clear but stilted even so, as if self-conscious, as if knowing the name was hurled in vain, would only reach their own ears. The weather was foul that weekend — it was the August bank holiday, after all. The tail end of Hurricane Charley, lashing Britain with wind and rain. *'Eddie!'* I try again, as loudly as I can. The quiet, when my clumsy feet go still, is astounding.

I come out of the woods beyond the dew pond. The barrow is a vague growth on the horizon. I skirt the edge of the field, along the fence, back towards the house, and slowly I see figures coming into being by the water. Two large, one small. I heave a lungful of air, feel a chill slide down my back. I had not known how afraid I was. Harry, Eddie, Dinny. They could be the three protagonists of a boy's own story, and here they are, at the dew pond. Skimming stones in the near dark on Christmas Day.

'Who's that?' Eddie says, when they notice me. His voice sounds high, childish.

'It's me, you muppet,' I say, mocking my own fear at his expense.

'Oh, hi, Rick,' he says. Harry gives an odd hoot — the first real sound I have heard him make. He runs around the water's edge to me — big clumsy strides. I hold my breath, wait for him to slip, stumble in, but he doesn't. He presents me with a small stone, flat, almost triangular. I can just about see his smile.

'He wants you to have a go,' Dinny says. I walk carefully around to them. I turn the stone over in my hand. It is warm, smooth.

'I came to get Eddie. It's time he was in — it's pitch black out here,' I say to Dinny. I feel prickly, endangered. The water is nothing but a blackness at our feet.

'You just need to give your eyes time to adjust, that's all,' Dinny tells me, as the others go back to their stones, the flat black water, the counting of white blooms in the gloaming.

'Still, we should go back. My parents are here . . .'

'Oh? Tell them hello from me.'

'Yes, I will.' I stand next to him, close enough for our sleeves to touch. I don't care if I am crowding him. I need something near enough to catch, something to anchor me. I can hear him breathing, hear the shape he makes in the echoes from the pond.

'Aren't you going to skim that stone?' He sounds wryly amused by the idea.

'I can hardly see the water.'

'So? You know it's there.' He looks sideways at me. Just a silhouette, and I want to put my hands on his face, to feel if he's smiling.

'Well, here goes.' I creep to the edge, find a firm footing. I crouch, swing my arm, and when I let go of the stone I follow it, towards the surface, towards the obsidian water. *One, two, three* . . . I count the splashes and then I stumble, my vision skids vertiginously, my feet slide over the edge of the bank and I gasp. What a place, I have sent that innocent stone to – what darkness.

'Three! Rubbish! Harry got a seven a little while ago!' Eddie calls to me. I feel Dinny's hands under my arms, the reassuring weight of him pulling me to my feet. Panic fluttering in my chest.

'Not a great night for swimming, I think,' Dinny murmurs. I shake my head, glad he can't see my face, the tears in my eyes.

'Come on, Eddie, we're going in,' I say. A ragged edge to my voice.

'But I've just . . .'

'Now, Eddie!' He sighs, solemnly presents Harry with the rest of his stones. They make a warm, cheerful noise as they change palms. I walk away from the edge, back towards the house.

'Erica,' Dinny calls to me. I turn, and he hesitates. 'Happy Christmas,' he says. I can tell this is not what he had intended to say, and even though I wonder, I don't feel strong enough to ask right now.

'Happy Christmas, Dinny,' I reply.

Losing

1903–1904

The summer swelled and Magpie's body ripened in time with it, seeming to expand by the day as her baby grew. She moved with an odd grace, as purposefully as ever but never suddenly, neatly angling her new width around the furniture and through the narrow door of the dugout she shared with Joe. Caroline watched her. She watched, and she wondered, her heart full of suspicions that she went from discrediting to confirming to herself twenty times a day. And more than anything, she was jealous. She felt sick and weak and full of something dark and bitter each time she saw the growing inches of the Indian girl's body. And if anything could have driven her from the house and out into the summer sun, it was this.

The wooden house just could not keep out the heat as the thick brownstone walls of New York had done. And, Caroline reflected, when it was hot in New York, it was never as hot as this, and she had never before had to be active in such temperatures. But Magpie's composure and Hutch's exhortation to her at new year were at work upon Caroline's mind; so one day, which dawned slightly overcast and a little cooler than usual, she decided to get out of the house. She packed a basket with a newly ripe melon, some biscuits and a bottle of tonic water, tied the ribbon of her sun bonnet in a bow beneath her chin, and set off for the nearest neighbouring farm, which belonged to an Irish family called Moore. It was six miles to the north-west and Caroline, who had no idea what it felt like to walk six miles, had nonetheless over-heard Corin say that a man might easily walk four miles in an hour. Setting off early, she thought, she would be there in time to take coffee and maybe a bite of lunch, and then back again in plenty of time to help cook dinner. She told Magpie where she was going, and squared her shoulders when the Ponca girl gave her a level, incredulous stare and blinked slowly, like an owl.

She walked for an hour, at first admiring the flowers on the horse-mint and wild verbena and gathering a posy to present to the Moores, but soon found the basket a dead weight on her arm, bruising her skin. She was slick with sweat in spite of the clouds, and felt it prickling her scalp underneath her hat. Her skirts were fouled up and wadded together with sandburs and thistle barbs, and they swung ponderously around her legs, tripping her. The sandy ground, which undulated gently, pulled at her feet and was more strenuous to walk across than she'd thought. She battled slowly up a long rise, certain that from the crest of it she would see the neighbouring farm. She could not. Breathing hard, she saw the landscape roll away into the distance, as far as the eye could see. Putting the basket down, she turned in a slow circle, staring into the unbroken horizon. A hot wind blew, making waves in the long grass that looked, in the distance, like a green and gold ocean. The wind carried the scent of dry earth and sagebrush and it moaned a low note in her ears.

'There's nothing here,' Caroline murmured to herself. Something rose up in her then, something like panic, or anger. 'There's *nothing here*!' she shouted, as loudly as she could. Her throat felt raw and dry. The wind snatched her words away, and gave her no answer. She sank onto the prairie and lay back to rest. An endless sky above her, and endless land all around. If she did not rise again, she thought, if she stayed where she was, only wild dogs and buzzards would ever find her. It was an irresistible thought, a terrifying one.

Walking back at last, having never reached the Moore's place, Caroline nearly missed the ranch. She had veered to the north by a mile or more and only happened by chance to see smoke rising from the chuck hut to her right, where a silent Louisiana Negro called Rook would be cooking dinner for the ranch hands. Turning south, Caroline's legs wobbled with exhaustion. Her mouth was parched and her face, after a day in the harsh light and hot wind, was tight and stinging. Behind her she could feel the vastness of the prairie spreading out, watching, and beyond the ranch the grasslands stretched away to every point on the compass. The corrals, fences, wheat and sorghum fields her husband had mapped onto the land were pitifully small. The ranch was an island, a tiny atoll of civilisation in an endless patchy sea, and when she finally reached the house, gasping for breath and scattering wilted flowers behind her, she shut the door and burst into tears.

That night Caroline lay awake, in spite of her exhaustion. The clouds cleared as night fell, and the moon rose luminously full. It was not this that kept her awake, but the knowledge, the new understanding of how vast and empty the land she now lived upon truly was. She felt swallowed up by it; tiny, invisible. She wanted to grow, to expand, to take up more space somehow. She wanted to be significant. The air inside the bedroom was smothering, thick with the lassitude of summer. Beside her, Corin snored softly, his face pressed into the pillow, arms flung out to his sides. The moon caught the contours of the muscles in his arms and shoulders, and the sharp line where the tan of his neck became the pale of his back. Caroline rose, took a spare blanket and went outside.

She spread the blanket amongst the fecund orbs of the watermelons and lay down upon it. Something scuttled away into the foliage close to her face, and she shuddered. There were no other sounds, though her ears strained to pick up any movement from the bunkhouse, any sign of an approaching ranch hand. Then she pulled her nightdress up until it covered only her breasts, leaving the lower portion of her body bare to the night sky. Her hipbones stood proud, casting shadows of their own in the silvery light. Her heart beat fast in her chest, and she did not shut her eyes. Stars scattered the sky. She began to count them, lost her place and started again, and again; losing all idea of how long she had lain there and where on earth she was. Then the door banged behind her and she heard uneven steps, and Corin grabbed her beneath her arms and pulled her into his lap.

'What is it? What's wrong?' Caroline gasped. Painted in greys and blacks, Corin's face was pinched with fear and his eyes were wide. Seeing her awake and well Corin let her go, exhaling heavily, and put his face into his hands.

'What are you doing out here?' he mumbled. 'Are you all right?'

'I'm . . . fine. I just . . . it was so hot in the bedroom . . .' Caroline hurriedly pulled her nightdress down.

'But it's just as hot out here! What are you doing – why were you naked?' he demanded. Alarmed, Caroline saw that he was shaking. She bit her lip and looked away.

'Moonbathing,' she said.

'What?'

'I was moonbathing . . . Angie told me it might help,' Caroline said quietly. She had sneered inwardly at such superstition when their neighbour first mentioned it, but now it seemed she would try anything.

'Help with what? Love, you're not making sense!'

'Help a woman to get pregnant. To lie with the moon shining on her body,' Caroline said, shamefacedly.

'And you believed her?'

'No, not really. Not really. It's just . . . *why* aren't I pregnant yet, Corin? It's been over a year!' she cried. 'I don't understand.'

'I don't understand it either,' Corin sighed. 'But I'm sure these things happen when they're good and ready, that's all. A year is not that long! You're young and . . . it's been a big upheaval for you, moving out here to be with me. It *will* happen love, please try not to worry.' He tipped her chin up with his fingertips. 'Come back inside now.'

'Corin . . . why were you so afraid just now?' Caroline asked, as she rose stiffly to her feet.

'What? When?'

'Just now, when you found me out here. You looked so alarmed! Why? What did you think had happened?'

'There was a woman, on the other side of Woodward a couple of years ago . . . never mind. I just thought something might have happened to you. But you're fine, and it's nothing to worry about . . .' Corin reassured her.

'Tell me, please,' she pressed, sensing his reluctance. 'What happened to the woman?'

'Well, apparently she felt the heat badly, like you do too, and she was also pining for her home back in France, and she took to sleeping out in the yard to keep cool, but one night . . . one night she . . .' His fingers grasped the night air, searching for a way to tell her without telling her.

'She what?'

'She cut her own throat,' he said, in a rush. 'Three children waiting for her indoors and all.' Caroline swallowed convulsively, her own throat closing at the thought of such violence.

'And you thought I'd . . . done that to myself?' she breathed.

'No! No, love, no. I was just worried for you, that's all.' He ushered her back into the bedroom and said he would wait up until she slept, but soon his soft snores began again, and still Caroline's eyes stayed fixed upon the ceiling.

She wondered. She wondered where Corin went all day. It had never occurred to her to think about this before. He always gave an account of his day over the supper table, but how could she know that he was telling it true? How could she know how long it took to round up strays, to pursue rustlers, to brand the new steers, to set the stallion Apache to a brood mare, to mend fences, to plough or sow or reap the wheat fields, or cut hay, or do any of it? And Corin could, of course, send Joe anywhere if he wanted him out of the way. And Magpie had often already left, by an hour or so, before Corin came in for the evening. There were times, plenty of times, when she had no idea where either of them might be. And the way he had touched Magpie, that time – the way he had put his hands on her at the Woodward gala. These were Caroline's thoughts as she lay awake, and as she sat in the ringing silence at the end of each day, waiting for Corin's return. When Caroline saw her husband, her fears vanished. When she was alone, they flourished like weeds. Her solace was Magpie's plainness, as she saw it. The coarseness of her hair, the fat on her figure, the alien planes of her face. She noted these things and called to mind Corin's praise of her own beauty.

But one hard August day when a high, spiteful sun was bleaching the grassland, even this solace was taken from Caroline. Magpie was at the kitchen window, standing sideways so that she could lean her hip against the bench as she peeled carrots with a short, sharp blade. She was singing, as usual, her expression soft and her hands busy. Caroline watched her through the doorway from the main room, from behind a book she was supposedly reading, and a falter in the quiet song made her blink. Magpie stopped peeling, her gaze falling out of focus and one hand going to her distended belly. A tiny smile twitched her lips and then the song and the work continued. The baby had shifted, Caroline realised. It was awake, alive inside the girl. It was listening to its mother singing. Swallowing, Caroline put her hand to her own stomach. It was more than flat, it was concave; there was no welcoming fold of flesh, no fulsome vitality. She could feel her ribs and her hipbones, wooden and sharp. How dry and hard and dead her body seemed, compared to Magpie's. Like the dead husks, the chaff that the men beat out of the wheat. She looked at the girl again, and then her throat went tight and for a second she couldn't breathe. The sun streaming in through the window caught the gloss of Magpie's thick, black hair;

the wide, bowed curve of her top lip; the high slant of her cheeks and eyes; the warm glow of her skin. Magpie was beautiful.

Before dawn the next day, as Corin stirred and began to wake, Caroline went on soft feet to the kitchen. She poured him a cup of cold tea and cut two thick slices of bread from yesterday's loaf, which she spread with honey. She presented him with these offerings as he sat up, blinking in the charcoal glow of near-day.

'Breakfast in bed. I always used to have breakfast in bed on Saturdays,' she told him, smiling.

'Well, thank you. How grand I feel!' Corin cupped her face in the palm of his hand, and took a long draught of the tea. Caroline propped the pillows up against the wall behind him.

'Sit back for a moment, love. You don't have to rush out just yet,' she urged him.

'Putting off a chore never got it finished faster,' he sighed, ruefully.

'Just five more minutes,' she begged. 'Try some of the bread. I spread it with that honey Joe collected for us.'

'That man is a marvel with bees,' Corin nodded. 'I've never seen anything like it. Just walks right up to the nest and puts in his arm, and never once takes a sting.'

'Some Indian magic, perhaps?'

'Either that or he's just got the toughest hide of any man alive,' Corin mused. Caroline thought of this – of Joe with his unforgiving black eyes and skin like the bark of a tree. She shuddered slightly, wondering how Magpie could bear to bed herself with him.

'Corin?'

'Yes?'

'You know, it's been more than a year now since we were wed and, well . . . we never have been back to go swimming again, like on our honeymoon.'

'I know. I know it, Caroline. It's so hard to find the time,' Corin said, leaning his head back against the wall, his face still languid with sleep.

'Can we go? Soon? I just . . . I want to spend the day with you. The whole day . . . we hardly ever do that! Not with all the work you have to do.'

'Well, I don't know, Caroline. There's just so much to do at this time of year! We've got the stupidest bunch of beeves as I've ever had on the ranch and they've been busting through the fences every chance they get, wandering off and getting themselves stuck in the creek and caught up in wire and I don't know what else. Maybe in a week. In a week or two . . . how about that?'

'You promised me we would,' she said quietly.

'And we will. We will,' he insisted.

Soon afterwards he rose, pulled himself into his clothes, stroked one hand gently over Caroline's hair and kissed the top of her head before going through to the kitchen to make coffee. Caroline sat and listened to the rattle of the coffee beans, the clang of the kettle hitting the stove, and she felt a peculiar weariness wash over her. For a moment, she did not think she had the strength to rise, to see another day through to its end. Every bone in her body seemed leaden. But she drew in a long breath, and she stood, and began to dress herself slowly.

At the end of September, Joe appeared at the house one wet afternoon, his hat in his hands, eyes half shut against the steady downpour and an air of impenetrable calm about him. Caroline smiled, but she could not help but draw back from him, and she saw a hardening in his eye when she did this.

'Magpie's time is come. She asks for you to go there,' Joe said.

'To go where? Why?' Caroline said, not understanding.

'To go to her. To help the baby,' Joe explained, in his guttural accent. His tone was as neutral as his expression, but something told Caroline that he did not necessarily approve of his wife's request. She hesitated, and felt her pulse quicken. She would have to go inside the dugout. However used to having Magpie around the house Caroline had become, she could not help thinking of that low, half-submerged dwelling as some kind of animal's den.

'I see,' she said quietly. 'I see.'

'In this way, she honours you,' Joe told her solemnly. 'Such work is only for family.'

After a hung pause, pinned by Joe's inscrutable gaze, Caroline went back inside. She squashed her hat onto her hair, took off her apron and felt panic rising like bubbles in her throat. She had no knowledge of birth, no idea what she should do to help. She was not sure that she wanted to help at all.

Outside, Joe showed the first and only sign of impatience Caroline had ever seen any of the Ponca show. He repositioned his hat in his hands and looked over his shoulder towards where his wife lay in labour. Seeing this, Caroline felt a stab of guilt and she hurried out, turning her face to the ground as they went so that she would not see the terrifying spread of land around them. Ever since her abortive walk to the Moore's farm, she had felt a dizzying horror of the gaping landscape of Woodward County. The expanse of it seemed to pull her thoughts apart, building an unbearable pressure behind her eyes. She felt the urge to run, to throw herself back indoors before she disintegrated into the mighty sky. Their footsteps splashed and Caroline's hem was soon soaked with water, stained ruddy from the soil.

Three steps led down into the dugout, and they dropped into a soft, warm darkness lit by a kerosene lamp that battled against the gloom outside and in. There was a strong smell, made up of smoke from the stove, animal hides, and herbs that Caroline could not identify. The blood thumped at her temples as she felt all eyes turn to her – Magpie's, White Cloud's, and those of Joe's sister, Annie. Joe himself stayed outside and disappeared into the rain. Magpie's face was slick with sweat, her eyes wide and fearful. The other women's expressions were cautious; not unfriendly, but reserved.

'Joe . . . said I should come. He said you had . . . had . . . asked for me to come?' Caroline stammered. Magpie nodded and smiled slightly before her body convulsed, and she ground her teeth together, an expression that made her look savage. 'What should I do? I don't know what I should do!' Caroline quailed. White Cloud said something rapid in the Ponca language and handed Caroline a small wooden pail, filled with rainwater, and a clean cloth. The old woman motioned dipping the cloth into the water, and then pressed her hand against her forehead, gesturing to Magpie. Caroline nodded and knelt beside the labouring girl, wiping her drenched face with the cool water, afraid, as she performed this intimate duty, that the girl would somehow see into her troubled heart.

In the semi-dark, White Cloud began to sing a soft monotonous song that lulled them all; lulled Caroline so that she had no idea how much time was passing, whether hours or minutes or days. The words were blurred and dry, and the song sounded to Caroline's ears like the long, drawn-out rush of the warm prairie wind, lonely and reverent. As regularly as waves on the shore, Magpie heaved against the pain inside her, screwing up her eyes and bearing her teeth. She looked as feral as a cat, but she did not cry out. On and on these waves came, as the darkness deepened outside; and on and on White Cloud sang, mixing up a pungent drink that she gave to Magpie gradually, a spoonful at a time. Then, with a low sound in her throat like a strangled growl, Magpie's baby arrived into Annie's waiting hands, and White Cloud broke off her song with a sharp cry of joy, her wizened face breaking into a wide grin, and then into laughter. Caroline smiled with relief, but as Annie passed the wriggling, whimpering baby boy to its mother, she felt a splinter pierce her heart and lodge there. Tears sprang to her eyes and she looked away to hide them, seeing, in a dark corner of the dugout, a pair of spurs on leather thongs. A pair Corin had been looking for and had asked if she had seen about the place. She stared at them, and the splinter wormed its way ever deeper.

Two months later, the baby was chubby and delightful. He was named, in the Ponca tongue, *first born son*; but called by his parents and so everybody else, William. He rode around the ranch in a sling on Magpie's back, gazing out at the world with an expression of mild astonishment in his round eyes. And he slept there in a crumpled little heap, dribbling down his chin, not stirring as Magpie returned to work in the main house, her body not at all fatigued by the child. The cold, like the heat, seemed to have little effect on the girl's spirits. She appeared at the house swathed in her thick, brightly patterned blanket, her cheeks burnished dark red by the wind and her eyes as bright as jet beads.

And although it hurt her to hold William, Caroline often asked to do so. Like exploring a wound, or pressing a bruise. She cradled him in the crook of her arm and rocked him gently. He was a good-natured baby and did not cry for strangers. He had an array of fledgling facial expressions that melted her heart and eased the splinter from it. A tiny frown of puzzlement at the noises she made; the sagging of his mouth and eyes as sleep took hold; wide-eyed wonder when she showed him her peacock-feather fan. But the pain of handing him back to his proud mother was a little stronger each time, the hurt a little worse; and the only thing harder than this was watching Corin play with the baby, when he came in from working. His brown hands looked impossibly large around the tiny child's body, and he grinned foolishly when he managed, by tickling and mugging, to make William smile. Each time he succeeded in this endeavour he glanced at his wife, to share it with her, but Caroline found it hard to find the smile she knew he wanted. Seeing him love this child, this child that was not hers, was almost more than she could bear.

There was to be no christening for William, which surprised

Caroline, even though it made sense. She fretted briefly about the danger to the child's soul, but Magpie only laughed when she tentatively suggested that it wouldn't hurt him to go through the ceremony, just in case.

'Our ancestors are watching him, Mrs Massey. You don't have to worry,' she smiled.

Awkwardly, Caroline dropped the subject. But she suggested that they hold a welcoming lunch for him instead, and Magpie agreed to this. Caroline sent out some invitations, but only Angie Fosset was willing to celebrate the birth of an Indian baby, and she turned up on her tall horse with the saddlebags full of cast-off baby smocks and napkins.

'I'm stopping at three, so I've no need of these any more,' she told Magpie. Caroline had sent Hutch into Woodward the week before to collect the gifts she had ordered for William from Corin and herself. Magpie accepted each present with increasing embarrassment, and the atmosphere over the party grew awkward.

'Mrs Massey . . . this is too much,' Magpie told her, her eyes troubled. Annie and White Cloud exchanged a look that Caroline could not read.

'Oh, my goodness, what lovely things!' Angie exclaimed.

'Well,' Caroline smiled, feeling suddenly exposed. 'A lovely little boy should have lovely things,' she said, but felt that they could all see into her heart – that these were gifts she had wanted to give her own baby, not Magpie's. She turned to William in his carrier to hide her dismay, stroking one finger down his crumpled, sleeping face. But this was worse. Her cheeks flared red and her breath caught in her chest. 'Who'd like some cake?' she asked tightly; getting up and fleeing into the kitchen.

Caroline's second winter on the prairie was harder than the first. The four walls of the house became her gaol, trapping her with Magpie and William – two constant reminders of how she failed, day after day. For if Magpie's return to work, her cheery demeanour and the ease with which she coped proved anything to Caroline, it was that she would never belong on the prairie like the Ponca girl did. She would never get on as well, never thrive, never settle, never put down roots here, but remain blown about the surface like tumble weed. She found it harder and harder to talk to Magpie, to sing and tell stories as they'd used to. The words stuck in her throat and she feared that even genuine expressions of admiration for Magpie, for William, would come out tainted with the grief she felt, and would sound insincere.

When Hutch came to the house for coffee he would push her gently to speak her mind, to come out riding again, to do anything but stay cooped up inside the house. Caroline assured him, absently, that she was fine, and all was well; and the foreman had no choice but to drift away again, a thoughtful look in his eye. When the confinement got unbearable, and Caroline did gather her courage and venture outside, the wind hit her skin like knives, and the sky rained terror down upon her and, once chilled, it took hours for her to get warm again, however close to the stove she huddled. As she broke the ice on the water cistern one morning and felt the splashes on her hands burning coldly, she remembered the warm water of the pool where they had swum on their honeymoon; and she gazed down into the dark depths of the tank, rooted to the spot by sadness.

At night, Caroline and Corin often lay awake as the wind howled around the house, too loud to ignore. Beneath the blankets one such night, he drew lazy patterns on her shoulder that both soothed and aroused her. The smell of him was so dear to her, strong and rank and animal after a day's work under heavy clothes. She clung to him like a drowning person clinging to a float, keeping her eyes tightly shut, feeling as though the house, at any moment, might give in to the onslaught and be torn away with them inside it. The house was a fiction, she thought; a flimsy carapace between them and the empty fury outside; and it might vanish in a heartbeat. As long as Corin was there, she told herself. As long as he was there with her she didn't care. He seemed to sense her fears and he spoke to calm them, the way she had heard him speak to nervous horses. His voice was low and she fought to hear it above the din — words rolling in a steady rhythm, like water trickling, half awake and half asleep.

'I guess we should spare a thought for White Cloud and Annie, although I know the Ponca are born to this life and they are stronger than we are, still I would not want to have nothing but hides between me and the wind on a night like this. Hutch has told me of the Great Die-Up, in the winter of eighty-seven, which was before I had come out west, and we two, you and I, were still in New York City, unbeknownst to one another. Every bad winter we have, every time I mention the cold he just shakes his head and says it's nothing, not compared to the Great Die-Up. Whole herds of cattle froze where they stood. Riders died out on the ranges and they weren't found until the spring, when the snow melted back and left them sitting high and dry, with their knees drawn up to their chests in the last pose they ever struck, just trying to keep warm. The beeves were all skinny and weak because the summer before that winter had been a droughty one and there was precious little grass or feed to be had. And they just died in their *droves*. And the cows lost their calves before they were due to birth them, because there was hardly enough to fill one mouth, let alone two; and Hutch himself lost three toes — two on his right foot and one on his left. He'd been out riding in a blizzard so thick he strained to see his horse's ears, trying to keep the cattle moving so they didn't just huddle up and freeze into one great heap of dead meat, and when he climbed off his horse at the end of the day he couldn't feel his legs, let alone his feet. He told me he didn't get his boots off until three days later, and by that time his feet were big and black and the blood had just frozen right there in his veins. And it's true, too; I've seen the gaps where those toes of his should be. There were snowstorms the likes of which had never been seen, nor have been since; from Mexico to Canada and everywhere in between, and I remember – don't you remember having no beef one year, when you were little? Perhaps you were too young, but I remember there being no beef in New York. Cook tried everything she could to get some each week but there was none to be had. Not with nigh on every poor beast on the ranges lying under a snowdrift. So this storm, this wind – well, like Hutch says, it's nothing, my darling. This is the prairie being sweet to us, Caroline. And we're warm, aren't we? And we're safe, too. How could we not be when we have each other?' He spoke like this, on and on through the ragged night, as hailstones hit the roof like lead shot; and Caroline drowsed on the edge of sleep, drinking in the steady words and feeling a cold ache in her feet for Hutch's lost toes, a cold ache in her heart for cowboys hugging their knees to their chests, out in the sweet prairie wind.

By the spring of 1904 there seemed to be infants everywhere. Several of the mares had gangling foals running at their heels, the yard hens bobbed on a sea of fluffy chicks, William's howls could at times be heard in every far corner of the ranch, and a small wire-haired terrier belonging to Rook, the Negro cook, gave birth to a litter of blunt-nosed puppies following a chance encounter with a Woodward mongrel of uncertain provenance. The weather was turning warm again, the days longer. No more ice in the cistern, no more hailstorms and blue north winds. The young wheat and sorghum was pale green, and there was a brave scattering of blossom on Caroline's spindly cherry trees. But, try as she might, Caroline could not be rid of the weight of her dashed expectations, or her fear of the open land that her husband loved so much.

They sat outside on the porch one fair Sunday afternoon, after a travelling preacher had called by to read a service for all the ranch's inhabitants, and, because of the contentment she read in Corin's face, rocking gently in his chair, Caroline felt a hundred miles from him.

'What are you reading?' he asked her eventually, startling her because she had thought him asleep beneath his copy of *The Woodward Bulletin*. She smiled and raised the book so he could see the cover. 'What, *The Virginian* again? Don't you get tired of reading it?'

'A little. But it's one of my favourites, and until you take me to town to buy some others . . .' she shrugged.

'All right, all right. We'll go next week, how about that? Once Bluebell's foaled. You could always go by yourself, if you didn't want to wait for me? No harm would come to you—'

'You don't know that! I prefer to wait for you,' Caroline cut him off. Just the thought of striking out for Woodward alone was enough to turn her stomach.

'All right, then.' Corin retreated back beneath his paper. 'Read some of that one to me then. Let's find out what's so special about it.' Caroline looked at the page she had been reading. Nothing was that special about it, she thought. Nothing but that the heroine, a civilised lady of the East, had made such a life for herself, had found such happiness in the wilderness; had been able to see beauty that Caroline could not, and to understand her man as Caroline could not. Caroline scoured the pages as if the secret to this was hidden there somewhere, as if she might be taught how to settle in the West, how to love it, how to thrive. But the passage she had been reading described Molly Wood deciding to leave – the dark spell before that girl's sunshine happy ending, and Caroline hesitated before reading it out, sitting tall as she had been taught and holding the book high in front of her so her voice would not be hampered by a crooked neck.

'This was the momentous result of that visit which the Virginian had paid her. He had told her that he was coming for his hour soon. From

that hour she had decided to escape. She was running away from her own heart. She did not dare to trust herself face to face again with her potent, indomitable lover . . .'

'My, what drama,' Corin murmured sleepily when Caroline finished, and she closed the book, running her hands over the cover which had become dog-eared and creased with rereading.

'Corin?' Caroline asked hesitantly, a while later when the sun was getting fat in the western sky. 'Are you awake?'

'Mmm . . .' came the drowsy reply.

'I come into my money soon, Corin. I know I told you before, but I . . . I didn't tell you how much money it is. It's . . . a lot of money. We could go anywhere you wanted . . . you won't have to work so hard any more . . .'

'Go somewhere? Why would we go anywhere?' he asked.

Caroline bit her lip. 'It's just . . . so isolated here – so far from town! We could . . . we could buy a house in Woodward, perhaps. I could spend some of the week there . . . Or we could move everything closer, move the whole ranch closer! I could . . . join the Coterie Club, perhaps . . .'

'What are you saying, Caroline? Of course I can't move the ranch closer to town! Cattle need open grasslands, and the land nearer town is all given over to homesteaders now.'

'But you won't need to raise cattle any more, don't you see? We'll have money – plenty of money!' she cried. Corin sat up and folded the newspaper. He looked at his wife and she recoiled from the pained expression on his face.

'If money was what I was interested in, I'd have stayed in New York. Sweetheart! This life is everything I've dreamed of since my father took me to Chicago when I was a boy and I saw Buffalo Bill Cody's 'Wild West and Congress of Rough Riders of the World' at the Columbian Exposition . . . That was when I decided to come out here with him, when he came looking for fresh suppliers. I watched those ropers and riders, and I knew that *this* was what I wanted to do with my life! Ranching isn't just a job for me . . . it's our life, and this is our home, and I can't think I'll ever want to move or live anywhere else. Is that what you want? Do you want to live somewhere else? Somewhere away from me, perhaps?' His voice caught when he asked this question and she looked up quickly, shocked to see tears waiting in the corners of his eyes.

'No! Of course not! *Never* away from you, Corin, it's just . . .'

'What is it?'

'Nothing. I just thought . . . perhaps I might be happier, to have a little more company. More refined society than I have here, perhaps. And . . . perhaps if I was happier, we might start a family at last.'

At this Corin looked away across the corrals and he seemed to consider for a long time. Caroline, thinking the discussion over, sank back into her chair and shut her eyes, sad to her core and exhausted by this attempt to voice her fears.

'We can build. We could use some of the money to double the size of the house, if you like, and get a maidservant, perhaps. A housekeeper to take over from Magpie now that she has William to look after . . . An electricity generator, maybe. And plumbing! A proper bathroom for you, with running water indoors . . . How about that? Would that fix this?' Corin asked. He sounded so hurt, so desperate.

'Yes, perhaps. A bathroom would be lovely. Let's see when the money comes,' she said.

'And I'll take you to town very soon. We can stay the night, maybe even a couple of nights, if you like? Buy you as many books and magazines as we can carry back; and I need to go to Joe Stone's for some new spurs. I've been idiot enough to break my spare pair and I've still not yet laid hands on the original ones . . .'

'They're at Joe and Magpie's place. In the dugout,' Caroline told him tonelessly.

'What? How do you know?'

'I saw them in there, when I was helping with the birth.' Hating herself, Caroline watched him closely. For signs of guilt or embarrassment, or a telltale blush. Instead Corin smacked a palm to his forehead.

'Lord, of course! I loaned them to Joe, months and months ago! Way out towards the panhandle that day we chased those thieves down – his snapped and since Strumpet was behaving and that gelding of his was being a brute, I gave him my spurs. I never thought to ask for them back at the end of that long ride – I was that ready to fall down and sleep! Why didn't you say, if you saw them, love?'

'Well, I . . .' Caroline faltered, and shrugged. 'I . . . just forgot, that's all. The baby came and that was something of a distraction . . .' Corin sprang to his feet.

'You clever girl to remember them now! I'll go over and fetch them right away, before we both forget again,' he smiled, and strode away from the house. Caroline watched him go and then she put her face into her hands for all the times since William's birth that she'd pictured the spurs, lying there in Magpie's home; all the times she'd imagined the haste and the urgency with which they might have been discarded there, flung aside by passionate hands in the desire to reach that hidden, adulterous nest of blankets.

After her suggestion that they move to town, and as the second anniversary of their marriage approached, Caroline caught her husband watching her more closely – for signs of malaise, perhaps, or melancholia. He must have noticed, then, that she was increasingly quiet and visibly enervated, but there was little he could do about it. Caroline smiled when he asked after her, and assured him that she was quite well. She did not say that when she opened the door she felt as though she might fall out, might tumble into the gaping emptiness of the prairie without man-made structures to anchor her. She did not say that gazing into the distance made her heart wince and then bump against her ribs so loudly she was sure Magpie could hear it. She did not say that the sky was just too dizzyingly huge for her to look at. Only cradling William seemed to soothe her. She marvelled at his increasing strength as he struggled to reach for things, to grasp and chew her fingers. The movement of his small body against hers seemed to fill a dark and gaping hole inside her, and Magpie smiled to see the tender expression on her face. But Caroline always had to give the baby back to his mother, and each time she did the hole inside her returned.

The plants in the garden wilted and were choked beneath encroaching weeds. Unharvested vegetables split and rotted in the sun. Magpie agreed to take over the tending of the garden, but she too watched Caroline with a slight, appraising frown. She forced Caroline to oversee the pulling up of the spent winter plants and the rearrangement of the garden for summer crops.

'You must tell me what to plant, Mrs Massey. You must tell me where to plant,' the girl insisted, although they both knew that Magpie was by far the wiser in such matters. Caroline demurred, but the raven-haired Ponca girl, with calm insistence, would brook no argument. As Magpie dug and hoed, Caroline remained always in the shadow of the house, her hands behind her, resting on the rough wood of the wall as if for support. Magpie jumped back with a gasp when she uncovered a rattlesnake in the shelter of the dying leaves, but then she killed it deftly with her hoe and tossed the limp coils to one side. 'Think, now, if the white lady had done it this way in the Garden of Eda!' she called to Caroline, laughing. But the violence made Caroline sick to her stomach.

'Eden,' she whispered. 'It was the Garden of Eden.' She went back inside without another word, her fingers never leaving the side of the house.

One evening, Caroline saw Corin stop Magpie as the girl, with William slung across her back, headed for the dugout where she would prepare another dinner, and keep another household. She stood at the window and held her breath as Corin jogged over to Magpie, put a hand lightly on her arm to stop her. Caroline strained her ears as if she might hear what her husband asked, for even from inside the house she could see questions written all over his face. Magpie answered him in her usual contained way. No gestures, no telltale facial expressions – or at least none that Caroline could read. When Corin released the girl and started towards the house, Caroline turned away and busied herself plating up the meal Magpie had made for them. Roasted corn chowder, with thick slices of roast beef and warm bread.

Corin was troubled by whatever Magpie had told him, that much was clear. Caroline felt a stab of resentment towards the girl, but she smiled as she put food on the table, willing him reassured, willing him unconcerned about her, because she did not know what she would say to him, if he were to ask if she was happy. What he said, as they settled down to eat, was:

'I do think, sweetheart, that you should learn to ride and come out with me sometime to see more of the land we live on. There's nothing that lifts my heart more than a fast ride over the prairie, with the wind to buoy you up and the swiftness of a good horse . . .' But he broke off because Caroline was shaking her head.

'I just can't, Corin! Please don't ask me . . . I tried! The horses frighten me. And they know it – Hutch says that they can sense the way people feel, and it makes them act badly . . .'

'But you were afraid of Joe and Maggie, until I introduced you to them. You're not still afraid of them now, are you?'

'Well, no . . .' she reluctantly agreed. Magpie she no longer feared, of course, but on the rare occasions that Joe came up to the house to speak to Corin, or to deliver supplies fetched in from Woodward, a knot of tension still clenched in the pit of her stomach. His face looked fierce to her, no matter what Corin said. His features spoke of violence and savagery.

'Well, it would be just the same with the horses. That mare you rode – Clara. Why, she's as gentle as a lamb! And that side saddle I bought you is just sitting in the shed, gathering cobwebs . . . The season's changing now, the weather's better . . . If you would only come out with me and see the beauty of God's virgin country here . . .'

'I just can't! Please, don't try to force me! I am far happier staying here . . .'

'Are you, though?' he asked. Caroline stirred her soup around with her spoon and said nothing. 'Maggie tells me . . .' He trailed off.

'What? What has she said about me?'

'That you don't want to go outside. That you stay indoors, and you're too quiet, and she has much more work to do. Caroline . . . I . . .'

'What?' she asked again, dreading to hear what he would say.

'I just want you to be happy,' he said miserably. He watched her with his eyes wide and she saw nothing within them but truth and love, and hated herself anew for ever thinking he could have betrayed her, could have passed over her infertile body to make a son elsewhere.

'I . . .' she began, but could not think what to say. 'I want to be happy too,' she whispered.

'Then tell me, please. Tell me what I can do to make you happy!' he implored. Caroline said nothing. What could she say? He had done everything a man could do to give her a child, but she could not manage it. He had loved her, and married her, and given her a new life, and she could not ask again for him to give that life up. 'We'll go swimming again. We'll have our honeymoon again. This Sunday – we'll go. Hang the ranch, hang the work – just you and me, my love. And we'll make a baby this time, I just know it. What do you say?' he urged. Caroline shook her head and felt a tremor shake the core of her. It was too late, she realised. Too late for their second honeymoon swim. She could never go back to that pool, not now. It was too far, the way too open; it was too much for her now, too frightening. But what remained? What else could she suggest?

'Only . . . only promise me you'll never leave me,' she said, at last. Corin put his arms around her and held her tightly with quiet, helpless desperation.

'I will *never* leave you,' he whispered.

The first hot night of June, Caroline woke in the darkness with sweat cooling between her breasts, pooling in the hollow of her stomach and slicking her hair to her forehead. She had been dreaming of waking up alone, out on the grasslands, as if she had fallen asleep that day she set out for the Moore's place and not woken since. No house, no ranch, no people, no Corin. She lay still and listened to the blood rushing in her ears, listened to her own breathing as it slowed, grew quieter. Goosebumps rose along her arms. She looked beside her at the comforting outline of Corin, edged in grey light from around the shutters. The coyote song that always haunted the night echoed outside, reaching out unhindered for mile after boundless, borderless mile. Caroline closed her eyes and tried to shut out the sound. It shook her very soul to hear it, waking from such a dream, from such a nightmare. It told her, over and over, of the wilderness outside the walls; of the empty, pitiless land.

Suddenly then, Caroline faced what she had long known but refused to acknowledge. This was where she lived. Here was her husband, here was her life, and this was it. No change, no move; Corin had told her so. And no children. It was two years since she and Corin had been wed and the failure to conceive a child certainly did not stem from a want of trying. She would watch Magpie and Joe raise a brood, she thought; and never have a child of her own. It would be unbearable. If Magpie were to conceive again, she would not be able to have her in the house all day. So, this empty house then, when Corin was away buying or selling beeves, delivering a thoroughbred saddle horse to its new owner, or arguing the price of wheat in Woodward. This empty house in this empty land, for the rest of her life. *I will lose my mind*, Caroline realised, seeing this fact clearly, like plainly printed words scrolling in front of her eyes. *I will lose my mind*. She sat up with a cry and beat her hands against her ears to block out the howling and the resounding silence behind it.

'What is it? What's happening! Are you ill?' Corin slurred, stirred from his sleep. 'What is it, my darling? Did you have a nightmare? Please, tell me!' he begged, grasping her hands to stop the blows she was raining onto them both.

'I just . . . I just . . .' she gasped, choking and shaking her head.

'What? Tell me!'

'I just . . . can't sleep with those god*damned* coyotes shrieking all night long! Don't they *ever* let up? All night! Every night! They're driving me out of my goddamned *mind*, I tell you!' she shouted, eyes wild with rage and fear. Corin took this in and then he smiled.

'Do you know, that's the first time I've ever heard you swear?' he said, releasing her, brushing her dishevelled hair from her face. 'And I have to say, you did a mighty fine job of it!' he grinned. Caroline stopped crying. She looked at the shadow of his smile in the darkness and an odd calm befell her – the numbness of exhausted sleep as it stole in and overcame her in seconds.

The next morning, Corin went out briefly before breakfast and then returned, smiling at his wife with a twinkle in his eye. Caroline's eyes were puffy and they itched. In silence, she went about making breakfast, but she burnt the coffee beans in the roasting pan and the resulting drink was bitter and gritty. She warmed some bean pottage from the night before and made a batch of flat biscuits to go with it, all of which Corin wolfed down with great relish. Before long there was a shout from outside. Caroline opened the door to find Hutch and Joe outside, mounted on their dun-coloured horses with rifles jutting up from the saddles and pistols at their hips. Joe held Strumpet's reins and the black mare was also saddled and ready to ride.

'I didn't think you were riding out today? I thought you were mending fences?' Caroline asked her husband, her voice a small thing after the furies in the night.

'Well,' Corin said, swallowing the last of his coffee with only the faintest grimace and walking out of the house. 'This is a little extra trip I've decided to take, on the spur of the moment.'

'Where are you going?'

'We're going . . .' Corin swung into the saddle, 'to hunt some coyotes,' he grinned. 'You're quite right, Caroline – there are too many of them living close to the ranch. We've been losing some hens; you've been losing some sleep. And it's a fine day for a bit of sport!' he exclaimed, wheeling Strumpet in a tight circle. The mare got onto her toes and snorted in anticipation.

'Oh, Corin!' Caroline said, touched by his efforts for her. The men tipped their hats to her, and with a whoop and a drumming of hooves they were away, leaving nothing but tracks in the sand.

By lunchtime the sky had closed over, filling with thick clouds that rolled steadily out of the north-west. In the kitchen, Caroline sat at the table with Magpie, shelling peas whilst William slept quietly by his mother's feet. Every now and then he stirred and whimpered as if dreaming, and while this made Magpie smile, it made Caroline's heart ache as if with cold. How much longer, she wondered, before this chill became irrevocable and her heart would be lost to her just like three of Hutch's toes had been lost to him? Magpie seemed to sense her sadness. At length the Ponca girl spoke.

'White Cloud is a very wise woman,' she said. In the stillness of the house the crisp pop of the green pods and the rattle of peas falling into the pail were loud. Caroline waited for Magpie to say more, unsure of how to reply to this statement. 'She can make many medicines,' Magpie went on at last. Caroline glanced up and Magpie met her gaze with steady, black eyes.

'Oh?' Caroline said, with as much polite interest as she could muster.

'In the days before, when she lived among our own people, in the lands far to the north of here, many Ponca would go to her for advice. Many *women* would go to her,' Magpie said, with heavy emphasis. Caroline felt warmth prickle her cheeks, and she got up to light a lamp against the dull afternoon. The yellow glow shone on glossy braids and brown skin. Caroline felt like a wraith of some kind, as if Magpie were real and she herself were not quite so. Not quite whole, not quite flesh. The lamp did not light her in the same way.

'Do you think . . . White Cloud would help me?' she asked, in barely more than a whisper. Magpie looked at her with great sympathy then, and Caroline looked down, studying the peas as they blurred in front of her.

'I can ask her. If you would like me to ask her?' Magpie said softly. Caroline could not speak, but she nodded.

Later, Caroline stood and watched from the window as the first drops of rain began to fall. It was not a violent rainstorm, just a steady soaking that fell straight down from the sky. Not a breath of wind was blowing. Caroline listened to the percussion of it on the roof, the gurgle of it in the guttering as it sluiced down into the cistern. It took a while for her to work out what was making her uneasy. The rain had come on slowly, out of the north-west, the same direction in which the men had ridden away. They would have seen this rain closing in, drawing a grey veil over the horizon. It would have found them long before it found the ranch, and yet they had not returned. There would be no hunting in rain like this, and it was late. Magpie had put a rabbit stew in the stove and had left, over an hour ago. The table was set, the stew was ready.

Caroline had scrubbed her nails to get the stain of the pea pods out from underneath them. She stood at the window and her unease grew with each drop of rain that fell.

When at last she thought she saw riders coming, the end-of-day light was weak and made them hard to discern. Two hats only, she could see. Two riders only, and not a third. Her heart beat in her chest – not fast, but hard. A steady, slow, tight clenching that was almost painful. Two hats only; and, as they drew nearer, definitely only two horses. And as they drew nearer still, she saw two horses with dun coats and no black one.

For I was reared
In the great city, pent 'mid cloisters dim,
And saw nought lovely but the sky and stars.
    Samuel Taylor Coleridge, *Frost at Midnight*

5

On Boxing Day I wake up to hear voices in the kitchen, the clatter of the kettle on the Rayburn, the tap running, water clunking through the pipes in the wall by my bed. It sounds so like the mornings of my childhood here that I lie still for a moment, with the dizzying feeling that I have gone back in time. I expect I am the last one up, as I always used to be. Still full and heavy with yesterday's rich food, I go up to the attic in my dressing gown, unwrap the bone ring from Caroline's trunk and take it downstairs with me. On the stairs hangs the smell of coffee and grilled bacon; and against all logic my stomach rumbles.

The four of them are at the table, which is properly laid with plates and cutlery, coffee mugs and a huge cafetière, a platter of bacon and eggs, toast tucked neatly into a rack. Such quirks of the generation gap make me so fond. I would never think of setting the breakfast table, putting toast in a rack instead of on my plate. The four people I care most about in the world, sitting together at a laden table. I lean on the door jamb for a second and wish that it could always be this way. Warm steam in the air; the dishwasher grinding through its noisy cycle.

'Ah! You've decided to grace us with your presence,' Dad beams, pouring me a coffee.

'Cut me some slack, Dad, it's only nine o'clock,' I yawn, sauntering to the table, sliding onto a bench.

'I've been out already, to fetch in loads more wood,' Eddie boasts, smothering some toast with chocolate spread.

'Show off,' I accuse him.

'Ed, would you like some toast with your Nutella?' Beth asks him pointedly. Eddie grins at her, takes a huge bite that leaves a chocolate smile on his cheeks.

'Sleep OK?' I ask my parents. They took the same guest room they always did before. So many rooms to choose from, and we all of us have filed into our habitual ones like well-behaved children.

'Very well, thank you, Erica.'

'Here, Mum — this is that bell I was telling you about, that I found up in Caroline's things.' I hand it to her. 'The handle looks like it's bone, or something.'

Mum turns it over in her hands, glances up at me incredulously. 'It's not a bell, you dope, it's a baby's teething ring. A very lovely one, too. This is ivory, not bone . . . and the silver bell acts as a rattle. Added interest.'

'A teething ring? Really?'

'A very old-fashioned one, yes; but that's certainly what it is.'

'I saw something like that on *The Antiques Roadshow* not that long ago,' Dad adds.

'Ivory and silver — it must have been for a pretty rich kid,' Eddie observes, around a mouthful of toast.

'Was it Clifford's? Do you remember it?' I ask. Mum frowns slightly.

'No, I have to say I don't. But I may have forgotten. Or . . .' she reaches behind her, takes the family tree from the sideboard. 'Look at the gap between Caroline getting married, and Meredith being born — seven years! That's rather unusual. There's my great aunt, Evangeline — she died before her first birthday, poor thing.' She points to the name preceding Meredith's, the pitifully short dates in brackets beneath. 'Two babies in seven years is not very many. Perhaps she had a son that died, before she had Meredith, and this ring belonged to that poor little chap.'

'Maybe. But wouldn't he be on the family tree, even if he'd died?'

'Well, not necessarily. Not if he was born prematurely, or was stillborn,' Mum muses. 'I know that Meredith lost a child before I was born. These things can run in families.'

'Perhaps we could talk about something else at the breakfast table?' Beth says quietly. Mum and I button our lips guiltily. Beth miscarried a child, very early on, before Eddie was born. It was little more than a slip of life, but its sudden absence was like a tiny, bright light going out.

'What are we going to do today, then?' Dad asks, helping himself to more scrambled eggs. 'I, for one, feel the need to stretch my legs a bit – walk off some of yesterday's excess.'

'To make room for today's excess, David?' Mum remarks, peering at his plate.

'Quite so!' he agrees cheerfully.

It is brighter today, but grey clouds nose purposefully across the sky and the wind is brisk, penetrating. We take a route through the village, westwards past the little stone church that nestles into a green slope studded with the gravestones of generations of Barrow Storton's dead. In the far corner is the Calcott plot, and in unspoken unity we drift over to it. It is about two metres wide, and as long. A cold bed of marble chippings for our family to sleep in. Henry, Lord Calcott, is in there, and Caroline, with the little daughter she lost before Meredith. Evangeline. And now Meredith has joined them. So recently that the remnants of the funeral flowers are still here in a small, brass pot, and the cuts of her name on the stone are sharp and fresh. I can't help thinking she would rather have had her own place, or lie next to her husband Charles, than spend eternity cooped up with Caroline, but it is too late now. I shudder, make a silent pledge that I will never lie in this claustrophobic family grave.

'I suppose if Caroline had had a son, he'd be buried here, wouldn't he?' I ask, breaking the silence. Beth sighs sharply and walks away, over to where Eddie is climbing the gabled lychgate.

'I suppose so. Probably. But, who knows? If he was very tiny, perhaps they'd have given him an infant's grave instead,' Mum replies.

'What would that look like?'

'Just like a grave with a smaller stone, usually with an angel on it somewhere — or a cherub,' she says. Dad looks at me sidelong.

'I have to say, you're taking a pretty keen interest in this all of a sudden,' he says.

'No, I just . . . you know. I never could stand an unsolved mystery,' I shrug.

'Then I fear you were born into the wrong family.'

'Hey, Eddie!' I call to him. 'Look for small gravestones with angels on them, and the name Calcott!' Eddie rips me a smart salute, begins to trot up and down the rows of stones. Beth folds her arms and glares at me.

'Can we please stop looking for dead babies!' she shouts, the wind pulling at her voice.

'Give me five minutes!' I call back.

'Perhaps we should get on, Erica?' Mum says diffidently.

'Five minutes,' I say again.

I run my eyes along the ranks of stones, in the opposite direction to which Eddie has gone, but they all seem to be of regular size.

'Sometimes there's a special area for the infant graves . . .' Mum sets her gaze to the far corner of the churchyard. 'Try over there — do you see? Under that beech tree.' I walk quickly to where the wind is seething through the naked beech, sounding like the sea. There are perhaps fifteen or twenty graves here. On the older graves are little cherubs, their features blurred with lichen, chubby arms wrapped forlornly around the stones. There are a couple of newer stones too, carved with teddy bears instead; less celestial guardians which seem somehow out of place. But then that's the point, I suppose. An infant has no place in a churchyard. Lives that had no chance to start, losses that must have torn their parents' souls. All those broken hearts are buried here too, alongside the tiny bodies that broke them. It's a melancholy sight and I scan the names and dates hurriedly, walk away from the sad little party with a shiver.

I have never before found graveyards eerie, or particularly depressing. I like the expressions of love on the stones, the quiet declarations of people having existed, of having mattered. Who knows what secret feelings lie behind the carved lists of offspring, siblings and surviving spouses – or if the memories they had were truly loving. But there is the hope, always, that each transient life meant something to those left behind; cast a vapour trail of influence and emotion to fade gradually across the years.

'Anything?' I ask Eddie.

'Nope. There's an angel over there, but the lady was seventy-three and called Iris Bateman.'

'Can we go, now?' Beth says impatiently. 'If you're that desperate to know if she had a son, go and look it up in the births, marriages and deaths register. It's all online now.'

'Perhaps she *was* married before, in America,' Mum says, taking my arm in a conciliatory manner. 'Perhaps the baby in the photograph died there, before she came over.'

To the north of the village is a web of farm tracks and bridleways, dodging through the drab winter fields. We take a circular route, at a brisk pace, falling into pairs to pass along the narrow pathways. Eddie drops back to walk beside me. He is leaving later on today. I look at his sharp face, his scruffy hair, and feel a pull of affection. It gives me such an odd, desperate feeling for a second that I pause to consider how Beth must be feeling. As if reading my mind, Eddie speaks.

'Is Mum going to be OK?' A carefully neutral tone he is too young to have developed.

'Yes, of course,' I tell him, with as much certainty as I can find.

'It's just . . . when Dad came to pick me up last time, before Christmas, she seemed . . . really unhappy about it. She's getting thin again. And, like, today, just now, she was really snappy with you . . .'

'Sisters always snap at each other, Eddie. That's nothing out of the ordinary!' I find a fake laugh and Eddie gives me an accusing look. I drop the bravado. 'Sorry,' I say. 'Look, it's just . . . it's hard for your mum, being back at the manor house. Has she told you about your great-grandma's will? That we can only keep the house if we both come and live in it?' He nods. 'Well, that's why we've come to stay. To see if we would like to come and live here.'

'Why does she hate it so much? Because your cousin was kidnapped – and she misses him?'

'Possibly . . . possibly it's to do with Henry. And the fact that, well, this place is in our past now, and sometimes it can feel wrong to try and live in the past. To be honest, I don't think we'll come to live here, but I'm going to try to make your mum stay for a bit longer at least; even if she doesn't really want to.'

'But why?'

'Well . . .' I struggle for a way to explain. 'Do you remember that time your finger swelled up to the size of a sausage and it was so sore you wouldn't let us look at it properly, but it wouldn't heal up so finally we did look and you had a splinter of metal in it?'

'Yeah, I remember. It looked like it was going to explode,' he grimaces.

'Once we got the splinter out it healed, right?' Eddie nods. 'Well, I think your mum won't . . . heal because she has a splinter. Not of metal, and not in her finger, but she's got a kind of splinter inside her and that's why she can't get better. I'm going to get the splinter out. I'm going to . . . find out what it is and get rid of it.' I hope I sound calm, confident in this purpose; when what I feel is desperate. If I believed in God, I would be striking all kinds of fervent bargains right now. *Make Beth well. Make her happy.*

'How? Why do you have to be here to do it?'

'Because . . . I think this is where she got the splinter in the first place,' I say.

Eddie considers this in silence for a while, his face marked by worried lines I hate to see. 'I hope you do. I hope you can find out what it is,' he says, eventually. 'You will find out, won't you? And she will get better?'

'I promise you, Ed,' I say. And now I must not fail. I *cannot* let us come away from here without a resolution of some kind. The weight of my promise settles onto me like chains.

Our parents leave soon after lunch, and by teatime Maxwell has come for Eddie as well. Maxwell is grouchy, blotches of over-indulgence on his cheeks. He looks mealy-mouthed. I load carrier bags of presents into the boot, Beth watching me blackly as if I am colluding in the theft of her son.

'See you, Edderino,' I say.

'Bye then, *Auntie* Rick,' he says, and climbs into the back. He is calm, resigned. He goes from one place of welcome to the next; he is practical, does not fret. He lets himself be ferried, and pretends not to notice Beth's anguish. There's the smallest hint of cruelty in this, as if he means to say, you made this situation, you set it up this way.

'Did you tell Harry you were going today?' I ask, leaning into the car.

'Yes, but you might have to tell him again, if you see him around. I'm not sure how much attention he was paying.'

'OK. Call your mum later on, won't you?' I keep my voice low.

''Course,' he mutters, looking at his hands.

The brake lights of the car gleam red as they pull out of the drive. It's raining again. Beth and I stand and wave like idiots until the car is out of sight. Our hands drop, in near-perfect unison. Neither one of us wants to turn back to the house now this event is past. Christmas. The preparation of the house, the feeding and entertaining of Eddie, of our parents. Now what? No deadline, no timetable. Nothing to guide us but ourselves. I glance at Beth, see tiny drops of water beading the stray hairs around her face. I can't even ask what she wants for lunch, can't even impose this small future on us. The house is bursting with leftovers, ready to be grazed.

'Eddie's so great, Beth. You've done so well there,' I say, needing to break the silence. But there's a chilly, sad edge to Beth's eyes.

'I'm not sure how much of it comes from me,' she says.

'All the best bits,' I say, taking her hand, squeezing it. She shakes her head. We turn and go inside again, alone.

When she is this quiet, when she is this pale and still, like a carving, I think of her in the hospital. At least I didn't find her. I've only got Eddie's descriptions, making pictures in my head. She was in her bedroom, lying on her side, bent at the waist as if she had been sitting up and then tipped over. He couldn't see her face, he told me. Her hair had fallen right over it. He says he doesn't know how long he stood there before going over to her, because he was too afraid of moving her hair, of seeing what was underneath. His mother, or his dead mother. He needn't have touched her at all, of course. He could have just called an ambulance. But he was a child, a little boy. He wanted to make it right himself. He wanted to touch her and find her sleeping, nothing more. What courage he must have found. To do it – to push back her hair. I am so proud of him it hurts.

She had taken a lot of sleeping pills and then tried to cut her wrists – with the short-bladed paring knife that I had seen her use more than once, slicing banana onto Eddie's cereal – but the conclusion drawn was that she had hesitated. She had hesitated – perhaps because the first cut, deep enough to look bad but not deep enough to do any real damage, had hurt more than she expected. And while she hesitated the pills sank into her bloodstream and she passed out. She had cut her wrist the wrong way. Horizontally, across the vessels and tendons, instead of parallel to them as any serious suicide, these days, knows is best. The doctors called it a cry for help rather than a genuine attempt, but I knew different. I clattered into the hospital, waited while they pumped her stomach. Opposite me in the corridor was a window, blinds drawn. My reflection stared back at me. In the greenish light I looked dead. Lank hair, face drooping. I fed money into a machine; it expelled watery hot chocolate for Eddie. Then Maxwell came and took him away.

When she woke up I went in to see her, and I had no idea until I got to her that I was angry. *So* angry with her. Angrier than I have ever been.

'What were you doing? What about Eddie?' These were my first words. Snapping like a trap.

A nurse with hair the colour of sharp sand scowled at me, said, 'Elizabeth needs her rest,' in an admonishing tone, as if she knew her better than I. There was a bruise on Beth's chin, purple hollows around her eyes, in her cheeks. *What about me?* I wanted to add. Hurt, that she would want to leave me. The same feeling as when she ran off with Dinny, snowballing down the years. She didn't answer me. She started to cry and my heart cracked, let the anger run out. I picked up a matted length of her hair and began chasing out the knots with my fingertips.

It's been a long time since I spoke to my Aunt Mary, let alone telephoned her. I am still reluctant to, but I have got a ball rolling now. I have started to learn things, started to uncover secrets. If I keep going, sooner or later I will get to the ones I am looking for. I shift uncomfortably in the chair as I wait to hear Mary's voice. She was always mousy, quiet; so mild and meek that half the time we didn't even notice her. A pink-skinned woman with pale hair and eyes. Neat blouses, tucked into neat skirts. It was a shock to hear her scream; to hear her shout and cry and curse in the aftermath of

Henry's disappearance. Then when that stopped she was even quieter than before, as if she'd used up all the noise she possessed in that one burst. Her voice is fluting and quiet, as precarious as wet tissue paper.

'Mary Calcott speaking?' So timorous, as if she's really not sure.

'Hello, Aunt Mary, it's Erica.'

'Erica? Oh hello, dear. Happy Christmas. Well, I suppose it's a bit late for that now. Happy New Year.' There is little conviction behind these words. I wonder if she hates us, for surviving when Henry did not. For being around to remind her of it.

'And to you. I hope you're well? You didn't come down with Clifford, to collect those bits and bobs you wanted from the house?'

'No, no. Well, I'm sure you understand that Storton Manor is . . . not an easy place for me. It's not a place I like to think of often, or return to,' she tells me, delicately. I can't warm to her. To put losing her son in such limp terms, as if it was an embarrassing incident, best forgotten. I know how unfair I am being. I know she's not a whole person any more.

'Of course.' I struggle to find more small talk, fail. 'Well, the reason I was calling, and I hope you won't mind me asking, is that I wanted to pick your brains a little about the family research you did, the year before last.'

'Oh, yes?'

'I've found a photo of Caroline, you see, dated 1904, and it was taken in New York . . .'

'Well, that certainly sounds right. She came to London in late 1904. It's hard to be absolutely sure of the date.'

'Yes. The thing is she has a child with her, in the picture. A baby that looks about six months old or so. I just wondered if you had any idea who the baby might have been?'

'A child? Well. I can't think. That can't be right.'

'Was she married before, in the States? Only, the way she's

holding the baby . . . it just looks like a family portrait to me. She looks so proud . . . It looks to me like it's her baby, you see.'

'Oh, no, Erica. That can't be right at all. Let me just get the file down. One moment.' I hear rustling, a cupboard door creaking. 'No, I've got a copy of her marriage certificate to Sir Henry Calcott here, and it clearly says, in the 'condition' column, that she was a spinster. A spinster at twenty-one! Hardly seems an appropriate label, does it?'

'Could she have . . . got a divorce, or something?' I ask, dubiously.

'Goodness me, no. It was very rare in that day and age, and certainly not without it being well talked about. Or mentioned on the occasion of her subsequent marriage. The child must belong to somebody else.'

'Oh. Well, thank you . . .'

'Of course, Caroline was always rather reticent about her early years in America. All anybody could discover was that she had grown up without any close family and had come to England to make a fresh start when she came into her money. She married Henry Calcott very soon after meeting him, which, I have always thought, perhaps shows how lonely she was, poor girl.' Twice now, she has said his name.

'Yes, it does sound that way. Well, thanks for looking it up for me, anyway.'

'You're welcome, Erica. I wonder whether I might ask you to send me the photograph? To add to my presentation files? Early pictures of Caroline and her generation are so very scarce.'

'Oh, well actually, my mother has already asked me to give her any pictures I find. But I'm sure she'd be happy to send you copies of them . . .'

'Of course. Well, I shall ask Laura when I next see her.'

There's a pause and I can't quite bring myself to say goodbye, to admit that this piece of information was all I was after, and that I do not want to talk to her. There is so much to say, so much not to say.

'So . . . how was Christmas?' I ask. I hear her draw in a breath, steeling herself.

'It was fine, thank you.' She pauses again. 'I still buy Henry a present every year, you know. Clifford thinks I am quite mad, of course, but he has never really understood. What it's like for a mother to lose a child. I can't just put it aside and move on, as he has managed to do.'

'What did you get him?' Before I can stop myself.

'A book about the RAF. Some new football boots, and some DVDs,' she says, her voice growing, as if she is pleased about choosing these gifts. Gifts she will never give. I can't think what to say. I would be strangely fascinated to know whether she buys child-sized football boots, or has hazarded a guess at his adult shoe size. 'Do you ever think about your cousin, Erica? Do you still think about Henry?' she asks, rushing the words.

'Of course. Of course I do. Especially now we're . . . back here again.'

'Good. Good. I'm glad,' she says, and I wonder what she means. I wonder if she senses guilt, hanging around Beth and me like a bad smell.

'So there's been no news? Of him – of Henry?' Ridiculous thing for me to ask, twenty-three years after he vanished. But what conclusion can I draw, from the gifts she still buys him, but that she expects someday to have him back?

'No,' she says flatly. A single word; she makes no effort to elaborate.

'Eddie's been here with us for Christmas,' I tell her.

'Who?'

'Edward – Beth's son?'

'Oh yes, of course.'

'He's eleven now, the same age as . . . Well, he had a fine old time, anyway, carousing around out in the woods, getting filthy.'

'Clifford wanted to have another, you know. After we lost Henry. There might still have been time.'

'Oh,' I say.

'But I told him I couldn't. What did he think – that we could just replace him, like a lost watch?' She makes an odd, strangled sound that I think is meant to be a laugh.

'No. No, of course not,' I say. There is another long pause, another long breath from Mary.

'I know you never got on. You girls and Henry. I know that you didn't like him,' she says, suddenly tense, offended.

'We did like him!' I lie. 'It's just . . . well, we liked Dinny too. And we kind of had to choose sides . . .'

'Did it ever occur to you that Henry used to . . . act up, sometimes, because you always left him out of your games and ran off to play with Dinny?' she says.

'No. I . . . never thought he wanted to play with us. He never seemed like he wanted to,' I mumble.

'Well, I think he did. I think it hurt his feelings that you couldn't wait to get away,' she tells me, resolutely. I try to picture my cousin this way – try to shape the way he treated us, treated Dinny, in these terms. But I can't – it won't fit. That's not the way it was, not the way *he* was. A flare of indignation warms me, but of course I can say nothing and the silence buzzes down the line. 'Well, Erica, I really must go,' she says at last, in one long exhalation. 'It was . . . nice to talk to you. Goodbye.'

She hangs up the phone before I can respond. She does not do this crossly, or abruptly. Absently, rather, as if something else has caught her attention. She's had lots of fads and projects in the years since Henry died. Tapestry, watercolours, horoscopes, brass rubbing, Anglo Saxon poetry. The family genealogy was the longest running, the one she really followed through. I wonder if she did it because she got to say his name, over and over again, when Clifford would not allow her to speak of their son. *Henry Calcott, Henry Calcott, Henry Calcott.* Learning everything she could about his ancestors, the source of each component part of him, as if she could rebuild him.

He's dead. This I know. He was not carried off. It wasn't him, lying in the back of a car in a Devizes car park. It wasn't him, being carried by a mysterious hobo on the A361. I know it because I can feel it, I can feel the memory of his death. I can feel it at the dew pond, even if I can't see it. The way I could hear the shape of Dinny in the darkness on Christmas Day. We were there, Henry was there; and Henry died. I have the shape of it. I just need to colour it in. Because I've stalled. I'm blocked. I can't go in any direction until I can fill this hole in my head, until I can work Beth's splinter free. Every other thought must detour around these missing things, and that will not do. Not any longer. And if I must start in 1904 and work my way towards it, then that is what I will do.

Through the kitchen window I see Harry, lingering by the trees at the far end of the garden. It's still raining, harder now. His hands are thrust into the pockets of his patchwork coat and he is hunched, damp, forlorn looking. Without thinking, I pull leftovers from the fridge and larder and start to carve fleshy slices from the cold turkey with its burnt leg stumps. I slather mayonnaise onto two bits of white bread, cram in turkey, and stuffing the consistency of chipboard. Then I take it down to him, wrapped in foil, my coat draped over my head. He doesn't smile at me. He shifts from foot to foot, in an apparent agony of indecision. Rain drips from the ends of his dreadlocks. I catch the scent of his unwashed body. A soft, animal smell, strangely endearing.

'Here, Harry. I made this for your lunch. It's a turkey sandwich,' I say, handing it to him. He takes it. I don't know why I expect him to speak, when I know he won't. It's such a fundamentally human thing, I suppose. To communicate with noise. 'Eddie's gone back to his dad's house now, Harry. Do you understand what I'm saying?

He's not here any more,' I tell him, as kindly as I can. If I knew when Eddie was coming back, I would add this information. I don't. I don't know if we'll be here. I don't know anything. 'His father came today and took him home with him,' I explain. Harry glances at the sandwich. A tiny metallic tune, as rain hits the foil. 'Well, at least eat this,' I say gently, patting his hand on the sandwich. 'It'll keep you going.'

Beth finds me in the study. I am curled up in a leather bucket chair. I stood on the desk to get this book of wild flowers down from the top shelf. It brought a shower of dead flies with it, a smell of past lives. Now it's open, heavy across my knees, at a double-page spread of yellow marsh flags. Ragged, buttery irises. Nonchalantly drooped petals on tall stems, like pennants on a still day. I recognised them as soon as I saw them. Marsh flags.

'The rain's stopped. Do you fancy a quick walk?' Beth asks. She has plaited her hair, put on clean jeans and a jumper the colour of raspberries.

'Absolutely,' I say, all astonishment. 'Yes, let's.'

'What were you reading?'

'Oh, just about wild flowers. There were three old pillowcases up in the press. They had yellow flowers embroidered on them, and I wanted to know what they were.'

'What were they?'

'Marsh flags. Does that ring any bells with you?'

'No. Should it? What kind of bell?'

'Probably a misplaced bell. I'll just get some wellies on.'

We don't walk very far, since the sky is like charcoal on the horizon. Just down into the village and then up to the barrow. I am sure I see one of the girls from the solstice party through the window of the pub. Sitting by the fire, accepting a fresh pint from a man whose back is turned to me. There's a welcoming drench of wood smoke and beer and voices from the doorway, but we carry on past. Lots of villagers out and about today. Walking off the cake and puddings. They all greet us, although I am sure we are not recognised. A few faces tug at me. They slot into my memories somewhere, but too seamlessly for me to pick them out. A stout woman rides past on her horse, silver tinsel woven into its tail.

We cross the tawny grassland up to the barrow, scare up two dozen glossy rooks that had been strutting purposefully. The wind whisks them away, and from a distance they look like ragged shot-holes in the sky. Beth links her arm through mine, walks with a swinging step.

'You seem happy today?' I ask her, carefully.

'I am. I've come to a decision.'

'Oh? What kind of decision?' We've reached the barrow. Beth lets go of my arm, conquers the mound in three long strides and turns to gaze over my head into the distance.

'I'm going. I'm not staying,' she says, throwing her arms wide, girlish, dramatic. She takes a huge breath, lets it out with emphasis.

'What do you mean? Going where?'

'Going home, of course. Later today. I've packed!' she laughs, as if she is wild, reckless. 'I'm taking *that* road,' she says, squinting and pointing to the line of tall poplars that march along the lane out of the village.

'You can't!' The thought of being alone in the house fills me with a dread I can't define. I would rather dive to the bottom of the pond, let it suck me down. I feel something like panic sputtering in my stomach.

'Of course I can. Why stay? What are we even *doing* here? I can't even remember why we came. Can you?'

'We came to . . . we came to sort things out. To . . . decide what we wanted to do!' I grope for words.

'Come on, Erica. Neither of us wants to live here.' She drops her arms as she says this, looks at me suddenly. 'You don't, do you? You don't want to live here? You don't want to stay?'

'I don't know yet!'

'But . . . you can't want to. It's *Meredith's* house. Everything about it says *Meredith*. And then there's . . . the other thing.'

'Henry?' I say. She nods, just once. Short and sharp. 'It's *our* house, Beth. Yours and mine now.'

'Oh my God, you want to stay. You do, don't you?' She is utterly incredulous.

'I don't know! I don't know. Not for ever, perhaps. For a while, maybe. I don't know. But please don't go, Beth! Not yet. I'm . . . I'm not done. I can't go yet and I can't stay here on my own. Please. Stay a bit longer.' On top of the barrow Beth sags. I have stabbed her, let out all the air. We are quiet for a while. The wind rolls over the ridge, trembles the grasses. I see Beth shiver. She looks impossibly lonely up there.

At length she comes down to me, her eyes lowered.

'I'm sorry,' I say.

'What do you mean, you're not done yet?' Her voice is flat now, lifeless.

'I need to . . . find out what happened. I need to remember.' A half-truth. I can't tell her about her splinter. I can't let her know what I am working towards. She would snatch herself away, not let me touch; just like Eddie with his swollen finger.

'Remember what?'

I stare at her. She must know what I'm talking about.

'About *Henry*, Beth. I need to remember what happened to Henry.' She glares at me now, eyes reflecting the grey sky. She searches my face, and I wait.

'You remember what happened. Don't lie. You were old enough.'

'But I don't. I really don't,' I say. 'Please tell me.' Beth looks away, past the rooftops and chimney trails of the village below and into the east, as if projecting herself there.

'No. I won't tell you,' she says. 'I won't tell anyone. Not *ever*.'

'Please, Beth! I have to know!'

'No! And if . . . if you love me, you'll stop asking.'

'Does Dinny know?'

'Yes, of *course* Dinny knows. Why don't you ask him?' She flicks her eyes at me. There's a chilly touch of resentment there. For an instant, then it's gone. 'But you know, too. And if you really don't remember then . . . then maybe that's a good thing.' She walks away from me, along the ridge towards the house.

She stops at the dew pond. This is the first time she's been back to it, that I know of, and it halts her so abruptly that I almost run into her. The wind skids over its surface, turns it matt and ugly. I expect to see her crying, but her eyes are dry and hard. The sad lines on her face, etched deeper than ever. She stares down into it.

'I was so scared, the first time you swam here,' she murmurs, so quietly I can hardly hear. 'I thought you wouldn't be able to get out. Like the hedgehog in the pond at home, that time. Do you remember? It had swum around and around until it was too exhausted to swim any more, and then it just drowned. All those videos we were shown at school — never to swim in quarries or rivers. I thought water without chlorine in it had some dreadful, lurking power that waited and watched and ate little kids.'

'I remember you yelling at me like a harpy.'

'I was scared for you,' she says, shrugging minutely. 'Now you spend all your time being scared for me. Except today. *Why* do I have to stay? You must see that . . . it's bad for me, being here?'

'No, I . . . I think it could be good for you,' I force myself to say.

'What do you mean?' she asks me, darkly. My heart beats faster.

'I mean what I say. You can't keep running from this, Beth! Please! If you would just talk about it—'

'No! I've told you — over and over. Not to you and not to anybody!'

'Why not to me? I'm your *sister*, Beth, nothing you could tell me would make me love you any less! Nothing,' I say firmly.

'That's what you think, is it? That there's something despicable in me that I'm trying to hide?' she whispers.

'No, Beth, that's what I *don't* think! You're not listening to me! But you *are* hiding something – you can't deny it. I have no secrets from you!'

'Everybody has secrets, Erica,' she snaps. It's true, and I look away.

'All I want is for us to be able to leave this place behind . . .'

'Good! That's what I want, too! So let's do it – let's leave.'

'Leaving it isn't the same as leaving it *behind*, Beth! Look at you – since we've been back here it's been like sharing the house with a ghost! You're . . . miserable and you seem determined to stay that way!' I shout.

'What are you *talking* about?' Beth shouts back at me, spreading her hands in fury. '*You're* the one determined to keep me here – you're the one determined to make me miserable! I only came here at all because you pressured me into it!'

'I'm determined to get rid of whatever it is that's keeping you down, Beth. And it's here – I know it is. It's here at this house – don't walk away from me!' I grab her arm, stop her. Beth is breathing hard, will not look me in the eye. Her face is pale.

'If you don't let me go, I might not ever forgive you. I don't know what I will do,' she says, her voice trembling. Startled, I drop my hand from her arm but I don't think this is what she means. I am afraid of what she will do. My resolve wavers, but I fight to hold on to it.

'Please, Beth. Please stay here with me. At least until the new year. Let's just . . . figure this out. Whatever it is.'

'Figure it out?' she echoes me, bitterly. 'It's not a riddle, Erica.'

'I know that. But life can't go on the way it has been. This is our *chance*, Beth – our chance to put things right.'

'Some things can't be undone, Erica. The sooner you accept that the better,' she whispers. Tears are bright in her eyes, but when she looks up at me they are full of anger. 'It can't be put right!' she snaps, and storms away from me. I pause before I follow her, find that I am shaking.

For the rest of the day we play hide and seek. This house always was perfect for it. The rain comes in sideways, draughts creep down the chimneys. I bring Harry inside and make him a cup of sweet tea. He sits at the kitchen table sucking it from his teaspoon like a child. He drips water onto the floor, fills the room with the smell of wet wool. But I can't find Beth to give her a cup of tea. I can't find her to ask what she wants for dinner, if she wants to go out anywhere, if she wants to rent a film from the garage on the road to Devizes. I feel it is my job, now, to fill her time. Time I am forcing her to spend here. But she melts into the house like a cat, and I stomp from room to room in vain.

Henry once left her hiding for hours. Left her alone, trapped, panicked. He made me part of it, again. I was small. I must have been – Caroline was still alive. Earlier that day she'd been wheeled outside to the terrace. She had one of those grand old wicker wheelchairs. No grey NHS metal and plastic for her. It creaked as it rolled along, fine spokes glinting, but Henry said it was Caroline that creaked, because she was so old and mummified. I knew it was nonsense but even so, each time I heard it, I would think of papery skin tearing; of hair that would crumble to dust if you touched it; of a tongue gone stiff and woody in a shrivelled mouth. We were never made to kiss her, if we didn't want to. Mum saw to that, and thank goodness.

By then she was mostly bedridden, but it was a fine day and we were all there – Clifford and Mary, my parents. She was wheeled to the table, presented with her lunch on a tray that slotted into the frame of the chair. The housekeeper brought out the soup in a white china tureen shaped like a giant cauliflower, and there were potatoes and salad and ham on the table. I was told off for dipping my fingers into the melted butter at the bottom of the potato bowl. Meredith helped Caroline to eat, sometimes feeding her the way you feed a baby. Meredith frowned as she did it; pinched her lips tightly together. Caroline's hair was thin. I could see her scalp through it and it *did* look papery. The conversation went on around her, and I kept my eyes carefully on my plate. Only once did she speak up and, though her voice was louder than I expected, the words crept out ponderously.

'Is that man Dinsdale still alive?' She dropped her fork as she spoke, as if holding it and speaking were too many things to do at once. It clattered loudly, down onto the paving slabs.

'No, Mother. He's not,' Meredith answered, and I burned with the knowledge that there were in fact many Dinsdales, alive and well not two hundred metres from where we sat. I knew better than to speak at the table. Caroline made a small sound, high and wavering, which could have been anything. Satisfaction, perhaps. 'I believe his son is, however,' Meredith added.

'Can't you get *rid* of him, child?' Caroline asked, and I was as puzzled to hear Meredith called *child* as I was outraged at the question. Across the table, Henry smirked, kicked me in the shin.

'No more than you could,' Meredith countered.

'Travellers,' Caroline mumbled. 'They were meant to go. They were meant to move on,' she said.

'They go. And then they come back again,' Meredith muttered. 'And sadly there is very little I can do about it.' At this Caroline went still. An unnatural pause, as if she was going to say something else. Everybody at the table waited, but she did not speak again. Meredith folded her napkin crisply onto her lap, began to serve herself with salad. But the frown stayed, knitted between her brows, and when I looked at Caroline she was staring out across the lawn, eyes boring into the far trees as though she could see straight through them. Her head wobbled on her neck, and from time to time her hands would twitch involuntarily, but that far, pale gaze never wavered.

After that lunch we children were sent to have an afternoon nap — because I was small and cross, Henry had been rude at lunch, and that left Beth with nobody to play with. Henry instigated the game. He hid first, and we found him at length in the attic room, behind the same crumbling, burgundy leather trunk I have so recently rediscovered. We stirred up motes of dust that flashed and swirled in the light from the eaves, circling slowly. I found a peacock butterfly, wrapped in spider webs and as mummified as I feared Caroline to be. I clamoured for it to be my turn to hide, but Beth had found Henry first, so it was her turn. Henry and I knelt at the bottom of the stairs, shut our eyes, counted.

I don't think I could count to a hundred at that age. I was relying on Henry, and he normally counted *one, two, miss a few, ninety-nine, a hundred*; so after what seemed a long time, listening to the housekeeper clattering dishes in the kitchen, I opened one eye to check on him. He wasn't there. I looked up and saw him coming down the stairs. He smiled nastily at me, and I cast my eyes around. I did this instinctively, whenever I found myself alone with that look on Henry's face. In case help was at hand. My heart quick in my chest.

'Is it time to find Beth yet?' I whispered at last.

'No. Not yet. I'll tell you when,' he said. 'Come on, then, come with me.' He used his fake-nice voice, a high pitch that he also used to trick the Labradors. He offered me his hand and I took it unwillingly. We went into the study; he put the TV on.

'Is it time now?' I asked again. Something was wrong. I made for the door but he put out his leg, blocked me.

'Not yet! I told you — you can't go and look until I say it's time.'

I waited. I was miserable. I didn't watch what was on the TV. I looked at Henry, at the door, back again. What's time, when you're five years old? I have no idea how long I was made to wait. It must have been over an hour, and it felt like an eternity. When the door creaked open, I ran to it. My father came in, asked where Beth was. He studied my anxious face and asked again. Henry shrugged. Dad and I went all over the house, calling. On the top floor corridor we heard her – banging, and faint sounds of distress. The final set of stairs, up to the attic, had a cupboard underneath, an iron key in the lock. Dad turned it, lifted the latch and Beth tumbled out, her face pale and streaked with dirt and tears.

'What on earth?' Dad said, gathering her up. She was breathing so hard that her own sobs half choked her, and her eyes stared out in a way that frightened me. It was as if she had closed herself off from me, from the world. Fear had made her hide inside her own head. The cupboard was cramped and cobwebby, and the light switch was on the outside. Henry had turned it off and turned the key in the lock while I kept my eyes closed and assumed he was counting. Left her alone in the dark with the spiders and no room to turn around. I knew all this, I told my dad, and he demanded the truth from Henry. Beth stood behind him, unnaturally quiet. There were pale patches of dust on her knees, grazes on the heels of her hands; something had caught a lock of her hair, pulled it out of her Alice band in a sagging loop.

'It was nothing to do with *me*. I've been down here all the time. We got bored of looking for her,' Henry shrugged, swinging his legs to and fro with excitement although he managed to keep his face straight. Beth had stopped crying. She was looking at Henry with a bright hatred that shocked me.

It's mid-afternoon and I am upstairs, wedged onto the window sill in my bedroom. My breath has steamed up the glass, obscured the view, but I am reading so it doesn't matter. More of Meredith's letters to Caroline. I am surprised that Meredith kept them all – that she stowed them away with Caroline's things, as a record of their troubled relationship. Letters belong to the recipient, I know, but it would have been easy, and understandable, for her to destroy them after her mother died. But perhaps she wanted them for exactly what they recorded. The fact that she tried to have another life, even if she failed.

Dear Mother,

Thank you for the card you sent. I can only say that I am as well as can be expected. I have my hands very full with Laura, who has recently started walking and has consequently taken to running rings around me — it is nigh on impossible to keep her out of mischief. Her particular passion this week is for mud and worms. I have an excellent nanny, a local girl called Doreen, who has a calming influence on the child — and on me, I must say. Nothing seems to fluster her, and in these troubled days, that is a virtue indeed. I have given your invitation to return to live with you at Storton Manor a great deal of thought, but for the time being I intend to remain in my own home. I have the support of my neighbours, who have proved themselves most sympathetic in my hour of need. Many of the local women have sons and husbands away fighting, and each time the much dreaded telegram arrives a contingent is dispatched to make sure that there is food in the house, and the children clothed, and the wife or mother still breathing. I dare say you would not approve of the social classes mingling in this way, but I was greatly moved to receive just such a visit myself when word of Charles' death got about. I went to London last Friday, to collect what belongings of his remained at his club and offices. You would not believe the scenes of devastation I witnessed there. It was enough to chill the very heart of me.

So I will stay for as long as I can manage to do so, because, though it pains me greatly to commit such a thing to paper, I have not yet forgiven you, Mother. For not coming to Charles' funeral. Your objections to him as a husband were never as great, and your dislike of travelling never so strong, that either should have prevented you from attending, and insulting him in this way. The snub did not go unnoticed amongst our acquaintances. And what of me? Do you not realise that I should have liked to have you there, that I needed your support on such a day? Surely there are limits to the stoicism a new widow should have to display? That is all I will say for the time being. I must grow accustomed to life without my husband, and I must take care of myself, little Laura and my unborn child. For now I do not think you or any one can ask anything more of me.

Meredith.

As I finish reading I am interrupted by the clang of the doorbell. I climb down from the sill, wincing, the blood rushing into my stiff legs. I make my way to the top of the stairs, pause when I hear Beth open the door, and Dinny's voice. My first impulse is to carry on, rush down the stairs to see him, to ease things for them. But my feet don't respond. I stay still, my hand on the banister, listening.

'How are you, Beth?' Dinny asks, and the question carries more weight than it normally would. More significance.

'I'm very well, thank you,' Beth answers, something odd in her tone that I can't identify.

'Only . . . Erica said that you—'

'Erica said that I what?' she says sharply.

'That you weren't happy to be back. That you wanted to leave.' I can't hear Beth's reply to this. If she makes one. 'Can I come in?' he says, almost nervously.

'No. I . . . I think you'd better not. I'm . . . busy right now,' Beth lies, and I feel her tension, making my shoulders ache.

'Oh. Well, I really just came up to say thanks to Erica for the baby things she took down to Honey. Honey even smiled when I got back – it was amazing.' I smile as I hear this, but I don't know if Beth will understand how rare Honey's smiles seem to be.

'Oh, well . . . I'll pass that on. Or shall I call her down?' Beth asks stiffly.

'No, no. No need,' Dinny says, and my smile fades. There's a pause. I feel a draught from the open door, whispering up the stairs to me. 'Listen, Beth, I'd like to talk to you about . . . what happened. There are some things I think you don't understand—'

'No!' Beth interrupts him, her voice higher now, alarmed. 'I don't want to talk about it. There's nothing to talk about. It's in the past.'

'Is it, though?' he asks softly, and I hold my breath, waiting for Beth's answer.

'Yes! What do you mean? Of course it is.'

'I mean, some things are hard to leave behind. Hard to forget about. Hard for me to forget about, anyway.'

'You just have to try hard,' she says bleakly. 'Try harder.'

I can hear the movement of feet, on the flagstones. I can picture Beth twisting, trying to escape.

'It's not that simple, though, is it, Beth?' he says, his voice stronger now. 'We used to be . . . we used to be able to talk about anything, you and I.'

'That was a very long time ago,' she says.

'You know, you don't get to call *all* the shots, Beth. You can't just pretend nothing happened, you can't wash your hands of it – of me.'

'I *don't want to talk about it.*' She emphasises each word, hardens them with feeling.

'You may not have a choice. There are things you need to hear,' Dinny says, every bit as firmly.

'Please,' Beth says. Her voice has shrunk, it is meek and afraid. 'Please don't.'

There's a long, empty pause. I daren't breathe.

'It's good to see you again, Beth,' Dinny says at length, and again this is not the flippant remark it usually is. 'I was starting to think I never would. See you again, that is.'

'We shouldn't be here. I wouldn't be, if it weren't for . . .'

'And you'll go again soon, will you?'

'Yes. Soon. After New Year.'

'Never a backward glance?' he asks, a bitter edge to the words.

'No,' Beth says, but the word does not sounds as firm as it should. The cold air makes me shiver and I am shot through with desperation again, to know what it is that they know, to remember it.

'I'll go, then.' Dinny sounds defeated. 'Thank Erica for me. I hope . . . I hope I'll see you again, Beth. Before you disappear.' I do not hear Beth's reply, only the door shutting and a sudden loud sigh, as if a thousand pent-up words rush out of her at once and echo around the hallway.

I stay on the stairs for a short while, listen as Beth goes into the study. I hear the whoosh of a chair as she sits down abruptly, then nothing more. It would be easier, I think, to squeeze truths from the stones of these walls than to squeeze them from my sister. In frustration, I return to the attic, flip open the lid of the red trunk with none of my usual care, and run my fingers through Caroline's possessions once more. There has to be something more, something I have missed. Something to tell me who the baby in the photo was and what happened to him. Something to tell me why she hated the Dinsdales so much that there was no room left inside her to love her own child. But once I have taken everything out, I am none the wiser. I stop, sit back on my heels, notice that my hands are shaking. And as I pick up a paper parcel, reach in to put it back, something catches my eye. A tear in the lining paper at the bottom of the trunk; a tear that has left a loose flap. And, half hidden beneath the paper, an envelope. I reach for it, see that the hand-writing is not Meredith's, and as I read the letter inside my pulse quickens.

Scrambling to my feet, I rush down to the study. The fire is devouring a huge pile of wood, pouring out heat.

'Beth – I've found something! Up in Caroline's things,' I tell her. She looks up at me, her face drawn. She has not forgiven me yet, for the things I said at the dew pond.

'What is it?' she asks flatly.

'It's a letter to Caroline – it had got lost. I found it in the lining of her trunk, and it's very old – from before she came to England. Listen to this!' The envelope is another very small one; the paper inside it so old that the ink has faded to a weak brown colour. The pages are spotted and torn, as if much handled; read and reread over a spread of long years. When I open it out, the sheets tear along the folds a little. I touch it as gently as I can. In places, I can hardly make out what it says, but there is enough here, enough to prove a theory.

'*April 22nd, 1902*,' I read. '*My Darling Caroline – I received your letter and was much dismayed to hear that you had not received mine – nor the one before it, it would seem! Please rest assured that I have been writing – that I do write, almost every night. There is so much work to be done here, to ready it for your arrival, that I am ending each day fairly well beat, but nevertheless I think of you every night, I swear it to you. We have been greatly hampered by spring storms here – the day before yesterday hailstones the size of my fist came down in a shower that could have killed a man! This wild land needs a gentle female hand to tame it, love. And I know that I will not be troubled by any such tempests once you are here at my side.*

'*Please do not fret about your Aunt's departure – here you will have all the home and family that you will ever need! I know it troubles you to part on bad terms with her, but surely* . . . I can't make out what it says next. In fact, most of this paragraph . . .' I squint at it. '*I have seen to it that* . . . *It pains me to* . . . *Be patient for just a little while longer, my darling, and before you know it we will be together. I have found a place beside the house where I am going to make you a garden.*

I remember you told me once how much you would love to have a garden. Well, you shall have one of your very own, and you can grow in it whatever you wish to. The soil here is a little sandy, but many things will flourish in it. And we will flourish here, I know it. My heart reminds me of your absence every day, and I thank God that we will soon be reunited.

'There's a huge chunk here that I can't make out at all – it looks like it got wet or something, at some point,' I interrupt myself, scanning down the rest of the page. 'Then he finishes: *I long to see you again, and it gladdens my heart to know that you will soon be setting out to journey here to me. Be at ease, darling – very soon we will begin the rest of our lives. Yours always, C.* How about that, then?'

'So, she was married!' Beth exclaims.

'It would seem so . . . nothing actually says that they were but I can't think of another reason, back then, that he would write a letter like that – about starting their lives together and her having a new family and all the rest of it.'

'Where was she travelling to? What does the postmark say?' I study the envelope.

'I can't make it out. It's totally worn away.'

'Shame. What if she was meant to travel out to marry him and something happened before she got there?'

'But then what about the baby?'

'True. So she lost a husband and a baby before she even came over here. And she was how old at that point?'

'Twenty-one, I think. She'd just come into her money.'

'How amazing – that none of it was on her marriage certificate, or was known until now! I wonder how it was forgotten?' Beth muses.

I shrug. 'Who knows. If she divorced him, maybe she wanted it kept quiet? Mary said that Caroline never wanted to talk about her early years – perhaps she had something to hide. And remember that letter from Aunt B I showed you – that mentioned things that happened in America staying in America. She was definitely worried about a scandal of some kind. If her husband had died, it would have just said widow on her marriage certificate to Lord Henry. She must have left him. And if her baby died, that might explain why she was always so frosty, so impenetrable.' At this Beth falls quiet.

She has not mentioned Dinny's visit to the house. She has not passed on his thanks to me, and I can't find out if this is deliberate, or an oversight, without letting on that I was listening. But it is niggling me. I itch to hear what it is he wants to say to her.

'What's wrong?' I ask.

'Erica, why are you so keen to know all this? To know everything?' She looks across at me from the shadow of her hair, her long eyelashes. The fire behind her gives her an orange gleam.

'Don't you find it interesting? I want to know why . . . why our family hates the Dinsdales. Hated the Dinsdales,' I correct myself. 'I want to know how Meredith got as cruel as she did – as bitter and twisted as she did. And the answer seems to be that she inherited it from Caroline. And I just want to know *why* . . .'

'And you think you've found out?'

'Why they hated the Dinsdales? No. I have no clue about that. It couldn't just have been class prejudice – it had to be more than that. It *was* more than that. It was *personal*. And anyway, in her letters it sounds like Meredith wasn't that bothered when class barriers started to come down during the war. But at least I think I know why Caroline was so cold. Why, as Mum said, she never loved Meredith.'

'Because she lost a child?'

'Lost a whole life, by the sounds of it. You remember that time, at that summer ball, when Caroline thought she recognised the waitress?'

'Yes?'

'I wonder who she thought it was. I wonder why she was so upset by her.'

Again Beth doesn't answer, blocks herself from me in that way I can't stand. 'And I can't get those blasted marsh flags out of my head! I'm sure I remember something about them . . .' But Beth isn't listening to me any more.

'Losing a child . . . I can't imagine how that must feel. A child that has had the chance to grow, to become a real person. When your love for it has had years to deepen. I just can't imagine.'

'Neither can I.'

'No, but you can't even begin to, Erica, because you don't know what it feels like – you don't know how strong that love is,' she tells me intensely.

'There's lots I don't know,' I aver, hurt. In the silence, the fire pops, shifts as it burns down.

'We never missed Henry,' she murmurs, sinking back into the shadow of the armchair so that I cannot see her face clearly. 'We saw the search for him and the way it nearly pulled the family apart. In a way, we saw the consequences of . . . what happened. But we never *missed* him. We were only ever on the edges of it . . . of the mess. The pain it caused . . .'

'It was hard to miss him, Beth. He was vile.'

'He was vile, but he was just a little boy. Just a little boy, Erica. He was so young! I don't know . . . I don't know how Mary survived it,' she says, her throat tightening around the words. I don't think Mary did survive it, not entirely. For a hideous moment I picture Beth being like Mary. Beth, twenty years from now, every bit as empty and deadened as Mary. For surely that is how it will go, if I do not manage to heal her. If I have got it wrong – if I have made it worse, bringing her here. I do not trust myself to speak. In my hands the letter to Caroline is as light as air; so insubstantial, the words of this lost man barely touching the pages, his voice whispering down the years, fading into the past. I touch my fingers to the *C* with which he signed himself, send out a silent thought to him, back through time, as if he might somehow hear it, and take comfort.

It's late now and Beth went to bed hours ago. Only two days since Christmas Day, since I last saw Dinny, and yet there's a kind of quiet desperation gathering beneath my ribs. If Beth won't tell me what happened then Dinny has to. He has to. Which means I have to ask him; and I know, I *know* he does not want to be asked. Pitch black outside but I haven't bothered to draw the curtains. I like sitting in full view of the night. There's some stupid film on the television, but the sound is turned down and I have been staring at the fire as it dies, and thinking, thinking. Nobody else to hear this wild weather but me, but it's comforting to know she is up there. The house gives me an empty feeling. Without her it would be unbearable. Now and then a drop of rain makes it down to the embers, hisses as it lands. A shred of what was wrapping paper, now a grey ghost of itself, is stuck to the grate. It bends this way and that in the vacillating updraft, as the wind curls into the chimney pots. I am hypnotised by it.

What would have happened, if Henry hadn't vanished? Perhaps Meredith wouldn't have grown ever more unpleasant, as she did. Mum might not have fallen out with her as she did, finally driven to the end of her patience, the end of her forgiveness. Clifford and Mary would have kept on coming, would not have been passed over for the house when the time came. I know it irks Clifford terribly, to be missing out on the house. A king without a castle. He kept on visiting but it wasn't enough. Mary's refusal to come near the place peeved Meredith sufficiently. *Does she want to be a Calcott or doesn't she, Clifford? Such cowardice!* Henry would be the Honourable Henry Calcott, just waiting for Clifford to die before he could slip on the *Lord*. Beth and I would have spent more summers here. Perhaps we would have grown up with Dinny. Beth and

Dinny, together; awkward, tentative, passionate teenagers. I shut my eyes, banish the thought.

There's a knock behind my shoulder, and a face at the black glass that makes me gasp. It's Dinny, and I stare stupidly, as if he's walked right out of my thoughts. The rain has slicked his hair to his forehead and his collar is turned up against the cold. I open the window and the wind snatches it, almost pulls it out of my hand.

'I'm sorry to . . . sorry it's so late, Erica. I saw the light was on. I need help.' There is rainwater on his lips, and I can taste it. He is breathing hard, looks scattered.

'What's wrong? What's happened?'

'Honey's gone into labour and . . . something's wrong. Erica, something's going wrong and all the vans are bogged in after all this pissing rain . . . We need to get to hospital. Can you take us? Please? It'll be quicker than waiting for an ambulance to find the place . . .'

'Of course I will! But if I drive down to you my car will just get stuck too . . .'

'No, no – just go to the top of the green lane, can you? I'll carry her up to you.'

'OK. OK. Are you sure you can carry her?'

'Just go, please – we need to hurry!'

Dinny vanishes from the window, back into the dark. I scrabble for my car keys, my coat, pause only for a second to think I should tell Beth. But she is probably asleep and I can't wait to explain it to her. I shove my mobile into my pocket and run for the car. The rain streams over the windscreen in an unbroken wave. In the short sprint from the house my shoulders are soaked. I am breathing hard, too hard. My hands shake as I try to find the ignition and I have to stop, make myself calmer. The driveway is potted with puddles and I splash out onto the road, wipers flailing.

There's no sign of them as I pull in at the top of the green lane. My headlights flare on the hedgerow, flood away towards the camp. I trot down the track, slipping. The ground is slimy. Grass pulls away beneath my feet, dissolves to nothing. I hear the wind plaguing the trees in the darkness. They crash like an invisible ocean. I stop at the far reach of the car's headlights and stare into the blackness. Rain comes in through the seams of my shoes. Then I see them, making slow progress, and as I lurch towards them Dinny slips and falls onto one knee, fighting to keep his balance with the bulk of the pregnant girl teetering in his arms. Honey grips his shoulders, fear turning her hands into claws.

'Can you walk?' I ask Honey, as I reach them. She nods, grimacing. 'Dinny, let go! Let her get to her feet!'

He tilts to the side, lowers Honey's feet to the ground then levers her up. She is upright for a second before she doubles over, cries out.

'*Fuck!*' she howls. I take her other hand and her nails bite into me. Drenched hair shrouds her face. 'This can't be right . . . it can't be right,' she moans.

'Her waters broke discoloured,' Dinny tells me.

'I don't know what that means!' I cry.

'It means trouble. The baby's in trouble,' he says. 'It means we need to move!' But Honey is still doubled up and now she is sobbing. In pain or fear, I can't tell.

'It's going to be OK,' I tell her. 'Listen – really, it's going to be OK. Are you sure you can walk? The car's not much further.' Honey nods, her eyes tight shut. She is breathing like bellows. My heart is racing but I feel calm now. I have a purpose.

We reach the car and manoeuvre Honey into the back seat. I have mud up to my knees. Honey is soaked to the skin, pale and shivering.

'I'll drive. You help Honey,' Dinny says, moving towards the driver's door.

'No! She needs you, Dinny! And it's my car. And the steering is a little snappy in the wet. It'll be safer if I drive,' I shout.

'One of you fucking well drive!' Honey shouts. I push past Dinny, take the driver's seat, and he climbs into the back. We skid off the verge, slalom down the lane, make for the main road.

I take us to Devizes at a reckless pace, as fast as I dare, squinting into the tunnelling rain. But when I corner Honey is thrown about in the back seat and so I slow down, unsure of what is best. She cries quietly between contractions, as if to herself, and Dinny seems dumbstruck.

'Not far now, Honey! You're going to be fine, please don't be scared! They'll whip that baby out faster than you can say *epidural*,' I shout, glancing at her in the mirror. I hope I am not lying to her.

'It's not far?' she gasps, eyes on my reflection, pleading.

'Five minutes, I promise. And they'll take good care of you and the baby. It's going to be fine. Right, Dinny?' He jumps as if I've startled him. His knuckles around Honey's hands are white.

'Right. Yes, right. You're going to be fine, sweetheart. Just hang in there.'

'Have you thought of any names?' I ask. I want to distract her. From her fear, from the cold, wet night, from the pain shining her face with sweat.

'Er . . . I think, um, I think . . . Callum, if it's a boy . . .' she pants, and pauses, her face curling up as a contraction ripples across her midriff.

'And for a girl?' I press.

'Girl . . . for a girl . . . Haydee . . .' she groans, tries to sit up taller. 'I need to push!'

'Not yet! Not yet! We're nearly there!' I press the accelerator flat as the orange glow of town grows in front of us.

I pull up right in front of the hospital and Dinny is out of the car before it stops. He comes back with help, and a wheelchair.

'Here we go, Honey.' I turn around to her, take her hand. 'You'll be fine now.' She squeezes my hand, tears rolling down her face, and there is no trace of her attitude, her fire, the disdainful tilt of her chin. She looks little more than a child. The rain batters the roof of the car for one quiet moment, then the back door is pulled open, and they take her out, and she shouts at them, and swears, and we pile into the building, blinking in the harsh light. I follow them as far as I can, along three clattering corridors, through several doors, until I am lost. At the last set of doors somebody stops Dinny and me. A hand on my upper arm, kind but implacable.

'Partners only from here, I'm afraid. You can wait back down the hall – there's a waiting room there,' the man tells me, pointing back the way we have come.

'You're Honey's partner?' he asks Dinny.

'Yes – no. I'm her brother. She's got no partner,' he says.

'Right. Come on then.' They disappear through the doors, leave them swinging in their wake. The doors make a sweeping sound and a thump, as they pass each other, once, twice, three times. My breathing slows with them, and then they fall still. Dinny is her brother.

The clock on the wall is just like the one that used to hang in my classroom at school. Round, white plastic with a yellowing fade, the thin red second hand ticking around with a tremble. It says ten to one as I sink into a green plastic chair, and I watch as it creeps round and round, wondering how it hadn't occurred to me that Dinny might have a sister. He didn't have one when we were little, so I assumed he still didn't have one. They look nothing alike. I think back, rake through all my memories, try to remember ever seeing them touch each other, or speak to each other as if they were a couple. They never did, of course. A feeling appears in me, to know he is not hers, it is not his baby. I feel a tentative hope.

Half past three and I am still the only person in this square waiting room. People go along the corridor occasionally, their shoes squeaking on the floor tiles. My legs are heavy from sitting too long. I am drifting into a kind of daze. I see Dinny's camp in my mind's eye, on a summer day – early summer, with spent tree blossoms raining down on a light breeze, and sunshine glancing from the metal grilles of the parked vans. Grandpa Flag dozing in his chair – the wind lifting the coarse ends of his graphite hair, but otherwise he would sit so still. He never said that much to us, but I always thought of him as kind, safe. He would slump, as if fast asleep, but then suddenly laugh at something that was said or done. A loud guffaw, booming from his chest. Always a battered hat, pulled low over his face; and in its shadow, dark eyes gleamed. Leathery cheeks, deeply scored. A lifetime outdoors had tanned him the colour of hazelnuts. The colour of Dinny's arms in the summertime. They made him move, again and again. The police, in the days after it happened. Grandpa Flag watched them with his calm, penetrating gaze. They made everybody move their vans, time and time again, with a roar of engines and plumes of diesel smoke. One trailer, belonging to a man called Bernie, needed a tow to move it. Mickey and the other men put their shoulders to it, shifted it, did as they were told even though Bernie's trailer was high enough from the ground to make looking underneath it easy. I asked Mum what they were looking for. *Fresh earth*, she told me shortly, and I didn't understand.

A figure passing the door rouses me – Dinny, walking slowly. I run clumsily into the corridor.

'Dinny – what's happened? Is everything OK?'

'Erica? What are you still doing here?' He looks dazed, battered and amazed to see me there.

'Well, I . . . I was waiting to hear. And I thought you'd want a ride back.'

'I thought you'd have gone – you needn't have waited all this time! I can take the bus back . . .'

'It's half past three.'

'Or a taxi then,' he amends, stubbornly.

'Dinny – will you tell me how Honey is? And the baby?'

'Fine, she's fine,' he smiles. 'The kid was upside down but she managed to do it, eventually. It's a girl and she's doing well.' His voice is rough, he sounds exhausted.

'That's great! Congratulations, Uncle Dinny,' I say.

'Thanks,' he grins, a touch bashfully.

'So, how long do they have to stay in?'

'A couple of days. Honey lost a fair amount of blood and the baby's a little jaundiced. They're both fast asleep now.'

'You look shattered. Do you want a ride home?' I offer. Dinny rubs his eyes with his forefinger and thumb.

'Yes, please,' he nods.

The weather has not let up. I drive at a more cautious pace. The countryside is so black, empty. I feel as though we're carving a tunnel through it, the only two people in the world. I am light-headed with fatigue but too tired for sleep. I have to concentrate hard on driving safely. I open my window a little; cold air hits me, flecks of rainwater. The roar of it fills the car, cloaks the weight of the silence between us.

'You never said Honey was your sister. I didn't realise,' I say, not quite lightly.

'Who did you think she was?'

'Well . . . I thought she was . . . I don't know . . .'

'You thought she was my girlfriend?' he asks incredulously, then laughs out loud. 'Erica – she's fifteen years old!'

'Well, I didn't know that!' I say defensively. 'What was I supposed to think? You didn't have a sister the last time I saw you.'

'No, I didn't. She was born well after you left. A late bonus, my mother called her.' He smiles slightly. 'Now she's not so sure.'

'What do you mean?'

'Well, you've met her. Honey doesn't have the easiest temperament.'

'So what happened? How come she's been staying with you?'

'The baby. When she got pregnant Mum wanted her to get rid of it. She thought it would ruin her life, having a baby so young.

Honey refused. So Mum said fine, have it adopted, and again she wouldn't. They had a massive row and then Keith weighed in as well. So Honey flounced out and was told not to come back.' He sighs. 'They're just angry with each other, that's all.'

'Keith's your mum's new husband?'

'They're not married, but yes, to all intents and purposes. He's OK. A bit strait-laced.'

'I can't really imagine your mother with somebody strait-laced.'

'No, well, neither can Honey.'

'But Honey must be used to a more . . . conventional sort of life, mustn't she?'

'She travelled with us until she was seven, when Dad died. I guess it got into her blood. She's never really settled into the mainstream.'

'But now, with the baby . . . surely she can't stay with you for ever?'

'No, she can't,' he says firmly, and I glance across at him. He looks careworn, and the silence settles back into the car.

'What happened to the father?' I ask cautiously.

'What happened to him? Nothing, yet. That may change if I ever get my hands on him,' Dinny says grimly.

'Ah. He's not been a knight in shining armour about it all, then?'

'He's a twenty-year-old townie idiot who told Honey she couldn't get pregnant on her first time.'

'That old chestnut.' I wince. 'And twenty years old? He must have known he was lying . . .'

'Like I say, if I ever catch up with him . . . Honey won't tell me his full name, or where he lives,' Dinny says, blackly.

I cast him a wry glance, smile slightly. 'I wonder why,' I murmur. 'Still, it must be a great way to raise a child – living the way you do. Travelling around, wherever you feel like. No mortgages, no nine-to-five, no juggling with childcare . . . The great outdoors, no keeping up with the Joneses . . .' I venture.

'It's fine for the likes of me, but for a fifteen-year-old with a fatherless kid? She hasn't even finished school yet,' he sighs. 'No. She needs to go back home.'

I park in front of the house. The study light I left on blooms out, lighting the stark tree trunks nearest the house.

'Thanks, Erica. Thank you for driving us. You were really great with Honey, back there – you've been great,' Dinny says, reaching for the door handle.

'Why don't you come in? Just to warm up. There's brandy, and you could have a shower, if you want. You're covered in mud,' I tell him. He looks at me, tips his head in that quizzical way.

'You're offering me a *shower?*' he smiles.

'Or whatever. I could dig out a clean T-shirt for you,' I flounder.

'I don't think that's a good idea, Erica.'

'Oh, for goodness' sake, Dinny! It's just a house. And you're welcome in it, now. You're not going to *catch* convention, just by using the plumbing.'

'I'm not sure how welcome I am. I came up to talk to Beth. She wouldn't let me in,' he says quietly.

'I know,' I say, before I can stop myself. He shoots me a questioning glance. 'I was listening. At the top of the stairs,' I say apologetically.

Dinny rolls his eyes. 'Same old Erica.'

'So are you coming in now?' I smile. Dinny looks at me for a long moment, until I start to feel pinned; then he looks out at the hostile night.

'All right. Thanks,' he nods.

I lead Dinny through to the study. The fire has gone out but it's still very warm. I go to draw the curtains.

'God, it's black out there! In London you have to shut out the light, here you have to shut out the dark,' I say. The wind throws a dead leaf against the glass, holds it there. 'Still think there's no such thing as bad weather?' I ask him wryly.

'Yes, but I'll admit that I'm *definitely* wearing the wrong clothes for it tonight,' Dinny concedes.

'Sit. I'll get brandy,' I tell him. I creep to the drawing room, fetch the decanter and two crystal tumblers, make as little noise as I can. I shut the door softly. 'Beth's asleep,' I tell him, filling the glasses.

'The house looks just the same as I remember it,' Dinny says, taking a swig of amber spirit, grimacing slightly.

'Meredith was never one for unnecessary change,' I shrug.

'The Calcotts are part of the old guard. Why would she want anything changed?'

'*Were* old guard. You can hardly say that of Beth and me – I'm an impoverished schoolteacher, for God's sake, and Beth's a single working parent.'

Dinny smiles a quick, ironic smile at this. 'That must have really pissed the old bird off.'

'Thanks. We like to think so.' I smile. 'Do you want another?' I ask as he drains his glass. He shakes his head, then leans back in his chair, stretches his arms over his head, arches his back, catlike. I watch him, feeling heat in my stomach, the blood pounding in my ears.

'I might take you up on that shower, though. I'll admit it's been a while since I had access to facilities like these.'

'Sure.' I nod, casually. 'This way.'

The room the furthest away from Beth's is Meredith's and its en suite has the best shower – the large glass cubicle is opaque with limescale, but it has one of those huge shower roses that pours out a wide cascade of hot water. I find new soap, a clean towel, and I turn on a bedside lamp because the main light is too bright and if Beth is awake she might see it as a strip under her door, might come and investigate. Dinny stands in the middle of the room and turns, taking in the huge bed, the heavy drapes, the elegant antique furniture. The carpet over the uneven boards is a threadbare sage green. That familiar faint smell of dust and mothballs and dog.

'This is her room, isn't it? Lady Calcott's?' Dinny asks. In the low light his eyes are black, unreadable.

'It has the best shower,' I say nonchalantly.

'It feels a bit . . . wrong, to be in here.'

'I think she owes you a shower, at least,' I say gently. Dinny says nothing, starts to unbutton his shirt while I hurry from the room.

Creeping softly away along the corridor I hear the shower come on, the pipes gurgling and popping in the walls, and I shut my eyes, hoping Beth won't wake up. But even as I think it she appears, looking at me around the side of her door at the far end of the corridor. Her hair hangs down at either side of her face, bare feet white and vulnerable.

'Erica? Is that you?' Her voice is taut with alarm.

'Yes – everything's fine,' I say quietly. I don't want Dinny to hear that she is awake.

'What are you doing up? What time is it?' she yawns.

'It's very early. Go back to bed, love.' Beth rubs her face. Her eyes are wide, confused, newly awake.

'Erica? Who's in the shower?' she asks.

'Dinny.' I look at my feet in my grubby socks, shifting guiltily.

'What? What's going on?'

'It's no big deal. Honey had her baby tonight – I had to drive them to Devizes and we got soaked and muddy and . . . when we got back I said he could have a shower here, if he wanted,' I tell her, all in one breath.

'You've been to *Devizes*? Why didn't you tell me?'

'You were asleep! And I had to go in a rush – Honey didn't feel right and . . . and it was all in a bit of a hurry, that's all.' I crush one of my feet beneath the other. I am reluctant to meet her eye. I flash her a grin. 'Imagine how Meredith would have gone off – to know a *Dinsdale* was in her shower!' I whisper, but Beth does not smile.

'Dinny is in the shower and you're waiting outside the room like . . . like I don't know what,' she says.

'I'm not waiting outside the room! I was just going to grab him a clean T-shirt . . .'

'Erica, what are you doing?' she asks me, seriously.

'Nothing! I'm not doing anything,' I say, but even though it's true it doesn't sound it. 'Are you going to tell me that I shouldn't have invited him in?'

'Maybe you shouldn't have,' she says shortly.

'Why not?'

'It's . . . he's . . . virtually a stranger, Erica! You can't just go inviting in random people in the middle of the night!'

'Not random people. Dinny,' I say firmly. I hold her gaze, see that I have won this argument. She can't explain her objection, not without explaining other things. She says nothing more, turns slowly and shuts the door.

I hurry to my room, pull one of the over-sized T-shirts I wear for pyjamas out of my case and drop it outside Meredith's door. Steam leaks out from under it, and the mineral smell of hot water. I hasten away down the stairs, retreat into the study, knock back the last of my brandy.

I emerge when I hear Dinny jogging down the stairs. The hallway is sunk in shadows. He pauses when he sees me.

'Erica! You made me jump,' he says, sounding tired, putting one hand up to his hair, raking it roughly with his fingers. Water drips from the ends of it, soaking the shoulders of my Rolling Stones T-shirt.

'So much for the dry clothes,' I say.

'Dry-er, anyway,' he smiles. 'I'll be wet again as soon as I go outside, but thanks all the same. That, I have to admit, is a great shower.'

I can't seem to answer him; I can't seem to breathe right. I feel as if I've forgotten how, as if breathing in no longer follows breathing out, as if I have lost the logic of it. He reaches the bottom of the stairs, is by my side, and I feel as if I am standing too close to him. But he does not move and neither do I. He tips his head, gives me a bemused look. The same look from decades ago, when I told him I saw trolls in the hollow on the downs, and I am suddenly beset by memories of him: teaching me to duck dive, watching my countless failed attempts; showing me how to suck the nectar from the white flowers of the dead-nettles, plucking one and offering it to me. Gradually his expression changes, grows more serious. I could dissolve under his scrutiny, but I can't seem to turn as I should, or move away. I watch a drop of water trickle down his arm; watch the faint scattering of goose pimples in its path. My hand moves without my bidding.

I touch the place where the droplet stops, trace my fingers along his forearm, wiping away its cold trail. The shape of the muscles over the bones. The warmth of his blood beneath the skin. My skin feels raw where it touches him, but I leave my hand on his arm; I am grounded, I cannot move. For a second he is still too, as still as I am, as if I have frozen us both with this uninvited touch. The vast hall, ceiling scattered with echoes, seems to shrink in around me. Then he moves away; just slightly, but enough.

'I should go,' he says quietly. 'Thanks for . . . all your help this evening – really.' He sounds puzzled.

'No . . . no problem. Any time,' I say, blinking, startled.

'I'll see you around.' He smiles awkwardly, lets himself out into the bleak early morning.

Lament

1904

Caroline found herself outside, found herself soaked and shivering, without even realising she had moved. Water ran into her eyes and through her hair and down the back of her cotton dress, and as the two horses trotted into the yard she splashed over to them from the house, caught the rank stink of hot, wet horse in her nostrils. She recognised Hutch and Joe, their hats pulled low over their faces, and as she drew breath to ask she saw the third rider, hanging bonelessly across the front of Hutch's saddle; bare-headed, the rain streaming from bronze hair gone slick and dark.

'Corin?' she whispered, putting her hand out to shake him slightly. She could not see his face, could not make him look up at her. 'Where's his hat? He'll get a chill!' she shouted at Hutch. She didn't know her own voice; it was too high, too brittle.

'Mrs Massey, come now, step aside. We have to get him inside the house. Quickly now!' Hutch told her sternly, trying to steer the horse around her.

'Where's Strumpet? What happened to Corin — what's wrong with him? Tell me!' she asked, frantic now. She knotted her fingers around the horse's reins, pulled its head around, stopped it walking past with its precious cargo. Hutch said something terse, and Joe swung down from his horse, taking Caroline's hands and freeing the reins. Joe shouted something, his voice loud and deep. Caroline paid no heed. More men arrived, to take the horses, to gather Corin up. Caroline stumbled behind them to the bottom step of the house; she fell, and could not rise again. She could not remember how to walk, how to make her legs bend or her feet rise or fall. Strong hands lifted her and even though they bore her in the direction she wanted to go, she fought them savagely, as if she could resist what was happening, and make it not so.

They laid Corin down on the bed. Caroline dried his hair carefully with a linen towel, peeled his wet shirt from his torso and pulled his sodden boots from his feet, splattering rainwater onto the floor. She fetched clean blankets and covered him thickly. His hands were like ice and she held them in her own, feeling the familiar calluses, trying to rub some warmth into them when she had none to give. She brought a bowl of the rabbit stew, steaming and fragrant, and set it by the bed.

'Won't you have some? It will warm you,' she murmured to him.

'He was riding hard after a big dog coyote. It was the last one we were going after, since we'd seen the rain coming in. Strumpet – she always was the quickest. Fast on her feet too – and that's not the same thing. She was nimble, that mare. Quick thinking. I never saw a horse and rider move so well together as Corin and that mare . . .' Hutch spoke in a low monotone; his eyes fixed on Corin and his hands working in circles, wringing and twisting and wringing again. Caroline hardly heard a word he said. 'But then, with no warning she just went over. High in the air, heels right up over her head. Whatever she stepped in, and I think it was some sinking sand, she never saw it coming or she'd have avoided it for sure. Corin was thrown down hard and . . . and then Strumpet came down on top of him. It was so fast! Like God reached down and turned that poor horse over with a flick of his finger. Her two legs were broke in front. Joe shot her. He shot her and we had to leave her out there for the damned coyotes. That brave horse!' He broke off, tears coursing down his cheeks.

Caroline blinked. 'Well,' she said eventually, slowly, like a drunken person. 'You'll have to go and fetch her back. Corin won't have any horse but her.' Hutch looked at her in confusion. 'Is the doctor here yet?' she asked, turning back to the bed. A dark water stain was ruining the silk squares of the quilt, seeping out around Corin. Patches of angry colour bloomed beneath the skin of his chest and arms, like an ugly blush. His right shoulder sat at a wrong angle and his head lolled to the left, always to the left. Caroline slipped her hands beneath the blankets to see if he was warming up, but his flesh was cold and solid and wrong somehow. She lay her head close to his and refused to listen to the quiet, terrified corner of her mind that knew he was dead.

They buried Corin on his own land, at the top of a green rise some hundred and fifty feet from the house and a good distance from the sweet-water well. The parson came out from Woodward and tried to persuade Caroline that it would be more seemly for the burial to be in the churchyard in town, but since Caroline was too numb to answer him Hutch had the final say, and he insisted that Corin had wanted to be buried on the prairie. Angie Fosset and Magpie were responsible for Caroline's attendance that day, and for lacing her into a borrowed black dress that was too big and hung from her thin frame in folds. They also found her a veiled hat with two long, black ostrich feathers that swept out behind her.

'Have you written to his people, Caroline?' Angie asked, pulling a brush through Caroline's matted hair. 'Sweetheart, have you written to his mama?' But Caroline did not answer her. She had no will left to draw breath, to form words. Angie shot Magpie a dark look, and took the Ponca girl aside for a whispered consultation that Caroline did not attempt to overhear. They led her up the rise to stand by the graveside as the parson read the sermon to a crowd of ranchers, neighbours and a good portion of the population of Woodward. The sky was tarnished. A warm wind shook the wreath of white roses on the coffin and carried a few sprinkled raindrops onto the congregation.

When the proper prayers were said and done, Hutch walked a

few steps to stand at the head of the coffin. The mourners waited, eyes turned respectfully downwards, and when Hutch did not speak they waited some more, glancing up at him from time to time. Even Caroline, eventually, raised her shrouded eyes to see what was happening. Then, at last, Hutch pulled in a long breath and spoke in a deep voice, soft and steady.

'The minister here has made a pretty speech, and I know he meant for it to be a comfort. And it may well be a comfort to some, to think of Corin Massey gone ahead of us into the kingdom of heaven. I daresay that, in time, I might be able to draw some comfort from that same thought. I hope he likes it there. I hope there are fine horses, and wide green spaces for him to ride. I hope the sky there is the colour of a spring dawn over the prairie. But today . . .' he paused, his voice cracking. 'Today I hope that God will forgive me if I object to him taking Corin from us so soon. Just for today, I think we can feel hard done by that our great friend has gone. For we will miss him sorely. I will miss him sorely. More than I can say. He was the best of us, and a fairer or a kinder man you could not hope to meet.' Hutch swallowed, two tears sliding down his cheeks. He wiped them away roughly with the back of his hand, then, clearing his throat, he began to sing:

> 'Where the dewdrops fall and the butterfly rests,
> The wild rose blooms on the prairie's crest,
> Where the coyotes howl and the wind sports free,
> They laid him there on the lone prairie.'

His song was as mournful as the empty wind and it blew right through Caroline. She felt as insubstantial as air, as intangible as the clouds above. Her eyes returned to the pale wooden casket. Nothing about it spoke of Corin, nothing about it reminded her of him. It was as if he had been wiped from the earth, she thought, and it seemed an impossible thing to have happened. She had no photographs, no portraits of him. Already his scent was fading from his pillow, from his clothes. Hutch, Joe, Jacob Fosset and three other men stepped either side of the coffin, gathered the ropes into their weathered hands and took the strain. The parson spoke again but Caroline turned and stumbled away down the hill, the folds of the borrowed dress trailing her like a dark echo of her wedding gown. She could not bear to see the weight on those ropes, the tension in those hands. She could not bear to picture what was weighing that coffin down; and the blackness of the open grave awaiting it appalled her.

'Don't you leave her alone for a second. Not for a second, Maggie. She was lonely enough when Corin was alive, God help her,' Angie whispered to Magpie as she got ready to depart after the funeral. Caroline was standing right next to them, but Angie guessed that she did not care. Angie turned to her, put firm hands on her shoulders. 'I'll be back on Tuesday, Caroline,' she said, sadly, but as she opened the door Caroline found her voice at last.

'Don't go!' she croaked. She could not bear to be left, could not bear the emptiness. The spaces inside the house were as terrifying as those outside it now. 'Please . . . don't go, Angie,' she said. Angie turned, her face twisted up with pity.

'Oh, Caroline!' she sighed, embracing her neighbour. 'My heart is breaking for you, it truly is,' she said, and Caroline wept, her body sagging helplessly against Angie's.

'I . . . I can't bear it . . . *I can't bear it!*' she cried, and her anguish seemed fit to pull her slowly to pieces. Magpie dropped her face into her hands and bowed her head in sorrow.

But Angie had to leave at some point – she had a family of her own to look after. Magpie was around as much as she could be. She slept on a folded blanket in the main room, with William beside her. His cries in the night woke Caroline in a panic because they were so loud and unfamiliar. She thought coyotes were inside the house, or that Corin was back and crying in pain. But once fully awake a persistent, dull lassitude returned to her. One night she peeked at Magpie through a crack in the door and watched the dark-skinned girl nurse the baby by candlelight, singing so softly that the sound might have been the breeze, or the blood moving in Caroline's own ears. She felt the darkness at her back like a threat, like a ghoul she was too afraid to turn and see. The darkness of the empty bedroom, as empty now as everything else. The ache of missing Corin, as she lay in that dark bed, was like a knife lodged in her heart, slowly twisting. So she stayed at the crack in the door for a long time, clinging to the candlelight like a moth; and eventually Magpie stopped singing and changed her posture subtly, just enough to show that she felt herself watched.

The heat of high summer was hardly worth fighting now. Caroline did as she was told, and ate as long as Magpie sat with her and forced her to. In the evening, Magpie spoke softly of unimportant things as she undressed Caroline and brushed out her hair, just as the maid Sara had once done. Caroline shut her eyes and thought back to that time, to the dark spell after her parents had died and how she had thought that she would never again feel as lost and sad as she did then. But this was worse; it was much, much worse.

'Do you remember the time my father took us to the circus, Sara?' she murmured, with the ghost of a smile.

'Who is Sara?' Magpie asked sharply. 'I am Magpie, your friend, Mrs Massey.'

Caroline opened her eyes and caught the Ponca girl's gaze in the mirror.

'Yes, of course,' she said tonelessly, to hide the fact that for a moment she'd had no idea who or where she was.

As she went about the chores, Magpie took to putting William into Caroline's lap. She did this particularly when Caroline had not spoken for several hours, or was not responding to questions, her face fixed and unchanging. The child, by then ten months old, soon began to wriggle and climb about her person, and she would be forced to take hold of him, steady him, and focus her attention on him.

'Sing to him, Mrs Massey. Tell him the story of the Garden of Eda,' Magpie urged; and although Caroline could not find any stories or songs in her heart, she did find traces of a smile for the baby, and her hands woke up enough to tickle him, to hold and reposition him. She did not wince when her hair was pulled. William regarded her with his curious, velvet dark eyes and grinned wetly from time to time; and from time to time Caroline gathered him up and held him close, her eyes shut tight, as if drawing strength from his tiny body. Magpie hovered nearby when she did this, ready to take the child back when the embrace grew too much and made him cry.

Throughout the summer, Caroline spent long hours sitting out on the porch, tapping the runner of Corin's rocking chair with her toe and then shutting her eyes, listening to the sound it made as it creaked to and fro, to and fro. She tried not to think. She tried to not wonder how things might have been if she had not blamed the coyotes for her fears in the night. She tried not to wonder how things might have been if she had not had that nightmare, if she had not been afraid of the wild, if she had been a stronger person; a better, more adaptable person. A braver one. Any other kind of person than the kind that sent a husband out to die chasing wild dogs. She wept without realising it, and went about with her face encrusted with salt. And she had no child of his to keep and raise and speak to with quiet sorrow of how bronze and gold and glorious its father had been. Not even this trace of him was left to comfort her. She stared into the wide, far horizon and let herself be afraid of it. All day she sat, and was afraid. It was the only way she knew to punish herself, and she felt that abject misery was no worse than she deserved.

Some weeks later, Hutch came into the house with a respectful knock. Had Caroline not been so remote, so inward facing since Corin's death, she would have noticed the man's suffering, and that he avoided her, shouldering the blame for Corin's accident upon himself. He was thinner because he could not bring himself to eat. The accident had cut him too deeply. The lines on his face seemed deeper, although he could not yet be thirty-five. Guilt weighed heavy upon him and grief was ageing him, stamping its mark on him, just as it was on Caroline, but she did not have it in her to offer comfort. Not even to Hutch. She made coffee for him and noticed, solemnly and without satisfaction, that she had finally brewed a good strong cup, not weak, not bitter, not burnt. She pictured Corin sipping it, pictured the smile that would have spread over his face, the way he would have complimented her on it — slipping an arm around her waist, planting a kiss on her face. *Sweetheart, that's the best coffee I ever tasted!* Even her smallest triumphs had made him proud. Thoughts like this made her sway. Thoughts like this knocked her legs out from under her.

'Mrs Massey, you know I hate to bother you, but there are things that require your attention,' Hutch said, taking a cup from her. With a slight wave of her hand, Caroline invited him to sit, but although Hutch turned to look at the proffered chair, he remained standing.

'What things?' she asked.

'Well, with Mr Massey . . . gone, you're the owner of this ranch now. I know that may sound alarming, but it needn't be. I don't want you to worry about a thing. I'll stay here and run it for you. I know the workings of it more than well enough, and I've been here long enough to call this my home. Your husband trusted me with his business concerns, and I hope you can too. But there are things I can't do, and one of those things is pay the hands and riders their wages.'

'Pay them? But . . . I haven't got any money,' Caroline frowned.

'Not here, perhaps. Corin always drew the wages every couple of months from his bank in Woodward, and I can't see that there'll be any trouble in you doing the same.'

'You . . . want me to go to Woodward? I can't,' she refused, as completely as if he'd asked her to go to the moon.

'I'll drive you. We can stay one night only if that's what you want; or you can go visiting some of the ladies while we're there. I think . . .' Hutch paused, turning the cup around in his hands. 'I think you need to go to Woodward, ma'am. I think you need to see some people. I think you need to get some air into your lungs. And if we don't pay them, those boys'll go elsewhere. They're good and loyal, but they've had no money for two months now, and that's just not right. And I can't run the ranch without them.' Finally, he sipped the coffee, and his look of surprise at its rich flavour did not go unnoticed. Caroline imagined the trip to Woodward, and a great weariness came over her. She rocked back on her heels and fought to keep her balance, grasping the back of a chair for support.

'All right then, if it's the only way. Corin . . . Corin would have wanted the ranch to carry on.'

'That he would, Mrs Massey,' Hutch agreed. He paused, and lowered his head sadly. 'Your husband was a good man and no mistake. The best I ever knew. And this place was his pride and joy, so I reckon we owe it to him to keep it running, to make it bigger and better than ever,' he said, looking up to hear Caroline echo the sentiment, but she was gazing out of the window and hardly heard him. 'This is damn good coffee, pardon my language, Mrs Massey,' Hutch told her, draining the cup. Caroline glanced at him and gave a small nod of agreement.

She forgot her parasol and felt the sun burning her skin as soon as they set out for Woodward. With her eyes screwed up against the light, she thought of the lines that would take root in her face, and found that she didn't care. The wind was blowing, hot and dry, and a pall of dust sat around Woodward. Sharp grains got into Caroline's unblinking eyes, so that as they travelled down Main Street her face streamed with tears. She rubbed at it roughly, pushing hard with her fingers, feeling the odd solidity of her eyeballs behind the lids.

'Stop now. Stop it,' Hutch told her softly. He wet his handkerchief with water from his flask and held her hands still in one of his while he wiped the sand from her face. 'There,' he said quietly. 'That's better. I reckon your poor eyes have shed enough tears of late to last a lifetime.' The hand holding hers relaxed its grip, but did not relinquish them completely, and, tenderly, he brushed a final grain of sand from her cheek with his thumb.

'Is this the place?' she asked dully. They had pulled up outside Gerlach's Bank, a large building with a grand, handsome sign.

'This is it. Do you want me to come in with you?'

'No.' She shook her head. 'I'll be fine. Thank you.'

Inside the building it was quiet and cool, and Caroline's boots sounded loudly on the wooden floor as she entered. She approached the neat young clerk and saw him recoil from the disarray of her face and clothes and hair. A long-case clock ticked ponderously against the wall, a sound Caroline hadn't heard since leaving New York. She looked at the gleaming clock, very similar to one that had stood in Bathilda's hallway, and it seemed an object from another world.

'May I help you, madam?' he asked.

'I would like to make a withdrawal,' she said, realising that she had no idea how this would be achieved, having never made such a request before.

'Do you have an account with Gerlach's, madam?' the clerk asked, making this prospect seem unlikely. Caroline looked at the precise trim of his moustache, and his immaculate suit and collar. His expression was haughty, she thought, for a boy who worked in a bank. She drew herself up and fixed him with a steady gaze.

'I believe my husband has kept an account here for many years. I am Mrs Corin Massey.' At this an older man appeared behind the young clerk and smiled kindly at her.

'Mrs Massey, do come and sit down. My name is Thomas Berringer. I've been expecting you. Everything has been put in order and you may of course have access to your late husband's account. May I bring you a glass of water?' Mr Berringer ushered her into a seat and waved a hand at the clerk for the water to be brought.

When it came to how much money should be withdrawn, Caroline realised that she had no idea. No idea how much a rider or a ranch hand should be paid, how much was owing, or even how many young men there were to be paid. She withdrew half of the available funds, and although Mr Berringer looked surprised, he filled out the necessary forms and passed them to her to sign without comment. The date he had written at the top gave Caroline a small jolt.

'It's my birthday,' she said dully. 'I'm twenty-one today.'

'Well, now.' Mr Berringer smiled, looking slightly uncomfortable. 'Many happy returns of the day, Mrs Massey.'

The resulting packet of bank notes was thick and heavy. Caroline weighed it in her hand, unsure of where to stow it. Seeing her predicament, Mr Berringer again beckoned to the clerk, and a cloth bag was found to conceal the money from prying eyes. Outside, Caroline stood on the raised sidewalk and gazed at all the people and horses and buggies. She had once felt so at home amidst people. Now she felt at home nowhere, she realised. Now was her chance to visit the town's stores, to buy books or foodstuffs or clothes, but she could not think of anything she wanted. Seeing a haberdashery, she bought a soft, white crocheted blanket for William, and an open carrycot made of close-woven straw.

'It'll be cooler in this heat than that leather papoose carrier he has currently,' she explained to Hutch.

'That's mighty kind of you, Caroline. I'm sure Maggie will be very pleased,' Hutch nodded, stowing the gifts beneath the seat of the buggy. A long while later, too late for her to comment, Caroline realised that Hutch, for the first time, had called her by her Christian name.

They stayed just one night, in the same hotel where they had stayed the night of the gala. Caroline asked for the same room, but it was occupied. She had wanted to be in a place where Corin had been, like a pilgrim visiting a shrine. As if the place would remember Corin, as if his essence would still be felt there. She watched from the window for a long time as the sun went down, painting the town in lavish shades of pink and gold. She watched the people who passed, and listened to snatches of their conversation, bubbles of their laughter, and she tried to remember what it had been like to be one of them. As dark was falling she saw Hutch go out, with his hair combed flat and a clean shirt on. He sauntered away along Main Street, and Caroline watched until she lost sight of him amidst the jumble of people.

The men were paid, and the wad of banknotes thinned by barely a third. Caroline returned the remainder to the cloth bag and put it into her vanity case. Her hand brushed something soft and she drew it out. It was her blue velvet jewellery fold, with her mother's emeralds and some other fine pieces inside. She unrolled it and looked at the bright stones, thinking of the last time she had worn them, the night she had first met Corin. When had she thought she would wear them out here? They looked ridiculous in the simple bedroom. Like glossy hothouse blooms in a field of wheat. She held them up against her skin and looked in the mirror. How different she looked now! So gaunt, so tanned; her nose a swathe of freckles, her hair dull and untidy. She looked like a lady's maid trying on her mistress's jewels, and she realised that she might never wear them again. They had no place on the prairie. She rolled them away and put them back in the case. Then, without thinking, she packed away some other things too – some clean undergarments and blouses; a nightdress with long sleeves too warm for the summer; some hair combs and face powder. She closed the lid and fastened the clasps tightly, wondering where on earth she thought she could go.

Late in August the ranch grew quiet. Hutch, Joe and several of the other men had gone out onto the grass with near a thousand head of cattle, for the final weeks of fattening up before the animals would be loaded onto trains and shipped north, to the meat markets of the eastern states. Many of those men who remained on the ranch were laid low with an illness that passed quickly from person to person, consigning them to their beds with a debilitating fever and tremors. Sitting on the porch early one morning, thinking of nothing and feeling nothing inside, Caroline saw Annie, Joe's sister, ride out of the ranch on Magpie's grey pony. She headed east, urging the pony into a brisk canter. The Ponca woman's face, as she passed, was set into deep lines of disquiet. Caroline watched until she was out of sight; then she thought for a while and realised that she had not seen Magpie since the previous afternoon. She stood and walked slowly across the yard.

The dugout was hot and rancid. Magpie lay still on the bed and William mumbled and grizzled to himself in the straw carrycot Caroline had bought for him. There was an unmistakable smell of ammonia and faeces coming from the baby, and a rank, metallic smell behind it which instinctively made Caroline afraid. With her heart beating fast, she knelt beside Magpie and shook her gently. The girl's face was deep red and dry. When she opened her eyes they had an odd, dull gleam and Caroline drew back slightly, frightened.

'Magpie, are you sick? Where has Annie gone?' she asked hurriedly.

'I am sick. White Cloud too. Her medicines have not cured us,' Magpie whispered. There was a wooden cup by the bed and Caroline picked it up. There was some concoction within, which smelt sharp and vinegary. She held it up to Magpie but the girl turned her head away weakly. 'No more of that stuff. No more of it,' she whispered.

'If you have a fever, you have to drink something,' Caroline said. 'I'll get some water. You have to get up, Magpie. William's dirty . . .'

'I cannot get up. I cannot change him,' Magpie replied, sounding so unhappy that Caroline faltered. 'You must do it. Please.'

'But I don't know how!' Caroline said. 'Magpie, why didn't you send word to me that you were sick?' she asked. Magpie gazed at her, and she read the answer there. Because none of them had thought she would be any help. Tears welled in her eyes. 'I'll clean him. I'll fetch you water,' she said, wiping her face. The smell of the sick girl and her soiled baby was nauseating, and a rush of dizziness assailed her. But she moved with a purpose, grabbing a pail and heading over to the cistern. 'Where's White Cloud? Where's Annie gone?' she asked again, from the doorway.

'White Cloud is sick too. She is in the teepee, resting. Annie has gone east, to our peoples' lands on the Arkansas River . . . she goes to fetch medicine . . .'

'The *Arkansas River*? That's nigh on two hundred miles! It will take her days and days!' Caroline cried.

Magpie just looked at her, her face slack with exhaustion and despair. 'Please, clean William,' she said again.

Caroline fetched a pail of water and a ladle. It took all of her strength to lift Magpie's head and shoulders so that the girl could drink, but Magpie could only manage tiny sips and found it hard to swallow.

'Please drink some more,' Caroline begged, but Magpie did not reply, lying back on her fetid bedding, her eyes closing. Searching the dugout, Caroline found clean napkins and a towel. She took William out of the carrycot and went outside with him. The filth she found when she undressed the baby made her gag, and she threw the rags onto the coals of the dying cook fire. The water was cold and William began to cry as she dunked him into the pail, swilling the congealed mess from his backside. His cries were weak though, his voice a little hoarse, and he seemed to tire himself out with it, falling into a kind of doze as Caroline finished bathing him and positioned a new napkin between his legs as best she could. Sitting on the ground, she lay him along her thighs and was stroking his arms, entranced, when she realised how warm he was and how flushed his cheeks had grown. She put her fingers to her own forehead to check, and the difference was unmistakable. Hurriedly, she gathered him up and went back into the dugout.

'Magpie . . . William's very hot. I think he has a fever too,' she said, bringing the baby to the bedside for Magpie to see. The Ponca girl's eyes filled with tears.

'I don't know how to help him. Please . . . he will get sick too. You must take him . . . take him to the house! Clean him, feed him. Please!' she said weakly.

'I have cleaned him, see? He will be fine . . . you'll both be fine, Magpie,' Caroline declared.

'White Cloud . . .' Magpie murmured indistinctly. Caroline lay William back in his cot and went over to the teepee. She hesitated outside, afraid to go any further. She thought of White Cloud's iron gaze, her alien voice raised in song.

'White Cloud? May I come in?' she called tentatively, but there came no reply. Breathing fast, Caroline lifted the tent flap and went inside. White Cloud lay crumpled on the ground like so many old rags. Her grey hair was slick with sweat, matted to her scalp. With her bright eyes closed she was just an elderly lady, small and weak, and Caroline felt ashamed for fearing her. 'White Cloud?' she whispered, kneeling beside her and shaking her as she had done Magpie. But White Cloud did not stir. She would not wake. Her skin radiated heat and her breathing was fast and shallow. Caroline had no idea what to do. She went back outside and then faltered, standing alone with her hands shaking, surrounded by people who suddenly had need of her help.

At Magpie's insistence, Caroline took William back to the house with her. He was fast asleep, his fist wedged into his mouth. She put him in the coolest, shadiest spot she could find and began to explore the kitchen cupboards, looking for food she could take over to Magpie. Steeling herself, she went over to the bunkhouses and found three of the beds occupied. The stricken riders murmured in helpless embarrassment when she entered, assuring her that they were quite well even though they were too weak to rise. Caroline fetched pails of water and made each of them drink, before leaving a further cup of water beside each man's bed. She had been hoping to find somebody able to ride to town and fetch the doctor, but there was no way any of those remaining could do so. The thought made panic close her throat. She went back to the house and began to make a soup from dried beans and the carcass of a chicken Magpie had roasted two days before. She also fetched a pumpkin up from the root cellar and cooked it up into a mash for William.

In the night William woke her up with thin cries of distress and she rose, holding him to stop his crying with comforting words and kisses. She laid him back down as he went back to sleep, then sat on the edge of the bed and cried quietly to herself, because it was all she had ever wanted to have a baby sleeping next to the bed, and to comfort it and love it. But this child was not hers, and Corin was not lying beside her, and this tiny taste of what should have happened, of how things should have been, was so bitter and sweet.

By morning, there was no denying that William had caught the fever as well. He slept too much, he was hot, and was groggy and limp when he woke. Caroline went over to the bunkhouses with the soup she had made, and then to the dugout to Magpie, pausing outside the teepee. She knew she should go in and try to wake White Cloud again, try to make her drink some water. But fear gripped her, a new and horrible fear born of instinct rather than conscious thought. It made the hair stand up on the back of her neck as she forced herself to lift the tent flap. White Cloud had not moved. She did not move. Not at all. Not even her chest, with the rise and fall of breathing. Caroline dropped the tent flap and backed away hurriedly, horror squeezing her insides, shaking her from head to foot. Breathing fast, she went down into the dugout.

Magpie was weaker, and harder to wake. The whites of her eyes looked grey, and her skin was even hotter. Caroline washed her face with a wet cloth, and ladled more water through her cracked lips.

'How is William? Is he sick?' Magpie whispered.

'He . . .' Caroline faltered, unwilling to speak the truth. 'He has a fever. He is quiet, this morning,' she said gravely. Fear lit a dull light in Magpie's eyes.

'And White Cloud?' she asked. Caroline looked away, busying her hands with the cloth, the water pail, the ladle.

'She is sleeping,' she said shortly. When she looked up Magpie was watching her, and she could not hold the girl's gaze.

'I don't know what to do. I don't know how to help myself or White Cloud,' Magpie whispered, despairingly. 'We must hope for Annie to come back soon, and to bring medicine.'

'That will take far too long!' Caroline said desperately. 'Some-body will have to go! You can't wait for Annie!' She stood up, pacing the dugout. 'I'll go,' she said in the end. 'I'm well enough. I'll go, and . . . I'll take William with me. The doctor can see to him straight away and then come back with me and look after you and everybody else. It's the best way.'

'You will take William with you . . . ?'

'It's the best way. You can't look after him, Magpie! I can do it. I'll take the buggy and that way the doctor will see him this evening. Tonight, Magpie! He could have medicines *tonight*! Please. This *is* the best way.' Now that she had decided, she was desperate to start. She thought of White Cloud – her denuded, too-still form. 'It might be too late, otherwise,' she added. Magpie's eyes widened with fear, and she blinked tears away.

'Please, take care of him. Please come back quickly,' the girl implored.

'I will! I'll send the doctor to you at once. It will be fine, Magpie – truly it will,' Caroline said, the speeding of her heart making her voice tremble. She took Magpie's hand and squeezed it hard.

She loaded her vanity case, the carrycot and a bag of William's things into the buggy and drove it as quickly as she dared, steering the horse between thickets of brush as she had watched Hutch and Corin do. The North Canadian was low between its banks and cool droplets of water spun up from the wheels as they took the ford, stirring up the sweet, dank, mineral smell of the river bottom. Pausing to rest herself and the horse, Caroline lifted William into her arms. He was still hot and cried fitfully each time he woke, but now he was sleeping, and his face had settled into a calm slump that so reminded Caroline of how Corin's face had looked when he'd slept in his chair that she caught her breath. Thinking again, even for a second, that this might be Corin's child stole the air from her lungs. She sat down in the sand with William in her lap, and she studied him, running a finger from his hairline to his toes. Long toes, spaced widely apart, just like Corin's. His hair was dark, but his skin was lighter than either Magpie's or Joe's. His eyes, although brown, had a greenish ring around the iris that lightened them. In the furrow of the tiny brow, and the pout of his lips above a tucked-in chin, Caroline thought she saw traces of her husband. She cradled the child to her chest and she wept. She wept for Corin's betrayal, and for the loss of him, and for the perfect, agonising feeling of holding his baby to her.

The doctor took one look at Caroline's frantic face and the child in her arms and ushered her inside. He took William and examined him closely, quizzing Caroline about the symptoms the adults at the ranch were showing and how long the illness had been rife. He listened to the baby's heart and breathing, and felt the heat glowing in the soft skin.

'I think he will be well. His fever is not too high as yet, and his heart is strong, so please, try not to worry too much. Are you staying in town tonight? Good. Keep him cool. The main thing is to bring his fever down as soon as possible. Cold wet cloths, changed regularly. Give him three drops of this on his tongue, with a teaspoon of water afterwards, every four hours. It's an anti-pyretic – it will help break the fever. And if he will eat or drink, try to let him do so. I believe he will recover quickly. Don't look so afraid! You brought him to me in time. But I must leave for the ranch, for if it goes unchecked this sickness could prove more serious. You will follow on tomorrow, so I can check the child again?' Caroline nodded. 'Good. Rest, for both of you. And cold cloths for your child. Are there any others at the ranch as young as this, or any of great age?' The doctor asked as he ushered her from the room. *Your child*.

'There are no other children. White Cloud . . . she is advanced in years, although I cannot say how old she is,' she whispered. 'But I think . . . I think she has died already,' she said, her throat constricting. The doctor shot her an incredulous glance.

'I must leave at once and travel through the night – I can hope to be there by sunrise. A fellow doctor can be found at this address – if William takes a turn for the worse, call upon him.' He handed Caroline a card, nodded briskly, and stalked from the room.

Caroline did not sleep. She fetched a basin of cold water from the hotel kitchens and laid damp cloths gently onto William's skin, as instructed. She was loath to take her eyes from him, studying each line of his face, each hair on his head. She checked the clock obsessively, giving him his dose when four hours had passed. He woke up from time to time and studied her in return, grasping her finger in a strong grip that reassured her. By morning she was light-headed with fatigue, but William's colour was better, and his skin was cooler. He ate some rice pudding that the landlady had made for him, studying the women with a calm appraisal that made them smile. Caroline wrapped him in the crocheted blanket, laid him in the carrycot, put a pacifier into his chubby hands and gazed at him. He could be hers – the doctor had immediately thought so. He could be the child of a respectable white woman – nothing about his person marked him out as a Ponca. Indeed, he could have been hers, she thought. He should have been hers.

Caroline was reluctant to go back to the ranch. She should have left hours before, with the sunrise, but the thought of starting back made her so tired inside that she averted her eyes from the black buggy, parked outside in the yard, and from the corral where the buggy horse had spent the night, chewing hay and scratching its sweaty head against the fence. The doctor would see to the sick, and when Caroline returned she would have to give William back. She thought of White Cloud's body, lying untended in the teepee. She thought of Magpie, helpless and sick. She thought of life, stretching on for year after empty year, and all of them without Corin. But when she looked at William she smiled and felt something swelling up inside her. Something that pushed the other thoughts aside and made it bearable to go on. She could not go back. It was a prospect as black and terrifying as the grave Hutch had cut into the grassland to take Corin's coffin. *She could not go back*.

Across town, plumes of steam rose from the railway track. Caroline walked in that direction, her case in one hand, the carrycot in the other. The weight of these two items made her unsteady on her feet, but she moved purposefully, her mind now empty of thought, because her thoughts were too dark. The platform was wreathed in steam and the hot metal smell that had accompanied her to Woodward in the first place. But this immense, black locomotive was facing the other way. Northwards, to Dodge City, Kansas City and beyond. Back the way she had come, away from the prairie that had torn out her heart.

'Look, William, look at the train!' she exclaimed, holding the baby up for his first sight of such a thing. William eyed it distrustfully, putting out a hand to grasp at a wisp of steam as it scrolled by. Then the guard's whistle startled them both and the train exhaled a vast, ponderous cough of steam, its wheels easing into motion. A latecomer ran onto the platform, wrenched open a carriage door and leapt aboard, just as the train began to inch slowly along the platform.

'Come along, ma'am! Quickly now, or you'll miss it!' the man smiled, holding out his hand to her. Caroline hesitated. Then she took the man's hand.

6

Meredith's laughter was the rarest of things. Even at the summer ball, or at the dinner parties she sometimes hosted – where children were not allowed and we would creep from our beds to eavesdrop – I hardly ever heard it. She would just smile, and sometimes make a single, satisfied sound in the back of her throat when something pleased her. Like most little girls, laughter came as easily to me as breathing. I remember thinking it must be something that got used up as you got older, as if laughter was like a mass of coloured ribbons, bundled up inside you, and once it had all spooled out, that was it.

But I did hear it once, and I was stunned. Not just by the sound – high and loud, with a rusty edge like an old hinge – but by what had caused it. An overcast day, not long before Henry disappeared, with a quiet breeze blowing. We were in Mickey and Mo's motor home, listening to the radio and playing rummy with Dinny, who had a slight temperature and had been told to stay indoors, much to his disgust. I tried to tempt him out, up into the tree house to play there instead, but he did what Mo told him. He was more obedient than Beth and I. The camp was quiet, most of the adults out working. Outside, sheets were drying on a line strung between the vehicles. They drifted in and out of view through the window, moving with a regular swell and fall. I could see them, in the corner of my eye, as I shifted my thighs against the vinyl bench and silently urged Beth to discard a four or a Jack. So I saw it first – the change in the view from the window. The sudden oddness of the sheets, the colour, the way the sky above them thickened.

The sheets were on fire. I gaped at them, stunned by this unexpected thing. Pale yellow and blue flames tore across them in odd patterns, scribbling lines of charred black, pouring smoke up in clouds, reducing the fabric to dark shreds that tore away like cobwebs. There was a shout from outside and Dinny got up, leaned past me to look out of the window.

'Look!' I gasped uselessly.

'Erica! Why didn't you say!' Beth admonished me as Dinny ran out and we followed. Outside, two women who had been laid up with the same bug as Dinny were yanking the sheets from the line, stamping at them frantically. The plastic-coated line itself had melted and fallen into pieces, scattering the burning remains of the sheets on the ground, which was perhaps for the best. On the side of the motor home, an ugly, brownish smear showed how close the flames had got.

'How the *bloody hell* did that happen?' one of the women swore, catching her breath as the last flames went out. Hands on hips, surveying the smouldering remnants.

'If we hadn't been here . . . Mo only hung those just before she went off – they can't even have been all the way dry yet!' the other exclaimed, fixing us kids with a serious eye.

'We were inside playing cards! Swear to God!' Dinny said emphatically. Beth and I nodded in frantic support. The smoke got into my nose, made me sneeze. The first woman crouched, picked up a shred of fabric with her fingertips, sniffed at it.

'Paraffin,' she said grimly.

Beth and I left then, running as soon as we were out of sight. We skirted the stables, looked in the coach house, found Henry in the woodshed. He had a flat plastic bottle of something, with a squeezy red nozzle on it. I thought of the patterns the flames had made, almost as though they'd been following lines. He put the bottle back on a high shelf, turned to face us, smiling.

'What?' He shrugged.

'You could have set the vans on fire. You could have killed

somebody,' Beth said quietly, watching him with such a grave and serious look that I was even more upset, even more afraid.

'I don't know what you're talking about,' Henry said loftily. The stink of paraffin clung to him, was on his hands.

'It *was* you!' I declared.

'Prove it.' He shrugged again, smiling now.

'I'm telling. You could have killed somebody,' Beth repeated, and now Henry stopped smiling.

'You're not supposed to go to the camp. You won't tell,' he sneered. Beth turned on her heel, stalked away towards the house. I followed, and so did Henry, and soon it became a race, and we thundered into the hall, shouting for Meredith, out of breath.

We thought that it was too serious not to tell. We thought that, even though Henry was her favourite, she would have to reprimand him for this. Making dogs sick was one thing, but Beth was right. The fire could have killed somebody. Even for Henry, it was too much.

'Henry set fire to the Dinsdales' washing!' Beth got her words out first, gasping them as Meredith looked up from the letter she was writing, sitting at the davenport in the drawing room.

'What is all this racket?' Meredith asked.

'We were at the camp, and I know we're not supposed to go, but we were only playing cards, and Henry set fire to the sheets that were hanging out on the line! He did it with paraffin from the shed! And the motor home nearly caught on fire, and somebody might have been killed!' Beth said, all at once but enunciating clearly.

Meredith took off her glasses, folded them calmly. 'Is this true?' she asked Henry.

'No! *I* haven't been near their filthy campsite,' he said.

'Liar!' I shouted.

'Erica!' Meredith silenced me, the word like a whip crack.

'So how did this fire start, if indeed there has been a fire?'

'Of course there's been a fire! Why would I say—' Beth protested.

'Well, Elizabeth, you also said you weren't going to associate with the tinkers, as I have repeatedly requested, so how am I to know when you are lying and when you are not?' Meredith asked, evenly. Beth clamped her lips together, her eyes fierce. 'Well, Henry? Do you know how the fire might have started?'

'No! Except – well . . . these two seem to get on with the gyppos like a house on fire. Perhaps that's what did it,' he said, looking up at her carefully, almost smiling, gauging her reaction. Meredith studied him for a moment, and then she laughed. That rare, loud sound that startled us all, even Henry. Two bright spots of pleasure bloomed in his cheeks.

In spite of the fact that Caroline never, apparently, went to visit her in Surrey, in spite of her no-show at Charles' funeral, Meredith did come back to live here with her. Perhaps life got too hard, with no husband and two children. Perhaps Caroline needed looking after, and Meredith loved her in spite of everything. And she was to be the next Lady Calcott, after all; perhaps she thought it was her duty to return to the family seat. I'll never know, of course, because the letters stop upon her return. I think of the care and attention she showed Caroline when she was ancient – feeding her, dressing her, reading to her. What if she did all that and still got no love back for her pains? What if she'd hoped for some deathbed confession that never came – that her mother had always loved her, that she had been a good daughter? What if she'd had dreams of marrying again, of starting over? Perhaps she expected Caroline to die soon after she returned, and had ideas about bringing the house back to life, of tempting a new husband with it, of having more children to fill it? But like the queen, Caroline lived on and on; and the heir grew old, waiting to ascend. I think it must have been something like that – some crushed hopes, some vast disappointment. To make Meredith turn out the way she did. To make her treat our mother so harshly, when our mother refused to make the same sacrifices.

These are my thoughts on Monday morning, as I dress in warm cords and slide the teething ring into my pocket. The bell makes a cheerful little giggling sound. I go to the study, look in the desk drawers for a pen and a pad of paper and stuff them into my bag. Outside is another of those crystal-clear days, painfully bright. I try to feel the optimism I felt the last time the sky was this blue, and we went to Avebury, and Eddie was here to make us glad. I leave Beth on the phone to Maxwell, bargaining for the return of her son. She sits by the kitchen window in a shaft of incandescent light that blanches out her expression.

The sun is low in the sky, inescapable. It stabs at me through the windscreen, lances up from the wet road so that I must drive through a blinding wall of light. I turn gingerly out of the village onto the main road and see a familiar figure walking along the frosty white verge. Light clothes, as ever; hands thrust into his pockets the only concession to the biting cold. Something leaps up inside me. I pull over, wind down the window and call to him. Dinny shades his face with one hand, hiding his eyes, leaving only his jaw visible – that flat line of his mouth that can look so serious.

'Where are you headed?' I ask. The cold stabs at my chest, makes my eyes water.

'To the bus stop,' Dinny replies.

'Well, I gathered that. Where then? I'm going into Devizes – do you want a lift?' Dinny walks over to the car, drops his hand from his face. With the sun this strong, I can see that his eyes are brown, not black. The warm colour of conkers; touches of tortoiseshell in his hair.

'Thanks. That'd be great,' he nods.

'Shopping?' I ask, as I pull away from the verge, the engine sluggish with frost.

'I thought I'd get something for the baby. And I need a few supplies. What about you?'

'I'm going to the library – they'll have internet access there, won't they?'

'I don't know – never been in, myself,' he admits, a touch sheepishly.

'For shame,' I tease.

'There's more than enough drama in the newspapers, without reading made-up dramas as well,' he smiles. 'Checking your email?'

'Well, yes, but I'm also going to look something up in the births, marriages and deaths index. I've been tracking down a Calcott family secret.'

'Oh?'

'I found a picture of my great-grandma, Caroline – do you remember her?'

'Not really. I think I saw her from afar a couple of times.'

'She was American. She came over to marry Lord Calcott late in 1904, but I've found this picture of her in 1904, in America, with a baby.' I fumble blindly in my bag and pass it to him. 'Nobody seems to know what happened to that baby – there's no record of her marrying before, but I've also found a letter that suggests otherwise.'

'Well, the baby probably died there, before she came over.' He shrugs slightly.

'Probably,' I concede. 'But I just want to check – just in case he's mentioned in the records. If he is . . . if I can prove that Caroline lost a child – another child, since we know she lost a daughter here in Barrow Storton – it might help explain why she was the way she was.'

Dinny says nothing to this. He studies the photo, frowning slightly.

'Perhaps,' he murmurs, after a while.

'I've been trying to find out, you see, why the Calcotts – the earlier Calcotts – had such a bee in their bonnets about you Dinsdales. Caroline and Meredith, I mean. I've been trying to find out why they behaved the way they did towards your family,' I say, suddenly keen to have his support in this quest.

'A bee in their bonnets?' he echoes quietly. 'That's a gentle euphemism.'

'I know,' I say apologetically. I change the subject. 'So, how's Honey doing?' We chat about his sister for a while, until I try to park in Devizes and am met by swarms of people, row upon row of parked cars.

'What on earth is all this?' I exclaim.

'Sale mania,' Dinny sighs. 'Try Sheep Street.'

Eventually, I creep the car into a space, bumping the one next to me when I open the door. Skeins of exhaust twist up into the sky and the town hums with voices, the ring of purposeful footsteps. It all seems too loud, and I feel as though the quiet at Storton Manor has snuck into me, somehow. It's performed a stealth coup; and now I notice its absence like something vital gone.

'Do you want a lift back as well?' I offer.

'How long will you be?'

'I'm not sure. An hour and a half? Maybe a bit longer?'

'OK – thanks. I'll meet you back here?'

'How about in that café on the High Street – the one with the blue awning? It'll be warmer if one of us has to wait,' I suggest. Dinny nods, twists his hand in salute and strides away between the packed cars.

The library is on Sheep Street, so I don't have far to walk. The fan above the doors pours out a stifling wave of warmth and I stop the second I am through, struggle out of my coat and scarf in the cloying heat. It's almost empty inside, with a few people perusing the shelves and a severe-looking woman at the desk who is busy with something and does not look up at me. Seated at a computer, I search for deaths in 1903, 1904 and 1905, to cast a wide net, and the names Calcott and Fitzpatrick, in London and in Wiltshire. I skim these results for the deaths of children under the age of two. My pad of paper remains blank on the desk beside me. After an hour, I scrawl on it: *He's not here*.

I stare at the last list of names on the screen, until my eyes slide through the pixels, focus on a point in the middle distance. The baby probably died in America. That, and whatever happened to make Caroline leave the man who signed himself C, might even be what made her come over to England in the first place, and could certainly have contributed to her distance, her frigidity. So why can't I let it go at that? What is it that is pulling at a far corner of my mind, begging me to grasp it? Something else – another thing – that I know and have forgotten. I wonder how many of these things are lurking in my head, waiting for me to chase them out. I pull the teething ring from my pocket, run my fingers around the smooth, immaculate ivory. Inside the bell, on the rim, is the hallmark. A tiny lion cartouche, an anchor, a gothic letter G, and something I struggle to make out. I turn it to the light, hold it close to my face. A flame? A tree – a skinny tree like a cypress? A hammer? The light bounces from it. It's a hammer head. Vertical, as if viewed from the side when striking something.

I turn back to the computer, search for *American silver marks G*. Several online encyclopedias and silver-collecting guides appear. Searching entries under the letter G, it takes no time at all to find the stamp on the bell. Gorham. Founded in Rhode Island in 1831. An influential silver maker – made various tea sets for the White House, and the Davis Cup for tennis, but their primary trade was in teaspoons, thimbles and other small gift items. I find the vertical hammer head in the list of Gorham's date marks – 1902. This then I have managed to prove – whoever the baby in the photo is, and whoever his father was, and whatever became of him, this silver and ivory teething ring belonged to him. He was the fine son it was offered to. Not Clifford, not any other child Caroline lost once she had come over to England. I close my hand around it, feel my skin warm the metal; the stifled movement of the clapper inside, like a tiny, tremulous heartbeat.

It is slow work, making my way to the High Street, through knots of purposeful browsers. Shop windows ablaze with lurid banners promising unmissable bargains, ludicrous discounts; music and heat blaring out; people with four, five, six fat carrier bags, sprouting from the ends of their arms. I am barrelled this way and that and the café, when I reach it, is full to the brim. I feel a wash of irritation, until I see Dinny already at one of the small tables in the steamed-up window. The reek of coffee grounds is strong and delicious in here. I edge my way through the crowded tables.

'Hi – sorry, have you been waiting long?' I smile, draping my coat over the empty seat opposite him.

'No, not long. I got lucky with this table – a couple of old dears were just getting up as I came in.'

'Do you want another coffee? Something to eat?'

'Thanks. Another coffee would be good.' He clasps his hands on the sticky table top and looks so odd suddenly that I stare, can't work out what I am seeing. Then I realise – this is one of only a scant handful of times I have seen Dinny indoors. Actually sitting at a table, in no hurry to be outside again, doing something as mundane as having coffee in a café. 'What's up?' he asks me.

'Nothing,' I shake my head. 'I'll be right back.'

I buy two big mugs of creamy coffee, and an almond croissant for me.

'Didn't you have breakfast today?' Dinny asks, as I sit.

'Yes, I did,' I shrug, tearing off a corner, dunking it. 'But it is Christmas,' I add, and Dinny smiles, tips one eyebrow in concession. The sunlight through the window gives him a bright halo; he is almost too dazzling to look at.

'Did you find what you were looking for?'

'Yes and no. There's no record of the baby dying this side of the

Atlantic, so I suppose he must have died on the other side of it, like you suggested.'

'Or . . .' Dinny shrugs.

'Or what?'

'Or, the baby didn't die at all.'

'So where is he?'

'I don't know — it's your project. I'm just pointing out one reason why there might be no record of his death.'

'True. But on her marriage certificate, it says spinster. It couldn't have said that if she'd come over with another man's baby,' I counter. Dinny shrugs again. I pass him the teething ring. 'I checked the mark on this, though. It's a—'

'Teething ring?' Dinny says.

'Which apparently everybody knows but me.' I roll my eyes. 'It's an American mark — and it was made in 1902.'

'But didn't you already know the baby was born in America? What does that prove?'

'Well, if nothing else, I think it proves that Caroline was his mother. When I showed Mum the photograph she suggested Caroline could have been its godmother, or it could have been a friend's baby, or something. But for her to have kept his teething ring this whole time — she has to have been his mother, don't you think?'

'I suppose so, yes.' Dinny nods, hands me back the ivory ring.

I gulp the hot coffee, feel it bring blood into my cheeks. Dinny casts his eyes back out to the thronging street, seems deep in thought.

'So, how does it feel to be the ladies of the manor? Are you starting to get used to it yet?' he asks suddenly, still looking out of the window, away from me.

'Hardly. I don't think we'll ever feel that the place is ours. Not really. And as for staying on to live . . . well. Aside from anything else, the upkeep costs alone would stop us.'

'What about all the Calcott riches village rumour has it you've inherited?'

'Just rumour, I'm afraid. The family wealth has been in decline since the war – and I mean the *first* war. Meredith was always complaining to my parents that they didn't help enough – with the upkeep of the place. That's why she had to sell off so much of the land, the best paintings, the silver . . . the list goes on. There was some money left, when she died, but it'll be spent once the death duties are paid.'

'What about the title?'

'Well, that's gone to Clifford, Henry's father.' As I say his name I raise my eyes, lock with Dinny's for a fleeting moment. 'My great-grandfather, who was also a Henry, changed the letters patent by act of parliament, because he had no sons. He fixed it so that the barony could pass to Meredith, and then revert to male offspring. Her heirs-male of the body, or whatever they call it.'

'So that's why Meredith stayed Calcott, even though she married? And why your mother is a Calcott too? But how come you and Beth are Calcotts, then?'

'Because Meredith bullied my parents into it. Poor Dad – didn't stand a chance. She said the Calcott name was too important to cast off. Apparently, Allen just doesn't have the same clout.'

'Odd, that she left the house to you girls if the title was going to your uncle, and she was so keen to keep the family line going and all the rest of it,' he muses, swirling his coffee around the bottom of the mug.

'Meredith *was* odd. She had no say in where the title went, but she could do what she liked with the house. Perhaps she thought we represented the best chance of keeping the family going.'

'So, after Clifford, it will be . . . ?'

'Extinct. No more title. Theoretically, Clifford could go to court again, and have it pass to Eddie, but there's no way in the world Beth would allow it.'

'No?'

'She wants nothing more to do with it. Or the house, really. Which kind of makes my decision for me, too – we would both have to live here if we wanted to keep it.' Dinny is silent for a while. I can feel the shape of Beth's reluctance, the reason for it, trying to coalesce in the air between us.

'Not really surprising,' Dinny murmurs at last.

'Isn't it?' I ask, leaning forward. But Dinny shrugs, leans back from the table.

'Why are you here, then? If you know you aren't going to stay?'

'I thought it would be good. Good for Beth. For both of us really. To come back for a while and . . .' I wave one hand, struggle for words. 'Revisit. You know.'

'Why would it be good for her? It doesn't seem to me like she even wants to think about it, let alone revisit it. Your childhood here, I mean.'

'Dinny . . .' I pause. 'When you came up to the house to see her, what did you mean when you said there were things she needed to know? Things you wanted to tell her?'

'You really were eavesdropping, weren't you?' he says, his tone ambiguous. I try to show contrition.

'What things, Dinny? Something about Henry?' I press, my heart thumping.

Dinny looks at me with lowered brows.

'I think I owe it to her . . . no, not owe. That's the wrong word. I think she ought to know some things about when we were young. I don't know what she thinks, but . . . some things might not have been what they seemed,' he says quietly.

'What things?' I lean forward, make him meet my eye. He hesitates, stays silent. 'Beth keeps telling me you can't turn back the clock, and we can't go back to the way things were,' I flick my eyes up at him, 'but I just want to tell you that . . . that you can trust me, Dinny.'

'Trust you to do what, Erica?' he asks, and his voice has an edge of sadness.

'To do whatever. I'm on your side. Whatever happens, or happened,' I say. I know I am not making myself clear. I don't know how to. Dinny pinches the bridge of his nose, screws his eyes shut for a second. When he opens them again I am shocked to see tears there, not quite ready to fall.

'You don't know what you're saying,' he says quietly.

'What do you mean?'

Again he pauses, lost in thought.

'You all done in town, then?' he says, ready to leave.

When I check my phone, there are three missed calls from my flatmate, Annabel. The name seems to come from another time, another world entirely. I wonder absently if there is some problem with the rent, or the radiator in my room that keeps leaking, staining the carpet. But these questions seem so very distant, irrelevant. And then I realise: that is not my life any more. It was the life I was living, and at some point, without me even realising it, I stopped living it. And I don't have very long to work out where that leaves me. I go up to my room to read letters, to think. I listen to the quiet, which resounds after the bustle of town. The muted yelping of the rooks outside. No musical bird song to charm the ear, no church bells pealing, no children laughing. Just the deep quiet that so upset me at first. I let it sink back into me. How amazing, that this could ever feel like home.

On Tuesday I drive to West Hatch, squinting into the lazy sun. It's not a big village. I drive around it twice until I see what I'm looking for. In front of a compact brick bungalow, a piece of sixties-built convention, there's a battered old motor home taking up the whole of the driveway. It was new once, cream coloured with a wide coffee-brown stripe running along each side. Now it's green with algae, bald of tyre. But I know it at once. I have been inside it, sat on a padded, sticky plastic bench and gulped down savage home-made lemonade. I am almost choked up at the sight of it now. Mickey Mouse's house. I picture Mo as she was, round and slightly wry, leaning on the door jamb drying her hands on a blue cloth as Dinny and Beth and I turned our backs to her. Mickey with his elaborate moustache, in overalls always streaked with engine oil, black grime in the creases of his hands.

At the door I find my nerves fluttering. Excited rather than scared. The bell makes a soft, electronic *ping . . . pong*. I never thought Mo would answer to such a bell, but answer she does. She looks smaller, older, slightly denuded, but I recognise her at once. More lines on her face, and her hair a solid, unlikely chestnut colour, but the same shrewd eyes. She looks at me with a steady, measuring gaze and I'm glad I'm not trying to sell her anything.

'Yes?'

'Um, I've come to see Honey? And the baby. It's Erica. Erica Calcott.' I smile slightly, watch her recognise the name and search my face for the features she knew.

'Erica! By Christ, I would never have known you! You look so different!'

'Twenty-three years might do that to a girl.' I smile.

'Well, come in, come in, we're all in the front room.' She ushers me inside, gestures to a doorway on the left and suddenly I'm nervous about going in. I wonder who *we all* are.

'Thanks,' I say, hovering in the hall, hands clammy on the plastic flower wrapper.

'Go on in, go on,' she says, and I have no choice. 'I hear you nearly met little Haydee already, on the way to the hospital!'

'Nearly!' I reply. I find myself the only one standing in a room full of seated people. It's stiflingly hot. The view from the window wobbles slightly in the radiator haze and I feel my face flush crimson. I glance around, smile like an idiot. Dinny looks up sharply from one end of the sofa, and he smiles when he sees me.

Honey sits next to him, an empty carrycot at her feet and a bundle in her arms. There's another young girl I don't recognise, with shocking-pink hair and a crystal in her lip. Mo introduces her as Lydia, a friend of Honey's, and an older man, thin and beady, is Mo's partner Keith. There's nowhere for me to sit so I dither awkwardly in the small room, and Honey struggles to sit up straighter.

'Oh, no – don't get up!' I say, proffering the flowers and chocolates, then shunting them onto the table through a clutter of empty coffee mugs and a plate of rich tea biscuits.

'I wasn't. I'm passing her to you,' Honey says, flicking her kohled eyelids and carefully manoeuvring the baby towards me.

'Oh, no. No. You look comfortable.'

'Don't be chicken-shit. Take her,' Honey insists, half smiling. 'How did you find us?' she asks.

'I went down to the camp first – bumped into Patrick. He told me you were home.' I glance at Dinny, I can't help it. He is watching me intently, but I can't guess his expression. I drop my bag and take Haydee from her mother. A small pink face, still creased and angry, below a shock of dark hair finer than cobwebs. She doesn't stir as I perch on the arm of the sofa, or as I kiss her forehead and smell the baby smell of brand-new skin and milky spit. I am suddenly curious to know how it would feel if this baby were mine. To be in on those secrets – the strength behind Beth's gaze when she watches her son; the way he raises her up, makes her whole, just by being in the room. These little creatures that have such power over us. The beginnings of a need in me that I hadn't known was there.

'She's *tiny*,' I say, breathlessly, and Honey rolls her eyes.

'I know. All that heaving and all this flab for a five pound midget!' she says, but she can't hide how pleased she is, how proud. This initiation over, the atmosphere in the room seems to ease.

'She's beautiful, Honey. Well done you! Is she a screamer?'

'No, not so far. She's been pretty chilled out.' Honey leans towards me, can't stay even arm's length from the child for long. Up close I see the dark shadows under her eyes, skin so pale that blue veins show through it, winding across her temples. She looks tired, but thrilled.

'She'll get the hang of the yelling, don't you worry,' Mo says ruefully, and Honey flashes her a mildly rebellious look.

'I'll put another brew on,' Keith says, levering himself from his chair and collecting empty mugs onto a tin tray. 'You'll take a cup, Erica?'

'Oh, yes please. Thanks.' I can feel eyes on me and I look to my right. Dinny watches me, still. Those dark eyes of his, black as a seal's again now; unblinking. I hold his gaze for two heartbeats and then he looks away, stands up abruptly. I suddenly wonder if he minds me gatecrashing his family like this.

'I have to get going,' he says.

'What? Why?' Honey asks.

'Just . . . things to do.' He bends down, kisses his sister on the top of her head, then he hesitates, and turns to me. 'We're all heading to the pub tomorrow night, if you and Beth want to come?' he asks.

'Oh, thanks. Yes – I'll ask Beth,' I say.

'Raise me a glass,' Honey grumbles. 'New Year's Eve and I'll be at home and in bed by nine.'

'Oh, you'll soon get used to missing out on all sorts of occasions, don't you worry,' Mo tells her brightly, and Honey's face falls in dismay.

'I'll be back later. Bye, Mum,' Dinny smiles, briefly presses his hand to the side of Mo's face and then stalks from the room.

'What have you done to him, then?' Honey asks me, and she smiles but she's guarded.

'What do you mean?' I reply, startled.

'He jumped like a rabbit when you walked in,' she observes; but her attention is back on Haydee, and I pass the baby back to her.

Keith returns with a fresh tray of steaming mugs, and the lights on the Christmas tree in the corner wink on and off; slow, then fast, then slow again. Mo asks me about the house, about Meredith and Beth and Eddie.

'Nathan tells me young Eddie was out playing with our Harry, when he was here,' she says.

'Yes, they got on brilliantly. Eddie's such a great kid. He never judges,' I say.

'Well, Beth was always such a good girl. It's no wonder really,' Mo nods. She blows on her tea, her top lip creasing like Grandpa Flag's did. It gives me a shock to notice this resemblance, this sign of how much time has passed. Mo, becoming an old woman.

'Yes. She's . . . a wonderful mum,' I say.

'God! It makes me feel ancient, to see you all grown up, Erica; and Beth too . . . with her own child, no less!' Mo sighs.

'Well, you are a grandma now, after all.' I smile.

'Yes. Not something we were quite ready for, but I am a grandma now,' she says, giving Honey a wry glance.

'Oh come *on*, Mum. We've had this conversation about a *hundred* times already,' Honey says, exasperated. Mo waves a conciliatory hand at her, then passes it wearily over her eyes.

'God, haven't we though?' she mutters; but then she smiles. We sit quietly for a moment, as Haydee murmurs in her sleep.

'Mo, I wanted to ask you about something – if you don't mind?'

'Fire away,' she says, but she laces her fingers in her lap, as if bracing herself, and there is tension around her eyes.

'Well, I was wondering if you'd tell me again why Grandpa Flag was called Flag? I know someone told me before, when we were little – but I can't remember it properly now . . .' At this she relaxes, unknots her hands.

'Oh! Well, that's an easy enough one to tell. His proper name was Peter, of course, but the story goes, as it was told to me, that he was a foundling. Did you know that? Mickey's grandparents found him in the woods one day, in a patch of marsh flags – those yellow flowers, you know them? It was something like that, anyway. He'd been ditched by some young lass who'd got herself in trouble, no doubt' – a mutinous scowl from Honey, at this – 'so they picked him up and took him in to raise as their own, and called him Peter; but more often than not Mickey's grandma just called him 'her baby of the flags', or some such fancy, and the name just stuck.'

'I remember. In a patch of marsh flags . . .' I say, and everything else about the story I remember being told before, except this part. With a tingle of recognition, I realise that this detail is not exactly right. 'Do you know when that was? What year?'

'Lord, no! Sorry. In the early years of the last century, it would have been; but I couldn't say any surer than that. Poor little mite. Can you imagine, leaving a baby out like that? No knowing if anyone would find it or if it would just lie there and suffer to the end. Terrible thing to do.' Mo slurps her tea. 'Mind you, in those days once you had a kid no one would touch you, I suppose. Not for work or for marrying or nothing else.' She shakes her head. 'Rotten bastards.'

'Do you know where they found him? Where in the country, I mean?'

'Well, here, of course. In Barrow Storton. He was a local baby, whose ever he was.'

I take this in, and I almost tell them what I think, but I don't. It seems suddenly too big, the incredible, disturbing, seasick idea that I have; and the way it chimes with something Dinny said to me in the café yesterday.

'Why do you ask?' Mo says.

'Oh, just curious. I've been looking into the history of the

Calcotts, and what have you, since I've been back. Shuffling through what I remember, trying to fill in the gaps,' I shrug. Mo nods.

'It's always the way. We wait until the people who could answer our questions are dead and gone, and only then do we realise we had questions to ask them,' she says, somewhat sadly.

'Oh, I'm not sure Meredith would have answered any questions of mine, anyway,' I say wryly. 'I was never her favourite.'

'Well, if it's the history of the house you're after, you should go and talk to old George Hathaway, over at Corner Cottage,' Keith tells me, leaning his sinewy elbows on his bony knees.

'Oh? Who's George Hathaway?' I ask.

'Just a pleasant old boy. He ran the garage on the Devizes road most of his life. Retired now, of course. But his mother was a maid at the big house, back in the day.'

'How far back?' I ask eagerly.

'Oh,' Keith flaps a gnarled red hand over his shoulder, 'right back. You know, they used to go into service at an early age, back then. I think she was only a girl when she started there. Before the first world war, it would have been.' I breathe deeply, excitement tickling the palms of my hands. 'You know which one Corner Cottage is? On the way out of the village, towards Pewsey, where the lane bends sharp to the left? It's the little thatched place with the green gates just there.'

'Yes, I know it. Thank you.' I smile. I leave them shortly afterwards, as Honey starts to drowse on the sofa and Mo takes the baby from her, puts her down in the carrycot.

'Come again, won't you? Bring Beth – it'd be nice to see you both,' Mo says, and I nod as the cold outside makes my nose ache.

I go straight to Corner Cottage, which sits by itself on the outskirts of Barrow Storton; walls that were once white now streaked and grey. The render is cracking in places, the thatch is dark and sagging. The gate is closed, but I let myself in, cross the weed-choked driveway. I knock three times, hard; the heavy knocker so cold it burns my fingers.

'Yes, my love?' An old man, short and spry, smiles at me, keeps the chain on the door.

'Um, hello. Sorry to bother you – are you George Hathaway?' I say, hurriedly marshalling my thoughts.

'That's me, my love. Can I help you?'

'My name's Erica Calcott, and I was wondering if—'

'*Calcott*, you say? From the manor house?' George interrupts.

'Yes, that's right. I was just—'

'Just a tick!' The door shuts in my face, opens a second later without the chain. 'Never in all my years did I expect a *Calcott* to arrive at my door. What a turn up! Come in, come in; don't dawdle on the step!'

'Thank you.' I step inside. The interior of the cottage is clean, tidy, warm. Pleasantly surprising, compared to the exterior.

'Come on through. I'll put the kettle on and you can tell me whatever it is that brings you here.' George bustles ahead of me along a narrow corridor. 'Coffee suit you?' The kitchen is low and crowded. The usual build up of paraphernalia – biscuit tins, spatulas, rusting sieves and onion skins; but other things besides. Things that speak of the absence of a woman about the house. A black and greasy engine part on the table. A set of spanners on top of the fridge. George moves with a speed and deftness that belies his years. Neat curls of white hair around a thin face; eyes a startling pale green, the colour of a driftwood fire.

'I've only just got back myself, last night – you're lucky to find me home. Been at my daughter's for Christmas, over in Yeovil. Lovely to see her, and the grandkids of course, but just as lovely to be home again, isn't that right, Jim?' He addresses a small, fat, wire-haired mongrel, which waddles from its basket to investigate my legs. It has the penetrating aroma of elderly dogs everywhere, but I scratch behind one of its ears, all the same. Pungent grease gathers under my nails. 'Here you go. Sit down, my love.' He passes me a mug of instant and I cup my hands around it gratefully, slide onto a chair at the enamel-topped table. 'You've moved into the big house, now, have you?'

'Oh, not really, no. We've been here for Christmas — my sister and I. But I don't think we'll be staying on permanently,' I explain. George's face falls.

'Now that's a shame! Not selling up, I hope? Shame for the place to fall out of the family, when it's been in it so many years.'

'I know. I know it is. Only, my grandmother was rather specific about the terms of her will, and . . . well, let's just say it might be very hard for us to keep to them,' I say.

'Ah, well, say no more. None of my business. Families is families, and they all have their ins and outs, Lord knows, even the grand ones!'

'Perhaps especially the grand ones.' I smile.

'My mother worked for your family you know,' George tells me, pride in his voice.

'I know. That was why I've come to see you, actually. The Dinsdales put me on to you—'

'Mo Dinsdale?'

'That's right.'

'Lovely lady, Mo. Bright as a button. Normally, it's the menfolk that brings a car in for work — I used to run the garage, you know, on the Devizes road. But when that big wagon of theirs needed fixing it was always Mo that came in with it, and she watched me like a hawk! Needn't have — I knew better than to try to pull the wool over her eyes. Lovely lady,' George chuckles.

'I was wondering if your mother ever used to talk about the time she spent working at the manor?' I ask, sipping my coffee, letting it scald my throat.

'If she ever talked about it? Well, she never *stopped* talking about it, my love — not when I was a lad.'

'Oh? Did she work there a long time, do you know? Do you know when she started there?' I am keen, I lean towards George. Beneath the table, Jim sits on my foot, plump and warm. George grins at me.

'It was the length of time she worked there that was the cause of all the natter!' he says. 'She was let go, you see. Only eight or nine months after she started. It was a bit of a source of shame, in our family.'

'Oh.' I can't hide my disappointment, because I doubt that she can have learnt much in so short a time. 'Do you know why? What happened?'

'Lady Calcott fingered her for stealing. Mother denied it with every breath she had, but there you go. The gentry didn't need proof back then. Off she went packing, with no character reference or nothing. Stroke of luck that the butcher here – my dad – was in love with her from the second he set eyes on her – she married him soon afterwards, so she wasn't without means for very long.'

'Which Lady Calcott was it? Do you know the year your mother was there?'

'Lady Caroline, she was. 1905, as I remember Mother telling me.' George rubs his chin, squints into the past. 'Must have been,' he concludes. 'She married my old man in the autumn of '05.'

'Caroline was my great-grandmother. Would you like to see a picture of her?' I smile. I have it with me, in my bag. The New York portrait. George's eyes widen with delight.

'Why, yes, look at that! She looks much the same as I remember her! Nice to know the old grey cells haven't packed all the way up just yet.'

'You knew her?' I am surprised at this.

'Not *knew* her, so much – the likes of her didn't come around to tea with the likes of us. But when I was a lad we used to see her, from time to time. She opened the church fête a couple of times, you know; and then there was the big bash we had for the coronation in fifty-three. They opened up the manor gardens, put some bunting around and the like. About the only time I remember them doing something so community-minded. The whole village poured in to have a gander, since, even for a bunch of toffs, and if you'll pardon my saying, miss, the Calcotts have always been tighter than a gnat's chuff. None of us was ever invited in for any other reason.'

'Please, call me Erica,' I tell him. 'So, did your mother say anything else about her time working for Caroline? Like why she was accused of theft, if she said she didn't do it?' At this, George looks a little sheepish.

'It's a bit of a wild story, that one. Mother was always very straight, very honest. But most people had trouble believing what she claimed, so after a long old while she finally stopped talking about it. But I do remember, from when I was a lad, that she reckoned she knew something she wasn't supposed to. Found something out she wasn't supposed to—'

'What was it?' The air expands in my chest, makes it hard to breathe.

'I'll tell you, if you give me half a chance!' George reprimands me with a smile. 'She said there was a *baby* vanished from the house. She didn't know whose baby it was – it just appeared one day, which was one of the things that made people doubt her. Babies don't just appear, after all, do they? Some gal had to have carried him and birthed him. But she swore it – that there was a baby in the house, and that it vanished again, just as quick as it arrived. And about the same time, one was found out in the woods and the tinkers – Mo's people – took it all round the village, asking who it belonged to. Nobody put their hand up, so they raised the child. But my mother could not let it lie – she swore blind to anybody that'd listen that that baby was in the manor house one day, and that Lady Calcott took him out and left him. So, of course

Lady C wanted her gone. Accused her of stealing some trinket, and that was that. She was out of there so fast she never had time to get her coat on. Make of that what you will. Some in the village said my mother cooked this baby story up, to get her own back, you understand? To bring some heat on the Calcotts who'd left her without a job to go to. And maybe, maybe there's some truth in that. She was so very young when all this went on, my mother. No more than fifteen or so. Perhaps she was too young for such a responsible position. But I can't credit her just lying about something like that. Nor stealing, for that matter. She was straight as a die, my old mum.' George stops, stares into the past, and I realise I am holding my breath. My heart bumps painfully, makes my fingers shake a little. I tap one nail on the blurred baby in the New York picture.

'That's the baby. That's the baby that appeared at the manor. The baby that Caroline dropped out in the woods. Your mother wasn't lying,' I tell him. George goggles at me and I feel the blessed relief of closure, of solving a puzzle, however distant from me it may be.

I tell him what I know, what I have gathered from her letters, from this photo, the teething ring, and the missing marsh flag pillowcase. And the age old animosity towards the Dinsdales. I talk until my mouth is dry and I have to swig cold coffee to wet it. And when I am done I feel bone weary but glad. It feels like finding something precious I thought I'd lost; like filling in a huge hole in my past – in our past. Mine, Beth's, Dinny's. He is my cousin. Not two families at war, but one family. At length, George speaks.

'Well, I'm staggered. Proof, after all these years! My mother – if she can hear you from wherever she is, believe me, my love, she's doing a little victory dance right now! And you're sure about all this, are you?'

'Yes, I'm sure. It probably wouldn't stand up in a court of law, or anything, but I'm as sure as I can be. That baby came with her from America, and somehow she kept him hidden while she married Lord Calcott. But then he wound up here at the manor, somehow, and she had to get rid of him. That's the part I'm most in the dark about – where he'd been in the meantime, and if she was married before and had a baby, why keep it hidden? But it's too much of a coincidence. The baby that vanished and the one that was found *have* to be one and the same.'

'It is a pity that all those people who called my mother a liar aren't around to find out better.'

'What was your mother's name?' I ask, on a whim.

'Cassandra. Evans, as she would have been back then. Hold on, I'll show you a photo.' George moves over to the dresser, opens a drawer and rifles through it. The picture he gives me is of Cassandra Evans on her wedding day. Cassandra Hathaway, as she had recently become. A small, delicate-looking girl with a determined glint in her eye and a broad smile. Smooth skin, dark hair caught up in coils, a garland of flowers pinned to it. Her dress is simple, shift-shaped with a panel of lace in the bodice and touches of net at the collar. This girl saw Grandpa Flag while he was still Caroline's *fine son*. She might have known what it was that Caroline longed to confess to her Aunt B. I stare into the grainy dark spots of her eyes, trying to see that knowledge there.

I leave Corner Cottage a short while later, promising to go back and visit. 'A new entente cordiale between Calcotts and Hathaways!' George announced, quite delighted, as I left. I hadn't the heart to say I might never be back; to the village, the manor, any of it. Unexpected, the way this thought makes me feel, when for twenty years or more I have lived away quite happily. I feel at the edge of a terrible sadness, a deep pool of it that I could fall into, never climb out of; just as Beth feared I would at the dew pond. And yet I haven't even unpacked, back at the manor. My clothes are still in my case. They are in disarray, like me. I've lurched out of my established trajectory and now I am freewheeling, uncertain of where to go next.

I think about blood as I drive back to the manor. About those little traces, the little tendencies all our ancestors have left in us. My propensity to clown in awkward situations; my mother's ability to draw; Beth's grace; Dinny's straight brows and jet eyes. A blizzard of tiny traces, whirling at the core of each of us. I think about my blood and Beth's. About Dinny's, about Grandpa Flag's. And Henry's of course. Henry, the last scion of the Calcott line. He showed us Dinny's blood once, up at the barrow. I think even Henry was a little shocked by it, just for a second. Shocked and then pleased, of course. Jubilant. It was the summer he disappeared, but it was early in the holidays. It might have been the first time they'd seen each other that year, but I don't know for sure.

I'd seen boys fight before, of course. At school, in the far corner of the playground where the side of the games hall shielded the combatants from the watchful eyes of the break monitor. *The corner*. That's what it was called. Whispered from ear to ear during lessons – the next assignation, the next death match. *Gary and Neil in the corner at lunchtime!* The scandal always thrilled me, although the fights never lasted long. Coat pulling; somebody spun around, thrown to the ground. Hair yanked, perhaps; a kicked shin, bruised knees. Then the monitor would notice the crowd, or one boy would start to cry. The victor won the right to escape, the loser had to stay and protest that nothing had happened.

But with Dinny and Henry it was different. We'd gone up to the barrow to test-fly the model aeroplanes we'd spent all morning making from brown paper and ice-lolly sticks. We needed a good launch site, was the verdict – proper thermal updraughts, Dinny said. Meredith was stirring trouble in the village, as ever. She'd forbidden the estate's tenant farmers to give work to any kind of itinerant worker, which left the farmers without the help they needed and could afford, and the Dinsdales without the summer jobs that they relied upon finding here. That was her aim, of course — although I'm not sure of that now. She must have known she'd have to back down eventually. I think she just did it to remind them. Remind them that she was there, and that she hated them. There were all sorts of arguments at the house, and we'd overheard a lot of them. And so had Henry, of course. He followed us up to the barrow with this as his ammunition.

'Shouldn't *you* be out begging? Your whole family will have to go out begging soon, I expect; or thieving of course.' Sneering at Dinny; no preamble. 'There's no way you'll be able to *buy* any food. Not if you stay around here.'

'Shut up, Henry! Go away!' Beth ordered, but he curled his lip at her.

'*You* shut up! You can't tell me what to do! And I'm going to tell Grandma you've been playing with the dirty gyppos!'

'Tell her! See if I care!' Beth cried. She was rigid, as taut and straight as a javelin.

'You *should* care — if you're friends with him then you might as well become a gyppo too. You already smell like one. You're stupid enough to be one too, I suppose . . .' He was breathing hard from running up the hill to us; spite made his neck mottle. Dinny glared at him with such fury that I launched my paper plane in anxious desperation.

'Look! Look — look how far it's going!' I cried, jumping up and down. But none of them looked.

'What's the matter with you? Haven't you learnt to talk yet? Are you too stupid?' Henry taunted Dinny. Dinny stared at him, knotted his jaw, said nothing. His silence was a challenge, and Henry didn't back down. 'I saw your mother just now, actually. She was looking in our dustbin for your supper!' Dinny flew at him. So fast that I wasn't aware he'd moved until he cannoned into Henry and they both went staggering down the hill.

'Don't!' Beth shouted, but I don't know which of them she was talking to. I stood stock-still, rooted with shock. This was no playground scuffle, there was no coat pulling. They looked like they wanted to kill each other. I saw bared teeth, fists, young muscles straining.

Then Henry landed one lucky punch. Truly blind luck, because Dinny was clawing at his face so his eyes were shut. Henry flailed his arms, raining blows, and got lucky. His fist cracked Dinny's nose and knocked him down. Dinny sat for a second, astonished, and then a rush of bright blood poured from his nose and began to drip from his chin. Beth and I were mute with horror. That Henry had won. That Dinny was bleeding so much. I had never seen blood like that. So red, so quick. Not like the dull smears on the butcher's block when I went shopping with Mum. Dinny cupped his hand under his chin and caught the blood as if he wanted to keep it. It must have hurt. Tears welled in his eyes, slipped mutinously down his cheeks to join the blood. Henry, when he realised what he'd achieved, stood over Dinny and grinned. I remember his nostrils flaring whitely in triumph, how haughty he looked. He walked away with a swaggering step. Dinny watched him, and I watched Dinny. His eyes blazed, and for a long moment Beth and I were too afraid to go near him.

New Year's Eve is a Wednesday and it really just feels like a Wednesday. None of the old excitement. It was always excitement tinged with dread anyway, I can tell myself now. The buzz and riot of the fireworks over the Thames, the grim knowledge of how long it would take to get clear of the crowds afterwards. Now it's just a Wednesday, but with an encroaching deadline of another kind. Beth said she would stay until the new year. That's what I begged from her – just until the new year. Tomorrow. There's only one thing that I can think of that might make her stay longer, and that's if she won the argument with Maxwell. If Eddie is coming again before school starts, then she might stay.

I am excited about something, of course. Excited about the announcement I plan to make this evening. It's wild outside. I turn the radio up to drown out the moaning wind, harrying the corners of the house. It took a long time to convince Beth to come to the pub – I had to lie, say it might be the last time she sees Dinny before we leave. The wrenching sound of the wind might be all it would take to dissuade her.

'Hair up or down?' I ask Beth as she comes into the bathroom, holding my hair up in a twist to show her, then dropping it, shaking it out. She considers me, tips her head to one side.

'Down. We're only going to the pub, after all,' she says. I rake my fingers through my hair.

'Yeah, I'm only going to put jeans on,' I nod. She stands behind me, bends to put her chin on my shoulder, peers at her own reflection. Can she see? That the bones of her face are so stark, compared to mine? That her skin looks too thin, too pale?

'I know it's New Year's Eve. But I just . . . I just don't really feel like going out. We don't *know* these people . . .' she says, moving away again.

'I'm starting to – you would, if you came out more. Please, Beth. You can't just stay in on your own. Not tonight.'

'Why are you so obsessed with spending time with him, anyway? What good will it do? We don't *know* him any more. We live utterly different lives! And soon we'll have left and we'll probably never see him again anyway.' She paces the floor behind me, agitated.

'I'm not obsessed,' I murmur, drawing silver powder across my eyelids and examining the effect in the mirror. I can feel her looking at me. 'It's *Dinny*,' I shrug. 'He's about *the* most important person from our childhood. Look,' I turn to her, make her look at me. 'Let's just not even think about any of that this evening, OK? Let's just go out, drink the new year in and have a good time. OK?'

I give her a little shake. She takes a deep breath, holds it for a moment.

'OK! You're right. Sorry,' she relents. She sounds relieved, and smiles a little.

'That's better. Now, go and pour us some whisky. *Lots* of whisky,' I command.

'Here you go,' she says, as I come down to the kitchen.

'This should get us a bit more in the party spirit.' I smile and take a glass from her. We clink, and drink. Beth's smile looks a little forced, but she is trying. 'How was Maxwell? Is Eddie coming back to stay?'

'What, here? No,' she says. 'I want him to come and stay with me at home for the last weekend of the holiday. Max says they're going to his parents . . . I don't know,' she sighs. 'I always feel like the one who has to fight to get the better slots in the timetable.'

'Well, we did have him for Christmas . . .' Disappointment bites me. Nothing will keep her here now. Something scrambles inside me, twists, tries to find a way to hold on to her, to hold on to our time here. I am not finished. I am jittery with need.

'A few days out of a four week holiday! It's hardly fair.'

'A few pretty important days, though,' I argue, my voice high. I have lost track of the conversation. I should be urging her to fight harder, to get Eddie back – back here to his friend Harry. Beth sips her whisky. I watch the cartilage in her neck move as she swallows.

'I know. I just . . . I miss him so much, Rick. I don't really see what the point of me is, when I don't have him to look after,' she says forlornly.

'The point of you is to be his mother, whether he's in the room or not. And to be my big sister. And, more importantly right now, your purpose is to drink whisky with me, because I don't intend to be the only one starting the new year with a headache,' I say.

'Bottoms up, then,' Beth says gravely, tipping the entire contents of her glass down her throat, spluttering and laughing as it burns her nose.

'Now, that's more like it!' I laugh.

It's bitter outside. The air bites right through our clothes, and the glow of the alcohol; makes our eyes stream, our lips crack. We walk quickly with gritted teeth, hunched and inelegant. It's clear; the sky is inky, torn across by the unrelenting wind. There are lights on all through the village, warding off the lonely night, and the heat and humanity of the White Horse crashes out like a wave when I pull the door open. It's cheek by jowl. We breathe in the breath of others, swim through it; the heavy, happy stink of alcohol and bodies. Voices so loud, so close. I am sure the silence at the heart of Beth will be battered into submission. I thread us a path to the bar, searching the crowd for Patrick or Dinny, or anybody else I recognise. It's Harry's dreadlocks that I spot, in the snug room at the back of the pub. I buy two whisky and waters, tip my head and smile at Beth to follow me.

'Hi!' I shout, arriving next to the table. I recognise faces from the solstice party, faces I have seen coming and going around the camp. Denise, Sarah and Kip. Dinny and Patrick, of course. Patrick grins at me, and Dinny smiles, his eyes widening with surprise as they alight on Beth. A second later I wonder if it was Beth he was smiling at, not me, but I can't be sure.

'It's the ladies of the manor! Come join us, ladies!' Patrick calls, waving a magnanimous arm over the group. His cheeks are pink, eyes bright. Harry pats my arm and on impulse I bend to him, kiss his cheek, feel the brush of his whiskers. Dinny stares. There's a shuffling, a bunching together along the horseshoe-shaped bench, and room is made for Beth and me at either end.

'I've never actually been in here before,' I shout. 'We weren't old enough the last time we came to stay!'

'That's a crime! Well, this is your local now, so let's get you acquainted with it. Cheers!' Patrick clatters our glasses together. Cold liquid see-saws out, catches the back of Dinny's hand.

'Sorry,' I say, and he shrugs.

'No problem.' He sucks the whisky from his skin, grimacing. 'I don't know how you can drink that poison.'

'After the fourth of fifth nip you get used to it,' I reply jovially. 'So, how are you getting used to being an uncle?'

'I'm not! I still can't believe she's had a baby – five seconds ago she was a baby herself, you know?' Dinny tips his head wryly.

'Make the most of her when she's tiny,' Beth tells him, her words struggling to rise above of the mash of voices. 'They grow so quickly! You won't believe how quickly,' she tries again, louder now.

'Well, I do have the best of both worlds, I suppose. I get to have fun with the kid and then give her back when she stinks or starts howling,' Dinny smiles.

'That's always been my favourite part of being an aunt,' I say, smiling at Beth. And so just like that we chat. We sit and talk like neighbours, like nearly friends. I try not to think about it, how miraculous it is; I don't want to break the spell.

'How's your family research going?' Dinny asks me a while later when my body is warm, my face slightly numb. I peer at him.

'You mean *our* family history?' I ask.

'Do I? What do you mean?'

'Well, what I've found out, basically, is that we're cousins,' I say, smiling widely. Beth frowns at me, Dinny gives that quizzical look of his.

'Rick, what are you talking about?' Beth asks.

'Quite distant – half cousins, twice removed, or thereabouts. Seriously!' I add, when I am met with scepticism all round.

'Let's hear it, then,' says Patrick, folding his arms.

'Right. We know that Caroline had a baby boy before she

married Lord Calcott in 1904. There's a photograph, and she kept hold of the kid's teething ring for the rest of her life—'

'A baby boy who more than likely never came over the water with her, or she would have had trouble remarrying as a spinster, which she apparently did not,' Beth interjects.

'Just hear me out. Then there's a pillowcase missing from one of the antique sets in the house – a pillowcase with yellow marsh flags stitched onto it. Now, Dinny, your grandpa himself told me the story of how he got his name, and your mum reminded me the other day, when I was over there. But I think some of the finer details have got scrambled over the years – Mo said Flag was found in a patch of marsh flags and got the name that way, here, in the Barrow Storton woods which slope and are pretty well drained and aren't really good ground for marsh flags to grow in. I'm *sure* I remember Grandpa Flag telling me himself that he was found in a blanket with yellow flowers on it. It has to be the pillowcase – it has to be!' I insist, as Patrick scoffs and Dinny looks even more sceptical. 'And today, I met George Hathaway—'

'The bloke who used to run the garage on the main road?' Patrick asks.

'That's him. His mother worked at the manor house when Caroline first arrived there. She was sacked – ostensibly for stealing, but she insisted, George says, that she was sent away because she knew there had been a baby in the house – right at the time the Dinsdales found Flag. There was a baby in the house and then it vanished. Your grandpa was my great-grandmother's son. I'm sure of it,' I finish, jabbing a tipsy finger at Dinny. He studies me, rubs his chin, considers this.

'That's . . .' Beth gropes for the word. 'Ridiculous!' she finishes.

'Why is it?' I demand. 'It would explain Caroline's hostility to the Dinsdales – she dumps the kid, wants rid of him, and they pick him up and raise him right on her doorstep. Every time they came back here, they brought that baby with them. It must have driven her mad. That was why she hated them so much.'

'Answer this, then,' Dinny says. 'She brings the baby over with her. She has him with her while she remarries – for some reason her previous marriage is not recorded, but there's no way she'd have wound up marrying a lord if the baby was illegitimate. So, she keeps the baby until she gets here, to Barrow Storton, and then she dumps it in the woods. My question would be why? Why did she do that?'

'Because . . .' I trail off, study my drink. 'I don't know,' I admit. I think hard. 'Was your grandpa disabled in any way?'

'Fit as a fiddle, sharp as a tack,' Dinny shakes his head.

'Maybe Lord Calcott wouldn't let her keep another man's son?'

'Then he would have just not married her, surely, if he minded that much?'

'Isn't it possible,' Patrick begins, 'and indeed rather more plausible, that Caroline's baby died in the States, one of the *servants* at the manor got herself in trouble – perhaps Hathaway's mum – took a pillowcase from the house in a moment of desperation, and got rid of her illegitimate baby? It would hardly be surprising if she lied about it, or got fired for it,' he suggests cheerfully.

'He has a point,' Beth tells me. I shake my head.

'No. I *know* it was the baby in the picture. It has to be,' I insist.

'And as for her attitude towards me and mine,' Patrick goes on with a shrug, 'she was just a product of her time. God knows we come up against enough prejudice these days, let alone a hundred years ago! Vagrancy used to be an actual crime, you know.'

'All right, all right!' I cry. 'I still think I'm right. What do you say, Dinny?'

'I'm not sure. And I'm not sure I want to be a Calcott. They haven't been very kind to the people I love, over the years,' he says, and his gaze is so direct that I have to look away.

'Well, drink up, cousin,' Patrick says. Conciliatory, but not convinced. The subject is changed, my parade rained upon.

'It was a good theory, though,' Beth says, chucking me with her elbow.

By midnight my ears are buzzing and when I turn my head the world blurs past, takes a while to settle back into the right order. I lean against Harry, who sits up straight and has drunk so much cola that he climbs over me go to the toilet every twenty minutes or so. There is talk all around me and I am part of it, I am included. I am happy, drunk, blinkered. At midnight the barman turns the radio up loud and we listen to Big Ben, waiting with our breath paused in the gap before the first toll of the new year. The pub erupts and I think of London, of hearing those bells all the way from there, of my old life carrying on without me. I find I don't want it back. Patrick and Beth and several others kiss me and then I turn to Dinny, proffer my cheek, and he plants a kiss there that I can still feel long after it's gone, wonder if it will leave an indelible mark.

Not long afterwards Beth pulls my arm, says that she's going. The crowd is thinning out, leaving the drunker people behind, of which I am one. I want to stay. I want to keep this party going, maintain the false impression that I belong with these people. Beth shakes her head and speaks into my ear.

'I'm tired. I think you should come too, so we can see each other safely back. You've had quite a bit to drink.'

'I'm fine!' I protest, too loudly, proving her point.

Beth gets up, smiles her goodbyes, starts to pull on her coat and hands me mine.

'We're off,' she says, smiling in general but not meeting Dinny's eye.

'Yep. Party's pretty much over,' Patrick yawns. His bright eyes have turned pink.

'You can all come back to ours, if you want. Plenty of booze there,' I offer expansively. Beth shoots me a worried glance, but nobody takes me up – pleading lateness, drunkenness, impending headaches. I pull on my coat. I am clumsy, can't find the arms. I knock the table as I climb out from behind it, rattling the glasses. As we turn to go Dinny catches Beth's arm, pulls her down to him and speaks into her ear.

'Good night, cousin Erica!' he calls as I weave away.

'I'm right!' I insist, tumbling out of the pub.

'Erica! Wait for me!' Beth shouts into the wind as she emerges from the pub behind me. But I can't seem to slow down. There's a fire in my blood and it's working my body, and I have no control. 'Wait for me, will you!' She jogs to my side. 'That was actually quite fun,' she says.

'Told you,' I say, loud above the buffeting air. I can't quite name what I'm feeling. A huge impatience, the boundless frustration of knowing nothing for sure.

'What were you and Dinny whispering about back there?' I ask.

'He, uh . . .' She looks taken aback. 'He just said to . . . see you safely to bed, that's all.'

'That's all?'

'Yes, that's all! Erica, don't start – you're drunk.'

'I'm not that drunk! You two always did have your secrets and not much has changed. Why won't either of you tell me what happened back then?'

'I . . . I've told you – I don't want to talk about it and neither should you. Have you asked Dinny, then?' She sounds alarmed, almost frightened. I think back, muzzily, realise that I haven't. Not outright.

'What did he really say just now?'

'I just *told* you what he said! My God, Erica . . . are you *jealous*? Still – after all this time?' I stop walking, turn to look at her in the last scatterings of light from the village. It never occurred to me that she knew. That they knew, that they noticed me clamouring for attention. Somehow, it's worse that they did.

'I'm not jealous,' I mutter, wishing it were true. We walk on, stumble up the driveway in silence. As we get to the house I realise that I am uneasy. Some warning bell is trying to ring, beneath my drunken haze. It's Beth's silence, I think. The quality of it, its breadth and depth.

Beth opens the front door but I step back from the darkness inside. In the graphite glow of the moon, it looks like a grave mouth. Beth steps in, flicks on a blinding yellow light, and I turn away.

'Come on – you're letting all the heat out,' she says at last.

I shake my head. 'I'm going for a walk.'

'Don't be ridiculous. It's half past one in the morning and it's freezing. Come inside.'

'No. I'll . . . stay in the gardens. I need to clear my head,' I tell her flatly, backing away. She is an outline in the doorway, faceless and black.

'I'll wait for you to come in, then. Don't be long.'

'Don't wait. Go to bed. I won't be long.'

'Erica!' she calls, as I turn away. 'You're . . . you're not going to let it drop, are you? You're not going to leave it alone.' Real fear in her voice now. It sounds as brittle as glass. I am frightened too, by this change in her, by her sudden vulnerability, the way she braces herself in the door frame as though she might fly apart. But I steel myself.

'No. I'm not,' I say, and I walk away from her.

I won't let this evening end until I have something, until I have resolved something. Until I have remembered something. I stride across the choppy lawn, my legs running away with me, joints swinging, elastic. Under the trees, the dark is solid. I look up at the sky, put my hands in front of me to feel the way, continue. I know where I am going.

The dew pond is just more blackness at my feet. The stone-and-mud smell of the water rises to greet me. Above me the sky hangs motionless, and it seems unreal that the stars should not move, should not be swept away in the wind. Their stillness makes me dizzy. Here I sit in the dead of winter, in the dead of night, a woman with a head full of whisky trying to go back, trying to be a child full of fantasies under a hot summer sky. I stare at the water, I take myself there. My breathing slows and I notice the cold for the first time, the press of the ground through my jeans. I hug my knees into my chest. *Have you pissed yourself, Erica?* Henry laughing, Henry smiling that nasty smile of his. Henry bending down, looking around. What was he doing? What was he looking for? What was I doing? I went back into the water. I'm sure I did. It was a diversion – I was trying to break the tension. I turned and took a run up, and made as big a splash as I could, scrabbling under the surface because my knickers threatened to desert me. And when I came up . . . when I dashed the water from my eyes . . . had Henry found what he was looking for?

Before I know what I am doing, I am in. I have put myself there. I take a run up, I make as big a splash as I can; and then reality comes pouring all around me and my skin catches fire at the cold of the water. The pain is incredible. I have no idea which way is up, no idea where to go, what to do. I have no control over my body, which flails and contorts itself. The air has vanished from my lungs, they have collapsed, my ribs are crushed. I will die, I think. I am sinking like a stone. I will reach the bottom at last, just like I always strove to. The water has no surface, there is no sky any more. And I see Henry. My heart seems to stop. I see Henry. I see him, looking down at me from the bank, eyes wide and incredulous. I see him teetering, and I see blood running down into his eyes. So much blood. I see him start to fall. Then I am in the air again and it is a blessing – so warm, so full of life after the knife strike of the water. A gasp rushes air into my lungs; I cry out in pain.

I can see the bank. It tips and blurs in my view as my body threatens to sink again. I try to make my arms work, to kick my legs. Nothing will move as it is supposed to. My heart beats wildly now, too fast, too big in my chest. It's trying to escape from me, from this leeching chill. I can't get air to stay in my lungs. It whistles out as the water squeezes me. I am flayed alive; I am burning. One hand hits the bank and I can't feel it on my skin, only the resistance of it. I claw at it, force my fingers into the mud, try to make my other hand reach it, try to pull myself out. I struggle. I am a rat in a barrel, a hedgehog in a pond. I am whimpering.

Then hands grab me, under my arms, pulling me further out until my knees are grounded. One more pull and I am out, water streaming from my clothes and hair and mouth. I cough and start to cry, so happy to be out, hurting so much.

'What the *fucking hell* are you *doing*?' It's Dinny. His voice echoes oddly in my ears and I can't look up at him yet, can't move my heavy head on my wooden neck. 'Are you trying to kill yourself, for fuck's sake?' He is rough, furious.

'I'm . . . not sure,' I croak, and concentrate on coughing again. Behind his head the stars judder and wheel.

'Get up!' he commands. He sounds so angry, and the last of my will leaves me. I give up. Lying down on the ground, I turn my head away from him. I can't feel my body, can't feel my heart.

'Just leave me alone,' I say. I think I say. I'm not sure if I have formed words, or just exhaled. He turns me over, stands behind my head and pulls me up by my armpits.

'Come on. You need to warm up before you can lie down and have a rest.'

'I am warm. I'm boiling hot,' I say, but tremors are starting to come, from my feet to my fingertips, convulsing every muscle. My head pounds.

'Come on, walk now. It's not far.'

A short time later I become aware of myself, of the peeled feeling of my skin, the ache in my ribs and arms and skull. My fingers and toes are throbbing, agonising. I am sitting in wet underwear in Dinny's van. Wrapped in a blanket. There's hot tea beside me. Dinny pours in sugar by the heaped spoonful, instructs me to drink it. I sip it, burn my tongue. I'm shaking still, but less now. The inside of the ambulance is warmer than I'd imagined. The embers in the stove light our faces. Narrow bunks along one side, cupboards and shelves and a worktop along the other. A space for billycans. A kettle on the stove top, pans hanging on hooks.

'How come you were at the dew pond?' I ask. My voice has an unhealthy rattle to it.

'I wasn't. I was going home when I heard the bloody great splash you made. You're just lucky the wind's blowing in from the east or I wouldn't have heard it. I wouldn't have come. Do you know what could have happened if I hadn't? Even if you'd managed to get out and then lain on the bank for half an hour . . . do you understand?'

'Yes.' I am contrite, embarrassed. There is no trace of the whisky in me now. My swim has washed it all away.

'So what were you doing?' He sits opposite me on a folding stool, rests one ankle on the opposite knee, crosses his arms. All barriers. I shrug.

'I was trying to remember. That day. The day Henry died.' *Died*, I say. Not *disappeared*. I wait to see if Dinny will correct me. He doesn't.

'Why would you want to remember?'

'Because I *don't*, Dinny. I don't remember it. And I have to. I need to.' He doesn't answer for a long time. He sits and he considers me with hooded eyes.

'Why? Why do you have to? If you really don't remember, then—'

'Don't tell me I'm better off! That's what Beth says and it's not true! I am not better off. There's a bit missing . . . I can't stop thinking about it . . .'

'Try.'

'I know he's dead. I know we killed him.' As I speak I shudder again, scattering drops of tea onto my legs.

'*We* killed him?' Dinny glares at me suddenly, his eyes alight. 'No. *We* didn't kill him.'

'What does that mean? What *happened*, Dinny? Where did he go?'

The question hangs between us for a long moment. I think he will tell me. I think he will. The silence stretches.

'These are not my secrets to tell,' Dinny says, his face troubled.

'I just want things to be as they were,' I say quietly. 'Not things — people. I want Beth to grow up the way she should have grown up, if it hadn't happened. It all starts there, I know it does. And I want for us to be friends, like we were . . .'

'We could have been, perhaps.' His voice is flat. I look up for an explanation. 'You just stopped coming!' he exclaims, eyes widening. 'How do you think that felt, after everything I—'

'After everything you what?'

'After all the time we'd spent, all the growing up . . . You just stopped coming.'

'We were kids! Our parents stopped bringing us . . . there wasn't much we could do about it . . .'

'They brought you here the summer after. And the one after that. I saw you, even if you didn't see me. But you never came down to the camp. My family were turned *inside out* by the police, looking for that boy. Everybody treated us like criminals! I bet they didn't turn the manor upside down, did they? I bet they didn't keep looking in the herb garden for a grave.' I stare at him. I can't think what to say. I try to remember the police searching the house, but I can't. 'At first I thought you'd been forbidden to come down here.

But you'd always been forbidden before and that had never stopped you. Then I thought perhaps you were scared, perhaps you didn't want to talk about what had happened. Then I finally hit on it. You just didn't care.'

'That's not true! We were just children, Dinny! What happened was . . . too big. We didn't know *what* to do with it—'

'*You* were just a child, Erica. Beth and I were twelve. That's old enough. Old enough to know where your loyalties lie. Would it have killed you to come? Just once? To write down your address, to write a letter?'

'I don't know,' I say. 'I don't know what happened. I . . . watched Beth for all my cues. Even now I can't tell if I knew what we'd done, what had happened. I don't know when it went out of my head. I can hardly remember anything I thought or did in those summers afterwards. And then we stopped coming.'

'Well, no wonder. If you were both acting so vacant, your mother must have thought it was damaging you.'

'It *was* damaging us, Dinny.'

'Well, there you go. What happened, happened. There's no changing it now, even if you want to.'

'I *do* want to,' I murmur. 'I want Beth back. I want *you* back.'

'You're lonely, Erica. I was too, for a long time. Nobody to talk to about it all. I guess we have to take what's due to us.'

'Whose secrets are they, Dinny, if they're not yours or mine?'

'I never said they weren't yours.'

'Mine and Beth's?' He stares at me, says nothing. I can feel tears in my eyes, feel them start to run, impossibly hot.

'But I don't *know*!' I say quietly.

'Yes. You do.' Dinny leans towards me. In the low light I can see every dark eyelash, outlined by the orange glow from the stove. 'It's time you went home to bed, I think,' he says.

'I don't want to go.' But he is on his feet. I wipe my face, notice that my hands are red and angry, mud under the nails.

'You can keep the blanket for now. Give it back to me whenever.' He rolls my wet clothes into a bundle, hands them to me. 'I'll walk you back.'

'Dinny!' I stand up, stagger slightly. In the small space we are centimetres apart but that is too far. He stops, turns to face me. I can't think of any words to say. I clasp the blanket close to me and lean towards him, tilt my head so my forehead can touch his cheek. I take one step closer, shut my eyes, put one hand on his shoulder, curling my thumb into the hard jut of his collarbone. I stay that way for three heartbeats, until I feel his arms circle me. I lift my chin, feel his lips brush mine, and I lean into his kiss, clumsy with desire. His arms tighten around me, chase my breath away. I would halt the world, if I could; stop it spinning, make it so I could stay here for ever, in this dark space with Dinny's mouth against mine.

He walks me back to the manor's ponderous front door and as I shut it behind me, I hear a sound that makes me pause. Water running. The sound of it echoes faintly down the stairs; and in the walls, the corresponding wrenching of the pipes.

'Beth?' I call out, my teeth chattering. I struggle out of my soaked boots, make my way to the kitchen, where the light is on. Beth is not there. 'Beth! Are you still up?' I shout, flinching from the glare of the lights, my head thumping. The water running still, drenching my thoughts with nauseating unease. I fight to focus my eyes, because there is something not right in here, in the kitchen. Something that makes the blood beat in my temples, dries my throat. The knife block, knocked roughly over and lying on its side on the worktop, and several of the knives pulled out, discarded beside it. For the second time on this black night, I cannot breathe. I turn, race to the stairs on legs that won't move fast enough.

Lasting

The stationmaster at Dodge City was most sympathetic. He listened patiently to Caroline's tale of her lost ticket and allowed her to pay there and then for her whole journey, from Woodward to New York. She spent the long days of the train ride watching out of the window, at grey storm skies and blistering white skies and china-blue skies so pretty they hurt her head. She thought of nothing, but tested the kernel of grief inside herself from time to time, to see if it would diminish with distance when it hadn't with time. William, still recovering from his fever, slept a great deal, whimpering fretfully when he awoke. But he knew Caroline and allowed her to soothe him. She sacrificed lunch at the Harvey hotel in Kansas City to shop instead for clean napkins, blankets and a bottle for the baby, hurrying back to the train with her heart fluttering anxiously, in case it left without her. The train was the only home she had at that moment. It was her only plan, the only thing she knew.

'Oh, he is just *beautiful*! What's his name?' a woman exclaimed one evening, pausing on her way through the carriage to bend over the carrycot and clasp her hands together over her heart.

'William,' Caroline told her, swallowing; her throat suddenly, painfully, dry.

'That's a handsome name, too. Such dark hair!'

'Oh, yes, he takes after his father in that respect,' Caroline smiled. She could not keep the sorrow from her voice as she spoke, though, and the woman glanced at her quickly, saw her red-rimmed eyes and the paleness of her face.

'Just you and William now, is it?' the woman asked kindly. Caroline nodded, amazed by how easily the lie came to her.

'I'm taking him to live with my family,' she said, smiling a wan smile. The woman nodded in sympathy.

'My name's Mary Russell. I'm sitting in the third car and if you need anything – even if it's just company – you come and find my husband Leslie and me. Agreed?'

'Agreed. Thank you.' Caroline smiled again as Mary moved away, wishing that she could accept the offer, wishing that she could seek out some company. But that could only be in another world, where Corin was not dead and they were just visiting his family in New York, perhaps, and with a baby that Caroline had carried in her womb, not just in her arms. She returned to her quiet study of the landscape, and William returned to sleep.

New York was impossibly loud and huge. The buildings seemed to lean over from their vast heights, casting deep, murky shadows, and the noise was like a tidal wave, crashing and foaming into every corner of every street. Heavy with fatigue, and with her mind wound tight with nerves, Caroline hailed a hansom cab and climbed aboard. Her clothes were travel-stained and smelt stale.

'Where to, madam?' the driver asked. Caroline blinked, and her face grew hot. She had no idea where to go. There were girls whose addresses she knew, whom she would once have called her friends, but she could not think of calling on them after more than two years without a word, with a black-eyed baby and her face dirty with smuts from the train. She thought briefly of Corin's family, but William squirmed in her arms and she blinked back tears. There was no way she could have carried and borne them a grandson without Corin having written to them about it. And she did not want to be anywhere she might be found. This knowledge came like a sluice of cold water. She *could* not go anywhere somebody might look to find her.

'A . . . um, a hotel. The Westchester, thank you,' she answered at length, naming a place where she had once had lunch with Bathilda. The driver flicked the reins and the horse started forwards, narrowly missing a motorcar that drew to a halt to let them go ahead, tooting its horn impatiently.

Bathilda. Caroline had not thought of her, had deliberately not thought of her in months and months. She knew what her aunt would have made of her fears, and of the wreck that life had become out in Woodward County. Now Caroline shut her eyes and at once she could see Bathilda's knowing look, her scathing expression. She could imagine Bathilda hearing of Caroline's plight and responding with a weighty, sanctimonious *Well* . . . She would not have gone to her, even if the woman had remained in New York, Caroline told herself defiantly. She would not have gone to Bathilda even now, now that she knew nobody and had no idea where to go, or what to do. She suppressed the treacherous longing she felt just to see a familiar face, even if it was not a friendly one. For whose faces would remain friendly to her now? She thought of Magpie, waiting in the dugout – but only for a second. The thought was too terrible. She thought of Hutch, of what emotions his face would register when he rode back in from the ranges, found White Cloud dead, maybe others too, and she and William gone without a word. Her insides seemed to burn her, seemed to writhe around themselves, and pain snapped behind her eyes. With a small cry she buried her face in her hands and concentrated hard on staying upright on the cab's padded bench.

At the Westchester she paid for a respectable room, and enquired after a nursemaid for William, explaining that her own maid had been taken seriously ill and been forced to return to her family's care. One was found without delay, a pug-faced girl with bright ginger hair, called Luella, who looked nothing but terrified when Caroline handed William to her. William took one look at the strange girl's frightened eyes and garish hair and began to wail. Holding the child awkwardly, Luella backed out of the room.

Caroline went into the bathroom and, realising in a way she never had before just how miraculous indoor plumbing was, she ran herself a hot bath, sank into it and tried to quiet her mind, which rang with unanswered questions and thoughts and fears, and threatened at any moment to tip her into panic.

In the end she did not stay more than a week in the city where she had been born and raised. It no longer felt any more like home than the ranch house, or Woodward, or the railway car that had brought her back. The oily fumes of the motorcars that had proliferated in her absence stuck in the back of her throat, and the throng of people made her feel every bit as invisible as she had felt out on the prairie. The buildings were too close, too solid, like the cliff walls of some labyrinth from which escape was impossible. *There's nowhere I belong,* Caroline thought, as she walked William in his new perambulator down streets she had never seen before, had never heard of before, hoping in this way to reduce the risk of anybody recognising her. She paused on a corner and looked up, high above, to where a crane was swinging a steel girder that looked like a toothpick into the waiting arms of a gang of workmen. The men stood at the edge of this unfinished tower with nothing to keep them but their balance. Caroline felt a sympathetic clench in her stomach for the danger they were in, for the nearness of the fall. But she soon walked on again, recognising the feeling as one she had herself, one she'd had for a long time. The creeping knowledge of life's precariousness, of the transience of it.

Passing a photographic studio, with a handsome gilt sign that read *Gilbert Beaufort & Son,* Caroline paused. Inside the cluttered, stuffy shop she recoiled from the vinegar stench of the developing chemicals. Not quite finding a smile for the camera, she commissioned several portraits of herself and William, arranging to have them delivered to the Westchester when they were ready.

Her fingers shook as she opened the package. She had hoped to create something permanent, to prove to herself, in some way, that she existed; and that even though she was widowed, she had Corin's child, the child that was rightly hers, to show for her marriage. She was part of a family. She would have some record of herself and of her life, which she was so unsure of that she sometimes wondered if she might still be lying out on the prairie somewhere, dreaming everything that had happened since. But in nearly every picture William had moved, blurring the image of himself so that his face was tantalisingly obscured; and in nearly every picture Caroline, to her own eyes, stared out from the paper every bit as ghostly and insubstantial looking as she felt. One photo alone had captured an intangible trace of what she'd hoped to see – in one shot she looked like a mother, proud and calm and possessive. She slid this picture into her case and threw the rest into the grate.

On the fourth day she saw Joe. She was walking with William in search of a park or a garden, a green space of some kind to feel a breeze and, she hoped, to calm the child. Fully recovered from his illness and returned to his strength, William was loud and unsettled. He cried in the night and snatched his arms away when Caroline tried to comfort him, squirming in her embrace as she rocked him and tried to sing to him as Magpie had done. But she could no more capture the Ponca girl's odd melodies than she could howl like a coyote, and her efforts were drowned out by William's shouts. Thinking it was the open prairie he missed, Caroline walked him most of the day, growing increasingly aware of how different the noises and smells and sights must be for the child, and how heavy the unclean air must feel in his tiny lungs. This was not his home, any more than it was hers, she realised; but unlike herself, William did have a home. She should take him back. The thought stung her like a slap to the face. Even if he was Corin's, even if he should have been hers, he belonged in Woodward County. She stood rooted to the spot, knocked senseless by this realisation, whilst pedestrians flowed around her like a river. But how could she? How could she explain – how could she be forgiven? She could see the pain, the accusation in Hutch's eyes, the anger and fear in Magpie's. All the times they had helped her, all the times they had encouraged her. And this was how she had repaid their belief in her — she was an outrage, a despicable failure. It was not possible. She could not face them. There *was* no going back.

And then she saw Joe, coming around the corner towards her, his face set into a grimace of hard fury, his black hair flying behind him as he strode towards her, knife ready in his hand to kill her. Caroline went cold from her head to her toes and stood petrified as the man walked past her, the black hair in fact a scarf, the knife a piece of rolled up paper, the face not Joe's at all but belonging to a swarthy, Mexican-looking man who was late for something and hurrying. Shaking uncontrollably, Caroline sank onto a nearby bench, the din of the city receding as a strange, muffled thumping invaded her head. Black speckles swirled like flies at the edges of her vision, and when she shut her eyes to be rid of them they turned brilliant white and danced on undeterred. In the distance, a passenger liner sounded its whistle as it slid gracefully into the docks. The deep blast echoed all around and brought Caroline back to herself, and to William's cries. Swallowing, she stroked his cheek, made some broken, soothing sounds, and then she stood up, turning to cast her eyes southwards towards the docks, the ship, and the sea. Five hours later she was aboard a steamer, bound for Southampton.

Joe was indeed in New York, but not on that very day. He and Hutch arrived two days after Caroline's ship had departed, where they made their way directly to the home of Mrs Massey, Corin's twice-bereaved mother, ignoring the stares that their country clothes and Joe's Indian blood elicited. No trace of Caroline or William had been found since she had been seen taking breakfast at the hotel, the morning after she'd left Woodward. The manager of Gerlach's Bank confirmed that there had been no transactions on the Massey account since the recent wages withdrawal. Word was sent out with every passing traveller, and to every outlying rancher, to report any sighting or signs of her; and although the ticket office clerk at the station swore that no fair-haired women carrying babies had bought a ticket for any train from him that day, or indeed that week, Hutch followed a hunch of his and took Joe and himself to New York, making fruitless enquiries at each station after a Mrs Massey.

Mrs Massey Senior had not, of course, seen or heard anything of her daughter-in-law, and was most distressed to hear that she and a young child had vanished. She was able to supply the men with Caroline's maiden name and former address, but their enquiries in the city after Miss Fitzpatrick were every bit as fruitless. They retraced their steps, trying the name Fitzpatrick instead of Massey, and then had little choice but to return to the ranch, to where Magpie had fallen into a trance, at times tearing at her hair and making long cuts down her arms with a blade that sent rivulets of bright blood to drip from her fingertips. Joe let his wife mourn in this way; he was impassive, the rage had burned from him, and his own heart was empty without his son. Between them, the men raised the money to pay a Pinkerton man for one month, but this was just enough time for the detective to follow the same path that Joe and Hutch had, and he finished the term unable even to say whether Caroline and William had been abducted or had run away. Hutch lay awake night after night, mystified and suspicious at once; scared for Caroline and for the ranch, which, having no owner, no longer had a future either.

Dreading her arrival more with each mile that passed, Caroline took the train from Southampton to London, and upon arriving found a hotel she could afford once the shrinking packet of dollars from Gerlach's Bank had been converted into pounds sterling. William was heavy in her arms and his cries made her ears wince, as if withdrawing inside her skull to protect themselves. During the long days of the sea crossing she had felt sick, distracted by a pounding at her temples that made it hard to think. William had cried for hours at a time, seemingly without pause, and although Caroline told herself that he must be feeling the same sickness as she, the same pain in his head, she could not shake the belief that he somehow knew he was being carried further and further from home, and that his cries were of rage at her for doing it. She saw an accusation in his face each time she looked at him. She stopped trying to quiet him, to sing to him or to hold him, leaving him instead to cry in the carrycot that he was rapidly outgrowing, so that she herself could remain in bed, curled against the cabin wall in misery.

Now, in an unfamiliar city, so tired she could barely think and with the ground still rolling beneath her feet, Caroline hefted the child higher in her arms and propped him against the smooth marble counter in the hotel lobby.

'I need a nursemaid,' she announced, with a note of panic in her voice. 'My own has been laid low with some fever.' The man behind the counter, tall and thin with immaculate hair and clothing, inclined his head condescendingly at her, twitching one eyebrow at her accent. She knew she was creased and careworn, and that William smelt bad, but these facts only served to make her crosser with the hotelier.

'Very well, madam. I shall make enquiries,' he told her smoothly. Caroline nodded, and toiled up the stairs to her room. She bathed William in the porcelain bowl of the washstand, trying not to ruin the towels with the filth smearing his bottom and legs. He stopped crying as she washed him, and made small, happy noises, slapping his feet in the water. Clearing her raw throat, Caroline hummed a lullaby until he began to drowse. Her ears rang with the quiet left by his absent cries, and she held him tightly to her, still humming, forgetting everything else but the warmth of him, the trusting weight of him, as he slept. There was no more water to wash herself with, and she put William to sleep on the bed as she fruitlessly paced the corridors of the hotel in search of a maid to remove the foul water, and to ask about the possibility of a hot bath.

Later a woman came to the room, announcing herself with a quiet knock. She was plump and florid with pale, frizzy hair and grimy smears on her dress, but her eyes spoke of warmth and intelligence as she introduced herself as Mrs Cox, and they lit up when they fell upon William.

'Is this the little chap in need of a nursemaid?' she asked. Caroline nodded and waved her forward to gather him up from the bed.

'Whereabouts in the hotel do you stay? In case I have need of you or the child?' Caroline asked.

'Oh, I'm not attached to the hotel, ma'am, although I have often been called upon to look after the young children of guests when they find themselves in unusual situations, like you, ma'am . . . I live with my own children and my husband not far from here in Roe Street. Mr Strachen downstairs will always know where to find me, if you need him to. How long will you be needing me to watch him, ma'am?'

'I . . . I don't know. I'm not sure yet. A couple of days, perhaps? A little longer . . . I'm not sure.' Caroline hesitated. Mrs Cox's face fell, but when Caroline paid in advance she smiled again, and was jouncing a startled-looking William merrily on her hip when she left with him not long afterwards. Caroline's heart gave a sickening little lurch as William disappeared from view, but then a vast and numbing weariness pulled at her. She lay down on the bed in her dirty clothes and, with her stomach rumbling, fell instantly asleep.

The next day, wearing the cleanest, least creased clothes she could find in her bag, Caroline gave the slip of paper upon which Bathilda had written a Knightsbridge address to a cab driver and let him transport her there with all the quiet resolution of a person going with dignity to the scaffold. The house she arrived at was four storeys high and built of pale, grey stone clamped into a strict row of identical such houses with handsome, red front doors. Caroline reached for the doorbell. Her arm felt as heavy and stiff as the iron railings, and by the time her finger was near to its target it was trembling with the effort. But she rang it, and gave her name to the elderly housekeeper, who admitted her to a gloomy entrance hall.

'Please, wait here,' the housekeeper intoned, and moved away along the corridor at no great speed. Caroline stood as still as stone. She looked inside her head and found no thoughts at all. Nothing but an echoing space, hollowed out like a cracked and discarded nutshell. *Oh, Corin!* His name rushed into that space like a thunder-clap. Reeling slightly, Caroline shook her head, and the emptiness returned.

Bathilda was fatter, and the hair at her temples was a brighter white, but other than that the two years since they had last met had wrought few changes upon her. She was occupying a brocaded couch with a cup of tea in her hand, and she stared at her niece in astonishment for several seconds.

'Good gracious, Caroline! I should never have known you if you weren't announced!' she exclaimed at last, raising her eyebrows and adopting her old familiar *froideur*.

'Aunt Bathilda,' Caroline said in a quiet voice, quite tonelessly.

'Your hair is quite wild. And you're so tanned! It's disastrous. It does not suit you at all.'

Caroline accepted this criticism without blinking, saying nothing while Bathilda sipped her tea. She was aware of her heart beating, hard and slow, just like when they had brought Corin home from the coyote hunt. This was another kind of death, but a death all the same.

'Well, to what do I owe this honour? Where is that cow-herding husband of yours? Has he not joined you on this foreign expedition?'

'Corin is dead.' It was the first time she had said the words. The first time she had had to. Tears scalded her eyes. Bathilda absorbed this news for a moment and then she relented.

'Come and sit down, child. I'll send for some more tea,' she commanded, in a softer tone of voice.

Bathilda soon took control of Caroline and seemed happy enough to do so now that the younger woman was meek and broken, and no longer defiant. Caroline went back to the hotel to collect her things that afternoon, and moved into a spare bedroom at the pale grey town house with the smart red door. She was introduced to the owner of the house, Bathilda's cousin by marriage, Mrs Dalgleish, who was thin and dry and wore a censorious look above a lipless mouth.

'Where is Sara?' Caroline asked hopefully.

Bathilda merely grunted. 'The foolish girl has wed herself to a grocer. She left last year,' she said.

Caroline's heart sank a little more. 'Did she love him?' she asked wistfully. 'Was she happy?'

'I really don't know. Now, to the matter in hand,' her aunt swept on.

Bathilda took Caroline to the bank and arranged for her money to be transferred from her parents' New York bank into an English account. She took Caroline shopping, accepting the story that all of her old clothes had been ruined on the ranch. They visited a hairdressing salon, where the rough ends and stray wisps of Caroline's hair were trimmed and tamed and curled neatly against her head. She applied to a chemist for Sulpholine Lotion, which was wiped, stinging, over Caroline's face and hands to bleach the tan from her skin. Fingernails were shaped and buffed, calluses worked from the skin with pumice stone. And, for the first time in over a year, Caroline's tiny form was tied tightly into corsets once again.

'You are too thin,' Bathilda said, scrutinising the end product of this beautification. 'Was there no food, out in the wilderness?' Caroline was considering the answer to this when Bathilda continued. 'Well, you are almost fit for society. You will have to remarry, of course. Two widows in this household are more than enough already. I know of just the gentleman, and he is in town now, to see the newest girls. A Baron, if you please – land-rich but cash-poor, and in need of an heir. He would make you a *lady* . . . from farmer's wife to nobility in the space of a couple of months! What a resolution that would be!' Bathilda exclaimed, reaching out for Caroline's shoulders and pulling them back a little straighter. 'But, although he is not as young as once he was, he's known to prefer fresh young things . . . not the world-weary widows of backwater cattlemen. It will be best if we do not mention to anyone your unfortunate first marriage. Can you do that? There's no evidence to the contrary? Nothing you haven't told me?' she asked, fixing Caroline with stern blue eyes.

Caroline took a deep breath. Words clamoured to be spoken, and her pulse raced. But she knew that if she confessed to having brought a child with her, this new life Bathilda was building for her would fly apart like a mirage and she would instead have to remain in this agonising present, with no chance of a more bearable future. She would have to remain with Bathilda, or alone, for ever. Neither could she stand. Caroline knew the answer she was expected to give, and she gave it. Biting down on her tongue to silence it, she shook her head. But when she raised her left hand and worked the wedding ring free, it left a perfect white band on her skin. She kept the ring in a closed fist and later slipped it into the satin lining of her vanity case, next to the photograph of herself and William.

The white band soon faded, kept hidden under satin and kid gloves until it was wholly invisible. Caroline met Lord Calcott at a reception that Bathilda took her to the following week, and she remained obedient and demure and nearly silent as he spoke and they danced and he looked at her with a heat in his eyes that left her cold inside. He was lightly built, not tall, perhaps forty-five years old, and he walked with a slight limp. His hair and moustache were speckled with grey amidst the dark, and his fingernails were neatly manicured. His hands left damp patches on her silk gowns when he held her waist to waltz. They met twice more, at a ball and a dinner party, in rooms stuffily heated against the late autumn chill. As they danced he asked her about her family, and her favourite pastimes, and how she liked London, and the English cuisine. Later he spoke to Bathilda and enquired after Caroline's temperament, her lack of conversation, and her income. After one such evening she accepted his proposal of marriage with a nod of her head and a smile as fleeting as winter sun. He drove her back to Knightsbridge in a smart black carriage pulled by a team of four, and his goodnight kiss roamed from her cheek to her mouth, his hands shaking with rising lust.

'Darling girl,' he whispered hoarsely, pushing up her skirts and kneeling between her legs to shove his way inside her, so abruptly that she gasped in shock. *Do you see?* She hurled the anguished thought out, silently, to wherever Corin had gone: *Do you see what has happened because you left me?*

Caroline spent Christmas of 1904 with Bathilda and Mrs Dalgleish, and she arranged to marry Henry Calcott late in February the following year. This time her engagement was properly announced, and a picture of the happy couple, taken at a celebratory ball, was published in *The Tatler*. As the wedding approached Caroline began to suffer from a consuming lassitude, the taste of copper in her throat, and a sickness in the mornings that made her long for the strong, cowboy coffee that Bathilda and her cousin considered too vulgar to keep in the house. Bathilda kept a stern eye on these developments.

'It seems the wedding won't come a day too soon,' she

commented one morning, as Caroline lay in bed, too dizzy and weak to rise. When the nature of her condition dawned upon her, Caroline was stunned.

'But . . . but I . . .' was all she managed to reply to her aunt, who raised an eyebrow and ordered beef tea for her, which she could not look at without gagging. Caroline remained still for several hours, and thought and thought, and tried not to see the clear implications of her pregnancy. For she was every bit as thin as she had been in Oklahoma Territory, if not thinner; and every bit as unhappy, indeed if not more so. The only thing that had changed was the man with which she lay.

Storton Manor seemed unlovely to Caroline. It was grand, but graceless; the windows too stern to be beautiful, the stone too grey to be welcoming. The driveway had been colonised by leggy dandelions and couch grass, the paint was peeling from the front door and the chimney stack was missing several pots. Her money was much needed, Caroline realised. The staff lined up crisply to meet her, as if determined to outshine the shabbiness of the house. Housekeeper, butler, cook, parlourmaid, chambermaid, scullery maid, groom. Caroline descended the carriage steps and swallowed back a threatened storm of weeping as she pictured the scruffy ranch hands who had lined up for her presentation to her first marital home. *And you left them*, she accused herself. *You just left them all without a word.* She smiled and nodded for each as Henry introduced them, and they in turn bobbed a curtsy to her, or made a short bow, muttering *Lady Calcott* in lowered voices. She took hold of her real name, *Caroline Massey*, and squeezed it tightly to her heart.

Later, walking around the broad sweep of the grounds, Caroline began to feel a little better; the snowstorm pieces of herself began to settle, just softly, into a kind of order. The air of the English countryside had a sweetness, a kind of soft greenness to it, even at the far end of winter. No clamour of city streets, horses, carts, or people; no empty prairie wind, or coyotes crying, or mile after unbroken mile of horizon. She was neither too hot, nor too cold. She could see the rooftops and smoke plumes of the village through the naked trees around the house, and it soothed her to know that within a moment's walk there were lives, being lived. A swathe of bright daffodils lit up the far end of the lawn, and Caroline walked slowly through them, her hem brushing them flat and then springing them free again. She meditated on the emptiness of her mind, on the hollow feeling she couldn't shake, but she allowed herself to think, just for a moment, that she was safe and could bear it all.

Henry Calcott was a lusty man, so Caroline suffered his conjugal attentions every night in the first few weeks of their wedded life. She was passive and turned her face away from him, amazed at how different love-making felt when undertaken with a person for whom she felt nothing. Her mind and senses completely free of passion, Caroline noticed the wet sounds enjoined by the meeting of their bodies; the fleshy, slightly fetid smell; the way her husband fought for breath, and the way his eyes crossed as he neared his climax. She tried to keep her face neutral and not let her distaste show.

Workmen appeared at Storton Manor and began to tidy the grounds and make repairs to the house, both inside and out.

'Will you be all right, if I go up to town? The men shan't bother you?' Henry asked Caroline at breakfast, three weeks after her arrival at the manor.

'Of course they won't bother me,' she replied calmly.

'You are more than welcome to come to town with me . . .'

'No, no, you go. I prefer to remain here and get better acquainted with . . . with the house, and . . .'

'Very well, very well. I'll only be a week, I should think. Just a few matters of business to attend to,' Henry smiled, returning to the morning's papers. Caroline turned to look out of the widow at the overcast day. *Matters of business*, she repeated to herself. At one London ball, a thin-faced girl with platinum hair had whispered to her that Henry Calcott loved a game of poker, even though he almost always lost. Caroline did not mind as long as his habit took him to London every few weeks, and left her well alone.

The second day after his departure was a day of steady rain that hung a wet curtain around the house. The view from the window was of greys and browns and muted greens, a sludgy smear of countryside blurring through the glass. Caroline sat close to the fire in the drawing room, reading an overblown romance by a woman called Elinor Glyn. Her eyes skimmed the text and her thoughts were on the child inside her: why she could not tell how she felt about it; when she should tell Henry; and why she had not done so already. This last answer at least she knew – because it was unbearably bitter, to have to give Henry Calcott the news she had yearned, fruitlessly, to give Corin. The parlourmaid, a timid girl called Estelle, interrupted her reverie with a quiet knock.

'Begging your pardon, my lady, but there's a woman here to see you,' Estelle announced in her wispy voice.

'A woman? What woman?'

'She wouldn't state her business, my lady, but she gave her name as Mrs Cox. Should I show her in?'

Caroline sat mesmerised with shock. There was a long pause, in which the sound of approaching feet could be heard.

'No!' Caroline managed at last, standing up abruptly but too late, as Mrs Cox pushed past Estelle and stood before Caroline with rainwater dripping from her hem onto the Persian rug. She fixed Caroline with a fiery eye and a determined set to her jaw. 'That will be all, thank you, Estelle,' Caroline whispered.

Mrs Cox looked immense but as she unbuttoned her raincoat the reason for this became clear. William was asleep, safely warm and dry beneath the coat, in a sling the woman had fashioned from a length of cotton canvas.

'I don't know what you mean by it!' Mrs Cox exclaimed at last, when it became clear that Caroline was lost for words. 'Leaving the child with me all these many weeks . . . I don't know what you can mean by it!'

'I . . .' But Caroline had no answer to give. Her careful neutrality, her passive acceptance of her fate, had written William out of the script. She had distanced herself from all thoughts of him, all responsibility. Seeing him again, waking up now as light and fresh air reached him, gave her a feeling like a blow to the stomach, a hard spike of love that was riddled with guilt and fear. 'How did you find me?' was all she could think to ask.

'It wasn't that hard, not with news of your wedding published in all the papers. I waited a bit longer, thinking you'd wanted the child kept safe and quiet while you got wed, but then I saw you weren't going to come for him at all! You weren't, were you? And him such a good, healthy boy . . . I don't know what you mean by it!' Mrs Cox repeated, her voice growing thick. She took a handkerchief from her pocket and dabbed at her eyes. 'And now I've had the expense of bringing him here on the train, and the trouble of walking him here through all this rain without him catching his death . . .'

'I can pay you. For the train, and . . . for the time you've had him. I can pay you more than that, even – here!' Caroline rushed to the dresser, withdrawing a purse of coins and holding it out to the woman. 'Will you keep him?' she asked suddenly, fear making her voice shake. Mrs Cox stared at her.

'*Keep him?* What can you mean? I'm not running a baby farm, I'll have you know! You're his mother – a child belongs with its mother. And look at the life he'll have here!' She gestured at the grand surroundings. 'I've enough mouths to feed and enough bodies to find beds for without taking on another one!' The woman seemed distraught. Caroline could only stand and stare in desperation as Mrs Cox began to work at the knot holding the sling around her shoulders. 'Here. I've brought him back to you now. Fit and well. All his things are in this bag – all but the carrier, for which he has grown too big, and I could not carry it as well as him to come down here. I . . . I hope you'll love him, ma'am. He's a good boy and he deserves to have a mother's love . . .' She seated William on the red silk cushion of a winged armchair. He held his arms up to her and smiled. 'No, lovey, you're staying with your real mam now,' she told him, her eyes again filling with tears. Now that it came to leaving him, Mrs Cox hesitated. She looked from William to Caroline and back again, and then her face creased in anguish and she knotted her hands in the folds of her skirts. 'Take good care of your boy, Lady Calcott,' she said, and hurried away. William sat quietly for a minute, his eyes darting around the room from one unfamiliar object to another. Then he began to cry.

Frantic to hide him, Caroline scooped William up and went quickly via the back stairs to her bedroom. She put him down on the bed and stepped back, clasping her hands to the sides of her head, trying to still her thoughts, and her heart, which was clattering far too fast in her chest. Her breathing came in short, panicked snatches. Quickly, she found a pacifier in William's bag of things and gave it to him to distract him. He stopped crying and grasped at the familiar, tinkling object, making small conversational noises to himself. Gradually, Caroline calmed down. He had grown so much! But then, he was a year and a half old now. His skin was darker and his hair was thicker. His face was beginning to show the high, slanting cheeks and straight brows of the Ponca. How could she ever have thought he was Corin's child? William was Indian, through and through; it would have been obvious even if she had not come to realise that her failure to give Corin a child had more to do with Corin than with herself. Which meant that she had stolen Joe and Magpie's baby. The enormity of this heinous crime hit Caroline like a poleaxe, and she sank to the floor, cramming a fist into her mouth to stifle uncontrollable sobs that surged up from her stomach and near strangled her. And she could not undo this terrible thing. There was no redress she could offer to Magpie — kind, gentle Magpie, who had been nothing but loyal and friendly, who was missing her child thousands of miles from where he now lay. Thousands of miles that neither she nor William would ever traverse again. It was another world, another lifetime. In bringing him here she had crossed a one-way boundary. In that moment, Caroline did not know how she was going to live with what she had done. She sat slumped on the carpet, and she wished to die.

Half an hour later, the maids and the housekeeper, Mrs Priddy, saw Lady Calcott struggling across the waterlogged lawn, carrying something heavy in what looked like a cloth bag. They called after her, and wondered whether to accompany her and make sure she was well, but if Lady Calcott heard them she showed no signs of pausing. She vanished with her burden into the trees at the furthest edge of the gardens, and when she appeared again, pale and shivering, at the mudroom door, she was without it.

'What a day for a walk, my lady!' Mrs Priddy exclaimed, as they found clean towels for her and unlaced her muddy boots. In truth it was a mild day, beneath those soggy English clouds, and certainly not cold enough to have brought on the storms of shuddering that wracked their new mistress's frail body. 'Let's get you up to your room. Cass will bring you some hot tea, won't you, Cass?' Mrs Priddy addressed the chambermaid, a girl of fifteen who goggled at Caroline with round, green eyes. If any of the staff thought anything more of Mrs Cox's short visit, Caroline's walk in the rain or the pillowcase missing from the bed, they knew better than to say anything about it. All except Cass Evans, that was, who whispered things late at night to Estelle, up in the small room on the top floor that they shared.

Caroline kept to her bed for several days. She lay in a state of dread and sorrow, which deepened when she slid her hand beneath her pillow and found William's pacifier there. The one she had given him, to quieten him as he lay on the bed; the one she and Corin had presented to him as a welcoming gift. She ran her fingers around the silken ivory, cradled the silver bell gently in her hand. She ought to get rid of it, she knew. She ought not to have anything in her possession that could link her to the child, to any child. But she could not. As if some essence of William, of Magpie, of life and love, remained caught up in that one precious talisman, she clasped it tightly in her fists and held it close to her heart. And when Lord Calcott returned from London with an empty wallet, she finally delivered the news of her delicate condition with an expressionless face and a calm demeanour.

The tinker family did not move on, as Caroline had assumed they would; as she had prayed they would. Instead, a few days later, they brought William to the door, to ask politely if anybody in the household had any idea to whom the child belonged, since their enquiries in the village had proved fruitless. Caroline saw them coming along the driveway from her position at the drawing room window. Her heart squeezed fearfully in her chest – just as it had when Corin had first told her she had Indian neighbours – and she jumped up to flee before realising that there was nowhere to go. She waited as the butler opened the front door, heard muffled words spoken, then the approach of footsteps and a subtle knock.

'Yes?' she called, her voice wavering.

'I'm sorry to disturb you, my lady, but Mr Dinsdale and his wife say they have found a child in the woods and they wonder if we have any idea to whom it might belong or what they ought to do with it?' The butler, Mr March, sounded puzzled, as if the etiquette surrounding lost babies was new to him. Feeling like she was going to be sick, Caroline turned on the man.

'What can that *possibly* have to do with me?' she demanded coldly.

'Yes, my lady,' Mr March intoned, every bit as coldly, making the slightest of bows as he withdrew. So the Dinsdales went away again, still carrying William and casting looks back at the house over their shoulders, as if bewildered by their dismissal. Caroline watched them go with increasing unease and a rush of blood to her head that dizzied her, and she traced this feeling to the way Mr March had referred to them – *Mr Dinsdale and his wife*. As if he knew them.

'Dinsdale? Ah, you've met our young campers, have you?' Henry exclaimed when Caroline asked him about the tinkers. She put down her knife and fork, her throat too tight to swallow. 'Harmless folk. Now, I know it may seem a little out of the ordinary, but I've given them permission to stay on that stretch of land—'

'What? Why would you do that?' Caroline gasped.

'Robbie Dinsdale saved my life in Africa, my dear – at Spion Kop, some years ago. Were it not for him, I would not be here today!' Henry announced dramatically, putting a huge forkful of potatoes *dauphinoise* into his mouth. A drop of hot cream ran down his chin, and Caroline looked away.

'But . . . they are *gypsies*. Thieves and . . . and probably worse! We *cannot* have them as our neighbours!'

'Now, my dear, I *will* not have that, I'm afraid. Private Dinsdale stayed with me in our pitiful trench when I was shot, and defended my prone body against a dozen Boer snipers until the Twin Peaks were taken and the buggers pulled back!' Henry waved his knife emphatically. 'He was wounded himself, and half dead with thirst, but by my side he stayed, when he could have run. All that was left of the rest of my men was a bloody mess like a scene from hell. The war changed him, though . . . He was eventually discharged on medical grounds, although they never did settle on what was wrong with the chap. Lost a few of his marbles out there, I would say. One day he just stopped talking, stopped eating, and wouldn't get up from his bunk no matter who ordered him to. I had to step in with a good word for the fellow. He's much improved now, but he was never quite able to fit back in to his civilian life. He was apprentice farrier in the village here, but that soon finished. He couldn't pay the rent and was thrown out of his cottage, so he took to the road. I told him he could stay here as long as he made no trouble, and he never has done. So here they stay.' Henry wiped potato from his moustache with a crisp, white napkin. Caroline studied her plate, fidgeting nervously.

'He took to the road, you say? So they move around the country, they're not often here?' Her voice was little more than a whisper.

'They're here a lot of the time. It's close to both their families, and Dinsdale can get work here and there where his name's known; mending metalwork and the like. So I fear you will have to get used to them, my dear. They need not trouble you – indeed, if you avoid that area of the grounds, you need not encounter them at all,' Henry concluded, and Caroline knew that the matter was closed. She shut her eyes, but she could feel them. She could sense that they were there – or rather that William was there, not two hundred yards from where she now sat at dinner. If he remained always there to remind her, she knew it would prey upon her, and slowly devour her. She prayed that they would give the child up, or move on, taking the object of her guilt and anguish with them.

When her baby was born, Caroline wept. A little girl, so tiny and perfect that she did not seem real, but wrought of magic instead. The soaring, consuming love that Caroline felt for her daughter only served to show her just how great the ill which she had done to Magpie truly was. The mere *thought* of being separated from this child of hers was painful enough. So Caroline wept, with love and with self-loathing, and nothing that was said could console her. Henry patted her head, at a loss, and did a poor job of hiding his disappointment that he had a daughter, not a son. Estelle and Mrs Priddy told Caroline, over and over, what a beauty the girl was, and how very well she had done, which brought fresh tears that they ascribed to exhaustion. At night she was beset by dreams of Magpie, her heart in flames, eyes fever-bright, failing, fading, dying of grief; and when she awoke the taint of her crime made her head throb as though it would burst. The baby was dressed in white lace gowns and named Evangeline. For four months Caroline loved her to distraction, and then the tiny girl died, one night in her crib, for no reason that any one of three doctors could ascertain. She flickered out of existence like a snuffed candle, and Caroline was shattered. What little will to go on she had kept since losing Corin now ran out of her like blood from a wound, and there was nothing left that could staunch it.

On a Tuesday, months later, Caroline went down to the kitchen and found Mrs Priddy and Cass Evans preparing a basket of vegetables from the garden with which to pay Robbie Dinsdale. He was out of sight in the scullery, sharpening the kitchen knives with a stone treadle wheel, sending sparks flying and filling the air with the piercing whine of stressed metal. Caroline would not have sought out the source of the racket if she hadn't seen guilt in Mrs Priddy's eyes; if the woman hadn't stopped what she was doing so suddenly, with such a start, when her mistress appeared in the room. Cass pressed anxious fingers to her mouth. They all knew how Lady Calcott felt about the Dinsdales, although they did not know why. Caroline strode through to the scullery and interrupted Dinsdale, who looked up at her with soft, amber eyes. Slowly, the wheel ground to a halt. Dinsdale was wearing rough clothing, and his hair was long and greasy, tied at the back of his head with string. His face was quite lovely, as fresh and innocent as a boy's, but somehow this only made it worse. Caroline's grief had turned her heart to stone. She knew herself to be punished, forced by fate to suffer the same anguish that she had inflicted upon Magpie, but so great was her pain that she did not accept it – she *could* not. She fought it, and bright anger coursed through her veins

'Get *out!*' she shouted, her voice vibrant with rage. 'Get *out* of this house!' Dinsdale started up from his stool like a jack-in-the-box and fled. Caroline turned on the housekeeper and the chamber maid. 'What is the meaning of this? I thought I had made my feelings about that man perfectly clear!'

'Mr Dinsdale has always done the knives for us, my lady . . . I didn't think any harm could come—' Mrs Priddy tried to explain.

'I don't care about that! I don't want him in the house – or anywhere near it! And what's this?' she demanded, gesturing to the basket of vegetables. 'Are you stealing from the gardens as well?'

At this Mrs Priddy swelled, and she pinched her brows together. 'I've worked here for more than thirty years, my lady, and never once been accused of any such thing! The excess from the kitchen garden has long been used to pay local men for their labour—'

'Well, not any more! Not that man, anyway. Do I make myself clear?' Caroline snapped. She fought to contain her voice. It was wavering, reeling; it threatened to rise to a shriek.

'They 'as extra mouths to feed!' Cass Evans piped up.

'Hush, child!' Mrs Priddy hissed.

'What?' Caroline said. She stared at the green-eyed girl in incredulous fear. *'What?'* she repeated, but Cass shook her head minutely and did not speak again.

Only Lord Calcott's intervention kept Mrs Priddy in her job in the wake of this misdemeanour. He did not understand his wife's objection to Dinsdale, and he did not try to. He merely silenced her and then took himself to London to avoid her vitriolic mood. The staff began to give Caroline a wide berth, fearing her unpredictable rages, her spells of sudden weeping. Late one night, after retiring, Caroline rose and went down to the kitchens in search of liver salts to calm her stomach. She went on soft feet, her slippers making almost no sound, and paused outside the scullery, hearing the girls still clearing up the dinner plates, and chatting to the stable boy, Davey Hook.

'Well, why else do you think she's took against them so fierce?' Cass's village accent was instantly recognisable.

''Cause she's a nob – they're all like that! Noses up in the air,' Davey said.

'I think she's half lost her reason since little Evangeline died, poor mite,' Estelle spoke up.

'I'm telling you, I heard it. There weren't no mistaking it – I *heard* it. That woman who came in from the station had something hidden under her coat, and then I heard a baby crying up in the mistress's chamber – I did! And then all of a sudden Robbie Dinsdale finds a lad out in the woods – and we *saw* her go over there, carrying something with her. We saw her.'

'But you never saw what it was she carried, did you?'

'But what else could it have been?'

'Why, anything at all, Cass Evans!' Estelle exclaimed. 'Why ever would the mistress take a child out and leave it in the woods?'

'You said yourself she's lost her reason!' Cass retorted.

'Only since she lost the little 'un, I said.'

'Maybe it's hers. Maybe that's her baby – another man's baby! And she had to keep it hid from the master – how about that, then?' Cass challenged them.

'It's you 'as gone soft in the head, Cass Evans, not her upstairs! Toffs don't go about dropping babies like farmers' daughters!' Davey laughed. 'Besides, you've seen that bairn the Dinsdales have got – swarthy as a blackamoor, he is! He's not her boy, he couldn't be. Not with her so pale. That there's a gypsy child, through and through. Some other lot probably cast it off, too many mouths to feed, and that's the beginning and end of it,' the boy said.

'You mustn't say such things about her ladyship, Cass,' Estelle warned her, softly. 'It'll fetch you nothing but trouble.'

'But I know what I heard. And I know what I saw, and it ain't right!' Cass stamped her foot. Outside the room, Caroline's chest was burning. A pent-up breath escaped her in a rush, not quiet enough, and the conversation within halted abruptly.

'*Shhh!*' Estelle hissed. Footsteps approached the door. Caroline turned on her toes and fled back to the stairs as silently as she could.

Henry Calcott was not at home when Cass Evans was dismissed. Caroline dealt with Mrs Priddy, Cass having been sent to her room to pack her meagre possessions.

'The girl's family is well known to me, my lady. I am certain she is not the thieving kind.' The housekeeper's face was clouded with concern.

'Nevertheless, I came in to find her rifling through my jewellery box. And now a silver pin is missing,' Caroline replied, marvelling at the dispassion in her voice when inside she was wrought with panic.

'What kind of pin, my lady? Perhaps it has been mislaid and is around the house somewhere?'

'No, it has not been mislaid. I want the girl removed from the house, Mrs Priddy; and that is all I have to say on the matter,' Caroline snapped. Mrs Priddy watched her, helplessly, with eyes so sharp that Caroline could not hold her gaze for long. She turned back to the mirror above the mantelpiece and saw no trace of fear, or guilt, or nerves in her own face. Her features were pale, immobile. Like stone.

'May I give her a good reference, at least, my lady? To give her a start elsewhere? She's a good girl, she works hard—'

'She steals, Mrs Priddy. If you write a reference, you must include that information within it,' Caroline said quietly. Behind her, she saw Mrs Priddy's expression change to incredulity. 'That will be all, Mrs Priddy.'

'Very well, my lady.' The older woman spoke coldly, and walked stiffly away. When the door closed behind her, Caroline sagged, holding the mantel for support. Her stomach churned, and she tasted bile. But she swallowed it down and steadied herself. Cass left via the kitchen door, with tears and highly vocal outrage, an hour or so later. Caroline watched from the upstairs hall window, and when Cass turned to look back at her former home she met Caroline's guarded gaze with a glare of such fury that it would have scorched a more feeling person.

Lord Calcott merely grunted when the new girl, who was fat and plain, opened the bedroom curtains one morning.

'What happened to that other lass? The brown-haired one?' he asked, idly.

'I had to let her go,' Caroline replied flatly. He said no more on the topic, since it was hardly an inconvenience to himself. Indeed, he was in residence less and less, and spent scant enough time with his wife for a second child to be conceived – the pregnancy was a long time coming. Caroline feared that nothing would ever again feel as wonderful as holding Evangeline for the first time, but the changing of her body brought with it an anticipation of love that was irresistible, and she succumbed to it, turning in on herself, humming softly to the unborn baby, feeling it wedged tightly beneath her ribs, a kernel of warmth and life in the dead husk of her being. But the boy, for boy it was, was born months too soon and had no chance of life. The doctor was all for taking it away with the bloodied sheets, but Caroline demanded to see her child. She studied the tiny, unformed face in wonderment – that she could still feel loss, that her eyes had tears left to shed. But it was the last of the love she possessed poured into that one gaze, that one long look she took at the dead baby's face. The very last touch of warmth inside her, she passed to him; and then the doctor did indeed take him out with the bloody sheets and all was lost.

Caroline's recovery was slow, and never complete. By the time she was well enough to receive visits from friends, and Bathilda, they found her slow and dull, her conversation near non-existent, her movements sluggish and her beauty much diminished. There were hollows at her eyes and cheeks, her hands were as bony as bird claws and there were touches of grey at her temples even though she was not yet near thirty. She seemed ghostly, as if part of her had left for another plane. People shook their heads sadly and thought twice before adding the Calcotts to any invitation list. Left alone, Caroline walked a great deal. Around and around the gardens, as if looking for something. One day she went through the woods, to the clearing where the Dinsdales still camped. They had learnt to give the house a wide berth, and never came again to swap labour for food. Caroline, therefore, had no excuse to argue for their removal, and to be thwarted this way made her ever more bitter towards them.

She waited in the trees, staring at their brightly painted wagon and the patchwork pony tethered nearby. Their home looked so jaunty, pitched there on the green summer grass; so practical, so wholesome. Caroline was reminded of White Cloud's teepee, and this, like any thought of the ranch, made her vision swim and her mind close up in misery. Just then the Dinsdales returned from the village. Mrs Dinsdale, whose blonde hair hung in angelic ringlets, had a babe in arms, and holding onto Mr Dinsdale's hand was a sturdy boy of about three years, dark coloured and round. His steps were sure but they made slow progress, pausing every few steps for the boy to crouch down and examine something on the ground with an endless curiosity. Caroline's breath caught in her throat. William so resembled Magpie that it was near unbearable to look at him.

She watched them for some time. Mrs Dinsdale put her baby down to sleep inside the wagon, then sat on the steps and called to

William, who came running to her with his arms aloft to be carried. She did not call him William, of course. It was some other name that she used, that Caroline could not entirely hear, but that sounded like *Flag*. Watching them, Caroline was so torn apart with sorrow and envy that she did not know how to contain it. But she was so angry too, that this family of drifters should flourish when her own had been snatched from her, twofold. She stared at William and she hated him. She hated them all. *No more*, she thought, *I can take no more*. The price she had been made to pay was far too high, and though some part of her thought that this injustice must, somehow, be redressed, she knew that it could not be. She sat down in the shadows and cried quietly for Corin, who could not help her.

Therefore all seasons shall be sweet to thee,
Whether the summer clothe the general earth
With greenness, or the redbreast sit and sing
Betwixt the tufts of snow on the bare branch
Of mossy apple-tree, while the nigh thatch
Smokes in the sun-thaw; whether the eve-drops fall
Heard only in the trances of the blast,
Or if the secret ministry of frost
Shall hang them up in silent icicles,
Quietly shining to the quiet Moon.

Samuel Taylor Coleridge, *Frost at Midnight*

7

The stairs take the last of my energy, so when I reach the bathroom door I am gulping, fighting for breath. The light is on inside, tendrils of steam creeping under the door. And the tap still running. With my hand on the door I freeze, shut my eyes for a second. I am so afraid; so afraid of what I might see. I think of Eddie, pushing back Beth's hair when he came home after school and found her. How I need his courage right now.

'Beth?' I call, too meekly. No reply. Swallowing, I give two tiny knocks then throw open the door.

Beth is in the bath, her hair floating around her, water perilously close to the rim, escaping into the over flow. Her eyes are shut and for an instant I think I have lost her. She is Ophelia, she will ebb away from me, float off into serene oblivion. But then she opens her eyes, turns her face to me, and I am so relieved I nearly fall. I stumble in, sit abruptly on the chair where her clothes are folded.

'Rick? What's going on? Where are your clothes?' she asks me, pushing the tap closed with her big toe. I dropped them and Dinny's blanket in the hallway, before I ran. I am wearing wet, muddy underwear, nothing more.

'I thought . . . I thought . . .' But I don't want to tell her what I thought. It seems a betrayal, to think that she would do that to herself again.

'What?' she asks, her voice flattening out, growing taut.

'Nothing,' I mumble. The light stabs at my eyes, makes me flinch. 'Why are you in the bath at this time of night?'

'I said I'd wait for you to get back,' she replies. 'And I was cold. Where have you been?' she asks, sitting up now, wet hair smoothing itself to her breasts. She bends her knees, wraps shining arms around them. I can see every rib, every bump of her spine, marching down into the water.

'I was with Dinny. I . . . fell into the dew pond.'

'You did *what*? What was Dinny doing there?'

'He heard me fall in. He helped me out.'

'You just fell in?' she asks incredulously.

'Yes! Too much whisky, I suppose.'

'And did you just . . . fall out of your clothes? Or did he help you with those as well?' she asks tartly. I give her a steady look. I am angry now – that she scared me so. That I scared myself so.

'Who's jealous now?' I ask, just as tart.

'I'm not—' she begins, then puts her chin on her knees, looks away from me. 'It's *weird*, OK, Erica? You chasing after Dinny is weird.'

'Why is it weird? Because he was yours first?'

'Yes!' she cries; and I stare, amazed by this admission. 'Just don't get involved with him, all right? It feels incestuous! It's just . . . wrong!' She struggles to explain herself, stretching her hands wide. 'I can't stand it.'

'It's not wrong. You just don't *like* the idea, that's all. But you needn't worry. I think he's still in love with you,' I say quietly, feeling my own heart sink inside me.

I wait to see her expression change, but it doesn't.

'We should go, Erica. Can't you see? We should leave here and not come back. It would be by far the best thing. We could go tomorrow.' Her voice gains conviction, she fixes me with desperate eyes. 'Never mind sorting out all Meredith's things – that's not why we came here, not really. The house clearance guys can do it! Please? Let's just go?'

'I know why I came here, Beth.' I am tired of not talking about it, tired of tiptoeing around it. 'I wanted us both to come because I thought I could make you better. Because I want to find out what it is that torments you, Beth. I want to bring it to the surface. I want to shine a light on it, and . . . show you that it's not so bad. Nothing is as bad in the light of day, Beth! Isn't that what you tell Eddie when he has nightmares?'

'Some things *are*, Erica! Some things are as bad!' she cries, the words torn from her, terrified. 'I want to *leave*. I'm leaving, tomorrow.'

'No. You're *not*. Not until we've confronted this. Whatever it is. Not until we've faced up to it!'

'You don't know what you're talking about!' she shouts harshly. She stands abruptly, sends water cascading onto the bathroom floor, reaches for her dressing gown and shrugs it on violently. 'You can't stop me if I want to go.'

'I won't drive you to the station.'

'I'll take a taxi!' she hisses.

'On New Year's Day? Out here in the sticks? Good luck.'

'God*damn it*, Rick! Why are you doing this?' she swears, anger snapping in her eyes, clipping her words. They echo from the tiled walls, attack me twice.

'I . . . I promised Eddie. That I'd make you better.'

'What?' she whispers.

I think carefully, before I speak again. I think about what I saw, as the dew pond closed over my head.

'Tell me what Henry was looking for at the side of the dew pond,' I demand softly.

'What? When?'

'At the side of the dew pond that day. The day he disappeared, and I'd been swimming in the pond. He was looking for something on the ground.' I hear Beth's sharp intake of breath. Her lips have gone pale.

'I thought you said you didn't remember?' she says.

'It's coming back to me. A little. Not all of it. I remember jumping back into the pond, and I remember looking up at Henry, and he had been looking for something on the ground. And then I remember . . .' I swallow, 'I remember him bleeding. His head bleeding.'

'Shut up! *Shut up!* I don't want to talk about it!' Beth shouts again, puts her hands over her ears, shakes her head madly. I watch, astonished, until she stops, stands snatching at the air, chest heaving. I take her arm carefully and she winces.

'Just tell me what he was looking for.'

'Stones, of course,' she says, quietly, defeated. 'He was looking for stones to throw.' She pulls away from me then, slips from the bathroom into the dark of the corridor.

No sleep for me. I try counting my breaths, counting my heartbeat; but when I do this my heart speeds up, as if startled by such scrutiny. It rushes along, makes my head ache. I shut my eyes so tightly that coloured shapes bloom in the dark and flounce across the ceiling when I open my eyes again. There's a bright moon tonight, and as I skim sleep, as the hours spin past, I see it sail heedlessly from one pane of the window to the next.

I feel dreadful when I get up: heavy and tired. My throat is sore; there's an ache behind my eyes that won't go. It was a hard frost last night – Dinny was right about what might have happened if I'd lain about on the ground, drunk and befuddled. Now there's a dense mist, so pale and luminous that I can't tell where it ends and the sky begins. The thing is, we ran. That day. Beth and I ran. I remember scrambling out of the pond as fast as I could, bruising my feet on flints. I remember Beth's fingers closing tightly on my arm like little bird claws, and we ran. Back to the house, back to lie low, to hide and stay quiet until the trouble started. Or rather, until the trouble was noticed. We didn't go back, I am sure of it. The last time I saw Henry he was by the side of the dew pond; he was teetering. Did he fall? Was that why I got out, so desperately fast? Was that why I told them all he was in the pond – why I insisted upon it? But he wasn't, and there was only one other person there.

There is only one person who can have moved Henry, who can have taken him somewhere else, because I know he didn't take himself. He was taken somewhere so secret and so hidden that twenty-three years of searching couldn't uncover him. But I am close now.

It could be this memory that I've fought so hard to regain that's hurting my head. I don't have to concentrate to recall it now. It capers in my mind's eye of its own accord, again and again. Henry bleeding, Henry falling. It worries me that I didn't want breakfast. I looked at the food and I remembered Henry and there was no question of eating anything. No question of putting anything into my mouth, of enjoyment or satisfaction. Is this how Beth has felt, for twenty-three years? The thought turns me cold. It's like knowing there's something behind you, following you. That neck-prickling feeling, a constant distraction. Something as dark and permanent as your shadow.

The doorbell startles me. Dinny is there, wearing a heavy canvas coat for once, his hands thrust deeply into the pockets. In spite of it all my cheeks glow and I feel a wave of something ill-defined. Relief, or perhaps dread.

'Dinny! Hello – come in,' I greet him.

'Hi, Erica, I just wanted to check you were all right. After last night,' Dinny says, stepping over the threshold but staying on the doormat.

'Come in – I can't shut the door with you standing there.'

'My boots are muddy,'

'That's the least of our problems, believe me.' I wave my hand.

'So, how are you? I wondered if . . . if you'd swallowed any of that pond water, it might have made you sick,' he says. An awkwardness about him that wasn't there before, a diffidence that touches me.

'I'm fine, really. I mean, I feel like death, and I'm sure I look like death, but other than that, I'm OK.' I smile nervously.

'You could have killed yourself,' he tells me gravely.

'I know. I know. I'm sorry. That wasn't my intention, believe me. And thank you for rescuing me – I really owe you one,' I say. At this he looks at me sharply, his eyes probing my face. But then he softens, puts out his hand and brushes cold knuckles lightly down my cheek. I catch my breath, shiver slightly.

'Idiot,' he says softly.

'Thanks,' I say.

There's a thump from upstairs. I picture a full suitcase, pulled off a bed. Dinny drops his hand quickly, puts it back in his pocket.

'Is that Beth?' he asks.

'Beth or the ghost of Calcotts past. I expect she's packing. She doesn't even want to stay for one more day.' I give a helpless little shrug.

'So you're leaving?'

'I . . . I don't know. I don't want to. Not yet. Maybe not at all.' I glance at him. I really don't think I could stay in this house by myself.

'No more Dinsdales or Calcotts at Storton Manor. It's the end of an era,' Dinny says, but he does not sound regretful.

'Are you moving on?' I ask. My heart gives a little leap of protest.

'Sooner or later. This is a rotten place to camp in the winter. I was only really here because of Honey—'

'I thought you said you saw Meredith's obituary?'

'Well, yes, and that. I thought there was a good chance you and Beth might be around.' For a moment we say nothing. I am still too unsure of him to test this tide that's towing us apart. Perhaps Dinny feels the same way.

'I'd like to say goodbye to Beth before you disappear,' he says quietly. I nod. Of course he does. 'I didn't get the chance, the last time you went,' he adds pointedly.

'She's upstairs. We had a fight. I don't know if she'll come down,' I tell him. I study his hands. Square shaped, smeared with grime. Black crescents under the nails. I think of the mud by the dew pond, him hauling me out. I think of the way he held me, just for a while, while the embers sank low and my body shook. I think of his kiss. How I want to keep him here.

'What did you fight about?'

'What do you think?' I ask bitterly. 'She won't tell me what happened. But she *has* to face up to it, Dinny – she has to! It's what's making her ill, I know it!' Dinny sighs sharply, shifts his weight onto the balls of his feet, as if he would run. He rubs a hand over his forehead, exasperated. 'You never did get to tell her the things you wanted to, Dinny. But . . . you can tell me instead,' I say.

'Erica—'

'I want to know!'

'What if knowing changes everything? What if, for once, your sister and I are right and you're better off not remembering?' Fierce eyes lock on mine.

'I *want* it to change everything! Change what, anyway? She's my sister. I love her and I'll love her no matter what she does. Or did,' I declare adamantly.

'I'm not just talking about Beth,' he says.

'Who, then? What then? Just tell me!'

'Don't shout at me, Erica, I can hear you. I'm talking about . . . you and me.' His voice grows softer. I am silent for two heartbeats. They come quickly, but seem to take for ever.

'What do you mean?'

'I mean . . . whatever this is . . . whatever it might have been, it would all change.' He looks away from me, folds his arms. 'Do you understand?' he asks. I bite my lower lip, feel my eyes stinging. But then I see Beth, in the bath, as she was last night; whole in body, but slipping away. I swallow the hot little flame that Dinny has just lit inside me.

'Yes. But I have to know,' I whisper. My nose is running. I scrub it with the back of my hand. I wait for him to speak, but he doesn't. His eyes dart from the floor to the door to the stairs and back again, focusing on nothing. Knots in his jaw, tying themselves tighter. 'Just tell me, Dinny! Beth and I ran off. I don't know what happened, but I know we ran off and left you and Henry at the pond. And that was the last anybody saw of him and I want you to *tell me*!' My voice sounds odd, too high.

'Beth should—' he begins.

'Beth won't. Oh, maybe she will, one day. Or maybe she'll try to kill herself again, and this time she'll manage it! I have to get this *out* of her!' I cry. Dinny stares at me, shocked.

'She tried to *kill* herself?' he breathes. 'Because of this?'

'Yes! Because she's depressed. Not just *unhappy* – ill, Dinny. And I want to know what caused it. If you don't tell me then you're just helping keep her like she is – haunted. Just tell me what you did with his body! Tell me where he is!' I plead. My blood is soaring like a tidal wave, roaring in my ears.

'Erica!' Beth's shout echoes across the hallway. Dinny and I jump, like guilty children. *'Don't!'* she cries, running down the stairs to us. Her eyes are wide, face marked with fright.

'Beth, I wasn't going to tell her—' Dinny starts to say, holding up a hand to placate her.

'What? Why not – because *Beth* has told you not to?' I snap at him.

'Don't tell anybody! *Ever!*' Beth says. I hardly recognise her voice. I grasp at her hands, try to make her look at me, but her eyes are fixed on Dinny's and something passes between them that I can't bear.

'Beth! Please – Beth, look at me! Look at what trying to keep this secret has done to you! Please, Beth. It's time to get rid of it. Whatever it is, let it go. Please. For Eddie's sake! He needs you to be happy—'

'Don't bring Eddie into this!' she snaps at me, her eyes awash with tears.

'Why not? It's *his* life that this is affecting too, you know! He's your responsibility. You owe it to him to be strong, Beth—'

'What would *you* know about it, Erica? What would you know about responsibility? You haven't even got a permanent job! You change flats every six months! You've been living like a student since you left home – you've never even had a pet so don't tell me about *my* responsibilities!' Beth shouts, and I recoil, stung.

'You're my responsibility,' I say quietly.

'No. I'm not,' Beth replies, holding my gaze.

'Beth,' Dinny says. 'I've been trying to talk to you since you got back here and I know you don't want to hear what I have to say, but it's important, and . . . I think Erica has a right to hear it too—'

'She was *there*, Dinny! If she doesn't remember then she doesn't need to. Now can we please leave it alone? Dinny, I . . . I think you should go.'

'No, he shouldn't! Why should he go? I asked him in. In fact,' I cross to the door, stand with my back to it, 'nobody's going until I have had the truth from one or both of you. I mean it. The truth. It's long overdue,' I say. My heart trips, hurls itself against my ribs.

'Like you could stop me,' Dinny mutters.

'Erica, stop asking!' Beth cries. 'Just . . . *stop asking!*'

'Beth, maybe it would be better to just tell her. She's not going to tell anybody. It's just the three of us. I think . . . I think she has a right to know,' Dinny says, his voice soft. Beth stares at him, her face so pale.

'No,' she whispers.

'*Christ!* I don't know why you even came back here!' he shouts, throwing up his arms in exasperation.

'Dinny, tell me. It's the only way to help her,' I say firmly. Beth's gaze flickers from me to Dinny and back again.

'No!' she hisses.

'Please. Tell me where Henry is,' I urge him.

'Stop it!' Beth commands me. She is shaking uncontrollably. Dinny grinds his teeth together, looks over his shoulder, looks back at me. His eyes are ablaze. He seems torn over something, undecided. I hold my breath and my head spins in protest.

'Fine!' he barks, grabbing my arm. 'If you think this is only way to help her. But if you're wrong, and when everything is different, don't say I didn't warn you!' He is suddenly angry, furious with us. His fingers bruise me; he tows me away from the door and wrenches it open.

'No! Dinny – *no!*' Beth shouts after us, as he pulls me outside.

'*Ow* – stop it! What are you doing? Where are we going?' On instinct I fight him, try to dig my heels in, but he is far stronger than me.

'You want to know what happened to Henry? I'll show you!' Dinny spits the words out. Fear grips my insides. I am so close to finding Henry, so close that it terrifies me. Dinny terrifies me. Such strength in him, in his grip; such an implacable look on his face.

'Dinny, *please* . . .' I gasp, but he ignores me.

'Erica! *No!*' I hear Beth's ragged shout chasing us but she does not follow. I look back over my shoulder, see her framed in the doorway, mouth distorted, hands grasping the jamb for support.

Dinny marches me across the lawn, out of the garden through the trees, and I think we are going to the dew pond. Suddenly I know, for absolute sure, that I do not want to go there. Dread makes my knees weak; I renew my struggle to get free.

'Come on!' he snaps, pulling me harder. He could wrench my arm clean away from my body. But we are not going to the dew pond. He is heading west now. We are going to the camp. I follow him like a reluctant shadow, weaving and stumbling behind him. My heart pummels inside me. Dinny pulls open the door of the nearest van, not bothering to knock. Harry looks up, startled;

smiles when he recognises us. Dinny propels me up the steps into the van, which smells of crisps and dog and damp clothing.

'What the hell is this?' My voice is shaking, I can't get my breath, I am ready to shatter.

'You wanted to know where Henry was.' Dinny raises his arm, points at Harry. 'There's Henry.'

I stare. My head empties, the plug is pulled. I'm not sure how long I stare, but when I speak my throat is dry.

'What?' The word is a feeble little thing, a faint shape around the last scrap of air in my chest. The floor is tipping underneath my feet; the earth has rolled off its axis, is wheeling away with me, dizzy and helpless. Dinny lowers his arm, shuts his eyes and puts a hand over them, wearily.

'That's Henry,' he repeats; and again I hear the words.

'But . . . how *can* it be? Henry's dead! How can this be Henry? Not *Henry*. Not him.'

'He's not dead. He didn't die.' Dinny drops his hand and the fire has gone out of him. He watches me but I can't move. I can't think. Harry smiles, uncertainly. 'Try not to shout. It upsets him,' Dinny says quietly. I can't shout. I can't anything. I can't breathe. Pressure is building inside my head. I worry that it will explode. I put my hands to my temples, try to hold my skull together. 'Come on — let's go. Let's go outside and talk,' Dinny murmurs, taking my arm more gently now. I snatch it away and lean towards Harry. I am so scared as I look at him. Scared enough for my knees to sag — there's a hollow thump as they hit the floor. Scared enough for a shocking nausea to sweep through me. I am chilled to the roots of my hair, and burning all over. I push stray dreadlocks back from Harry's face, peer into his eyes. I try to see it. Try to recognise him, but I can't. I won't.

'You're wrong. You're lying!'

'I'm neither. Come on, we can't talk about this here.' Dinny pulls me to my feet and takes me outside again.

For the second time in twelve hours I sit in Dinny's van, shivering, stunned, stupid. He makes coffee on the stove in a battered steel pot, the liquid spitting and smelling delicious. Sipping from the cup he gives me scalds my mouth, and I feel it revive me.

'I . . . I can't believe it. I don't understand,' I say quietly. Outside a door bangs. Popeye and Blot woof gently behind their teeth; more a greeting than a warning. Dinny has one ankle propped up on the other knee, his familiar pose. He looks both hard and nervous. He sighs.

'What don't you understand?' He says this quietly, in the spirit of genuine enquiry.

'Well, where has he *been* all these years? How come he was never found? They searched *everywhere* for him!'

'Nobody ever searches *everywhere*.' Dinny shakes his head. 'He's been here, with us. With my family, or with friends of my family. There's more than one traveller camp in the south of England. Mum and Dad had plenty of friends to leave him with, friends who looked after him, until it had blown over. As soon as I was old enough to keep an eye on him myself, I did.'

'But . . . I saw him bleeding. I saw him fall into the pond . . .'

'And then you two ran away. I fished him out and I fetched my dad. He wasn't breathing, but Dad managed to get it going again. The cut on his head wasn't as bad as it looked . . . head wounds just bleed a lot.' He looks at his boot, twists the frayed end of a lace between his finger and thumb.

'And then? Didn't you take him to the hospital? Why didn't you come and find somebody at the manor?' I ask. Twenty-three years of my life are rewriting themselves behind my eyes, unravelling like wool. I can hardly focus, hardly think. Dinny doesn't answer for a long time. He grips his chin in his hand, knuckles white. His eyes burn into me.

'I . . . wouldn't say what had happened. I wouldn't tell them how he'd got hurt . . . or by who. So Dad . . . Dad thought it was me. He thought Henry and me had got into a fight or something. He was trying to protect me.'

'But, you could have told them it was an accident—'

'Come off it, Erica. Everyone's always looking to be proved right about us – all my life, people have looked to be proved right. That we thieve, that we're criminals – that we're scum. The social would have leapt at the chance to take me away from Mum and Dad. A spell in juvy, then a *proper* home, with a *proper* family . . .'

'You don't know that . . .'

'Yes. Yes, I do. It's you who doesn't know, Erica.'

'Why is he . . . the way he is?'

'Not from the knock on the head, that's for sure. Dad took him to an old friend, Joanna, who used to be a nurse in Marlborough. This was that same afternoon, before anyone even knew he was missing. She put a couple of stitches in his head, said he might have a concussion but it was nothing to worry about. We were going to wait for him to wake up, make sure he was OK, then drop him within walking distance of the village and disappear. That was the plan. Joanna looked after him for the first few days. He was out of it for two days straight and . . . then he woke up.'

'You could have brought him back then. You could have left him somewhere he'd be found, like you said. Why didn't you?'

'By then the search was enormous. We were being watched. We couldn't move without some keen copper noting it down. Henry would have told them we'd had him – when he was found, of course. But we thought we'd have a head start to vanish. By the time we realised there was no way we could bring him back without being seen, it was too late. And he wasn't right, when he woke up. Anybody could tell that. Dad took me to see him, since I knew him best, out of all of us. *Just tell me what you think*, Dad said. I didn't know what he was getting at until I saw Henry and spoke to him. Sitting up in Joanna's spare bed, holding a glass of orange squash like he didn't know what to do with it. I'd rather have been anywhere else in the world than in that room with him.' Dinny pushes his fingers through his hair, grips his scalp. 'I tried talking to him, like Dad said I should. But he wasn't the same. He was wide awake, but . . . distant. Dazed.'

'But why? You said his head wasn't hit that hard?'

'It wasn't. It was the time he spent not breathing. The time before Dad got to him and got air back into his lungs.' Dinny sounds so tired now, leaden. There's a sparkle of pity, at the core of me, but I can't let it fill me yet. Too many other things to feel.

I've finished my coffee before I speak again. I hadn't noticed the silence. Dinny is watching me, tapping his ankle with one agitated thumb, waiting. Waiting for my reaction, I suppose. A defensive gleam in his eye.

'It didn't blow over, you know. Not for his parents. Not for our family . . .'

'Do you think it blew over for me? For *my* family? I've had to see him nearly every day since then, wondering if it would have been different if I'd tried to revive him myself, that bit sooner . . . If we *had* taken him to hospital.'

'But you've never told. You've kept him—'

'Not *kept* him. Looked after him . . .'

'You've kept him and let his family – let his *parents* think he was dead! You've let Beth and I think he was dead.'

'No, I had no idea what you and Beth were thinking! How would I know? You *ran*, remember? You ran and washed your hands of it! You never even came to ask me about it! You left him with me and I . . . we . . . did what we thought was best.'

This I cannot dispute.

'I was eight years old!'

'Well, I was twelve – still just a kid, and I had to let my parents think I'd nearly killed another boy. That I'd *brain-damaged* another boy. At least, that's what I thought I had to do. That's what I thought was right. By the time I realised you two were never coming back, it was too late to change anything. How much fun do you think that was?'

I feel the blood run out of my face when he says this. *I had to let them think* . . . A memory fights its way through the clash in my head. Henry bending down, surveying the ground, gathering four, five stones. Water in my eyes and in one ear, which boomed and wobbled, mangling their voices; Henry, taunting, throwing names at Dinny; Beth's shrill commands: *Stop it! Go away! Henry, don't!* Henry said, *Pikey! Filth! Dirty gyppo! Thieving dog! Tramp!* With each word he threw a stone, whipping it from the shoulder with that throw boys are taught at school, but girls never are. A throw that would have sent a cricket ball back from the boundary, and a good aim. I remember Dinny crying out as one hit him, grabbing his shoulder, wincing. *I remember what happened.* And I picture Beth, in the doorway just now; her shout following us, and the terror on her face. *No!*

'I have to go,' I whisper, stumbling to my feet.

'Erica, wait—'

'No! I have to go!'

I feel sick. There's too much inside me, something has to come out. I rush back to the house, tripping over my feet. In the cold downstairs toilet, where the frigid toilet seat makes your thighs ache, I collapse, throw up. But with my throat burning and the stink of it all around me, I somehow feel better. I feel justly punished. I feel as if some kind of retribution is beginning. Now I know what has tortured Beth all these years. Now I know why she has punished herself so, why she has sought such retribution. Splashing my face in the basin, I gasp for breath, try to find the strength to rise. I am cold with fear – I think I know what retribution she might seek from herself.

'Beth!' I call, coughing at the ragged feeling in my throat. 'Beth, where are you – I have to tell you something!' On trembling legs, I run in and out of all the downstairs rooms, my heart skittering, making me dizzy. *'Beth!'* My voice is rising, almost a scream. I pound up the stairs, run to the bathroom first then along the corridor to Beth's room. The door is shut and I throw myself against it. Inside, the curtains are closed, the room in darkness. And what I fear the most, what I dreaded to see is there in front of me. It fills my vision, hollows me out. *'No!'* I rush into the shadowed room. My sister, curled on the floor, her face turned away from me. Long-bladed scissors gripped in her fragile hand, and a dark pool around her. 'Beth, no,' I whisper, with no more air in my lungs, no blood in my veins. I fall to my knees, gather her up; she is so light, insubstantial. For a second I am struck dumb by the pain, and then she turns her face to me, and her eyes are open, focused on mine, and I laugh out loud with relief.

'Erica?' Her voice is tiny.

'Oh, Beth! What have you done?' I smooth her hair back from her face and then I realise. She has hacked it off, all of it. The dark pool on the floor is the severed length of her hair. Without it she looks like a little girl; so vulnerable. 'Your hair!' I cry, and then I laugh again and kiss her face. She has not cut herself, is not bleeding.

'I couldn't do it. I wanted to but . . . Eddie . . .'

'You *didn't* want to do it! You *don't* want to do it! I know you don't, not really,' I tell her. I pull her further into my arms, rock her gently.

'I did! I did want to!' she weeps angrily, and I think she would pull away from me if she had the strength. '*Why* did you make him tell you? *Why* wouldn't you *listen* to me?'

'Because it had to happen. It did. But listen to me – Beth, are you listening? This is important.' I glance up, catch my reflection in the dressing table mirror. I look grey, spectral. But I can see it in my own eyes – the truth, waiting to spill out. I take a deep breath. 'Beth, Henry's not dead. *Harry* is Henry! It's true! Dinny told me the whole story . . . he didn't die. They took him off to some friend of theirs for first aid and then they moved him around different camps for years and years. That's why none of the searches ever found him.'

'*What?*' she whispers. She watches me like she would a snake, waiting for the next strike.

'Harry – the Harry your son just spent the Christmas holiday playing with – Harry is *our cousin Henry.*' Oh, I want to release her; I want to mend her! In the silence I hear her breathing. The fluttering of air, pushed from her body.

'That's not true,' she whispers.

'It's true, Beth. It's true. I believe it. Dinny wouldn't tell anyone what had happened, so Mickey thought *Dinny* had done it, and they didn't want him to be taken away . . .'

'No, no, *no!* None of that is right! I killed him! I *killed* him, Rick.' Her voice rises to a wail, wanes to a sliver. 'I killed him.' She says it more calmly now, as if almost relieved to let the words out.

'No, you didn't,' I insist.

'But . . . I threw that stone . . . it was too big! I should never have thrown it! Even Henry wouldn't have thrown one that big. But I was so angry! I was *so* angry I just wanted to make him *stop*! It went so high,' she whispers.

I can see it now. Finally, finally. Like it was there all along. Girls aren't taught to throw properly. She flung her whole body behind it, let go of it too soon, sent it too high. We lost sight of it against the incandescent summer sky. Henry was already laughing at her, laughing at the ineptness of the throw. He was already laughing when it came back down, when it hit his head with a sound that was so wrong. Loud, and wrong. We all knew the wrongness of that sound at once, even though we'd never heard it before. The sound of flesh breaking, of a blow to the bone. It was that sound that made me sick just now. As if I were hearing it again for the first time, and only now rejecting it. And then all that blood, and his glazed look, and my scramble from the water, and our flight. I have it now. At last.

'I didn't kill him?' Beth whispers at last, eyes boring into my face, mining me for the truth.

I shake my head, smile at her.

'No. You didn't kill him.'

I see relief seep into her face, slowly, so slowly; like she hardly dares believe it. I hold her tightly, feel her start to cry.

Later, I go back to the camp. In the early afternoon, with the sun burning through the mist. As the first glimpses of sky appear — gauzy, dazzling shreds — I feel something in me pouring out, pouring up. I'm left with a neutral feeling that could become anything. It could become joy. Perhaps. I sit next to Harry on the steps of his van. I ask him what he's doing and although he doesn't speak, he shows me, opening his hands. A tiny penknife in one hand, a half-cylinder shard of tree bark in the other, and patterns scratched into it, geometric shapes bumping and overlapping. He is miraculous to me now. I try to take his arm but he shuffles, doesn't want me to. I don't force it. Miraculous. That Henry could grow into this gentle soul. Was he damaged or, rather, was something knocked out of him by Beth's blow? The spite? The childish arrogance, the aggression? All the base things, all of Meredith's legacy, all the hate she taught him. He is a cleanly wiped slate.

I let him keep working, but I tie his dreadlocks into a chaotic knot behind his head so I can see his face. I sit, and he works, and I watch his face. And slowly, familiar things surface. Some of his features settle back into the shapes I knew. Just here and there, just traces. The Calcott nose we all have, narrow at the bridge. The blue-grey shade of his irises. He doesn't seem to mind me watching. He doesn't seem to notice.

'He recognised you, I think,' Dinny says quietly, coming to stand in front of us. His arms hang loosely at his sides, hands in fists, as if he's ready for something. Ready to react. 'That first time you saw him in the woods and he stopped you passing by. I think he recognised you, you see.' I look up at Dinny, but I can't speak to him. Not yet. Tendons standing out on his forearms, ridges under the skin, tense with the clench of his hands. He was right. Everything has changed. Across the clearing, Patrick emerges from his van and gives me a solemn nod.

I go up to fetch Beth as the light is failing. She has been lying down for hours. Assimilating. I tell her who is downstairs and she agrees to see him. All the solemnity and the dread of one going to the gallows. Her bluntly cropped hair lies at odd angles, and her face is immobile, unnaturally still. Some force of will it must be costing her, to keep it that still. In the kitchen the lights are on. Dinny and Henry, sitting opposite each other at the table, playing snap and drinking tea as if the world has not just tensed itself up and thrown off everything our lives were based upon, like a dog shaking off muddy water. Dinny glances up as we come in, but Beth only looks at Henry. She sits down, at a safe distance, and stares. I watch and wait. Henry shuffles the cards clumsily, dropping a few onto the table that he slides back into the deck, one by one.

'Does he know me?' Beth whispers; her voice so thin, so precarious. Something about to break. I sit beside her, put my hands out to catch her.

Dinny shrugs slightly. 'There's really no way of knowing. He seems . . . comfortable around you. Around both of you. It usually takes him a while to warm up to strangers, so . . .'

'I thought I'd killed him. All this time, I thought I'd killed him . . .'

'You did,' Dinny says flatly. Her mouth opens in shock. 'You knocked him out and left him face down in the water—'

'Dinny! Don't—' I try to stop him.

'If I hadn't pulled him out, he *would* be dead. So just remember that before you start judging what *I've* done, what my family's done . . .'

'Nobody's judging anybody! We were just kids . . . we had no idea what to do. And yes, it was lucky you thought so fast, Dinny,' I say.

'I'd hardly call it lucky.'

'Well, whatever you want to call it then.'

Dinny draws in another breath, eyes narrowing at me, but Beth starts to cry. Not soft, self-pitying tears. Ragged, ugly sobs, torn out from the heart of her. Her mouth is a deep red hole. Low wails, rising from a darkness inside that's almost palpable, horrible to hear. I sit back down, put my arms around her as if I can hold her together. Dinny goes to the window, leans his forehead against the glass as if he wants nothing more than to be gone from this place. I press my cheek against Beth's back, feeling shudders pass up through her and into me. Henry sorts the cards into their suits in neat piles on the table. I can't begin to decipher what I feel about Dinny, about this secret he's been keeping. Henry, squirrelled away in England's labyrinth of lay-bys and green lanes; in vans and motor homes and caravans and lorries; a simple side-step but a world away from the door-to-door search for him in the neat and tidy villages. It's too big. I can't see it clearly.

We part some time later, to deliver our respective charges to bed. Dinny goes into the night with Henry; I walk up the stairs with Beth. She cried for a long time and now she's quiet. I think her mind is rewriting itself, like mine had to, and that she needs time. I hope that is all she needs. Her face looks raw. Not just red, not just rubbed. Raw like it is new-made, like it has yet to be shaped, yet to be marked by life. A childlike delicacy. I hope I see something wiped from it, some of her caginess, some of the shadow and fear. Too soon to tell. I pull the blankets up to her chin like a mother would, and she smiles a half-mocking smile.

'Erica,' she says, and sighs a little. 'How long have you been in love with Dinny?'

'What?' I shrug one shoulder to dismiss her, realise too late that it's a gesture of his that I've picked up.

'Don't deny it. It's written all over you.'

'You need to sleep. It's been a rough day.'

'How long?' she presses, catching my hand as I move away. I look at her. In this light her eyes are unreadable. I can't lie, but I can't answer.

'I don't know,' I say shortly. 'I don't know that I am in love with him.' I walk to the door, stiffly, feeling betrayed by every line of my body, every tiny move I make.

'Erica!'

'What?'

'I . . . was pleased, when you said you didn't remember what had happened. I didn't want you to remember. You were so young . . .'

'Not *that* young.'

'Young enough. None of it was your fault, I hope you know that. Of course you know. I didn't want you to remember, because I was so ashamed. Not of throwing a stone back at him, but of running. Of leaving him there, and never telling Mum and Dad. I don't know why. I don't know why I did that! I've never known!'

'It wasn't—'

'It was a thing to be decided on the instant. That's what I've come to think, as I've got older. A decision made in an instant and once it's made you can't go back on it. Do you face up to a mistake, even one so terrible, or do you run away from it? I ran. I failed.'

'You didn't fail, Beth.'

'Yes, I did. You only ever did what *I* did. I was the leader, the eldest. If I'd spoken up straight away he could have lived.'

'He did live!'

'He could have lived *normally*! Not been so damaged . . .'

'Beth, there's no point to this. He lived. It can't be undone now. Please stop torturing yourself. You were a child.'

'When I think of Mary, and Clifford . . .' Tears blur her eyes again, spill over. I can think of nothing to say to this. Clifford and Mary. Their lives were ruined more completely than ours. The thought of them settles like lead around my heart.

I am awake in the clinging darkness before sunrise, and creep quietly to the kitchen. That odd state, exhausted and electrified at once. I make coffee, drink it strong and too hot. The cold of the floor numbs my feet through my socks. The little clock on the microwave tells me it's half past seven. Silence in the house but for the creak of the heating as it fights its losing battle. I fetch yesterday's paper, stare at it blankly and fail to do the crossword. The caffeine bustles my brain awake, but it doesn't help me think. How can we not tell Henry's parents that he's alive? How can we not? We can't not. But they will want to know what happened. Even placid Mary, so broken, will want to know what happened. And Clifford will want *justice*. Justice as he would see it. He will want charges brought against the Dinsdales for kidnapping, for withholding medical treatment. He will probably want charges brought against Beth and me, although these would be harder to bring. Grievous bodily harm, perhaps. Perverting the course of justice. I have no idea what charges apply to children. But I can see him clearly, with the three of us in his teeth, shaking and shaking. So how can we tell them?

Outside the sky lightens slowly. Beth appears, fully dressed, at ten o'clock. She stands in the doorway with her bag on her shoulder.

'How are you doing?' I ask her.

'I'm . . . OK. I've got to go. Maxwell's dropping Eddie off after lunch tomorrow and nothing's ready, and . . . and I need to get to a hairdresser before he arrives. I've got him until he goes back to school on Wednesday.'

'Oh, right. I thought . . . I thought we were going to talk about it? About Henry?' I ask.

She shakes her head. 'I'm just not ready to talk about it yet. Not yet. I feel better, though.'

'Good, good. I'm glad, Beth. Really, I am. I want nothing more than for you to be able to put all this behind you.'

'That's what I want too.' She sounds lighter, almost bright; smiles in readiness to depart, grips her bag convincingly.

'Only . . . I don't know what we should do about Clifford and Mary. What we should do about telling them . . .' I say. Her face falls. She is on the same train of thought as me, I think, only I am some hours ahead of her. She licks her lips, quickly, nervously.

'Right now I have to go. But honestly, Rick, I don't think I should have any say in what happens next. I don't have the right. I don't want the right. I've done enough to him. To them. I don't think any idea of mine would be a good one.' Little shadows chase across her face again.

'Don't worry about it, Beth. I'll sort it out.' So sure of this, I sound. She smiles at me, diaphanous and wonderful as new butterfly wings; comes over and hugs me.

'Thank you, Erica. I owe you so much,' she says.

'You don't owe me anything.' I shake my head. 'You're my sister.'

She squeezes me with all the strength in her willow-switch body.

It starts to sleet from a flat grey sky as we get into the car, and I have just started the engine when Dinny appears from beneath the trees, knocks on the window.

'I was hoping I'd catch you. I guessed you'd be off this morning,' he says to Beth. Just the faintest hint of a rebuke, but enough to put a line between her brows.

'Beth has to catch the next train,' I say. He flicks his eyes to me and nods.

'Look, Beth, I just wanted to say . . . I just . . . when I said last night that you'd killed him, I didn't mean that . . . that you'd done it deliberately or anything,' he says. 'I used to ask my parents why Henry was such a bastard. Why he was such a bully, such a vicious little git . . . They told me over and over again that when children behave that way it's because they aren't happy. For whatever reason they're full of fear and anger and they take it out on other people. I didn't believe them then, of course. I thought it was just because he was an evil sod, but I believe it now. It's true, of course. Henry wasn't happy then, and, well, he is happy now. He's the happiest, most peaceful soul I know. I just . . . I just thought you should think about that.' Dinny swallows, tips his chin at us and steps back from the car.

'Thank you,' Beth says. She can't quite look him in the eye, but she's trying. 'Thank you, for what you did. For never telling anybody.'

'I'd never have done anything to hurt you, Beth,' he says softly. My knuckles on the steering wheel are white. Beth nods, her eyes downcast. 'Will you ever come back this way?' he asks.

'Perhaps. I think so. Sometime in the future,' she replies.

'Then I'll see you around, Beth,' Dinny says, with a sad smile.

'Goodbye, Dinny,' she says quietly. He smacks the roof of the car with the flat of his hand and I pull away obediently. In the rear-view mirror I see him standing there, hands in his pockets, dark eyes in a dark face. He stays until we have driven out of sight.

Saturday the third of January today. Most people will be back at work on Monday. I will call the Calcott family lawyer, a Mr Dawlish of Marlborough, and tell him he can put Storton Manor on the market. I have decisions to make, now that I can go forward again. There's nothing missing any more, no cracks, no excuses to stall. I am quiet as I move around the house. I don't want the radio on, or the TV for company. I don't hum, I try not to bang; I put my feet down softly. I want to hear the clear bell-tone of the truths I know ringing in my head. I could leave it all — leave the huge tree and all the holly I painted gold. They could stay, gathering dust and cobwebs until the auctioneer has been and gone with all the good stuff, and the house clearance men have been for the rest. Relics of this odd, limbo Christmas of ours. But I can't bear the thought of it. That shreds of our lives should be left like Meredith's apple core in the drawing room bin. Discarded and repugnant.

Industry is good. It keeps my thoughts from overwhelming me. Three things only I will keep: Caroline's writing case and the letters within it, the New York portrait and Flag's teething ring. The rest can go. I strip the tree of baubles and beads and clear the last of the Christmas leftovers from the fridge and the larder, scattering the lawn with anything the birds or foxes might fancy. I find pliers in a scullery drawer, climb the stairs to where the Christmas tree is fixed to the banisters, and cut the wire. 'Timber!' I cry, to the empty hallway. The tree sags slowly to one side, then flops to the floor like an elderly dog. A delicate, muffled crunch tells me I didn't find every bauble. Dry needles cascade from the branches, carpet the flagstones. With a sigh, I fetch a dustpan and brush and set to chasing them around the floor. I can't help conjuring a life for myself with Dinny, picturing staying with him. Sleeping on a narrow bunk in the back of his ambulance; cooking breakfast on the tiny stove; perhaps working in each new town. Short contracts, sick-leave cover. Tutoring. As if anybody would hire a supply teacher with no fixed address. Lying close each night, hearing his heartbeat, woken by his touch.

There's a knock, and Dinny's voice startles me from my reverie.

'Is this a bad time?' His head appears around the front door.

'No, it's perfect timing, actually. You can help me drag this tree out.' I smile, climbing to my feet and wincing. 'I've been on my knees for too long. And not for any of the best reasons,' I tell him.

'Oh? And what are the best reasons?' Dinny asks, with an arch smile that warms me.

'Why, prayer, of course,' I tell him, all sincerity, and he chuckles. He hands me an envelope.

'Here. A card from Honey. For your help the other night, and for the flowers.' He takes an elastic band from his pocket, holding it in his teeth while he gathers up his hair, pulls it back from his face.

'Oh, she didn't have to do that.'

'Well, after you'd left Mum's the other day she realised that she hadn't actually *said* thank you. And now that the hormones are settling down, I think she appreciates how vile she's been for the past few weeks.'

'She had good reason, I suppose. Not an easy time for her.'

'She didn't make it easy. But it all seems to be working out now.'

'Here – grab a branch.' I open both sides of the front door wide and we grasp the tree by its lowest branches, tow it across the floor. It bleeds a green wake behind it.

'Perhaps you shouldn't have swept up until after we'd moved the tree?' Dinny observes.

'Could be,' I agree. We abandon the tree on the driveway, brush the needles from our hands. Everything is dripping wet out here, weighed down with water. Dark streaks on the trees, like a fever sweat. The rooks clamour from across the garden. Their disembodied voices hit the house, come back again as metallic echoes; I think I can feel them watching us with their hard little eyes like metal beads. My heart is the quickest thing for miles around. My thoughts the least quiet. I look at Dinny, suddenly shy. I can't give a name to what's between us, can't quite feel the shape of it. 'Come for dinner tonight,' I say.

'OK. Thanks,' he replies.

*

I've made a meal with the last of anything edible from the larder, the fridge, the freezer. This is the last time. I will throw the rest away. Ancient tins of custard powder; dog biscuits; jars of treacle with rusted-on lids; sachets of ready-mix béchamel. The house will go from lived-in to empty, from home to property. Any time now. I said he could bring Harry, if he wanted. It seemed only right. I feel I ought to have some part in looking after him, in supporting him. But Dinny sensed this, and he frowned, and when he arrives at seven he's alone. A tawny owl shrieks in the trees behind him, heralds him. A still night, cold and dank as a riverbank pebble.

'Beth seemed a bit better when she left,' I say, opening a bottle of wine and pouring two large glasses. 'Thank you for saying . . . what you said. About Henry being happy.'

'It's true,' Dinny says, taking a sip that wets his lower lip, traces it with crimson.

All along, he has known. All this time, all these years. He can't know, then, how I feel now – looking down and seeing I wasn't walking on solid ground after all.

'What is this, anyway?' he asks me, turning the food over with his fork.

'Chicken Provençal. And those are cheese dumplings. Mixed bean salad and tinned spinach. Why? Is there a problem?'

'No, no problem,' he smiles, and gamely begins to eat. I take a forkful of dumpling. It has the texture of plasticine.

'It's horrible. Sorry. I never was much of a cook,' I say.

'The chicken's not bad,' Dinny says diplomatically. We are so unused to this. To sitting and eating together. Small talk. The idea of us together, in this new world order. The silence hangs.

'My mum told me that you were in love with Beth back then. Is that why you would never say what had really happened? To protect Beth?'

Dinny chews slowly, swallows.

'We were *twelve*, Erica. But I didn't want to tell on her, no.'

'Do you still love her?' I don't want to know, but I have to.

'She's not the same person now.' He looks down, frowns.

'And me? Am I the same?'

'Pretty much,' Dinny smiles. 'As tenacious as ever.'

'I don't mean to be,' I say. 'I just want to do the right thing. I just want . . . I want everything to be all right.'

'You always did. But life's not that simple.'

'No.'

'Are you going back to London?'

'I don't think so. No, I'm not. I'm not sure where I'm going.' I look at him when I say this and I can't keep the question from my eyes. He looks at me, steadily but without an answer.

'Clifford will make trouble,' I say at length. 'If we tell them. I know he will. But I'm not sure if I could live with myself, knowing what I know and letting him and Mary think Henry's dead,' I say.

'They wouldn't know him now, Erica,' Dinny says seriously. 'He's not their son any more.'

'Of course he's their son! What else is he?'

'He's been with me for so long now. I've grown up with him. I've seen myself change . . . but Harry just stayed the same. Like he was frozen in time the day that rock hit him. If anything, he's my brother. He's part of *my* family now.'

'We're all one family, remember? In more ways than one, it seems. They could help you look after him . . . or I could. Help support him . . . financially, or . . . He's their *son*, Dinny. And he didn't die!'

'But he did. Their son did. Harry is not Henry. They'd take him away from everything he knows.'

'They have a right to know about him.' I shake my head, I cannot let this lie.

'So, what — you're picturing Harry living with them, cooped up in a conventional life, or in some kind of institution, where they can visit him whenever they like and he'd be plonked in front of the TV the rest of the time?'

'It wouldn't be like that!'

'How do you know?'

'I just . . . I can't even imagine what it must have been like for them, all this time.' We are quiet for a long time. 'I'm not going to decide anything without you,' I tell him.

'I've told you what I think,' Dinny says. 'It would do them no good to see him now. And we don't need any help.'

He shakes his head and looks sad. I cannot bear this thought, that I am making Dinny sad. I put my hand across the table, mesh my fingers into his.

'What you did for us – for Beth – taking the blame like that . . . it's huge, Dinny. That was a huge thing that you did,' I say quietly. 'Thank you.'

'Will you stay?' I ask him, late in the evening. He doesn't answer, but he stands up, waits for me to lead. I won't take him into Meredith's room. I choose a guest room on the top floor, in the attics of the house, where the sheets are chilly with the long absence of warm bodies and the floorboards creak as we cross them. The silence makes us quiet, and the night outside the bare window sketches us in silvery greys as we undress. My skin rises where he touches me, the tiny hairs on me reaching out. He is so dark in this monochrome light, his face a depth of shadow I can't fathom. I kiss his mouth, bruise my lips against his, drink him in. I want there to be no space between us, no part of my body not touching his. I want to wind myself around him like ivy, like a rope, binding us together. He has no tattoos, no piercings, no scars. He is whole, perfect. The palms of his hands are rough on my back. He coils one through my hair, tips my head back.

I close my eyes and watch with my body – each sure move of his hands, the warm brush of his breath, his weight over me. I pull his elbows out from under him. I want him to cover me, to crush me. Nothing guarded about him now, no hesitation, no thinking. A frown of a different kind as he puts his hands under my hips, lifts me, fits me to his body, pushes hard. I want to ink my mind with this, always keep him in this room with me; keep the taste of him on my tongue, make the beat between each second last, unending. Salt sweat on his top lip, ragged words mumbled into my hair. I want nothing else.

'I could stay with you,' I say afterwards. My eyes are shut, trusting. 'I could stay and help you with Harry. I can get work anywhere. You shouldn't have to support him alone. I could help. I could stay with you.'

'And travel all the time, and live like we do?'

'Well, why not? I'm homeless now, after all.'

'You're a long way from being homeless. You don't know what you're saying.' His fingers are curled around my shoulder, and they smell of me. I lean myself against him. His skin is hot and dry beneath my cheek.

'I do know. I don't want to go back to London, and I can't stay here. I'm at your disposal,' I say, and the absurdity of this statement makes me chuckle. But Dinny does not laugh. There's a growing tension in his frame that makes me uneasy. 'I don't mean . . . I'm not trying to foist myself on you, or anything,' I add hurriedly. No grip of mine could hold him, if he wanted to go. He sighs, turns his head to press a kiss onto my hair.

'It wouldn't be so bad having you foisted on me, Pup,' he smiles. 'Let's sleep on it. We can sort it out tomorrow.' He says it so softly, so quietly that I decipher the words from the rumble in his chest beneath my ear. Deep and resolute. I am awake long enough to hear his breathing deepen, slow down, grow even. Then I sleep.

When I wake up I'm alone. The sky is flat, matt white, and a fine drizzle sifts down through the trees. A rook perches on a bare branch outside the window, feathers fluffed against the weather.

Suddenly, I long for summer. For warmth, and dry ground, and a mile-wide sky. I run my hand across the side of the bed where Dinny was when I fell asleep. The sheets aren't warm. There's no indent in the pillow, no echo of his head. I could have imagined him here with me, but I didn't. I didn't. I won't race down there. I won't be alarmed. I make myself get dressed, eat breakfast cereal with the last of the milk. Today I will either have to shop or leave. I wonder which it will be.

I slip across the sodden lawn, wellies slick with water, papered with dead leaves. I feel clear-headed today, purposeful. It's misplaced, perhaps, when I have not yet made the decisions that need making, but perhaps I am finally ready to make them, perhaps that's what this feeling is. I've got a box of things for Harry. I found them in some drawers in the cellar, had earmarked them for the bin when I realised he might like them. A broken Sony radio, some old torches and batteries and bulbs and small metal objects of unknown provenance. They rattle against the cardboard under my arm. My back aches from the strain of Dinny's weight, pushing against my pelvis. I shiver, cradle this physical memory close to me.

I stand for quite some time in the centre of the camp clearing, while the rain begins to soften the box I carry. No vans here now, no dogs, no columns of smoke. It is deserted and I am left behind – alone in an empty clearing churned muddy by feet and wheels; and me, churned muddy by him. By the getting of him, and now the losing. My long-lost cousin, my childhood hero. My Dinny. Perfect calm, and stillness. No breath of a breeze today. I can hear a car, speeding along the lane from the village, tyres crackling in the standing rainwater. I have no phone number for him, no email address, no clue in which direction he has gone. I turn in a slow circle, in case there is something behind me, something that waited for me, or someone.

Legacy

1911—

Caroline's last child was born in 1911, long after the occupants of Storton Manor had given up hope of there being a Calcott heir. There had been other pregnancies, two of them, both a long time in the conceiving, but Caroline's body had rejected the children and they had been lost before they even really began. The little girl was born in August. It was a long, hot summer the likes of which no one could remember, and Caroline sweltered, shuffling into the garden to lie swollen and prone in the shade, drowsing. The heat was such that sometimes, as she hovered on the edges of sleep, she imagined herself back in Woodward County, sitting on the porch and gazing out at the yard, waiting for Corin to ride home; so that when she was approached by a servant or her husband, she stared at them in no little confusion for a while, before remembering who they were and where she was.

The gardens were scorched and brown. A village boy, Tommy Westenfell, drowned in the dew pond. His feet got tangled in weeds at the bottom and he was found hours later by his distraught father; pale, still, and sleepy-eyed. Mrs Priddy took a bad turn walking back from the butcher with a whole leg of lamb and was consigned to her bed for three days, her skin mottled and puce. Estelle and Liz, Cass's plump replacement, worked hard to cover for her, with perspiration soaking their uniforms. The smell everywhere was of parched earth, sweat and hot, dry air. The stone flags of the terrace burnt Caroline's feet through the soles of her slippers. Henry Calcott, who was by then uncomfortable around his own wife, remained at home long enough to see the child safely born, and then quit Wiltshire to stay with friends by the sea in Bournemouth.

The labour was long and arduous, and Caroline was delirious by the end. The doctor forced fluids into her through a tube pushed down her throat, and she gazed at him from the bed with uncomprehending terror. Liz and Estelle kept the baby those first few days, taking turns to lay cold cloths onto their mistress's skin to cool her. Caroline recovered, at length, but when they brought the child to her, her gaze swept over it impassively, and then she turned her face away and would not nurse it. A wet nurse was found in the village and Caroline, who wanted to be sure that the girl would live before she dared to love her, found, as months and then years passed, that she had left it too late. The little girl did not seem to belong to her, and she could not love her. The child was two years old before she was given a name. Estelle, Liz and the wet nurse had been calling her Augusta all that time, but one day Caroline looked dispassionately into her cradle and announced that she would be named Meredith, after her grandmother.

Meredith was a lonely child. She had no siblings to play with and was forbidden to play with any of the village children that she saw roaming the fields and lanes around the manor house. The household was in decline by then, and the village of Barrow Storton was a sad, quiet place with most of the young men gone off to fight and die on the continent. Henry Calcott kept mainly to town, where his gambling consumed so much money that several of the staff, including Liz and the scullery maid, were laid off, leaving Mrs Priddy to keep the house as best she could with only Estelle to help her. Mrs Priddy was kind to Meredith, letting her eat the leftover pastry scraps and keep a pet rabbit in a pen outside the kitchen door, where she fed it carrot tops and ragged outer lettuce leaves. A tutor came, five mornings a week, to teach Meredith her letters, music, needlework and deportment. Meredith hated the lessons and the tutor both; and escaped into the garden as soon as she could.

But Meredith longed for her mother. Caroline was an otherworldly creature by then, who sat for hours in a white gown, either at a window or out on the lawn, staring into the distance and seeing who knew what. When Meredith tried to hug her, she tolerated it for a moment and then disentangled the child's arms with a mild smile, telling her vaguely to run along and play. Mrs Priddy admonished her not to tire her mother out, and Meredith took this instruction to heart, fearing that she was somehow responsible for her mother's persistent lethargy. So she kept away, thinking that if she did her mother would not be so tired, and would get up and smile and love her more. She played alone, watching pigeons on the rooftops courting and bowing to one another. She watched the frog spawn in the ornamental pond slowly grow tails and hatch into tadpoles. She watched the kitchen cats as they chased down hapless mice and then devoured them with swift, perfunctory crunches. And she watched the Dinsdales in the clearing through the woods. She watched them whenever she could, but she was too shy to ever let them see her.

The Dinsdales had three children: a tiny baby who went around in a sling on his mother's back, a little girl with yellow hair like her mother's, who was a few years older than Meredith herself, and a boy, a dark, strange-looking boy whose age Meredith was unable to guess at, who went everywhere with his father and played with his little sister, grinning as he teased her. Their mother was pretty and she smiled all the time, laughing at their antics and hugging them. Their father was more serious, as Meredith understood fathers should be, but he smiled often too, and put his arm around the boy, or lifted the little girl high into the air to sit astride his shoulders. Meredith could not imagine her own father ever doing such a thing with her – the very thought made her uneasy. So Meredith watched this family, fascinated, and even though they were happy and bright she came away from her clandestine visits feeling tearful and dark, unaware that she watched them because she envied them and was filled with yearning for her own mother to hug her that way.

One day she made a mistake. Her mother was on the lawn in her wicker chair, an untouched jug of lemonade on the table beside her with thirsty flies settling unafraid on the beaded lace cover. Meredith emerged from the woods and was startled to see her there, immediately brushing down her skirts and tucking her hair behind her ears. Her mother did not look up as she approached, but managed a wan smile once her daughter was standing right in front of her.

'Well, child, and where have you been today?' her mother asked her in a voice that was soft and dry and seemed to come from far away. Meredith went right up to her and tentatively took hold of her hand.

'I was in the woods. Exploring,' she said. 'Shall I pour you some lemonade?'

'And what did you find in the woods?' her mother asked, ignoring the offer of lemonade.

'I saw the Dinsdales—' Meredith said, and then put her hand over her mouth. Mrs Priddy had warned her never to mention the Dinsdales to her mother, although she had no idea why not.

'You did what?' her mother snapped. 'You know that's not allowed! I hope you have not been talking to those people?'

'No, Mama,' Meredith said quietly. Her mother settled back into her chair, pressing her mouth into a bloodless line. Meredith steeled herself. 'But, Mama, *why* can I not play with them?' Her heart beat fast at her own temerity.

'Because they are filth! Gypsy, tinker villains! They are thieves and liars and they are not welcome here – and you are *not* to go near them! Not *ever*! Do you understand?' Her mother leant forward in her chair like a whip cracking, and grasped Meredith's wrist so that it hurt. Meredith nodded fearfully.

'Yes, Mama,' she whispered.

They are not welcome here. Meredith took these words to heart. When she watched them next her envy became jealousy, and instead of wanting to play with them, and share their happy existence, she began to wish instead that they did not *have* their happy existence. She watched them every day, and every day she grew crosser with them, and sadder inside, so that it came to seem to her that it was the Dinsdales who were *making* her sad. Her and her mother both. If she could make them go away, she thought, her mother would be pleased. Surely, she would *have* to be pleased.

On a hot summer's day in 1918, Meredith heard the Dinsdale children playing at the dew pond. She edged closer, through the dappled light beneath the trees, then stood behind the smooth trunk of a beech and watched them jumping in and out of the water. It looked like tremendous fun, although Meredith had never been swimming so she could not know for sure. She wished she could try, though. Her skin was itchy with the heat, and the thought of all that clear, cold water washing over it was so tempting it made her weak. The Dinsdales were splashing up arcs of crystalline droplets, and Meredith noticed how dry her mouth felt. The boy's skin was so much darker than his sister's. It was a kind of nut colour, and his raggedy hair was inky black. He teased the girl and dunked her under the water, but Meredith saw that he secretly watched her and made sure she was still laughing before he dunked her again.

She leant out for a better view, and then froze to the spot. The Dinsdales had seen her. First the boy, who had climbed out and was standing on the bank, water streaming from the hems of his short breeches, then the girl, who paddled in a circle to see what her brother was looking at.

'Hello,' the boy said to her, so casual and friendly, when Meredith felt like her heart might explode in her chest. 'Who are you?'

Meredith was amazed that he didn't know, when she herself felt that she knew *them* so well. It outraged her that they did not know who she was. She stood, stock still and breathless, not knowing whether to stay or to run.

'Meredith,' she whispered, after a long, uneasy silence.

'I'm Maria!' the girl called from the water, her arms windmilling madly beneath the surface.

'And I'm Flag. Do you want to come in for a swim? It's quite safe,' the boy told her. He put his hands on his hips and examined her, head tipped to one side. His wet skin shone over the curves of his arms and legs, and liquid light from the water danced in his eyes. Meredith felt almost too shy to answer him. She thought him beautiful, and was not sure what to say.

'What kind of name is *Flag*?' she asked, haughtily, in spite of herself.

'My name,' he shrugged. 'Do you live at the big house, then?'

'Yes,' she replied, her words still reluctant to come.

'Well,' Flag continued, after a pause, 'do you want to swim with us or not?'

Meredith felt her face burn and she tipped her chin down to hide. She was not allowed to swim. She never had been — but the temptation was so strong and, she reasoned, who would ever find out?

'I . . . I don't know how to swim,' she was forced to admit.

'Paddle then. I'll fetch you out if you fall in,' Flag shrugged. Meredith had never heard the word *paddle* before, but she thought she understood. Fingers trembling with the illicit thrill of disobedience, she sat down on the cracked earth and pulled off her boots, then crept carefully to the water's edge. It wasn't *really* disobeying, she told herself. Nobody had ever said anything to her about not paddling.

She slithered the last few inches down the steep bank and gasped nervously as her feet stumbled into the water.

'It's so cold!' she squeaked, hastily scrambling backwards. Maria giggled.

'It's only cold when you first jump in. Then it's perfect!' she said.

Meredith edged forwards again and let the water rise to her ankles. The bite of it made her bones ache and scattered silvery shivers all over her. With a yell, Flag took a short run up and leapt into the middle of the pool, bending his knees and wrapping his arms around them. The splash caused a wave to engulf Maria and soak the bottom six inches of Meredith's dress.

'Now look what you've done!' she cried, afraid that Mrs Priddy or her mother would see and she would be found out.

'Flag! Don't,' Maria told him gaily as he surfaced, spluttering.

'It'll soon dry out,' Flag told her carelessly. His hair was plastered to his neck, as slick as otter fur. Meredith climbed out crossly, sat down on the bank and studied her feet, which had gone from pink to bright white after their wetting.

'Flag – say you're sorry!' Maria commanded.

'Sorry for getting your dress wet, Meredith,' Flag said, rolling his eyes at his sister. But Meredith didn't reply. She sat and watched them swim for a while longer, but her sullen presence seemed to spoil their fun and they soon climbed out and pulled on the rest of their clothes.

'Do you want to come and have tea?' Maria asked her, her smile a little less ready than before. Flag stood half turned to go. Water ran from his hair and wet his shirt, slicking it to his skin. Meredith wanted to look at him but her eyes slid away infuriatingly when she tried.

She shook her head. 'I'm not allowed,' she said.

'Come on then, Maria,' Flag said, a touch impatiently.

'Goodbye, then,' Maria shrugged, and gave Meredith a little wave.

It took nearly two hours for the thick cotton of her dress to dry out completely, and during that time Meredith kept to the outer edges of the garden where only the gardener might see her. He was ancient and didn't pay much attention to anything except his marrows. She thought about her paddle, and about Maria inviting her to tea, and about Flag's wet hair shining, and each of these things gave her a fizzing feeling quite at odds with the resentment she had felt before. It made her skip a little and smile excitedly. She imagined how it might be to go to tea, to see the inside of the covered wagon that she had watched so many times from the trees, to meet their blonde and affectionate mother, who put her arms around them and smiled all the time. *How do you do, Mrs Dinsdale?* She practised the phrase under her breath in the safe, silent confines of the greenhouse. But there could be no arguing that this would be a huge disobedience. And that talking to Flag and Maria had been one as well, even if she could argue her way around the paddling. Just thinking about what would happen if Mama found out about it brought her spirits low again, and when she was called in for tea she made sure that she was quiet and dull and gave nothing away.

For days, Meredith was consumed with thoughts and daydreams about the Dinsdales. She had so rarely encountered other children – only visiting cousins, or the children of other guests who stayed only fleetingly so she never really got to know them. She knew she was supposed to despise the tinkers, and she knew all the things her mother had told her about them, and she still longed more than anything to please her mother and to make her happy, but the idea of having friends was irresistible. A week later, she was playing in the barred shadow of the tall iron gates when she saw Flag and Maria walking along the lane towards the village. They would not see her unless she called out and for a second she was paralysed, torn between longing to speak to them again and knowing that she shouldn't – least of all from the gate, which was visible from the house if anybody happened to be at one of the east-facing windows. In desperation she came up with a compromise of sorts and burst loudly into song – the first thing that came to mind, a song she had heard Estelle singing as she pegged the laundry out to dry.

'*I'd like to see the Kaiser, with a lily in his hand!*' she bellowed, tunelessly, hopping from one bar of shadow to the next. Flag and Maria turned and, seeing her, came over to the gates.

'Hello again,' Maria greeted her. 'What are you doing?'

'Nothing,' Meredith replied, her heart yammering behind her ribs. 'What are you doing?'

'Going on to the village to buy bread and Bovril for tea. Do you want to come too? If we can get a broken loaf, there'll be a ha'penny left to buy sweets,' Maria smiled.

'Not necessarily,' Flag qualified. 'If there's enough left over we're to buy butter, remember?'

'Oh, but there's never enough for butter as well!' Maria dismissed her brother.

'You have to go to the shops yourselves?' Meredith asked, puzzled.

'Of course, silly! Who else would go?' Maria laughed.

'Suppose *you've* got servants to run around buying *your* tea, haven't you?' Flag asked, a touch derisively.

Meredith bit her lip, an awkward blush heating her face. She hardly ever went into the village. A handful of times she had accompanied Mrs Priddy or Estelle on some errand, but only when her father was away, and her mother laid low and guaranteed not to hear of it.

'Do you want to come, then?'

'I'm not allowed,' Meredith said unhappily. Her cheeks burned even more, and Flag tilted his head at her, a mischievous glint coming into his eye.

'Seems to be a fair bit you're not allowed to do,' he remarked.

'Hush! It's not *her* fault!' Maria admonished him.

'Come on – I dare you. Or maybe you're just scared?' he asked, arching an eyebrow.

Meredith glared at him defiantly. 'I am not! Only . . .' She hesitated. She *was* scared, it was true. Scared of being found out, scared of her mother's lightning-fast temper. But it would be so easy to slip away and back again without being noticed. Only the worst luck would mean she was discovered in this outrageous behaviour.

'Cowardy, cowardy custard!' Flag sang softly.

'Don't listen to *him*,' Maria advised her. 'Boys are *stupid*.' But Meredith was listening, and she did want to impress this black-eyed boy, and she did want to be friends with his sister, and she did want to be as free as they were, to come and go, and to buy sweets in the village and bread for tea. The gates of Storton Manor seemed to rear up above her head, ever higher and starker. Jangling with nerves, she reached for the latch, pulled open a narrow gap and slipped out into the lane.

Flag strode on ahead, leaving Maria and Meredith to walk side by side, picking wild flowers from the hedgerows and firing questions to and fro – what was it like living in a caravan, what was it like living in a mansion, how many servants were there and what were their names and why didn't Meredith go to school, and what was school like and what did they do there? In the village they stopped at the door to the farrier's shed to watch as he pressed a hot iron shoe onto the foot of a farm horse, whose hooves were the size of dinner plates. Clouds of acrid smoke billowed past them, but the horse did not blink an eye.

'Doesn't it hurt him?' Meredith asked.

''Course not. No more than it hurts you to have your hair cut,' Flag shrugged.

'Get on with ye, casting shadows o'er the work,' said the farrier, who was old and grizzled and stern of eye, so they carried on towards the grocer's. They bought a broken loaf and a jar of Bovril, and even though there was only enough left for two small sugar mice, the lady behind the counter smiled at Meredith and gave them a third.

'Not often we see you in the village, Miss Meredith,' the lady said, and Meredith caught her breath. How did the woman know who she was? And would she tell Mrs Priddy? Her face went pale and panicked tears came hotly into her eyes. 'Now, now. Don't look so aghast! Your secret's safe with me,' the woman said.

'Thank you, Mrs Carter!' Maria called brightly, and they went outside to devour their sweets.

'Why aren't you allowed to go into the village? No harm could come to you,' Flag asked as they stopped by the pond to watch the ducks circling idly. They sat down on the grass and Meredith nibbled at her sugar mouse, determined to make it last. She so rarely had sweets.

'Mama says it's not seemly,' Meredith replied.

'What's seemly?' Maria asked, licking her fingers with relish. Meredith shrugged.

'It means she's too good to go mixing with the hoi polloi. The likes of us,' Flag said, sounding amused. The girls thought about this for a while, in meditative silence.

'So . . . what would happen if your ma found out you was along here with us, then?' Maria asked at length.

'I would be . . . told off,' Meredith said uncertainly. In fact, she had no real idea. She had been told off for even watching the Dinsdales. Now she had sneaked out of the gardens and come into the village with them, and talked to them lots, and been seen in the grocer's by a woman who knew her name, and it had all been wonderful. Painfully, she swallowed the last of her sugar mouse, which had lost all its sweetness. 'I should go back,' she said nervously, scrambling to her feet. As if sensing the change in mood, the Dinsdales got up without argument and they began to walk back along the lane.

At the gates, Meredith slithered back through the gap as quickly as she could and pulled the gate closed, not daring to look up at the house in case somebody was watching. Her blood was racing and only once the gate was shut did she feel a little safer. She held on to the bars for support while she got her breath back.

'You're an odd one and no mistake,' Flag said, with a bemused smile.

'Come and have some tea with us tomorrow,' Maria invited her. 'Ma said you can – I asked her already.'

'Thank you. But . . . I don't know,' Meredith said. She was feeling exhausted by her adventure and could hardly think of anything except getting away from the gates without being seen talking to them. The Dinsdales wandered off and Meredith put her face to the bars to watch them go, pressing the cold metal into her skin. Flag pulled a leggy stem of goose grass from the hedge and stuck it to the back of Maria's blouse, and the blonde girl twisted and craned her neck, trying to reach it. As they passed out of sight Meredith turned and saw her mother standing in the upstairs hall window, watching her. Behind the glass, her face was ghastly pale and her eyes far too wide. She looked like a spectre, frozen for ever in torment.

Meredith's heart seemed to stop, and at once she thought desperately about running away to the furthest part of the garden. But that would only make matters worse, she realised in a moment of cold clarity. She suddenly needed to pee and thought for a hideous second that she would wet herself. On trembling legs she made her slow progress into the house, up the stairs and along the corridor to where her mother was waiting.

'How dare you?' Caroline whispered. Meredith looked at her feet. Her silence seemed to enrage her mother further. *'How dare you!'* she shouted, so loudly and harshly that Meredith jumped, and began to cry. 'Answer me – where have you been with them? What were you doing?' Mrs Priddy appeared from a room down the hall and hurried along to stand behind Meredith protectively.

'My lady? Is something the matter?' the housekeeper asked, diffidently.

Caroline ignored her. She bent forwards, seized Meredith's shoulders and shook her roughly.

'*Answer me!* How *dare* you disobey me, girl!' she spat, her gaunt face made brutal by rage. Meredith sobbed harder, tears of pure fear running down her cheeks. Straightening up, Caroline took a short breath that flared her nostrils whitely. She measured her daughter briefly, then slapped her sharply across the face.

'My lady! That's enough!' Mrs Priddy gasped. Meredith fell into shocked silence, her eyes fixed on the front of her mother's skirts and not daring to move from there. Caroline grasped her arm again and towed her viciously to her room, pushing her inside so abruptly that Meredith stumbled.

'You will stay in there and not come out until you have learnt your lesson,' Caroline said coldly. Meredith wiped her nose and felt her face throbbing where her mother had hit her. 'You're a wicked child. No mother could ever love you,' Caroline said; and the last thing Meredith saw before the door closed was Mrs Priddy's stunned expression.

For a week, Meredith was kept locked in her room. The staff were given orders that she was to have nothing but bread and water, but once Caroline had retired, Estelle and Mrs Priddy took her biscuits and scones and ham sandwiches. They brushed her hair for her, told her funny stories, and put arnica cream on her lip where the slap had made it swell, but Meredith remained silent and closed off, so that they exchanged worried looks above her head. *No mother could ever love her*. Meredith dwelt on this statement for a long time and refused to believe it. She would *make* her mother love her, she resolved. She would prove that she was not wicked, she would strive to be good and obedient and decorous in all things, and would win her mother's heart that way. And she would shun the tinkers. Because of them, her mother could not love her. *They are not welcome here*. She lay listlessly on her bed and felt her old anger at the Dinsdales, her old resentment, well up into a stifling pall that cast a dark shadow over her heart.

Epilogue

Spring is finally looking like it might win. We're through the muddy daffodils stage, past the week where soft tree blossoms were stripped by wind and rain and left to rot at the roadside in pink and brown drifts. Now there are tiny cracks in the earth of my sparse lawn, and fledgling sparrows line up along the fence, wide yellow mouths and fluffy feathers. I might get a cat, if it weren't for these absurd little birds, sitting shoulder to shoulder like beads on a string. I check their progress daily. The last tenant here parked his motorbikes on the lawn, and piled up the debris of his DIY, so there isn't much grass, but it will grow now, I think. The sun finally has some warmth. I sit out in it, tilt my face to it like a daisy, and I can feel the summer coming at last.

It was a relief, in the end, to have all my decisions made for me. Made by Dinny. What could I tell Clifford and Mary? That Henry was alive but damaged, and although I had seen him many times over Christmas and not told them, I now had no idea where he was? And why would I even try to stay at the manor, with all of them gone? Beth, Dinny, Harry. Henry. But I didn't go far. That was a decision I had already made, I think. There was no question of me going back to London – it would have been like walking backwards. And on the edge of Barrow Storton was this cottage to rent. Not pretty, not quaint, but fine. A 1950s two-up, two-down at the end of a short row of identical cottages. Two bedrooms, so Beth and Eddie can come and stay, and a great view from my bedroom at the front. It's on the opposite side of the village to the manor. I can see right across the valley, with the village at its bottom, and one corner of the manor is visible through distant trees. Less and less of it now that the trees are swelling into leaf.

Then the downs roll away, bounding up to the barrow on the horizon.

It makes me very serene, living here. I feel like I belong. I have no sense of there being anything else I should be doing, or working towards, or changing. I am not even waiting, not really. I make a special point of not waiting. I teach in Devizes, I walk a lot. I call in on George Hathaway for cups of tea and biscuits. Sometimes I miss the people I used to see in London – not specific people as such, but having so many faces around me. The illusion of company. But here I tend to notice the faces I do see all the more. People aren't part of a crowd like they were. I've made friends with my neighbours, Susan and Paul, and sometimes babysit for them for free because their little girls wear patched trousers far too short for them and don't go to ballet or judo or have riding lessons. There's no trampoline in their back yard. Susan's expression moved from suspicion to incredulous joy when I offered. The girls are good-natured and they do as they're told, most of the time. I take them on nature walks up on the downs or along the riverbank; we make cornflake cakes and hot chocolate while Susan and Paul go to the pub, the cinema, the shops, their bed.

Honey knows I'm here, and so does Mo. I went back to see Haydee and told them where I was and they've both been to visit since. I polished the tarnish from the silver bell on Flag's teething ring, brought it to a high shine and tucked it into Haydee's cot. She grabbed it with one fat hand, crammed it immediately into her mouth. *It was your great-grandpa's*, I whispered to her. I wrote down my address, told Honey to keep it in case anybody asked for it. She gave me a straight look, solemn, then arched one eyebrow. But she didn't say anything. She's back at school now and Mo comes around with Haydee in her pram. She walks from West Hatch, says the fresh air and movement is the only thing that makes the baby sleep. I revive her with tea at this, the furthest point of her journey. Mo walks with a waddle, her back aches, and when she gets to me she is usually hot, pulling at her T-shirt to unstick it from her breasts. But she loves Haydee. As I make tea she twitches the blanket over the child and can't keep herself from smiling.

I have the photo of Caroline with her baby in a frame on the window sill. I never did get around to giving it to Mum. I am still proud to have uncovered the child's identity, to have found the source of the rift between my family and Dinny's. Mum was astonished when I told her the story. I can't prove it all, definitively; but I know it to be true. I've decided to like the fact that I can't find out completely; that I can't fill in all the blanks – why Caroline hid her earlier marriage, why she hid her child. Where Flag was before he appeared at the manor and then fell into the Dinsdale's loving arms. Some things are lost in the past – surely that's why the past is so mysterious, why it fascinates us. Nothing much will be lost any more – too much is recorded, noted, stored in a file on a computer somewhere. It would be easy, not to be fascinated these days. It's harder to keep a secret, but they can be kept. Harry is living proof that they can be kept. I find I don't mind secrets half so much when they are mine to keep, when I am not excluded.

The manor house was sold at auction for a figure that gave me a sinking feeling inside, just for half an hour, imagining where I could have gone and what I could have done with such wealth. Clifford came to the auction but I hid from him, at the back of the conference room in a Marlborough hotel, as the figures bounced to and fro, got bigger and bigger. I could sense his anguish just by looking at the back of his head, rigid on stiff shoulders. I felt sorry for him. I think perhaps he'd hoped nobody else would come, nobody else would want to buy it; that he could snap it up for the price of a semi in Hertfordshire and tell everyone for ever that it was his birthright. But plenty of people did come, and a developer bought it. It's being converted into luxury flats, just like Maxwell suggested, because this is considered commutable now – from Pewsey to London and back every day. I can't imagine how it will look inside when it's done. What will my little back bedroom be? A kitchen with black granite worktops? A fully tiled wet room? I can't imagine it, and I'm half tempted to go and see the show flat when it's ready. Only half tempted though. I don't think I will. I don't want my memories of it muddied.

I think about Caroline and Meredith a lot. I think about what Dinny said – that people who bully and hate, people who are cold and aggressive are not happy people. They behave that way because they are unhappy. It is hard to find sympathy for Meredith when I have such memories of her, but now that she is dead I can manage it, when I try. Hers was a life of disappointment – her one bid to free herself from a loveless home over so soon after it began. It might have been harder still to feel sympathy for Caroline when I never really knew her, when she chose to abandon one child and then raised another without love. It would be easy to conclude that she just could not love. Wasn't able to. That she was too cold to be truly human, that she was born flawed. But then I found the last letter she wrote before she died; and I know better.

It lay undiscovered for weeks in the writing case, after I left the manor. Because she never sent it, of course, never even tore it from the writing pad. It was there, all along, beneath the cover, the line guide still in place underneath it. Her spidery writing tumbles across the page as if unravelling. 1983 is the date. No day or month specified, so perhaps that was the best she could do. She was over a hundred by then, and weakening. She knew that she was dying. Perhaps that was why she wrote this letter. Perhaps that was why she forgot, for a while, that she could never send it, that it would be read by nobody until me, more than a quarter of a century later.

My Dearest Corin,

It has been so long since I lost you that I cannot count the years. I am old now – old enough to be waiting to die myself. But then, I have been waiting to die ever since we were parted, my love. It is strange that the long years I have spent here in England seem, sometimes, to have passed by in a blur. I cannot recall what I can have possibly done to fill so much time — I really do not remember. But I do remember every second I spent with you, my love. Every precious second that I was your wife, and we were together. Oh, why did you die? Why did you ride out that day? I have been over it so many times. I see you mounting up, and I try to change the memory. I convince myself that I ran after you, told you not to go, not to leave me. Then you would not have fallen, and you would not have died, and I would not have had to spend these long dark years without you. Sometimes I so convince myself that I did run after you, that I did stop you, that when I realise you are gone it comes almost as a shock. It hurts me dreadfully, but I do it over and over again.

I did a terrible thing, Corin. An unforgivable thing. I ran away from it but I could not undo it, and it has followed me through all the years since. My only consolation has been that I never forgave myself, and that surely this life I have endured has been punishment enough? But no, there could never be punishment enough for what I did. I pray that you do not know of it, for if you did, you would not love me any more and I simply could not bear that. I pray that there is no God, and no heaven or hell, so that you cannot have been looking down, cannot have seen what crimes I committed. And I can never join you in heaven, if that is where you are. Surely, my soul belongs in hell when I die. But how could you not go to heaven, my love? You were an angel already, even on earth. Being with you was the one time in my whole life that I was happy, that I was glad to be alive, and everything since then has been ashes and dust to me. How long you have lain under that empty prairie? It is aeons since I saw you. The whole world could have been born and died again in the vast age since we touched.

I wish I could see you one more time, before I die. Part of me believes that there would be some justice in this — that if the world was a fair place, I would be allowed just a second of your embrace, to make up for

*losing you. No matter what I did in the madness of grief, no matter how
I compounded my mistake or how much worse I have made it – have
made myself – ever since. I would gladly give myself up to an eternity
of torment just to see you one more time. But it cannot be. I will die,
and be forgot, just as you died. But I never forgot you, my Corin, my
husband. Whatever else I did, I never forgot you, and I loved you
always.*

   Caroline.

I read and re-read this letter in the weeks after I found it. Until I
knew it by rote, and each word broke my heart a little. Such a vast
depth of regret and sorrow that it could cloud a sunny day. When I
feel it take hold of me, when I feel I have absorbed too much of it,
I remember Beth. Her crime will not follow her any more. She will
not compound it, or let the regret tear at her for ever. The chain
has been broken, and I helped to break it. I remember that, and I
let it cheer me, fill me up with hope. I will never know what
Caroline did. Why she took her baby and ran to England, why she
then abandoned him. One thing I do notice, though, from my
many readings of this letter: she does not mention her son. If the
child was hers, and Corin his father, why doesn't she mention him?
Why doesn't she tell her Corin about his son? Try to explain why
she abandoned him? This may well be the crime she hopes he
never saw, but surely that must have come before her flight from
America? And this abandonment seems inexplicable, really
unbelievable, when matched to the love she professes for the child's
father. I remember the dark young girl at the summer party – the
girl whom Caroline called Magpie. Her hair, as black as Dinny's. I
will never know for sure, but this omission from the letter hints at a
crime indeed, and makes me doubt the claim of kinship I made to
Dinny.

   Beth came to stay a couple of weeks ago. She wishes, I think, that I'd settled in a different village, but she's getting used to the idea. She doesn't shy away from this place any more.

'Doesn't it bother you, seeing the house over there?' she asked. Expressions fly across her face these days. They rise and jostle like balloons. Something tethered her features before and now it's gone. And I may well settle somewhere else, sometime; soon, or eventually. I'm not waiting, but I need to be where he can find me. Just until the next time he does. And he's got reasons to come back here, after all. More to pull him here than just me, and my desire for him. A mother, a sister, a niece. I think Honey would tell me, if he'd been back.

My happiness at seeing Beth improve bubbles up whenever I set eyes on her. No miracle cure, of course, but she's better. She can split the blame for what happened with Dinny now; she no longer has to think that she and she alone dealt fate to Henry Calcott. The truth of it, the right and wrong, is more diffuse now. She didn't take a life, she just changed one. There's even a fragment of leeway, just a hint of grey as to whether the change was for the better or worse. So no miracle cure, but she talks to me about it now – she'll talk about what happened, and because she's turned around and looked at it, it's not dogging her steps like it used to. I can see the improvement and so can Eddie, although he hasn't asked me about it. I don't think he cares what's changed, he's just pleased that it has.

It takes a while to see somebody differently when for years you've seen them in a particular way, or not seen them at all. I still saw Harry, when Dinny told me to see Henry. And I still saw Dinny as I had always seen him, always loved him. I tell myself that he needs time to see me differently, to see me as I am now and not see a child, or a nuisance, or Beth's little sister, or whatever else it is he sees. Perhaps the time is not now; but it will come, I believe. There was a legal wrangle over the plot of land where the Dinsdales are allowed to camp. The developer didn't want a load of travellers parking up in the communal gardens of his new flats. In the end that piece of ground, along with the rest of the woods and pasture, was sold to the farmer whose land adjoins it, and he has known the Dinsdales for years. So it's still there, waiting for them. Waiting for him. A beautiful place to camp in the summer, green and sheltered, and unmolested now.

I'm hoping for a hot summer. Weather to bake the bones and excuse this languid life I've adopted. Weather to give Honey freckles, and to make ice-lollies from lemon squash with Susan and Paul's girls, and to darken Dinny's skin. Weather to sneak to the dew pond, to paddle, to swim, to chase its ghosts away. And today a small parcel came in the post for me. Inside, crumbling, was a piece of tree bark with patterns scratched into it. Nothing I could distinguish in the designs, except the name at the bottom – *HARRY* – in crooked, angular, almost unreadable letters. A declaration, I take it to be, of who he is now, of who he wants to be. And an unspoken message from Dinny, who wrapped it up and posted it. That he knows where I am, and that he thinks of me. For now, I find I am quite happy with that.

Acknowledgements

My love and thanks to Alison and Charlotte Webb for their reading, critiquing and endless enthusiasm over the years; and to John Webb for never suggesting that I get a proper job!

Thanks to the members of WordWatchers in Newbury for all their support, comments and cake.

Finally, my thanks also to Edward Smith and the members of youwriteon.com for getting the book read, reviewed and noticed; and to Sara and Natalie at Orion for taking it the rest of the way.

Not
The End

Go to channel4.com/tvbookclub for more great reads,
brought to you by Specsavers.

Enjoy a good read with